ALSO BY ISABEL COLEGATE

ORLANDO KING

Isabel Colegate

BLOOMSBURY PUBLISHING

LONDON · OXFORD · NEW YORK · NEW DELHI · SYDNEY

BLOOMSBURY PUBLISHING
Bloomsbury Publishing Plc
50 Bedford Square, London, WC1B 3DP, UK

BLOOMSBURY, BLOOMSBURY PUBLISHING and the
Diana logo are trademarks of Bloomsbury Publishing Plc

Orlando King first published 1968 in Great Britain by The Bodley Head
Orlando at the Brazen Threshold first published 1971 in Great Britain
by The Bodley Head
Agatha first published 1973 in Great Britain by The Bodley Head
This edition published 2020

A catalogue record for this book is available from the British Library

ISBN: PB: 978-1-5266-1558-9; EPUB: 978-1-5266-1556-5

4 6 8 10 9 7 5 3

Typeset by Integra Software Services Pvt. Ltd.
Printed and bound in Great Britain by CPI Group (UK) Ltd, Croydon CR0 4YY

MIX
Paper from
responsible sources
FSC® C020471

To find out more about our authors and books visit www.bloomsbury.com
and sign up for our newsletters

Introduction

by Melissa Harrison

A boy with damaged feet, raised on a remote island by a man called King, accidentally kills his real father and goes on to marry the man's wife. Later, bereaved and half-blind, he goes into exile with his daughter; later still she will sacrifice herself to help her half-brother, a traitor.

These are not spoilers, for in her extraordinary account of the turbulent middle years of the last century Isabel Colegate intends the Greek myths of Oedipus and Antigone to be evident from the very first page: 'We know the story of course, so nothing need be withheld,' she says of her main character Orlando's fictional history – and of the legend behind Sophocles' tragedy, *Oedipus Rex*. It shimmers through *Orlando King* like the dreams of marble columns, towers and temples that plague Orlando and his daughter Agatha; it lends the domestic, the social and the political aspects of all three novels a kind of archetypal significance. 'We choose a situation in the drama to expose a theme,' Colegate writes. 'We are here profoundly to contemplate eternal truths. With ritual, like the Greeks. With dream, like Freud. Let us pray.'

Those first paragraphs of *Orlando King* make up one of the most extraordinarily confident openings of any 20th century novel. Utterly stylish, brilliantly sure-footed and deliberately, teasingly opaque, Colegate seems to revel in her powers as she introduces us to Orlando ('Here he is... our hero'), sets out her narrator's field of view and relationship to the reader ('The girls in the outer office look up. Nice, they think. He brings his air of seeming to matter'), nods to her guiding myth while pretending to correct herself ('But no, he does not know it is his father'), drops in some humour ('Miss Pyne is agitating behind him'), gives us some of the brilliantly differentiated dialogue that's one of her greatest strengths, then hops forward in time deftly and enigmatically – another stylistic trait – before calling a sudden halt and exhorting us to pay proper attention, for this is not just a comedy of manners or even a social novel: she intends something more. So much of the texture and style of the entire trilogy is there in the feinting, almost Woolfian dance of those opening paragraphs: the short, cinematic scenes, the dry humour, the deftly drawn characters, the acute psychological insight. We know from the off that while all has not yet been made clear, we're in safe hands.

Societies come to understand themselves through the production and enjoyment of culture: literature, the visual arts, films, music and all the rest. Art is key to how we process collective experience, how we bring to the surface our fears and hopes for the future, and how we digest the past. In that respect, *Orlando King* is a fascinating artefact: an attempt to look squarely at the deep transformation of the English social, political and economic systems as a result of the Second World War, and to pick through its lingering effects. It's also, of course, a window into the late sixties and early seventies, when the trilogy was being written: a period in which the country was in the grip of further alterations whose destabilising effects echo through all three books.

To read it now, during another period of seismic change, lends it particular resonance, for the questions Colegate's characters struggle with echo clearly today: how should we balance individualism with the good of the collective? Is real change desirable, or even possible any more? What of duty and patriotism and religious faith – do they have any currency? Has capitalism disrupted our moral instincts? Where, if anywhere, might hope lie?

In 1930, a 21-year-old Orlando arrives in London from an island in Brittany and finds it dazzling – particularly the women. He misses entirely the dole queues, hunger marchers and 'the possibility of panic, the earth tremors beneath the civilisation in decay.' He is good-looking and charismatic, and people from all walks of life take to him; his rise is fast and unearned, and he learns nothing from it because it comes at no cost. 'Perhaps it's his heart that will let him down,' writes his Communist friend and colleague Graham in his diary – prophetically, in more ways than one. 'A perfect human being would have a heart as well wouldn't he? And of course you can't have one of those and be a successful capitalist and lover of society ladies, which are the two things I think for the moment he's setting out to be.' Graham's eventual decision to join the International Brigade and fight in Spain is both principled and ultimately pointless, but the absolute seriousness Colegate affords his fate is in stark contrast to the frivolity of Orlando's early years, when, 'all his bright achievements in his hands' he is tempted into politics not out of principle, but for 'the sheer fun of the thing'.

The society lady Graham refers to is Judith, wife of Orlando's boss (and father) Leonard, and sister of Orlando's lifelong friend Conrad, Lord Field. She is one of the trilogy's most vivid characters: a fearless sailor and horsewoman, proud, often bitter, competitive and sometimes violent; she is not likeable, and does not much care. Yet it is almost unbearable to watch her life unravel as a result of Orlando's selfishness, and witness his indifference to her pain – all the more so for the way Colegate leaves us to judge him as we cannot fail to, while saying little herself. Judith's agony is mirrored in the final book by that of her daughter Agatha; both suffer as a result not only of the behaviour of individual men but of the wider benefits accorded them, a structural imbalance we're still struggling with today.

Like his sister, the widowed Conrad is also unforgettable: keeper of a moral code that today is lost, and in the years of the book was passing away. Born in India, his dream was to be Viceroy; now a conservative politician (like Colegate's father, Sir Arthur Colegate), late in life he recalls 'his father gently introducing to him the idea of duty, which seemed one of the most beautiful ideas in the world, and the love of God, and the fellowship of men, and wanting the village to be able to be proud of one'. Conrad is a sympathetic and even moving emblem of the fading powers of the English aristocracy and of the deep comfort of religious faith; but in the end, it is his moral code that leads him to a betrayal which exposes the ruthlessness, the inhumanity and inflexibility at its core.

Woven around the lives of Orlando, Judith and their children, and of Conrad and his son Henry, lies the warp and weft of mid-twentieth century politics and commerce, from the Great Depression and the Blitz to the Suez Crisis and at last the Cambridge Five. And behind that great tapestry lies the creaking loom of the English class system, an enduring theme of Colegate's and one which runs through all her novels and short stories, from her first, *The Blackmailer*, (1958) to her most famous, *The Shooting Party* (1980), and *Winter Journey*, published in 1995. 'The English will never turn Communist, they're such snobs,' writes Judith's son Paul to his half-sister, Agatha, in the final book of *Orlando King*. 'An English Communist could have a duke at gunpoint; if he asked him to stay for the weekend he'd drop the gun and dash off to Moss Bros to hire a dinner-jacket.' Much has been written and broadcast about the aristocracy in the early years of the twentieth century; it's less common to be given a window into the gradual fading of their influence, as the middle classes expanded and the country limped towards a less hide-bound, but perhaps more venal, way of thinking about itself. 'Capitalism has got to be modified not abolished,' Conrad opines to Orlando in the early 1930s, trimming the sail as ever. 'We want new capitalists, men of sense and sensibility who can make peace between capital and labour.' Much later on, Paul's wealthy, rapacious father-in-law Daintry is the absolute embodiment of this new kind of man; Conrad's early fascination with him, and later his intense dislike, are telling.

Orlando King's exploration of class and commerce is big-picture, state-of-the-nation stuff; coupled with Colegate's examination across three books of the influence of fascism and socialism on the country and it's clear how ambitious – and how far-sighted – a writer she is and how much her books deserve to be read again today, as similar influences bubble up afresh. One of Orlando's first friends in London, Penelope Waring, becomes a Mosley acolyte and is later interned with her husband under Defence Regulation 18B; after the War they move to Ireland, where 'we keep our boat always at the ready in Limerick harbour, all the stores and everything, wine at the right temperature and a crew of four – so that we can go straight over to America, of course, as soon as we hear the Commies have taken over.'

Not that any of the trilogy's other characters have much cleaner hands; Colegate is much too subtle a thinker to deal in moral absolutes. Conrad – utterly unforgiving of the next generation – somehow squares his Christian virtue with occasional visits to a certain discreet gentleman's establishment; while casually, for her own amusement, Judith attends a Blackshirts rally in Bath. Worst of all, in 1938 Orlando – chairman by then of a company that manufactures armaments, as well as an MP – speaks out in favour of appeasement: his speech to the House, in which he lists his concerns about the Nazi party's exploits but proclaims them 'nothing to do with politics' (politics being about 'flexibility' and 'conciliation') is a breathtaking piece of ideological equivocation to rival anything we have recently witnessed at the despatch box. Years later, Judith's deeply damaged son Paul will sell secrets to Russia ('the money only interested me in the sense that it was the handful of silver with which the traitor is rewarded, and I wanted to feel like a traitor').

So what might virtue look like? There are no easy answers to be found. Agatha, who once wanted to be a doctor and who tries all her life to be 'good', is led by the utter inflexibility of this goal into total self-abnegation – not to mention criminality and the infliction of trauma on her adored children. The world is too complex for anyone to be morally pure, Colegate seems to be telling us. Even love – romantic love, love of children or siblings, love of one's country – is no longer enough.

And the relationship of characters to country in *Orlando King* is subtle and profound. The pillars and porticos of Mount Sorrel, with its lake and estate wall dividing it from the village with church and chapel and 'mild green slope', *are* England; Conrad loves it deeply, of course, and longs for Henry to take an interest, but to Agatha, a generation younger, it seems cold and grey, an 'eighteenth-century landscape'. Orlando's first boss (and real father) Leonard loves the village too, but is drawn to signs of modernity rather than tradition: 'the trees closed about the little road, until looking up at the tallest you saw the viaduct taller behind through the leaves, its arches reaching from the damp shade of the stream bed to the open air fifty feet above where the train rollicked past from time to time. "Good old Somerset and Dorset," Leonard would say. (Orlando would think, he's lived here three years or something, what right has he to be so loyal to the railway?)'

It is the War which at last engenders a love of country in Orlando, who grew up, after all, in France. Broken by guilt and contrition he volunteers as an ARP warden during the Blitz, when 'he felt the stirring of an unfamiliar emotion, which he eventually recognized with some embarrassment as patriotism ... Britain Can Take It, said the posters. In his present state of mind it was as if, in love, he saw the name of his beloved scratched on the walls.'

It is a brief love, but one that transforms him. 'I have misunderstood everything,' he thinks in hospital; 'King tried to tell me, he spoke to me of love, good and evil, guilt... the true and the false, and I ignored it all and took the world on its own terms.' Having passed through fire, Orlando at last begins his necessary suffering.

The world turns, and society with it. Orlando may secede, but his daughter's generation have their own battle to fight – as do we, today. Caught in the mire of events we struggle for perspective, for a glimpse of the big picture, some kind of hint as to what the 'right side of history' might turn out to be.

But there's no view from nowhere, and perhaps the confusion of the mire is all we have. In the middle book of the trilogy, Conrad, who is fond of quoting William Morris ('it showed how open his mind was that he should quote from the works of a Socialist'), tells Orlando about 'how men fight and lose the battle ... and the thing they fought for comes about in spite of their defeat and when it comes turns out not to be what they meant, and other men have to fight for what they meant under another name.' *Orlando King* is about that battle, which belongs to every one of us and is unending. It is the unresolvable tension between conflicting principles and opposing outcomes that provides 'the singing wire on which we balance', as Henry writes to Agatha at the very end of the story – and on the first page of this remarkable book.

Melissa Harrison, June 2020

Orlando King

Here he is. In the doorway, going to his first interview with Leonard. Badly dressed. It is before Guy Waring has introduced him to his tailor. Here he comes. The girls in the outer office look up. Nice, they think. He brings his air of seeming to matter. He pauses. 'I am here, Father.' But no, he does not know it is his father. He says, 'Hallo.' Miss Pyne is agitating behind him. The way he just walked in! Leonard says, 'All right Miss Pyne.'

Orlando says, 'I'm afraid I'm a little early.' Our hero.

That night old King died.

Orlando went back to the island for the funeral.

We know the story of course, so nothing need be withheld. We can see it on television or in the cinema or read about it in popular histories of the time or, again, in less popular histories of the other time. This dear art in which our loved predecessors excelled has conceded ground; suspense may go. We choose a situation in the drama to expose a theme: passing curiosity must look elsewhere, we are here profoundly to contemplate eternal truths. With ritual, like the Greeks. With dream, like Freud. Let us pray.

[∗]

My dear Agatha, Henry wrote much later. You are right, and yet you are not right, because it is restlessness which distinguishes life from death, the search for new stimulus, the need for movement, and so we turn from you to Conrad and back again, seeking you but needing him; and it is this which makes the singing wire on which we balance, hoping always that it will be in your arms that we die.

But Agatha would have claimed that in her was all the movement of the spheres.

When Orlando was in hospital he often dreamt of the house where he and Judith used to live; and King would be there, stalking through the now unfurnished rooms, often covering his eyes with his hands and groaning; searching for the island, opening doors saying where is it; Orlando said it's there, you know, in the Morbihan, not here; but he said no it was never there. Orlando said how do you know and King replied my mother told me.

After all, it's always a bit different when it happens to someone you know.

'My mother told me,' shouted King from the top of the rock.

Orlando never listened when he talked like that. It was so boring.

Orlando, our hero, was the illegitimate son of a certain Leonard Gardner and a girl called Pauline who was one of King's students when he was a lecturer in Modern Languages at Cambridge in 1909. Pauline was a good-looking girl of advanced views, the daughter of a doctor. She and Leonard used to go for walking tours and talk about poetry and theories of sex. Some people found her alarming. There was no question of marriage; he was too young and poor and she wanted to make a career in teaching. When she found that she was pregnant she told no one, not even Leonard, because she thought that the responsibility for having failed to avoid such an event was hers and not his. She was planning to procure an abortion, though without yet much idea of how to set about it, when King, finding her in tears one day and learning the cause (they did all confide in him somehow), and overwhelmed with conscience and moral delicacy, interfered. It was an extraordinary thing to do, but by then he was already an eccentric. He had been planning for some time to leave the life he knew, and to live completely alone, and now he saw a new and marvellous part of the plan. He would take the child. This would give a purpose to it all. A woolly-haired, large, emotional don, he blinked away tears, begging her to do it. 'It'll be in the Long Vac... no one will know ... A nurse ... I'll pay ... I'll adopt it legally ...'

Then she was moved too and protested, 'But you might have one of your own one day.' (But of course he wouldn't.)

So it was done and in the end she paid, because she had been left some money by her grandmother, and King left for the island with the child and a nurse as soon as was practicable after the birth.

Orlando of course gained most by this arrangement because he gained life, which had he been capable of being offered the choice, he would have accepted on any terms at all. And King gained a love object who caused him little distress and much happiness until the day he left the island. Pauline gained nothing, and after it was all over she suffered severely from emotional disequilibrium. She ended her relationship with Leonard, and failed to pass her exams. Leaving Girton, she became governess to a family of plain and unoriginal girls and when she left them – it was in the war – she did not tell them where she was going, nor was the plain and unoriginal mother ever subsequently approached for a reference. King tried to trace her when Orlando was seven – it had been agreed that they should not try to communicate until then – but he failed.

He turned his attention to the boy.

He had so much he wanted to tell him.

'My mother told me,' he shouted. 'I am passing on the ancient message.'

As well as the ancient message she had left him a little capital, and with it he bought the island. Early schoolmastering holidays had brought him to Brittany, and on one occasion he had explored the south coast of that peninsula and discovered the strange islanded inland sea known as the Gulf of Morbihan, which was then remote and self-contained. When he had gathered the money and the resolution he returned to it and bought a small island.

'The principle underlying capitalist society and the principle of love are incompatible,' he said nevertheless. 'One must create the truth by love. Even the physical laws of the scientists are provisional in character. Theories are to be used. Good is always a provisional hypothesis whereas evil can be final. As one gets older the ultimate retreats. The imagination may be compared with Adam's dream, he awoke and found it true – have you read the book of Keats' letters I gave you?'

Orlando did not listen, scanning the patterns of the oyster parks at low tide, the wide white light through the ribs of the wrecked boat at the end of their island, the end where Sid lived. The island had two houses, the proprietor's house and the guardian's house. Sid was the guardian. He was also the cook, housekeeper, gardener, boatman, secretary, friend. King could do nothing for himself. Sid could do everything, and being a nihilist did not mind where he did it as long as it was not in Australia where he had been born. He was with them for all of the twenty-one years that Orlando and King lived on the island and he stayed there after Orlando had left and King had died.

It was Sid who took Orlando in the motor boat through the strong currents to the Catholic boys' school at Locmariaquer every morning until he was old enough to manage the boat himself. It was Sid who saw that they were always supplied with vegetables from his carefully cultivated garden and who once or twice when money was short took a job oystering for eight hours a day and came back with bruised and swollen hands. And yet he was hardly lovable.

Sid did not listen to what King said either.

Sometimes King experienced periods of crushing boredom.

'This is the only way of life,' he would insist at such times. 'The world of London, the world of Cambridge, stifling, agonizing, selfish, competitive, I know it all ...' And he would drink dreadful quantities of the local Muscadet, unconscious guilt no doubt directing his choice since he knew it left him with a worse headache than any other wine.

'False, false, they're all false.' And he would do a really terrible imitation of Margot Asquith.

'Of course it all leads to war,' he would go on. 'Capitalism is bound to lead to war – they've got to have markets – it's pure hypocrisy to talk about ending war.' But it was not war which had hurt him, it was the appalling difficulty of personal relations. 'Friendship,' he would proclaim into the sweet salt desolate air. 'Friendship,' to the Australian nihilist and the abstracted boy. 'Friendship is the only good.'

Sometimes after one of the heavy drinking evenings in which the periods of boredom culminated he would make physical overtures to Sid, who did not care one way or the other and never afterwards referred to such incidents (Sid never referred to anything). 'Love,' King would say to Orlando, 'is a word which hasn't been understood for years, least of all in the twentieth century. Love is as terrible as violence, as powerful as despair. Guilt,' he would cry tortured by guilt, 'guilt is the enemy of liberty.' With the boy he was delicate: he never even peed in front of him. The night before Orlando, aged twenty-one, left for England, King said to Sid, 'Do you suppose – I mean, physiologically – that is, ought I to tell him what are called the facts of life?'

'He knows,' said Sid.

When Orlando was old enough to handle the boats and to manoeuvre them through the strong currents of the inland sea, he would take King fishing or to other islands for picnics or to spend the day in the deep sheltered valleys of Belle He, two or three hours' journey out to sea; or they would go with knives and baskets to collect *fruits de mer* at low tide, recognizing the clams by the two tiny holes they left in the sand, finding crayfish in the tidal ponds, and sea-snails. In the spring the island would be covered with wild flowers, yellow juniper, thin poppies and cornflowers, and tiny wild dianthus. King planted a mimosa tree but it died.

Mimosa grew on the mainland, less exposed than their island. The winter climate was mild because of the sea currents, the summers warm though sometimes windy. Then Orlando would take the little sailing boat and coast on the currents, worrying King who knew they were dangerous.

King worried about religion too.

'If you start to believe you're drinking blood and eating flesh I'll never forgive you. He's after you, that curé, I can see it. They're all the same, these priests.'

'He hardly ever mentions religion,' said Orlando. 'He's more interested in football, I think.'

'That's their cleverness, it's all part of the trick. Farm Street all over. It's when they don't mention it that you really want to watch out. They nearly got me once, that's how I know about it. When I was at Cambridge.'

Orlando was not sent to a university, not only because of the predatory priests lying in wait there but of the inanities of an empty intellectualism, or else because King knew he could not live without him.

After he left school he joined two friends of his, brothers, who worked with their father in one of the small family oyster businesses of the Auray river. There was an uncle as well, and some cousins, and besides the *chantier* there was a small poor farm on the mainland where the old grandmother lived and a little bar and *crêperie* on the harbour at Locmariaquer. Orlando sometimes worked in the oyster parks or on the farm, and sometimes at sea, placing or collecting the white tiles on which the oyster larvae gathered, and which had to be towed out into the Bay of Quiberon every June, and sometimes even – on Sundays perhaps – in the bar, carrying plates of oysters and bottles of white wine to the customers, most of whom he had known all his life, for there were few tourists then even in August. Once he spent a season working with the sardine fleet from Quiberon. He did not play football in the cure's team because of his foot, but occasionally he went to Mass on Sundays if there was a girl he wanted to meet afterwards.

'Haven't you any ambition?' King asked him rather irritably when they were building the tower (they worked on it for years: it was *one* of King's schemes: he ordered an astronomical telescope from the Army and Navy Stores but told them to hold it until he sent word that the tower was ready: they may be holding it yet).

'What sort of ambition?' Orlando asked.

'To achieve something, to make your mark in the world of men,' said King. 'I know I've always told you that was the last thing you ought to want – but it's a bit disconcerting to find one's advice taken.'

'You mean I'm dull,' said Orlando helpfully.

'Not at all. But are you never discontented?'

'Oh yes,' said Orlando. 'But not very often.'

'Perhaps you could survive it. You're not very introspective, are you?'

'No,' said Orlando. 'You've put too much cement on that, it will look terrible. Survive what?'

'I shall have to think about it,' said King.

He thought about it.

'I've never been possessive, have I?' he said to Sid. 'No one could say I've been possessive, could they?'

'No,' said Sid.

'That was the whole point of sending him to school, encouraging him to have friends of his own age. He has got a lot of friends, hasn't he?'

'Yes.'

'They're nice boys round here, healthy handsome boys, fine faces. He's popular, isn't he? He's the most popular boy in the locality, wouldn't you say?'

'Probably.'

'Well, then ...'

Sid was scraping potatoes with a knife.

'He's well-educated, isn't he?' Those rows of damp books, that special arrangement with the London Library. But who will come with me in the boat to the post office in Vannes to collect the parcels, and zigzag back across the currents while I open the parcels ... don't go so fast Orlando, I say ... there was a letter once, from the Chief Librarian himself, about the salt water marks ... it was my own fault, of course, for not being able to wait until we got home to open the parcels.

'He doesn't read much by himself, though, does he?'

'No.'

'He is bilingual, of course.'

Sid scraped in silence.

'Do we smell, do you suppose?' King asked.

'Sometimes,' said Sid.

'There's no woman about the place. Are our habits – would they laugh at him, do you suppose, in London, say?'

'Thank God.'

'Thank God what?'

'No women.'

'Would they laugh at him for his hammer toes? And love, sex, oh God, must he go through all that, all that prestige aspect of male sex and competition and power and money and the wrongness of people's attitudes to every-thing, and success and money – oh no, I couldn't send him to all that.' Have I built my life here on a falsehood, was it cowardice not strength, was it that I wasn't tough enough, that I longed to be a success on their terms and couldn't do it? 'No, it wasn't that, there wasn't any right living, anywhere.' Is it wrong to impose one's own values, force the young to eat the fruit of one's own experience? 'But he's educated, isn't he? Properly educated. How can he come to any harm?' Easily, more easily than anyone who's been differently educated. 'Has he listened, has he taken it all in? I don't believe he listens to a word I say, does he, Sid?'

'Not too much, I'd say,' said Sid.

'I didn't always mean it as an experiment, if that's what you're thinking,' said King, needlessly aggressive since Sid was not thinking anything. 'I mean, to bring him up like that, in isolation, grounded in the truth, and then send him back, you know, like a kind of Christ – I mean, God forbid.'

'Why not send him to London for a few months, then, and see how he gets on?' said Sid.

King reached for the bottle of wine.

'I suppose I shall have to,' he said.

Orlando did not want to go. Not that he was alarmed by King's warnings. He expected to find life in London much the same as life in the Morbihan, except that it would be in a town, which was a bore. He would not like to live in St Nazaire, for instance, where he had been on a school outing to visit the shipyards. Nor was he much distressed at the thought of leaving his friends, since it was only to be for six months. And only in a rather pleasantly melancholy way did he mind leaving Anne Marie, the daughter of the family for whom he worked. She was seventeen and he was very fond of her and thought that in a few years' time he might marry her; but it was only for six months. All the same, he was afraid that six months was time enough for King's boredom to become a problem.

King's boredom was never openly referred to – he often said that no properly educated man was ever bored – but Orlando knew about it very well, and knew that he was the only person who could cure it. When King insisted that he must go to London, Orlando went to see several of his friends and asked them to keep an eye on the island when he was away, but he knew that his friends generally found King tedious – he was so talkative and helpless – and Sid unwelcoming: so Orlando was worried, leaving for London.

He was not as worried as King.

The year was 1930. King had come to the island in 1909. Only Coutts' Bank, the London Library and the Army and Navy Stores knew that he could be addressed Poste Restante, Vannes, and they had been asked not to disclose this to anyone else. At first he would look at an occasional newspaper. The local girls who looked after Orlando when he was a baby (the English nurse left after four days on the island) kept him in touch with local news, and told him of the imminence and then the outbreak of war. After that the outside world became less interesting to him as it became less comprehensible. Growing most of their own food, or fishing for it, they had no reason to know more of the war than the most distant of rumours, nor of peace than the news that it had come.

'Do you think everything has changed then, and everyone I knew disappeared?'

'Perhaps they were all killed in the war,' said Sid.

'Not all, surely?' said King. 'Look here, we must get some English newspapers.'

By ordering it from the newsagent in Vannes he procured a copy of *The Times*, a day or two old.

'It looks much the same,' he said, spreading it out on a table. 'Births, Deaths – Personal Column, that should be revealing. Lancing Old Boys' Dinner, Lady highly recommends her Parisienne dressmaker. Charming villa Ste Maxime, Unwanted false teeth. Not much change there. Two recently shot tiger skins. Give health to a little East Ender. Golf made easy.' He turned over a page. 'Domestic Sits. Vac. Lady housekeepers and housekeepers. Between-maids, generals and laundrymaids. Stars of the month, the evening sky in October. What could sound more stable than that?'

'I wonder if I could get a job as a general,' said Sid.

'Burial mounds in Hampshire,' read King. 'I am an unfortunate subscriber to the Post Office telephone service. Mr

Chaplin's new picture. The basket-maker's craft. Chinese salt loans. A farewell banquet was given to the Viceroy last night by members and Ministers of the Punjab Government.'

'Stinkeroo,' said Sid mechanically.

'Unrest in Cuba, crisis in Ecuador,' read King. 'Reduction in armaments: diverse views. Miss Mercedes Gleitze entered the water at Shakespeare Beach, Dover, at 8.47 last night in an attempt to swim the Channel for the Dover Corporation Gold Cup.'

'Isn't there anything more interesting?' said Sid.

'The King and Queen accompanied by Prince George returned to London from Balmoral,' offered King. 'The Queen wearing a long fur-trimmed coat of grey figured velvet and a toque of royal blue. Lord Birkenhead's death. Well that marks the passage of time at least.'

'Who was he?' said Sid.

'Orlando will tell you. Unemployment growing. Beauty of the Downs. The Duchess of Devonshire will return to London tomorrow from Ireland. She will leave on Friday for Chatsworth. What more do you want? City Notes, Money Market, Stock Exchange prices?'

'I'll have it for the crossword,' said Sid.

'You can't want the crossword,' said King irritably.

'Why not?'

'You don't know any words,' said King. 'I shall write to Guy Waring. He's the kind of person who couldn't possibly have been killed in the war.'

But then the question was whether to write to Leonard, and if so what to say.

'He'll be a civil servant, a respectable civil servant living in the suburbs with a respectable civil servant's wife. It will be a terrible shock. Wouldn't it be better to let them meet first and tell them later, if it seems wise? What do you think?'

'Why tell them at all?' said Sid.

'Do you think they ought not to meet? Would that be better for Orlando? Would it be unsettling?' Supposing they love each other? Like father and son? But father and son don't necessarily love each other. Besides Leonard hardly is his father. Biologically only, and what does that mean? Well everything perhaps and perhaps I am totally irrelevant. And so on.

In the end he gave Orlando letters of introduction to six people including Guy Waring and Leonard. The letters were very brief. They reminded the recipients of King's existence, introduced Orlando as his 'young English ward' and continued, 'He is ...' but what could he say? '... a nice boy.'

Which was true, though not the whole story.

Whose dream was it anyway, Orlando wondered, dreaming of King dreaming a dream.

Agatha was playing Tom Tiddler's Ground, with the others, in the clock golf circle on the lawn. Sometimes they danced together, he and Agatha, the gramophone playing 'All By Myself in the Moonlight'. Or was it only once?

Judith winding the gramophone, that was a typical gesture. Sometimes in beach pyjamas with a lipsticked disillusioned mouth like someone in an Aldous Huxley novel. But her little sideways sniff, that was her own.

The women.

What would you think he might have thought, coming to London for the first time in 1930? It was December. Nearly 1931. That's a year we've heard of. Would he have seen dole queues, hunger marchers? Would he have sensed the shabby political comings and goings, the presence, subdued, of the

possibility of panic, the earth tremors beneath the civilization in decay?

The first thing that struck him was the women.

And after that the luxury, the ease, the things to do and
see and eat and say, the quickness, cleverness and beauty.

London in 1931 was dazzling, Orlando found.

Penelope Waring took him to a Scavenge Hunt. They had
to race round London collecting objects from a list – a
Christmas tree decoration, a door-knocker, an egg-whisk, a
horseshoe, and so on. Orlando had no idea where to find any
of the things and anyway had to concentrate desperately on
driving Penelope's Hillman without accident. Guy had had to
go to Glasgow on some business to do with a ship. Orlando
had had very little driving experience, but fortunately it was
too late at night for the traffic to be heavy. He drove furiously
with Penelope bouncing on the seat beside him, squeaking
at every jerk, but urging him on because of the thrill of the
chase. Another couple leant over him from the back of the
car shouting instructions and intermittently screaming. He
found it all very exciting. They were nearly the last and had
not found a horseshoe so they were disqualified, and afterwards there was kedgeree and champagne in their hostess's
tremendously smart house. He talked to a pretty girl who
seemed very shy and reminded him of Anne Marie. He would
have liked to be alone with her but did not know whether it
would be all right to ask her to have lunch with him one day.
He was sorry when Penelope said that it was time to go home.

Penelope was tiny and thin with huge blue eyes and
fluffy fair hair which was flat on the top of her head and
bubbled out into curls round her ears. It amazed him that
someone so sophisticated and busy could find time to be as
kind to him as she was.

When they got back to the Warings' house it was beginning to get light. Orlando lay in bed thinking about the shy girl and Anne Marie. After a bit the door opened and Penelope came in wearing a pink silk negligee.

'Good heavens!' cried Orlando, jumping out of bed and reaching for his dressing-gown. 'Is something the matter?'

'Do get back into bed – don't bother about your dressing-gown, I won't stay a moment. It was just that I felt so terribly awake and wanted to talk to someone.'

So she sat on his bed and they talked and she told him that Guy was unfortunately not able to satisfy her physically and they both agreed that this was very bad luck on poor Guy.

At first he felt rather embarrassed to be talking so intimately to someone older than himself and a woman at that but he quickly became used to it and when he finally understood that she would like him to make love to her he did so, to their mutual satisfaction.

Men's voices singing.

'Rock of Ages, cleft for me.'

Conrad says, 'They sing it when there's an accident in the pit.'

Agatha is five. She is sitting on the piano with Jen's arms round her waist. Jen has said, 'He is blind. He plays by ear.' Agatha looks at the man's ear, obscurely shocked.

Before that it was 'Little Angeline, sweet sixteen, always sitting on the village green'. It is the Anglers' Club outing, and all afternoon they have been fishing in the lake. Now they have come in for tea in the servants' hall, and a sing-song.

Agatha has heard Conrad say quietly to Orlando, 'They sing it when there's an accident in the pit.'

She is uneasy because the miners' smell is not familiar. It is familiar to Jen, who is enjoying herself. Jen likes a song. She joins in with her thin voice, but not too loud in case Nanny tells her off afterwards.

> 'Rock of Ages, cleft for me
> Let me hide myself in Thee.'

Orlando is looking at Agatha, his daughter.

Often in hospital Orlando was filled with regrets for things he had hardly noticed at the time. Incidents would seem charged with significance, like the miners' singing and Agatha's absorption, and they would reappear in his dreams and his dreams would seem like parables.

> Or fairy stories.
> Once upon a time there was a king. His name was Leonard.

'A small company of which I happen to be Chairman,' said Leonard, 'has just gone into voluntary liquidation.'

He looked across his desk at Orlando, with a look of gravity, and of weight.

Orlando admired the look; and the rosy freshly-shaved face, the sleek hair, the big grey chalk-striped suit, cream silk shirt and paisley tie. He thought approvingly, here is a man of gravity and weight.

'This shows you the gravity of the situation,' said Leonard, weightily.

Orlando nodded.

'Fortunately for reasons too complicated to explain at the moment it happened to be to the advantage of the company concerned to take this step. However, I needn't bother you with all that. The point I want to make is that it's a bad time for a young man without qualifications or experience to be looking for a job. Old King, of course, wouldn't understand that. Tell me, what does he do out there all day?'

'He fishes, or reads,' said Orlando. 'Or mends the boats, or builds the tower, a sort of look-out tower he's building. He is usually very busy.'

'It's the ideal life of course,' said Leonard. 'It's the kind of thing I'm always dreaming of doing myself if only I could save a little money. Life's a good deal more expensive here than in France. You'll have found that out already, I don't doubt. The upkeep of an establishment, school fees – not that you need expect to face any of that for some time, but still, however modest one's demands, life's a pretty keen economic struggle here these days. It's my belief it's going to get worse too. I don't see how it can be avoided. The Government daren't face the issue. They won't cut down on unemployment benefits. I've told them. Day after day I've hammered at them in the House of Commons. There's quite a little group of us, and we never let them alone, trying to get them to face facts. Poor old King wouldn't be able to believe his eyes if he saw what has happened since he went off to that island. No one could have guessed at that time that we'd have the kind of irresponsible socialistic ideas we've got running around at the moment. That's the problem, capital and labour; and until people in this country will face the problem and realize which side their bread is buttered, we're going to have economic chaos. There's got to be drastic cuts, drastic cuts in expenditure.'

'Guy Waring would agree with you,' said Orlando politely.

'Very decent fellow, Waring,' said Leonard. 'Attractive wife, too. He's putting you up for a bit, is he, while you look round? I'd certainly like to help you if I could. A recommendation from Guy Waring means a lot. Quite apart from my affectionate memories of old King. Give him my love will you when you write? Will he ever come to England again do you think?'

'I'd like him to. Perhaps he will if I stay.'

'I wish I could help you. Unfortunately my interests are mainly in fields where some qualification is necessary. Of course if we could get you qualified as an accountant – but I'm afraid that's a long haul. I should have thought work on the land might be the answer. After all that's where your only useful experience has been. Of course agriculture's going through a bad time at the moment like everything else. My brother-in-law Lord Field – Guy Waring would know him – is having quite a bit of trouble down in Somerset with his farms. But I could arrange for you to see his agent. He's an awfully decent fellow – Hugh Grant, one of the Grants. You could have a talk with him.' A telephone rang on his desk. 'Forgive me. Yes, Miss Pyne?'

Orlando lowered his eyes and thought, stupid ass, in a phrase of King's. Guy Waring had said Leonard was the most successful businessman he knew, had made heaps of money, was a director of all sorts of important firms, could find him a job with no trouble at all, and here he was talking about work on the land and one of the Grants. Pompous ass. But he had said yes to someone's coming in, and now was standing up, buttoning his substantial coat and smiling.

Judith came in.

She brought scent and a flow of rapid talk, to which Orlando could not for a moment attend, because he was so struck by her appearance.

She was very thin. She wore a rather long black coat and a black beret. Her face was very white and pointed and she had thin scarlet lips and dark eyes. Her black wavy hair was cut short.

She tossed her bag and gloves and a black chiffon scarf into one chair and sat down herself in another, talking all the time.

'Orlando King. My wife,' Leonard had said.

She touched Orlando's hand.

'I wanted some money,' she was saying. 'I'm taking the boys to the dentist and they have to go to Fortnum's afterwards for a huge tea. Pauly's lying in a darkened room with a wet towel over his eyes. He says the thought of the dentist makes his head ache.'

'He's ten years old,' protested Leonard, moving irritably in his chair.

'Eleven,' said Judith. 'I was passing so I thought I'd look in and ask Miss Pyne for some cash.'

'This young man is staying with the Warings,' said Leonard, reaching for his wallet. 'How much do you need?'

'Tea at Fortnum's costs the earth,' said Judith. 'I've heard about you from Penelope. She made you sound so romantic.' She smiled coldly. 'Like that French person. You know, that one had to read about with one's governess.'

'Orlando may not have had a governess,' said Leonard with an indulgent smile.

Orlando looked coldly back at Judith, who sniffed. It was a quick twitch of a sniff, affecting one side of her face only, a sort of parlour-maid's sniff. Orlando found it extremely attractive.

'Are you offering him a job?' asked Judith.

'I was trying to explain to him how very difficult conditions in this country are at the present time,' said Leonard in a disapproving tone of voice. 'Particularly how difficult it is for a young man without qualifications or experience to find an opening with interesting prospects.'

'Can't he go into Lloyd's?' said Judith indifferently.

'There are certain obstacles.'

'I haven't any money,' explained Orlando.

Judith stared at him. It was the first time he had spoken to her.

She smiled.

'Why don't we introduce him to Noël Coward?' she said.

'I certainly wouldn't recommend a stage career,' said Leonard, frowning. 'In fact out of loyalty to old King I don't think I could even – I mean one gets a very degenerate type of person ...'

'I should like to meet Noël Coward very much,' said Orlando. 'But I don't want to be an actor.'

'I know,' said Judith. 'Why doesn't he come to Mount Sorrel, and work for Timberwork? He could have Tom Ford's job.'

'I hadn't thought of that,' said Leonard. 'I had thought of asking Conrad whether there was any opening on the estate management side of things. But perhaps Timberwork would be more interesting. It's certainly more likely to lead somewhere.'

'You're always saying you need young men,' said Judith. 'Thanks awfully, I must dash. He could stay with us for a bit if you like. If he doesn't want Ford's flat, that is. Goodbye. Wish me luck. I'm in for a deadly afternoon.'

She kissed Leonard on the cheek, and shook Orlando's hand.

Leonard led her to the door and returned to his chair looking refreshed.

'Let me tell you about this little firm, he said.

One in the eye for Penelope Waring, thought Judith clip-peting down the stairs.

When Orlando went back to the island for the funeral he found that Sid had moved a woman into his house. It was the first time he had ever done that. His sexual appetites had hitherto involved him in forays on to the mainland last-ing sometimes for days at a time, but he had never brought a woman to the island during King's lifetime, let alone allowed her to stay there. She was a squat little person of an unwelcoming appearance and Sid did not speak to her much.

The other house seemed as if no one had lived in it for years. It was only two days since King had died, but already the place smelt of damp books and mouldering bread. Perhaps it always had.

King had been working on the tower when Sid went to tell him that their supper was cooked. He had turned, started to walk towards Sid, thrown up his arms with a great cry and fallen to the ground, dead. He was sixty-six. Everyone agreed that it was a good way to die.

When Orlando's old schoolmaster, the curé of Locmariaquer, prayed over the coffin Orlando wept, reminding himself how King would have hated it, being so severe an atheist. But when he returned to the island with Sid he felt a kind of excitement at the finality of the parting. Everything was different now. King had made a will, leav-ing Orlando the island and two thousand pounds, all that remained of the capital his mother had left him. Orlando arranged for a monthly payment to be made to Sid for the upkeep of the house, and told him he would come back in the summer.

'OK,' said Sid.

'You'll stay here?'

'Sure. Good as anywhere.'

'I'll let you know when I'm coming.'

'OK.'

'This is where you can get in touch with me if you need me,' said Orlando.

'OK.' Sid put the piece of paper in his pocket without looking at it.

'I'll write and tell you if I move. I think I'm going to go and work in a furniture factory for a bit.'

'Jesus.'

'Well, goodbye, Sid, see you in the summer.'

He had seen Anne Marie at the funeral. He had taken her hand in his for a moment and received her condolences but he had not looked into her eyes. He did not believe he would come back in the summer, and he was right. It was eight years before he saw Sid again, and fifteen before he returned to the island.

Sometimes the thought of King throwing up his arms and dying would come very clearly into Orlando's mind and he would feel sorry, but for the rest of the time he did not much think about it. It was only a great deal later that he tried to rediscover King.

He went to Mount Sorrel.

He travelled by train from London to Bath, wearing a new suit, made for him by Guy Waring's tailor. It was the spring of 1931. The suit was made of brown chalk-striped flannel, the shoulders were padded but not excessively, the trousers wide but not ridiculously. With it he wore a dark cream shirt with a long pointed collar and a wide silk paisley tie. He carried a brown fedora with a wide ribbon. His hair had been cut by Guy Waring's barber and was a good deal shorter than it had ever been before. It was annointed with an oil called Royal Yacht. His shoes were dark brown suède, fairly heavy, and had been made for him by Lobb. His legacy was new to him and he travelled first class.

Although it was still cold, the sun was shining, and the train journey took him through agreeable country. He had bought a copy of the *Strand Magazine* but he hardly read it. He thought instead about whether a job in a small furniture factory in the West Country was likely to leave him enough time for going to parties in London. He had been to a great many of these since Penelope Waring first started introducing him to her friends, and he found that he enjoyed them very much. He was also pleased to discover that he was a success. Although he still felt himself to be very ignorant and unpolished he had become quite skilful at covering up these faults, by a judicious silence, or a significant smile, or a joke. Jokes presented little difficulty because King had been witty in a donnish kind of way and Orlando found most people very friendly and willing to laugh, especially the girls; but he knew that he did not yet think as quickly as many of the people he met, except Guy Waring, than whom he was quicker, and he also found himself short of topical allusions and the other common trivialities of a shared background.

He had soon found out that the background which he might have been supposed to have shared with his new friends, that is to say English literature and learning, played in fact little or no part in their lives – though many of them had shelves full of books in their houses – and was indeed regarded by them with a disrespect amounting altogether to scorn. Orlando soon dropped his bookish allusions, and began quite quickly to learn the commonly current attitudes, partly by reading a great many newspapers and magazines but mainly by talking to people. Penelope was useful to him in this respect because she was – so she assured him – very much in the swim. Later he discovered seas more secret, cool and rarefied than those in which Penelope demonstrated her brave little breast stroke, but for the time being he submitted himself to her authority. This authority extended – and here he became restive – to the extra-marital bed, wherever that might happen to be. The truth was, she was really rather bossy in bed, and sometimes when her thin hot body arched under his and she shrieked like a cat for satisfaction he wondered whether something a little more affectionate might not be nice; or, more accurately, a small part of his mind wondered, since most of his attention was too occupied by giving her satisfaction and gaining it for himself to be diverted by anything else. He still found her exciting. He felt too that their relationship put him under a considerable obligation to her, and though he had exchanged many warm embraces with delightful girls at dances when heated by wine he had walked with them in moonlit gardens or canoodled vigorously in taxis on the way home, he did not feel entitled to go further, or to enter into any other intimate relationship. He did sometimes imagine a more ideal one, though, a more loving one, one in which he himself was the leader rather than the follower. He imagined, however, though without specifically planning it, that before embarking on such an ideal relationship he would make a fortune, a fortune being an obvious necessity all round and therefore the sooner made the better.

He was met at Bath station by a chauffeur and a boy.

'God dammit,' he cried almost immediately. 'I've left my hat on the train.'

The boy, who was Paul, the son of Leonard and Judith, immediately rushed back into the station shouting, 'Oh please, please, stop the train.'

The train had already left and was halfway round the corner on its way to Bristol.

'Stop, oh please, everybody help, you must stop the train,' Paul shouted, dashing through the barrier and up the stairs to the up platform where he seized the ticket collector by the arm and gasped, 'Oh please, please, sir, your lordship, you must help me, help me, stop the train.'

Orlando and the chauffeur were now pursuing him up the stairs. He more or less swung, frail and pale and yellow-haired, on the sizeable arm of the ticket collector.

'Oh sir, oh please.' But now his look of terror, which had alarmed the few people standing on the platform, disappeared, and he began to giggle nervously. 'Oh sir, you must, your lordship ...' he faltered unconvincingly. 'My friend has, my friend ...' Here his giggles almost made him speechless but he burst out, 'My friend has left his hat on the train.'

Orlando had now reached his side, and Paul suddenly hung his head, still clinging to the ticket collector, then looked up with the confiding smile of a much younger child and said, 'You are my friend aren't you?'

'Not yet,' said Orlando firmly. 'I'm so sorry,' he went on to the ticket collector.

'That's all right. You want to get on to the Lost Property at Bristol. I thought at least it was his grandmother he'd left on the train.'

'I haven't got a grandmother,' said Paul wistfully.

Orlando led the way back to the car, avoiding the amused glances of the onlookers.

As they drove out of Bath, Orlando talked to the chauffeur about the weather and Paul sat in silence, until he said sadly, 'I don't think it was very kind of you to say that you weren't my friend.'

'I probably will be your friend,' said Orlando. 'But we'd only just met, you know.'

'I was trying to help you,' said Paul.

'How old are you?' asked Orlando in order to change the subject.

'Eleven. People often think I'm younger because I'm smaller than my brother. My brother's very nice. His name is Stephen. He does much better at school than I do.'

'Does he? What do you do better than he does?'

'Nothing. He's awfully good at everything. He really is. You must believe me. I'm quite good at swimming but I don't use ordinary strokes. I do dog-paddle. Can you swim? Would you like to swim with me? We swim in Uncle Conrad's lake. It's lovely.'

'What else do you like doing?'

'Reading Pip Squeak and Wilfred. It's a cartoon in the newspaper. Mummy says it's silly. Do you know Dagwood?'

'Who's Dagwood?'

'It's another cartoon. Mummy says that's silly too. Have you met my mother?'

'Yes.'

'She's nice, isn't she? She's in London today. Would you like to kiss her?'

'Yes. I suppose most people would.'

'Shall I tell her you'd like to kiss her?'

'I shouldn't bother. Oughtn't you to be at school today?'

'I've had chicken pox. Most people stay at school to have chicken pox, in the san. They have great fun. But I came home because Father said I ought to be under my own doctor because I once put a ball-bearing down my ear and I'm partly deaf. Did you know that?

'Is it still there?'

'No, they took it out. I screamed terribly Have you had chicken pox?'

'No.'

'Oh dear, because I'm afraid I'm still infectious.'

'Oh dear.'

'We are going to be friends though aren't we?'

'I suppose so,' said Orlando.

They drove through several stone-built villages. The countryside became less populated.

'It's pretty here, isn't it?' said Orlando.

'Here's Mount Sorrel,' said Paul. 'This is where Uncle Conrad lives. He's Mummy's brother. He's gone to India to tell the black people what to do. His son Henry is only five which is too young for Stephen and me but he's not bad all the same.'

'How old is Stephen?'

'Ten. I'm eleven. But everyone thinks he's older than me.'

'So you said. And who else lives in that house?'

'No one. Just Uncle Conrad and Henry. Aunt Alexandra died in agony when Henry was born. She split in half. I can remember it. I was three. I was only three but I can remember it.'

'If Henry's five and you're eleven you must have been six when he was born.'

'Oh. Oh yes. Five from eleven is six, isn't it? I thought I was three. It was awfully clever of you to work that out.'

'Nonsense.'

'It was, it was. I mean it. You must believe me. I really think it was awfully clever of you.'

They were driving beside the park wall, which was high enough to conceal the house from the road. Orlando had caught only one glimpse of it, through an entrance gate. He had seen a pillared portico and a lake, and had noticed with approval that it looked very grand.

As they came into the village he was able to see more of it because the back of the house was only divided from the village street by a yew hedge and the wall, which became higher here but over the top of which he could see some upper windows. The only means of access from the village street was through a door in the wall, the main entrance to the house being approached through the park.

'That's our door, that's Henry's and our door, that's where we leave our bicycles,' said Paul. 'No one's allowed to lock it because Uncle Conrad says it's a matter of principle even when someone came in and stole all the peaches out of the greenhouse. That's the church, it's a famous Somerset church tower, and that's where Desmond lives, the carpenter. He's my friend. He gives me nails whenever I need them. He just gives them to me.'

It was a small village of grey stone houses round an uneven green. As they drove out of it they passed a little Wesleyan chapel with the date 1817 carved over its wooden portico. A few hundred yards further on was what seemed to be a tall stone chimney, to one side of which were attached two dilapidated cottages with broken windows.

'That's the old coal mine,' said Paul. 'We're not allowed to go there. Uncle Conrad's going to pull down the cottages and fill in the shaft and then we'll be allowed to.'

'I didn't know there were coal mines here.'

'Oh yes, they're the Mendip coal mines. Uncle Conrad's got lots of them but they're not much good. They're very old. Further on over there, there are lead mines. The Romans used to use them. We learnt about them at school.'

'It's not what I think of as coal-mining country,' said Orlando, who had read about the Industrial North.

'It isn't coal-mining country,' said Paul. 'It's just that there are some coal mines. Uncle Conrad grows trees as well. That's why he started Timberwork. We're nearly home now. Our house is not as big as Uncle Conrad's and it hasn't got a lake. Do you mind?'

'No.'

'I expect you're very sad about your hat,' said Paul.

The house was two miles from Mount Sorrel. A sign pointed to Wood Hill, and Wood Hill turned out to be just the house, which was on a hill in a wood, a pleasant two-storeyed early Georgian house built of local stone and without ornament except for a pilastered doorway with a carved headstone. A wide vista had been cut through the woods so that from the front of the house there was a view down the valley towards Mount Sorrel, though the village itself was out of sight behind a fold of mild green slope.

The inside of the house was white. The small panelled entrance hall had been painted a matt white, so had the mahogany staircase. On the stone-flagged floor, in the angle of the staircase, stood a white peacock on a pedestal, staring towards the door. In the corner of the hall furthest from the door, beside a tall mirror of which the frame was also white, was a white vase containing pampas grass, the cream of whose plumes was the same as the cream carpet on the stairs.

Paul led Orlando into the drawing-room, which was a long low room with windows on two sides. Two of them were french windows opening on to the garden. This room was more or less ivory-coloured, a colour between the white of the hall walls and the cream of the pampas grass.

It had two big mirrors on either side of the fireplace which reflected the windows and the garden. The windows had curtains the same colour as the walls. Otherwise the room seemed full of fat white sofas and armchairs with brown cushions. It struck Orlando as smart but cold. He preferred the hall.

A butler, alarmingly dark amid the white, came to tell him that Mr Gardner was in the library. Orlando and Paul followed him and found Leonard sitting at his desk in a small book-lined room with flowery chintz curtains and a knole sofa.

'Ah,' he said, without rising but holding out his hand across the desk for Orlando to shake.

'Well, Paul,' he said. 'What are you up to? No Latin this morning?'

'I've done it.'

'Mathews, get the garden boy to bowl a few balls for Master Paul until lunchtime, would you?'

'As a matter of fact, I'm rather bored of cricket. I don't think I'm much good at it, as a matter of fact.'

'All the more reason to practise then,' said Leonard. 'Practice makes perfect, they say, don't they? Off you run now.'

Paul and the butler left the room and Leonard went on, 'The sooner that boy gets to his public school the better. They're too soft with him where he is at the moment. He plays them up.'

'Yes, I can imagine that,' said Orlando. 'He was very polite to me though.'

'Was he?' Leonard paused a moment and then asked, 'How do you find him?'

'Very nice,' said Orlando. 'I thought he was a bit young for his age perhaps.'

Leonard shifted irritably in his chair. 'He puts it on. It's a way of trying to attract his mother's attention. He's always done it. Children are a problem, you know.'

Orlando nodded understandingly, glad to think he was not Leonard's child.

Later, when he was an important man of affairs, he pushed the sofas and armchairs aside and danced with Agatha, his daughter.

For hours it seemed.

> 'All by myself in the morning
> All by myself in the night'

Judith was in London, the boys away at school.

> 'I sit alone in a cosy Morris chair
> So unhappy there
> Playing solitaire'

It was Nanny's night out and Jen was supposed to put Agatha to bed but she hadn't the heart to interrupt them, seeing them enjoying themselves, so went back to the nursery and knitted, listening to the baby Imogen talking to herself before falling asleep.

> 'I long to rest my weary head on somebody's
>   shoulder
> I hate to grow older
> All by myself'

They played the record over and over again, and another one about living in the sunlight, loving in the moonlight, having a wonderful time. Sometimes Agatha was seized with laughter and hung on his arm breathless but he did not stop. He fox-trotted, two-stepped, one-stepped, reversed, a touch

of tap, a soft-shoe shuffle, he was Fred Astaire, was Mrs
Irene Castle, was Charlie Chaplin, was, singing as well, Jack
Buchanan, Noël Coward. Agatha clapped and was Shirley
Temple and fell down laughing and was a smart Society lady
foxtrotting in pearls and they played the same records over
and over again while Jen upstairs knitted a comforter for her
father and thought let them enjoy themselves, Nanny's out.

'Me and Jane in a plane,' Agatha shouted.

It sounded worn and scratchy.

> 'In my two-seater
> What could be sweeter.'

They fox-trotted like mad, bouncing up and down as
they went.

> 'I'll be keeping my eye
> On the man in the moon
> He's a dangerous guy
> When he starts to spoon'

Bump bump bumpety bump

> 'No traffic cop
> Will ever stop
> Me and Jane in a plane'

Judith had Bix Beiderbeck and Jack Teagarden but
Agatha's favourite was Me and Jane in a Plane so they
hopped and jumped and jerked to it until even she admitted
she was tired and Jen's head round the door elicited only
token protests and she went not un-willingly to bed. And
he was alone, and walked down in the evening to the mill,
as Leonard used to do.

'This mill,' Leonard said to Orlando. 'Is my pride and
joy.'

Orlando did not believe him. He found it hard to believe Leonard when he spoke of anything which involved his emotions.

'It is my little kingdom,' said Leonard.

Orlando was prepared to concede that for the time being he probably meant it.

'Of course I have other more important interests.'

'Of course.'

'But this is something special.'

Leonard was not the sober civil servant of Proby's prediction, and the reason for this was the war. Coming from a dull respectable background, an intelligent young man who had done well at Cambridge but upon whom the cold fingers of a certain kind of conformity had already, as King had noticed, fastened themselves, he was plunged by the war into a milieu in which he unexpectedly shone, the military one. He volunteered, rose rapidly, and took his place in no time at all among a select few first-class officers. He was responsible and reliable and an implicit believer in military discipline. Only occasionally did he lose his outward calm and reveal himself to be more emotional than he appeared. On one of these occasions he won his D S O.

Leaving the Army with a whole network of new acquaintances, he found the City rather than the Civil Service a suitable environment for a man of his standing. He had proved to himself that he could rise in the world, and the discovery fed his ambition, social, financial and eventually political.

It was his ambition which drew Judith to him. Her eyes softened, describing their relationship, in the early days, to friends.

'It's fair exchange, you see,' she said. 'I can help him by giving him social position and sons and he can give me money and a job I can get my teeth into – pushing his career I mean. It's going to be the most successful marriage ever because we're going to be a team.' Her eyes shone with idealism. 'It's much better than if I'd married one of my own set.'

She needed money because, as she put it, it suited her, and because although she was not exactly poor herself the provision which had been made for her by her father, the bulk of whose property had naturally been inherited by her brother Conrad, was mainly in the form of an interest in certain of his agricultural estates, and this, though productive of a regular income, and useful as security for her overdrafts from the bank, was not an endless source of ready cash. Leonard, as a highly successful stockbroker, almost was.

He was so successful as a stockbroker that he was asked to exercise his financial wisdom on the boards of several companies; and he was of course the obvious choice to be Chairman of Timberwork.

Timberwork had developed out of various natural causes. One was Conrad's interest in the commercial growing of timber, another was the presence close to Mount Sorrel of a large disused paper mill which had been powered by the stream in whose valley it stood; and another was the increasingly rapid decline of the Somerset coal mining industry and the consequent need for employment, so that Timberwork both gave and received benefit from the local labour situation, an aspect of its function which gave gratification to its founder. Having founded it, Conrad handed its fortunes over to his brother-in-law, and so Leonard and Judith came to live at Wood Hill and Leonard devoted a day or two a week to the affairs of Timberwork and Judith kept two hunters in Conrad's stables.

The woods behind the mill were cool in the summer and smelt of garlic; the sound of water and of birdsong was in the air, the scrabble of a squirrel or clatter of pigeons; the sun through the beech leaves reached the dark mud by the stream, the deep azure dragonflies hesitating between big yellow king-cups. In the woods in the lunch-hour the employees wandered, the works manager belching after his sandwiches, the jaunty draughtsman swinging hands with one or other of the girls, the oldest joiner observing shyly the cheeky creature from the design office, who went arm in arm with her best friend the girl from accounts, he being haunted by the image of his shrewish wife; and Orlando walked there too in his time in the summer, liking the smell of mud and garlic and the occasional sound of the train crossing the viaduct.

He liked it but resisted Leonard's sentimentality. He was used to working in a small concern in rural surroundings. It had advantages and disadvantages. The atmosphere was friendly but sometimes restrictive, corporate loyalty came easily but so did petty discontents: a little matter like the works manager's indigestion could assume a disproportionate importance. It was not a modern kind of organization. Orlando was interested only in the efficiency or lack of it with which Timberwork fulfilled its function. When he spoke about it with Conrad he felt that Conrad thought as he did. When he spoke about it with Leonard he felt like screaming.

'They all know one here,' said Leonard, walking through the workshop. 'Some of these big firms, you know, lose all sense of personal contact. I'm on the board of a big heavy engineering firm up in Birmingham and I go up there once a month for a meeting but one has very little idea of what the day to day activities in a place like that are like. Here one's really in the midst of it. There's no barrier between manager and employee. How's it going, Desmond? All right?'

'Yes thank you, sir.'

'This is the big order for Harrods isn't it?' said Leonard. 'This is a big order for Harrods,' he told Orlando.

'It's those garden benches for Lady Judith I'm doing here as a matter of fact, sir,' said Desmond.

'Ah,' said Leonard. 'Ah yes, Judith's garden benches. Shall we go and have a look at the office? I must introduce you to young Graham.'

'Young Graham,' said Leonard, 'is not exactly what you would call a gent.'

You turned off the minor road a mile or two from Mount Sorrel, near a cottage with roses and gothic windows, the demure front of which belied its backyard, where racing pigeons and rabbits lived and a couple of mangy dogs who rattled chains and barked; and behind again were cabbages and hens. Leonard made representations but in vain. Important visitors, he said, were given a bad impression; but the cottage belonged to the Belgian who lived in it and nothing could be done. He had been a refugee in the war and had married a local girl of ill repute and they had bred excessively. Some of the smaller children who scuffed in the backyard with the hens and dogs and smelly rabbits were grandchildren, of doubtful paternity.

This thorn in Leonard's side you passed, and the trees closed about the little road, until looking up at the tallest you saw the viaduct taller behind through the leaves, its arches reaching from the damp shade of the stream bed to the open air fifty feet above where the train rollicked past from time to time.

'Good old Somerset and Dorset,' Leonard would say. (Orlando would think, he's lived here three years or something, what right has he to be so loyal to the railway?)

The road turned under one of the arches and led to the broad space where the mill stood, a fine stone building built in 1805 as a paper mill under a concession from Conrad's ancestor and inside now light and huge like a cathedral. Small uninteresting buildings behind housed a canteen and the new design office: the yard was there too, full of timber, and the lorries.

He drives under the viaduct in the old bullnose Morris he bought from Tom Ford, the general manager who left because he could not stand Leonard. The steering is not perfect and it lurches at speed out into the open space and round into the yard at the back.

And here he comes again in the new Model A Ford the firm provided when he in his turn became general manager. A source of pride for a matter of weeks only, he smashed it into a Keep Left sign one night in London rather late and swopped it for a second-hand Alvis speed 20 which annoyed Leonard because he had always had an Alvis himself.

Here now quickly in the new Lagonda 4½ litre, in the sunshine swirling confidently round the corner into the yard, the busy managing director, late for a meeting.

And here again – the good times now – in the Bentley Park Ward, slowly, with a blast of the horn, and slower still so they can all see. His first Bentley.

Orlando moved into a three-roomed flat over the stables at Mount Sorrel. Mrs Janson the wife of Conrad's butler cooked his breakfast and did his cleaning and washing. The flat had been adapted for Tom Ford the departing general manager. The stable yard was some way from the house, a big square of mid-eighteenth century buildings with a cupola over a clock. One side of the entrance formed a cottage where the Jansons lived, and there were two flats as well as Orlando's, lived in by the groom and his family and by the chauffeur who was a bachelor.

Conrad was not particularly interested in horses but he kept two for riding round the woods or accompanying his son on the pony or lending to visitors. His wife had been a keen rider. George Johnson the groom spoke of her with the deepest admiration and respect. George missed her. Most of his time apart from young Henry's riding lessons, was spent in looking after Judith's two splendid hunters, one of which he would hack or box to meet her when she was hunting so that she could change horses, but he did not speak of her with the devotion he showed towards the memory of Lady Alexandra. She was too bold, he said, as a rider, and she didn't take account of anybody, no matter who. Orlando thought this was probably true and admired her the more for it.

He liked to hear the horses being got ready for hunting early in the mornings before he had got out of bed. Once or twice he went with Judith but he had not the time to learn how to behave on the hunting field and felt out of place, although he rode well and later bought a comfortable retired hunter for riding with the children.

He was fond of his flat over the stables although he did little but sleep in it. He worked long hours at Timberwork and soon most of the rest of his time was spent either in London or in one or other of the two households, Mount Sorrel or Wood Hill.

One evening Graham Harper took Orlando to his cottage for a drink after work. They drove there on Graham's motor bicycle. Orlando sat on the pillion and thought that Graham drove too fast. The cottage was two or three miles from the mill and was on a main road. It was a one-storeyed stone building with a green corrugated iron roof. Behind it was a field full of pigs.

'Stinks, doesn't it?' said Graham, as they left the powerful machine on the pavement and went inside.

'Yes,' said Orlando.

Graham went to fetch some bottles of beer from the larder.

'Bottle-opener,' he said, coming back into the little dark sitting-room which faced the road. 'Can't find it.'

'Here,' said Orlando, bringing out his knife.

'That's a good knife,' said Graham.

'I know,' said Orlando. 'It's useful. I used to use it on the boats in France.'

'What boats?'

'Well, on the fishing boats, I really meant. When I used to go with the fishing fleet. In Brittany. Sardines.'

'Oh. Well, have a drink. Oh, glasses.' He found some in a cupboard and wiped them inside with his thumb. 'What do you think of our Leonard?'

'I find him rather irritating,' said Orlando. 'But I think he quite often knows what he's talking about all the same.'

'I'm in it for the money,' said Graham, thinking I must not talk too much. 'Only the money interests me.' It keeps me going while I bide my time, train, wait. 'It keeps me going while I look around. It's a rich man's toy, you know, it's nothing more. I'm in favour of it, mind you. It gives us all a living. These blokes round here used to work in the mines, you know, in this village they used to work in the mines. Or else on the land and that's nearly as bad. Do you know the latest unemployment figures? Two and a half million. And going up all the time. The chap who used to live in this house was carried off to a slave camp, that's how I got it.'

'A slave camp?' asked Orlando.

'Work camp for the unemployed. Slave camps, that's all they are. They carried him off to Wales somewhere to make baskets. I went to grammar school.'

'What's that?'

'What is it? Don't you know what it is then? Well it's ... I tell you what it's not, it's not a public school.'

'Eton and all that?'

'Eton and all that. So I'm not a gentleman and I don't have a gentleman's accent. Don't say you hadn't noticed.'

'I know it's very stupid but it's the one thing I can't seem to get right because of having lived abroad. It's very important to English people, I know, but I'm afraid my ear isn't properly attuned yet. You don't speak like the men in the factory, though, like Desmond, for instance.'

'Good Lord, no. They're lower class. I'm just common.'

'I see.'

Graham smiled. He did not smile often. He had a bad complexion and was small and skinny. He had long brown hair which Leonard was always asking him to get cut; it flopped over his forehead and he tossed it irritably back from time to time.

He walked up and down in the little sitting-room while Orlando sat on an uncomfortable chair.

'Look,' said Graham, picking up some drawings which were lying on a table and tossing them on to Orlando's knee. 'The new line. Same as the last as it happens. Awful, aren't they?'

Orlando blew the dust and cigarette ash off the drawings and looked at them carefully.

'Do they sell?' he asked.

'Of course they sell. That's what people want. It's no use being snooty about it. What's the good of designing anything decent when what people want is Tudor garden furniture?'

'Oh it's Tudor, is it?'

'Of course it's Tudor, can't you see? That's what they want, that's what we've got to give them, isn't it? They'll pay for it too. You've seen what they get for this stuff in Harrods.'

'I think something simpler and cheaper could be produced in larger quantities and make more money in the end,' said Orlando. 'It would be nicer too. I've been thinking about it. I'm sure it wouldn't be beyond our powers to produce plain furniture for simple rooms rather on the American pattern – playroom furniture, more or less, only for grown-ups – which could be used in various combinations, and painted or not as people wanted. If we found that any of it was really succeeding we could sell the licence to produce it to a bigger firm and take a royalty. So that we could expand without ourselves having to go into mass-production.'

'We certainly can't produce enormous quantities of anything here,' said Graham. 'We can spread a little but not much, not without building a new factory and importing more labour and God knows what.'

'I don't think it would be necessary to grow too large. But I don't think anything that can't be mass-produced is really going to be big business nowadays. Mass-production is the big new factor. Good designs can be mass-produced as well as bad designs. At least I don't see why they shouldn't be, if they are developed with mass-production in mind.'

'Maybe. I don't mind having a go. Mass-production in mind, oh dear, what would they say at the dear old Bristol Tech? Or rather, what would Lady Judith think? Have you met Our Lord yet?'

'Our Lord?'

'Lord Field. You wait.'

'Is he like his sister?'

'No. They don't get on all that well I don't think. At least I suppose they get on better than you'd think considering he's a saint and she's a scarlet woman.'

'A saint?'

'He tries to do good. I'm not joking. He tries to do good. But listen, I tell you what, he hasn't a chance. You don't know, you've lived abroad, but I tell you this country's in for something really big, really big, the whole system we live under's crumbling, Ramsay Macdonald himself has said so, he's said the system is breaking down as it was bound to break down, they all know it's only a matter of time. Listen I'll tell you, I've got this chum, he's just gone up to Cambridge – yes, Cambridge, I know you think some kind of stuck-up class thing but he's not like that, my God he's businesslike, that's what I admire about him, he believes in organization – and he's introduced me to these people, you know, they're really serious about it, about the revolution, and we go to demonstrations and so on and it's really serious. I tell you the organization's there. And listen, if you're interested I could let you have some literature. The Left is really beginning to organize itself, you'd be amazed. This chum of mine knows someone who's been to Russia, I could introduce you to him, I go to Cambridge most weekends on the bike, or London we go to if there's a meeting. There's this terrific feeling of, I know it sounds silly, serious purpose or something, you know, you'd know what I mean if you came to one of the meetings.'

'Isn't it rather a long drive from here to Cambridge?' asked Orlando.

'Four or five hours I suppose. I do it at night. I like being on the bike at night. Have some more beer.' He began to pace backwards and forwards faster than ever. 'The police and the communications and that's it. You know. Hardly any bloodshed. It's bound to come. It's the only thing that will stop war and cure unemployment. We're going to march with the hunger marchers on Saturday. They can't survive, even the good ones, even Conrad Field. And Leonard, Christ, you know he's on the board of some armament firm in the North somewhere? The armament firms and the big banks and the big insurance companies – they're international of course, they cut across patriotism and all that – and now the Left is doing it too, it used to be feeble and parochial and do-gooding, now it's getting some teeth at last. It's an international class struggle. Listen, you know how much a baby is allowed for food under the Means Test? One shilling, one shilling a week.'

'Perhaps that's for when it's being breast-fed?' suggested Orlando, who was listening carefully.

'How can the mother have any milk when she's half-starved herself?' said Graham with wild eyes. 'And the upper classes don't breast-feed, do they? In case they spoil their figures. Lady Judith and her friends. And I tell you what, this chum of mine knows someone else at Cambridge whose mother's her aunt, Judith's aunt, or something, and we all went there one night after a meeting, in chokers and caps, and there was this big party going on, and we were dead drunk most of us and he was sick on her doorstep, well I know? that probably seems rather childish to you and it is I suppose really but you see it represents something to them, it really does, and the real stuff, the real seriousness is there, it is there I tell you. Listen, would you like some stuff to read, because honestly I mean I can't talk to a soul in this damn place and I can't get away every weekend, I mean things have been pretty busy here lately and then these other chaps have their own work to do and everything.'

'I'd like to read some of your things. I don't think I take quite such a gloomy view as you do.'

'It's not gloomy, it's optimistic. It's optimistic, but terrible.'

'A friend of mine called Guy Waring says that all we need is a leader.'

'No, no, there's got to be a total upheaval. Leaders are nothing, it's the great inevitable forces that count. Take this and this, I'll get you some more if you're interested, I'll get some next time I go to Cambridge.'

'Thanks awfully. And if you have a moment will you think about those designs we were talking about, the indoor ones? We needn't bother Leonard with them yet.'

'I'll take you back on the bike.'

Graham drove faster than ever at night. He dropped Orlando at the stables and drove away again, the bike roaring and his thin hair whipped backwards by the dark wind.

'My experience is this,' said Leonard, 'and it's been proved to me time and time again. When you've got a good line, stick to it. Don't waste your resources in experiment. When you've got one good product concentrate on it.'

'When the rubber tube people called me in to advise them in 1927,' said Leonard, 'I said to them, look here, I'll be honest with you. I said there's nothing needed here that any suburban housewife couldn't tell you. Common sense. You've overspent, you're over-extended, you've got to consolidate. They were making two-thirds of the rubber tubing used in this country and they wanted to diversify. That was their cry. Diversification. I said, don't diversify, export. Spread your risk, that's all. But don't muck about with your basic product.'

[*]

'Timberwork is a small firm,' said Leonard. 'A small local family firm. I think we ought to keep it like that.'

'Harrods are perfectly satisfied with our garden furniture,' said Leonard. 'Of course you probably haven't realized quite what Harrods means in this country – all over the world in fact.'

'I like a young man to have ideas,' said Leonard. 'Let's wait until Conrad comes back. Let's not do anything in a hurry. I believe – I've always believed – that a gradual development in the direction of indoor furniture as well as garden stuff is the ultimate answer for Timberwork.'

'The time,' said Leonard, 'is not ripe for expansion. Now is the time to tighten our belts. We've got to get the country on its feet financially before we shall get a climate in which the small private company can afford to take risks.'

'I'd like to show you these new drawings of young Graham's,' said Leonard. 'It's all very speculative of course and far in the future, but I've always felt, as I was telling you the other day, that Timberwork has got to spread its wings a bit some day. I had a talk with him and these are what he's produced. You've seen them already? Good. The time's not ripe for taking risks of course, but I shall have a word with Conrad when he gets back and tell him I think we ought to go into some of these ideas quite seriously. Incidentally, you seem to be the only person young Graham ever speaks to in a relatively civilized manner. See if you can persuade him to get his hair cut, would you?'

Orlando went to London.

He stood opposite Penelope in her little grey drawing-room.

'I've hardly even seen Judith,' he said. 'She's always away.'

'If it isn't Judith it will be someone else,' said Penelope, intensely serious. 'I know the time is coming when you will want someone else and I can't bear ever to be a burden to you, I can't bear that we should part slowly, I want it to be quick, so that we can still be friends.'

'Of course I'll always be your friend, Penelope, but do you really want to end everything between us now? I never dreamt, when I came here this evening, that that would be what you would say.'

'It's right,' said Penelope. 'Anything else would be horrible. I know I'm right. We won't be lovers any more but soon we'll be friends.'

'Can I still come and talk to you?'

'Of course, but not for a few weeks.'

'I've never admired you more in my whole life. You know I like you very much. Must we really do this?'

'Yes.'

Love, pity, and self-pity, which had rushed to his heart and made it hard for him to breathe, moderated.

'I shall always – would you mind if I respected you?'

'No, that would be all right,' she said, pleased.

She looked, with her curls and cosmetics, rather old.

He kissed her on the cheek, and left.

Of course, in some small corner of her mind, she had hoped that he would say, come to me, we will run away together, Gerald can divorce you. There were no children, after all. But he was half her age and had no money. It would have been very unsuitable. She had done the right thing, rather well. She powdered her face and began the long routine of recovery.

Graham Harper kept a diary, in which he wrote, 'It seems that in this youth we have some kind of a phenomenon.'

He wrote it in his cottage after work. Leaving the office late he would call in as often as not at the pub in his nearest village and after a couple of pints and perhaps a game of darts with one of the three old men who frequented the public bar, he would drive his motor bicycle rather fast through the narrow lanes to his cottage and in the dark little sitting-room which smelt of damp and stale tobacco would pull out his notebook and sit writing until quite late, only pausing to fetch himself some bread and cheese from the kitchen, or to let the cat in. The cat belonged to his nearest neighbours up the road, an agricultural labourer's family with six children, three cats and a yard full of smelly hens. One of the cats had attached itself to Graham, who fed it intermittently on sardines and allowed it to sit on his knee while he wrote.

'It seems that in this youth we have some kind of a phenomenon. He's the same age as I am and as far as we know of equally undistinguished parentage. No one thinks a thing of me, but Orlando they load with their favours. Well, the girls in the office, that I can understand, because he's sexy, I can see that. But it's not his curly hair or his well formed torso that makes old Leonard bless him with his patronage, and Our Lord himself crown him with the accolade of his smile and an invitation to evening kippers at the Great House or whatever. Leonard's a hard-hearted bastard and Our Lord as distant as Hell on his old cloud, yet for him they soften, for him they unload their cornucopias. He's fluent, shall we say, can express himself, is articulate. That's because he lived with this educated fellow who talked all the time. He gives the impression of being self-reliant at the same time as being modest and willing to learn. (I am hopelessly dependent on others at the same time as being arrogant and prejudiced, so perhaps we're getting at the differences now.) He has what used to be known as a pleasing address (that I certainly lack – filthy manners and 33 High Street, Nalderton). He's sympathetic – wouldn't you tell him anything and know you'd get a sensible disinterested answer? Sensible. God he's sensible. And so alert, so balanced, so young – for with him youth is a phenomenon too. No one thinks of me as young, but youth sits on Orlando like the dawn on the mountains, religiously immanent, lending him the illusion – if it is an illusion – of warmth. Perhaps it's his heart that will let him down. I mean a perfect human being would have a heart as well wouldn't he? And of course you can't have one of those and be a successful capitalist and lover of society ladies, which are the two things I think for the moment he's setting out to be. Perhaps he'll change, and begin to understand and become one of us. Not likely, not when he's doing so well in the state of things as they are. He's going to be taken up by Them, all plausible and practical and promising as he is. Oh he's clever too and analytical and decisive. If I had a problem I'd take it to him. But I haven't a problem, only a cause, and that I wouldn't expect him to understand. He's too lucky, the lucky bastard.'

Leonard was beginning to think of Orlando almost like a son.

'He's getting too big for his boots,' he said to Judith in the bathroom. Leonard was in the bath, which was very full. Judith was wearing a white silk dressing-gown and was sitting on the lavatory seat, the lid being down. It was before dinner. They each had a martini glass beside them on the edge of the bath.

'You mean he's challenging your authority?' said Judith, smiling at him.

'Not exactly,' said Leonard. 'But he's got too many ideas and he can't sort out which are the good ones and which are the bad ones. They haven't any judgement at that age.'

'I don't think I'll have any judgement at any age,' said Judith. 'How lucky you are to have it.'

'You know I rely enormously on your advice,' said Leonard. 'It's entirely because of you that I employed him. What's this lemony smell? Do I like it?'

'It's some new marvellous thing made from Caribbean limes. Someone told me about it.'

'I like that ordinary Floris stuff better. Sandalwood. Or violet.'

'Oh I can't bear violet. How masculine of you to like violet. Go on.'

'What with?'

'Orlando.'

'Oh yes. He seems to be able to cope with young Graham. That I do admire him for. And indeed he gets on well with everyone. But he's ambitious. He wants to make Timberwork into something much bigger.'

'That would be all right wouldn't it, if it made us all more money?'

'It wouldn't make us all more money. He has no idea of the general business situation. Nor of the fact that a firm like that can exist economically if it's very big or very small but not if it's medium-sized.'

'Can't you tell him?'

'It's no use telling the young anything,' Leonard soaped his arms rather excessively with verbena soap. 'And another thing, it wouldn't in the least suit me personally if Timberwork were to become more of an undertaking. I haven't the time to give to it for one thing.'

'Couldn't Orlando run it?'

'He's too inexperienced. Besides, I don't want to get out of touch with it myself.'

'So he is challenging your authority in a way?'

'In a way, I suppose. But I don't mind that. It's perfectly natural. I should have done the same at his age. And he's a bright boy. I want to bring him on. And I will too, in my own good time and when he's ready for it.'

'Does he know that? I mean, that you want him to do well?'

'I don't know. Perhaps I seem to be always turning down his schemes. You might help me there. You could let him know I've nothing against him for being ambitious. I've told him myself but it's difficult to talk to the young. You have a word with him some time. We ought to ask him here more anyway. I don't suppose he has much social life in these parts.'

'All right, I'll ask him. You'd better get out, it's nearly quarter to.'

She held a towel for him. He rose splashing from the bath and walked into it. When she had wrapped him round she kissed him. He returned the kiss.

'What would I do without you?' he said.

She smiled and went to dress.

So Orlando went to dinner at Wood Hill, sometimes when Leonard and Judith were alone and sometimes when there were local neighbours there, or friends staying in the house.

Although he admired Judith and thought her extraordinarily attractive, he found her difficult to talk to. Mostly they gossiped about mutual acquaintances in London, and Orlando listened to her with attention since she was obviously an expert at this kind of conversation; but Leonard, sitting at the head of the table, made him uneasy. Judith made him uneasy too, for that matter, because she seemed to be teasing him. They often ended by talking rather stiltedly about Timberwork or the children, she ignorant on the first subject, he on the second, particularly since he had not then met Stephen, her second son, and had to some extent taken against Paul, her firstborn.

The child he did rather like was Henry Field, the son of Conrad, who was then five and living alone at Mount Sorrel with his governess and the servants. The governess it was who in fact had first attracted Orlando's attention, and it was through her that he had come to know and like Henry.

The governess's name was Flora McLeod and Orlando had noticed her one day when she brought Henry down to the stables for his riding lesson. Orlando was still in bed although it was Wednesday because he had been to a party in London the night before and had returned on the milk train to Bath and was feeling very tired. He also had a severe headache, so he had telephoned the mill to say that he thought he had flu but would come in later in the day if he felt better.

When he heard the sound of horses' hooves in the stable yard he made his way to his window and looked out. He saw the little boy being hoisted on to his Shetland pony and George Johnson preparing to accompany him on Conrad's cob. He also saw Miss McLeod, understood her to be the governess, and observed that she had a figure remarkably unsuitable for a governess, since though otherwise neat and ladylike she had an unusually well-developed bosom. He had noticed before that a hangover was not inconsistent with a certain kind of rather dreamy lecherousness. After watching her for a bit as she stood in the stable yard watching the riders ride away, he opened the window and leaning out dishevelled in his pyjamas asked her the time. Miss McLeod, whose family and friends were in distant Argyll and who was rather lonely in her present post, told him. Soon, on her Tuesdays and alternate Sundays, she would transport her fine figure up the narrow stairs to share with Orlando the pleasures it revealed. She was a nice girl, a strict Presbyterian, and never gave him a moment's trouble. Her warm heart had room for Henry in it too.

'Miss McLeod allows Henry to play too much with the village children,' said Judith. 'He's getting an accent.'

'I think he's rather lonely,' said Orlando.

Judith smiled knowingly at his so defending the governess but only said, 'I suppose he might as well get to know them since Conrad says he's going to send him to the village school until he's eight.'

Often in the evenings Orlando would look in on his way back from work, going through the door in the wall into the garden and into the house through the side entrance, past the tennis rackets and Conrad's old sleeping Labrador. If Henry was not yet in bed they would talk, and Orlando found him a sensible and self-reliant little boy, with a voice in which an echo of Miss McLeod's Scots already mingled with a Somerset softness picked up from his village companions. His having no other family than a father who was away made him touching. Miss McLeod and the servants spoilt him but he remained rather self-contained.

One evening Orlando walked in a little earlier than usual, through a minor hall containing a secondary staircase, through a passage room containing reference books, and out into the main staircase hall, through which he had to pass in order to reach the servants' sitting-room, where he expected to find Henry having his apple and his glass of milk before going upstairs. This main hall was a long room with pillars which balanced the pillars on the portico outside the front door: it was grand but not particularly agreeable; like most of the house it had been rebuilt in Regency times and was inclined to seem cold and pompous. At the far end of this hall was hung a portrait by Orpen of Conrad's late wife, and it was in front of this portrait that two figures were standing, their backs to Orlando and their faces raised to the picture.

Orlando hesitated, too surprised to go back the way he had come. He recognized that the man standing with the child was Conrad.

Conrad turned and looked at Orlando, down the length of the hall, without speaking. Henry looked up at him, turned too, and said, 'Hullo Orlando.'

'I'm so sorry, I had no idea ...'

'He's a friend of Flora's,' said Henry. 'This is my father.'

'How do you do?' Conrad began to walk across the hall. Orlando hastened to meet him. At the foot of the stairs they shook hands.

'I'm most awfully sorry to walk into your house like this. I knew you were expected back but I thought not until tomorrow. I'm living in your stables and working at Timberwork, and I've sometimes been coming in to say good night to Henry and to talk to Miss McLeod for a few minutes on my way back from work. I do hope you don't mind.'

'Not at all. It's very good of you. I'm afraid they've been a bit short of company.' Conrad looked seriously into Orlando's face as he spoke. In his glance there was no trace of irony or reserve. Orlando immediately felt violently ashamed of his relationship with Miss McLeod.

'I found that I could get back this evening instead of waiting until tomorrow morning,' said Conrad. 'I only arrived an hour or two ago and we've been walking about a bit seeing what's been happening while I've been away.'

'We always come to look at the picture of my mother after my father's been away,' said Henry. 'She's dead, you know. He's brought me a whole regiment of Indian soldiers, an army practically, shall I show you? And a lovely Indian shawl for Flora. Come and see.'

'I'd love to see them another day, Henry, but I must go home now.'

'Won't you just come and see the soldiers?' said Conrad. 'It won't take you a moment.'

Orlando followed them into the library where set out on a round leather-topped table there was indeed what seemed to be a whole Gurkha regiment in miniature.

'I have seen them marching like that through the streets of Delhi,' said Conrad.

'Were they going into battle?' Henry's face was flushed. His hand hovered over his regiment, not certain which warrior to touch.

'It was a ceremonial parade in front of the Viceroy,' said Conrad.

'Did they carry guns or only swords?' asked Henry.

Conrad explained about the parade. He told them that the Viceroy had had the most important Indian princes to dinner and what they had been wearing. He told them that he himself had been right up to the borders of Tibet, a land no foreigner might enter, and had seen a Lama passing on the other side with a group of followers, and everyone had bowed to the ground and Conrad had bowed to the ground too only he had looked up quickly out of curiosity and had seen the Lama staring at him, curious too. And he had seen the sun rise over Mount Everest.

Orlando soon excused himself and said good night to Henry and left. He wished he had been better dressed. That morning, knowing he was going to have to help to move furniture in the new design office, he had put on some corduroy trousers and one of his old fisherman's jerseys. He was afraid Conrad must have thought him too young to be of any significance.

Some days later Orlando was in the design office with Graham when Graham began to sing.

'Lo he-e co-o-omes with clou-ou-ouds de-esce-ending...'

Conrad and Leonard were crossing the yard.

'The Lord cometh,' said Graham. 'Isn't he glorious?'

In that year Conrad was forty-one.

'Gradually we shall progress towards self-government in India,' he said. 'It's a question of organization, of working out in detail the widening of the franchise. There need be no question of our leaving India. We should make it clear that we are going ahead with Federation as fast as we can, and we should try to legislate next year. I am convinced that fundamentally Gandhi is a force for peace.'

Walking outside the mill with Orlando, Conrad said, 'You'll notice the paper mills round here were always built as close to where the water comes out of the hill as possible. Have you been to Wookey Hole yet? There's a big paper mill there still in use, right up against the hill. Our own here managed to exist until the beginning of the century, but of course the introduction of steam and the new methods of producing paper meant that the thing had to be done on a larger scale than they could manage here. They only had a couple of vats, two papermakers and a dozen or so other workers. But it was beautiful paper. I've got some of it.'

'One can't help feeling that the day of the small business is passing,' said Conrad. 'The death of laissez-faire has seen to that. It makes sense that there should be a different kind of economic unit nowadays. It must be the way out of our industrial difficulties. I think we must face the fact that if and when Timberwork becomes a profit-making organization we've got to become part of a larger concern.'

Soon after Conrad's return the range of furniture devised by Orlando and Graham went into production.

Leonard's attitude to Conrad was complicated. Conrad was the largest shareholder in Timberwork but Leonard was its Chairman. Conrad was Leonard's social superior but Leonard was ten years older. Leonard had advised Conrad on the handling of his affairs in many directions, but Conrad was an active member of the House of Lords, had been for a short time a junior Minister under Baldwin, and had served on several commissions of national and even international importance. Leonard thought Conrad arrogant and Conrad thought Leonard limited.

'Tell me about Mr King,' said Conrad.

Orlando told him.

'Then you've no idea who your parents were?' said Conrad.

'When I asked King he said they were of no importance,' said Orlando. 'He said they were healthy, and that was all that mattered.'

'I expect he was right. He meant that you yourself were all that mattered.'

'Once he said that they were the equivalent of a doctor and a nurse. I don't know why but I lost interest in them after that.'

'I should like to have met Mr King. Tell me, coming here as a stranger – not that you were by any means a complete stranger because Mr King sounds an entirely English character – but did anything in particular strike you as a surprise?'

'The importance of class, I think,' said Orlando. 'And the amount people talk about it.'

'Yes. How very interesting. I'm sure you're right. Of course much of it didn't exist before the war. I suppose that was because differences in status were much less questioned, but certainly I think what's known as class antagonism hardly existed until after 1918. Of course the Socialists have put ideas into the heads of the working classes which certainly weren't there before, ideas of class warfare and so on which are thoroughly unnecessary. And I think that certain members of the so-called upper classes who should know better have been given such a sense of insecurity by this kind of thing that they've responded by becoming embittered too. Certainly I've heard members of my own class speak of the working classes in a way which I shouldn't dream of doing myself, nor would most of my friends. There's no doubt that there's a bitterness in the air which was not there before the war. It's one of the things we've got to work to get rid of in political life.'

Whenever Conrad came back to Mount Sorrel after being away he opened the door of the car before it drew up in front of the house so that the moment it stopped he could step out. He usually reached the front door before any waiting servant had time to open it for him, strode through the hall into the library, threw open the french window there, stepped out on to the terrace and stretching back his arms from the shoulders, elbows bent, breathed deeply several times. Then he turned back to whoever might be waiting to speak to him.

On the terrace they had an Easter egg hunt for the village children, and for Judith's sons Paul and Stephen, and for Henry. There was a cold wind. Henry wore an overcoat and carried a basket which Flora had given him. When he had collected his eight allotted eggs he gave her the basket to hold and went to play football with some other boys. Paul found five eggs and then panicked. He accused Stephen of having taken more than his share. Stephen pushed him into a flower bed where he crushed some primulas which were just coming into flower. Conrad explained to him that there were eight eggs for each child and that if he went on looking he would find his remaining three. Paul found one more among the primulas and took two from a village girl who was too young to be able to count.

Conrad joined the footballers, shouting, his rather long hair blowing in the wind; then Judith joined in too, running at great speed with a scarf tied round her head. Orlando knew that he could not run as fast because of his hammer toes and so he pretended to be helping the smallest children, who had still not found all their eggs. He was watching Conrad out of the corner of his eye. He was always on the alert when Conrad was there. He did not care whether or not each child found its allotted share of eggs. A few years later, Agatha being then still very young, he held her hand while she searched, jealous that she should have her due, or more if he could fix it.

Strong Indian tea with sugar in it, the warmth of the cup in both palms, the thick smooth china between his lips. They had said, drink this, and he did whatever they told him, listening carefully for their instructions through the darkness. They were rousing him from month-long dreams. Judith ran over the lawn towards Conrad, her scarf blowing

out behind her, her thin knees bent for speed, away into the
wood behind the mill, and Leonard by the viaduct stared,
and on the island King turned away from his unfinished
tower. Orlando remembered Agatha at Easter.

Leonard did not play football but walked up and down
the terrace, hunched in his overcoat, wondering if he could
decently ask Conrad for a whisky and soda, it was after tea
after all.

The profits of Timberwork climbed, in contradistinction
to the national trend.

Penelope's grey drawing-room bursting with people
drinking cocktails pressing up against the walls between the
Marie Laurencin prints and the daffodils and the canapés by
Searcys and the windows open to the grey spring day to let
out the smoke from the cigarettes and the roar of the voices.

Orlando talked to Guy about Conrad and Guy said,
'He's one of our most able men. If only he wasn't so fond
of being a country squire, if only he'd give himself whole-
heartedly to political life, don't you know? What does he
think about what's been going on in Germany? Doesn't he
think they're beginning to pull themselves together at last?'

'I don't know really,' Orlando was looking round for
pretty girls. 'I say, Guy, you know, I can't thank you enough
for all your help,' he added suddenly. 'Letting me stay with
you so long and giving me so much good advice.'

'Not at all, my dear fellow, nice of you to amuse Penelope.
She gets a bit bored, you know, with no children. All this
social life's a bit of a scramble really, I mean what we all
need is a purpose, isn't it, but it's dashed hard to find one
nowadays, now that everything's been de-bunked. I say, do
you know that pretty thing over there talking to the chap in
the dinner jacket? I'll introduce you shall I? She's awfully
nice.'

Guy was awfully nice. Years afterwards when people at just such parties were saying to each other with clever laughs, 'What's become of the Warings?' Orlando thought how awfully nice to him Guy and Penelope had been.

The girl was pretty. The man in the dinner jacket was a BBC announcer. The girl introduced Orlando to her brother, who worked for a big wholesale furniture manufacturers.

And so the process began. It took place in the early summer of 1932, when Orlando had been working at Timberwork for rather more than a year, and it was a common business manoeuvre. For Orlando it had a particular excitement because of the feeling which he was experiencing fully for the first time of things being achieved on a large scale, and of there being in the new circumstances almost nothing which he himself could not achieve, with the new means at his disposal.

There were talks, and lunches. There were proposals, and counter-proposals, and legal opinions.

One day Sir Giles Logan the chairman of Logan Holdings the holding company, a large proportion of whose interests was represented by Logan Furniture the manufacturers who employed the brother of the pretty girl Orlando had met at the Warings' party, spoke to Conrad Field in their club, where they had met by chance.

Conrad said, 'It's nothing much to do with me at this stage. I'm a director because I'm the major shareholder but I'm not a working director and I've always said I won't have anything to do with the running of the thing, because I know nothing about business. If the management and your people can work out a scheme which seems mutually satisfactory I'm in favour of it, because it seems to me to be logical. Though of course none of us want to see Timberwork lose its own identity.'

'That's one of the things we believe in, the autonomy of the individual firms within the groups,' said Sir Giles. 'So that needn't bother us. Tell me about young King.'

'I think very highly of him,' said Conrad. 'I think he has an extraordinarily good judgement for someone so young, and I think the reason for it is that he has a genuine flair for business. He's not a great reasoner. He often can't explain why he thinks one course of action better than another, but he's been more or less running that firm lately, first as General Manager and recently as Managing Director, and though of course it's too early to tell I would say that something like ninety per cent of his business decisions are the right ones.'

Sir Giles nodded. 'As you can imagine, it's that potentiality that we want to buy as much as any of the Timberwork products. Now your brother-in-law. He has a lot of other interests?'

'He's a stockbroker, as well as a director of various other companies, and naturally the recent situation has meant he's been very busy in the City. That's why he's handed over so much so quickly to Orlando.'

'To be quite frank with you, the usual pattern we follow in these cases would probably mean leaving King as Managing Director and putting in one of our chaps as Chairman. It wouldn't leave much room for your brother-in-law, who's not, I seem to remember, a considerable shareholder. I know him slightly and have always liked him, but frankly we've several men like him in our organization and not enough like King. I've told King that he can expect to come in on other of our things in due course. Indeed I'm sure that he sees himself on our main board in a few years' time, and he may well be right. To tell you the truth, we don't really need your brother-in-law. I'm putting it frankly to you like

this because I know it's a small family firm and considerations like this may sway the thing one way or the other
and I shouldn't like you afterwards to feel you'd been in
any way misled.'

'That's very fair of you,' said Conrad.

'I believe in fairness,' said Sir Giles. 'I imagine, and hope,
that in this case the fact that Timberwork has been more or
less a sideline for your brother-in-law...?'

Conrad leant back in his leather armchair, stretching his
legs in front of him.

'I can't speak for Leonard,' he said. 'And I think that
all things considered it is better that I should remain as
detached as possible from these negotiations. Leonard has
indeed many other interests, although I think he has a special
fondness for Timberwork. I imagine that your policy of
fairness will lead you to keep the people most concerned
in the matter as fully informed of what is entailed as seems
to you to be right. Apart from that I can only reinforce
your own feelings about Orlando. Indeed I'm beginning
almost to regard him as a sort of protégé. I'm hoping eventually, when he's a bit more experienced, to interest him in
politics.'

'We certainly could do with some good men there,'
agreed Sir Giles.

They began to discuss the political situation.

Leonard tapped briskly at his boiled egg.

'When the Chairman of the Party comes down for the
meeting next month,' he said, 'I think it would be a nice
thing to do to ask Orlando to meet him. Ask him to the
lunch or something.'

'My dear old thing,' said Judith, looking up from a letter
over which she was frowning, 'Conrad took Orlando to
dinner with him in the House a couple of weeks ago. Didn't

you hear about it? And he's going to let him know if there are any likely seats coming up.'

'Really? No one told me. Surely that's rather premature? I mean, the boy's only twenty-three or something, isn't he? He's no experience. And no money. How could he possibly afford it?'

'I daresay Conrad would stake him,' said Judith carelessly.

'Why on earth should he do that? Besides Orlando ought to give all his time to the business for a few more years yet. With this new deal we've just signed he's going to have a lot more scope and responsibility. He'll have to look to his laurels if he wants to keep his job. I shan't be able to protect him. I've told him things are going to be very different now that we're part of a huge impersonal organization. Did Conrad tell you about the lunch?'

'No, Orlando did.'

'You don't think you're seeing too much of Orlando?'

'You told me to make friends with him.'

'Not to the extent of causing a scandal.'

'A scandal?'

'It's not the same in a small country community as it is in London, you know.'

'What on earth are you talking about?'

'I'm talking about your relationship with Orlando.'

Her face, as he had known it would, took on its thinnest aspect.

'I find Orlando extremely attractive,' she said. 'Here is another letter about your son.' She tossed it to him across the table, gathered up her other letters and left the room.

'I wish you'd have breakfast in bed,' he said rather loudly.

He looked at the letter from Paul's headmaster. Its tone was familiar. '... seem able to get through to him ... confess myself baffled ... he must realize he cannot always be the centre of attention ... still wondering whether this is really the right school for Paul ... '

'Can't afford to keep him there any longer anyway,' said Leonard. He began to walk towards the door, then thinking that he would rather the servants did not read the letter he turned back and put it in his pocket.

Later he drove down to the mill.

He looked into Orlando's room. No one was there.

'Why does he never clear his desk?' said Leonard.

The desk was covered with papers. So were a couple of chairs and a corner of the floor. Leonard began to look through the correspondence in a tray marked In. He only came into the office once a week now. 'Orlando makes me a weekly report,' he had said a day or two ago to Conrad. 'I like to feel in close touch.' It was gratifying, of course, to find from the contents of the In tray that there seemed to be a great deal of activity in the business. Less gratifying perhaps to find so many thickly embossed invitation cards, some of them to parties to which he was not sure whether he and Judith had been invited, though he was certainly sure that they should have been; and then there was some dreadful violet paper on which was written in green ink and much too large writing, 'I didn't mean it I didn't I DID N'T – how could you think I did – I'm just a horrid putrid silly practical joker who deserves to be SMACKED! – PLEASE come on Friday – Mugs. P.S. Actually I think you're DIVINE, P.P.S. Slopey Macdougal has had THREE ! ! ! '

Three what, Leonard thought, scenting obscenity.

'A clear desk policy,' he said aloud, hoping Orlando would come in and hear him. 'A clear desk policy.'

Orlando did not come in.

Leonard walked along to his own room at the end of the passage. It was bare and tidy. The desk was clear except for one small pile of letters and Orlando's feet. Orlando was sitting in Leonard's chair, talking on the telephone. Without pausing in his conversation he took his feet off the desk, stood up, shook Leonard warmly by the hand, and sat down again on a corner of the desk.

'She told me she'd been dancing the night away with the Prince of Wales. What a liar she is. But listen I can't come on the 5th because I'm going to be in Ealing for the day. Well, it's the new smart place, terribly amusing, jellied eels and costermongers, merry folk-dancing by groups of unemployed. How did you know? You oughtn't to take an interest in your husband's work you know, it's bound to lead to trouble. Oh, his colleagues' work, that's another matter. Yes, I'm spending the day with Giles Logan really, that's where the main factory is as well as the head office. We're mutually fascinated, I by his money, he by my youth and good looks. No he's married actually. Not that that's anything to go by these days. Look I must go because Leonard's here frowning. Would you like to speak to him? All right. Yes. 'Bye.' He put down the receiver. 'Your wife says she won't be in for lunch,' he said. 'Sorry to be usurping your seat. I came in here to get some peace as a matter of fact. I'm writing a political speech.'

'Oh?'

'I'm getting quite keen on politics. It is rather fun, isn't it?'

'A rather sober sort of fun at the moment.'

'Oh I know. But it's a game as well, isn't it?'

'Some unscrupulous people treat it as such.'

'I'm only being frivolous, Leonard, I know people like you are rightly serious-minded about it. Shall I get you some coffee?'

'No, thank you.' Leonard sat down in the seat which Orlando had left and took some indigestion tablets out of a drawer. 'I shall have some sandwiches sent in later, I've a lot of work to do. I shall have to leave immediately after lunch because I've got to be in my London office before closing time. No better news from the City I'm afraid. Is there anything in particular you want me to deal with here?' He began to look through the letters in front of him.

'Nothing special, thanks awfully. I'll leave you to look through your mail and come back later.' Orlando went out of the room, rather hurriedly Leonard thought, almost immediately understanding with disagreeable clarity why he had done so, and finding himself confronting much too unexpectedly something to which his reaction was quickly that it was nothing; nothing serious, a misunderstanding, wrongly addressed, he'd have a word with Logan; only apparently awkward, Good Lord some people would say it looked like a plot; a little awkward, need a bit of skill here, some cunning; he might have known, he'd feared all along, he'd seen it coming, what to say, what people will think, a trick, a disaster, nothing less than a rotten trick, they're going to ditch me, he thought. They're going to ditch me.

He chewed an indigestion tablet and read the letter again more slowly.

It was from the Managing Director of Logan Furniture and it spoke of necessary developments from the decisions mutually reached and embodied in the signed agreement between the two firms, and of the constitution of the new board, and of 'the matter of your own compensation'; which being interpreted meant, 'We do not want you but are prepared to pay you to go.'

He put the letter into a drawer and rang for a secretary. A girl he did not know appeared.

'Where is Miss Wood?' he asked.

'She is taking some letters for Mr Orlando,' said the girl. 'Sit down.'

She had thick legs and thick fingers. Her round face turned towards him with an air of attentiveness which he felt was likely to prove misleading.

'Dear Mr Gore Jones,' he began rather fast. 'Thank you for your letter of yesterday's date on the subject of my son Paul. Paragraph. I have been meaning to write to you for some time. As you are no doubt aware, the financial situation in which this country finds itself is extremely serious, and we who in the City of London attempt to earn a livelihood in the maintaining of the vital functions of the nation's economy are needless to say the first to suffer. But though I may be among the first parents to write to you in the sense in which I do, I feel sure I shall not be the last. You may or may not be surprised to learn that many thinking people in this country are convinced that private education has had its day. Like many other institutions on which our Empire has been founded, the private school must give way before the onset of the new age of lowered standards, of the values of the hoi-polloi H-O-I-P-O-L-L-O-I.'

'New age of ... ?' she wavered.

'Lowered standards comma of the values of the H-O-I P-O-L-L-O-I'

'Values of the H-O-I-T-'

'P. P. P-O-L-L-O-I. Hoi-polloi. The values of the hoi-polloi. Paragraph. I have therefore to give you notice that both my sons will be leaving your school at the end of this term. Paragraph. I recognize of course that the term is nearly at an end and that therefore this is not the customary full term's notice. In view of the hardship which has necessitated this step, however, I imagine you will overlook the formality which would require another term's fees in lieu of notice. Paragraph.'

'In view of – sorry – I didn't quite …?'

He repeated his last sentence with exaggerated emphasis and continued, gathering speed as he went, 'I regret that this situation should have arisen before your failure with my elder son should have been redeemed. This difficult boy, who has inherited from his mother a highly nervous temperament, must indeed represent a challenge to any schoolmaster, and it will be interesting to discover whether the employees of the State are more successful in administering the necessary disciplines. Is that too harsh, would you say?'

'Challenge, sorry, I – oh me? Oh I couldn't say, I'm sorry.'

'Well leave it, leave it. The Editor, the *Financial Times*. Dear Sir …'

His sandwiches were sent in. Orlando went out to lunch with a buyer from Sheffield. Later Leonard went into his room in the hope of speaking to him about the letter but there were too many people coming in and out with questions or remarks or complaints, and the telephone kept on ringing and Orlando kept on talking. Leonard went back to his own room mumbling that he couldn't imagine how anyone could work in such conditions. He telephoned to his London office to say that he would not be there until the morning and Miss Pyne in her usual efficient way undertook to hold until the morning all the important matters awaiting his attention. After this conversation he felt much better and wished that Miss Pyne would come down to Timberwork once a week and then remembered that that wouldn't of course be necessary if his connection with the firm was to be severed; so then he sent for the secretary

again, whose name was Mary Baines, and dictated a memo-
randum on the financial situation to be used later should he
decide to make a speech on the budget; and then he sent for
a cup of tea and swallowed some more indigestion tablets
and waited for Orlando to be alone and for his letters to be
typed and for the day to come to an end, and now at last,
inactive, he allowed the injustice he had suffered to make its
way to the forefront of his mind where it began to assume
the proportions of a monstrosity. A monstrosity.

Miss Baines brought his letters in for him to sign at
half-past five. She was looking flustered and wearing an
overcoat.

'Why have you got your coat on?' he asked.

'It's half-past five,' she said.

'You will have to wait until these letters are signed, won't
you?'

'Miss Wright is here,' she said in her breathless way. 'And
Rodney does the post. I was leaving punctually tonight
because Mr Ryder was going to take me to see my mother.
He lives just by the hospital you see.' She smiled, appar-
ently confident that he would share her appreciation of Mr
Ryder's thoughtfulness.

But he had begun to read the letters.

'Dear Mr Gore James,' he read. 'Thank you for your
letter of yesterday's date on the subject of my son Bill.
Programme. I have been meaning to write to you for some
time as you are no doubt aware. The financial situation in
which this country finds itself is extremely serious and we
who in the City of London are tempted to earn a livelihood
in the manoeuvring of the vital fictions of the nation's economy are needless to say the last to suffer. But though I may
be among the last prints ...'

'Aaaaaaaah!' he shouted.

It was the cry of the wounded President as the assassin's dagger plunges into his breast.

Miss Baines trembled.

'God in heaven help us all!' he cried, and threw the letter at her feet. 'Pick it up, pick it up, look at it. Are you out of your mind, woman? Read it, read it. What kind of rubbish is this? Take it back, do it again, all of it, take these, take them all, do them all again, they are nonsense, madness, gobbledegook. What do you think I am that you can so totally disregard my instructions, treat my work with such total lack of seriousness? I am the Chairman of your company. Do you know that?'

'Yes, yes.' Eyes and mouth gaped at him. 'Yes, I, I ...'

'Who employed you? Who allowed you to come to me when I rang for someone? Where is Mrs Wood? Where is Miss Wright? Is my work considered so insignificant here that I am sent the duds, the dunces, to do it? Go away. Go away. Do it all again.'

She gathered up the scattered letters, awkward in her overcoat, the thick fingers trembling and the round glasses blurring her sight because of the tears that were misting them over.

'Bring them back to me as quickly as you can,' he said more calmly. Then she sniffed and nodded in a manner which he took as offensive and he suddenly roared, 'Don't snivel at me! What right have you to be sorry for yourself? It is I that should be weeping.'

She left the room, clasping the letters to her chest. She did not shut the door behind her and he saw her break into a shuffling run down the passage.

'God damn them all,' he said.

He took the letter from the Managing Director of Logan Furniture out of the drawer where he had put it earlier and went into Orlando's room. Orlando was talking on the telephone. Leonard took the receiver out of his hand and replaced it on the telephone.

'I am the Chairman of this company and I wish to speak to you,' he said. 'All through the day you have done nothing but ignore and humiliate me and I am not prepared to submit to it.'

Orlando looked at him with some concern, but did not speak.

'I am unable to do any work in this office,' Leonard went on. 'Or to get any sense out of anyone. My time is too valuable to be wasted like this. I have been tortured all afternoon by the idiocies of Miss Baines because Mrs Wood was with you. Mrs Wood, if you remember, was employed by me to do my work. I cannot waste my one day a week here dictating letters to imbeciles for them to render unintelligible.'

'I'm sorry, Leonard. I didn't know you needed Mrs Wood or I should have sent her to you. I'm afraid she's got used to doing my work now that you're not here very often.'

'Quite,' said Leonard. 'Quite. Exactly.'

Orlando was looking tired. He was tired. He knew he was not going to be able to cope with Leonard. What the hell, he thought, tired.

'Exactly,' said Leonard, recognizing and resenting Orlando's tiredness. 'But when you say "got used to" what you mean in fact is "been instructed to".'

'Been ...?' Orlando looked blank.

Leonard tossed the letter he had been carrying on to the desk between them.

'It is all part of that, isn't it?' he said, his heart beating faster because of the dramatic nature of his own gesture, of his tossing of the letter with so violent a movement of his wrist. 'I know very well what has been going on here.'

Orlando looked at the letter with reluctance. He could think of nothing to say.

'I brought you into this firm,' Leonard's voice had begun to tremble. 'And I am rewarded by this.'

'It has nothing to do with me,' Orlando looked hopelessly at the letter, rather than at Leonard. 'Something ...' He paused, trying to remember the truth. 'Something Logan said to me gave me the impression that whatever was to be agreed with you had been discussed with you and Conrad already.'

'Don't pretend that in the course of furthering your own ambitions you gave any thought at all to my position.'

Orlando was silent.

'Except that you wanted it for yourself,' said Leonard. 'My position. You wanted it. It's what you've wanted ever since you came here isn't it? To oust me and step into my shoes.'

Orlando shook his head.

Leonard's voice had begun to tremble again.

'I brought you into this firm, tried to encourage you in every way, treated you like a son – God knows my own will never be anything but a trouble to me – and all you wanted was to get rid of me. You wanted my job, my money – do you realize what my salary here means to me now? I'm close to bankruptcy. Close to bankruptcy. A year or two ago I was a rich man. Now through no fault of my own I can hardly pay my bills. Things have gone badly wrong for stockbrokers. You must have known that. I have a family to support. I have a very extravagant wife.'

A just perceptible movement of Orlando's head drove like another arrow into Leonard's bared breast.

'Oh yes,' he cried as it pierced him. 'Oh yes. I know very well. I know very well. You wanted my wife too, didn't you? My job, my money, my wife. Well, now you have them, and much good may they do you. You will lose them all when someone younger comes along.'

'Leonard,' Orlando began in a reasonable voice, 'I ... Judith and I ...' He shook his head.

'Judith has told me everything,' said Leonard.

'But there is nothing to tell,' said Orlando. 'Of course I admire Judith very much but I haven't, that is, there is nothing ...'

'You have seen to it that she should fall in love with you,' said Leonard. 'What else you have done, God knows.'

'What do you mean? Did Judith say ...?'

'Take that idiotic look off your face,' shouted Leonard. 'I'll tell you this. Once you start with Judith there's no end to it, no end to the misery. When you embrace Judith you are clasping a viper to your bosom. She will use you and throw you aside. She has no idea what decent behaviour is. If you treat her as an honest man would treat his friend she will repay you with perfidy.' He had begun to cry. 'Perfidy,' he repeated as if he had momentarily forgotten what he was going to say next. 'She will – she will play you false.' Tears were running down his cheeks. 'There is no such thing as friendship.'

Orlando rose slowly to his feet with some idea that his doing so might change the atmosphere.

'Don't touch me,' Leonard shouted, pointing at him. 'You are a traitor. Do you know that? A traitor. No, I am going now, there is nothing more to be said.' He turned and began to walk down the passage. 'Don't follow me. There is nothing more to be said.'

He hurried, staggering a little, to the car park, where his and Orlando's cars were the only ones now remaining. Orlando pursued him.

'No, no,' said Leonard, getting quickly into the driving seat of his car. 'Don't follow me. I may be going to do some violence.'

'Leonard, for God's sake wait. What do you mean? It doesn't make sense. What do you mean, do some violence?'

Leonard, his whole face trembling, had already started the car. Orlando stood on the running board. Leonard jerked the car forward. Orlando clung on. Leonard, violently excited, accelerated with another jerk.

'Get off, get off, get off.' Leonard turned the wheel from side to side, accelerating noisily in second gear. The car lurched. Orlando jumped off, stumbled and fell. Leonard accelerated again and side-slipped round the corner of the mill. Orlando ran after him. Leonard saw the running figure in his driving mirror, stamped on the accelerator, looked again into his mirror and misjudged the corner under the viaduct. He skidded. He hit the side of the arch head on. A crash, a tinny rattle, silence except for Orlando's running footsteps.

Orlando pulled open the car door. Leonard had been thrown into the back seat. He lay there, his head at an odd angle in relation to the rest of his body, and gazed at Orlando. Orlando stared back. The expression in Leonard's eyes appeared to be one of overwhelming affection.

Hearing another sound, Orlando turned to see Miss Baines hesitating at some little distance, clasping her hands.

'Telephone the doctor,' said Orlando.

Thinking that he ought not to move Leonard, Orlando climbed into the ruined car beside him and put his arm beneath his shoulders.

Leonard looked up at him with a calm though now more distant expression and said quietly, 'Judith. Please fetch Judith.'

And died.

Orlando said aloud, 'He's fainted,' knowing he was dead. The head he held on his arm was very heavy. He had seen a dead fisherman once, floated ashore on the island by the tide. He had seen King, laid out by the nuns.

Orlando held Leonard's head and waited for the doctor to come.

He knew a man, the managing director of an engineering firm making component parts for the aircraft industry, whose wife was killed in a car crash just about the time of Munich She was a little liverish creature with brown bobbed hair and a fringe. They had no children and he was always buying her expensive jewellery. In the weeks immediately after her death he went to bed with all the girls in the typing pool, one after the other, except for the recently married one and the one who didn't go in for that sort of thing; and when this became common knowledge in the firm, as it somehow inevitably did, everyone was very shocked. It was the way grief took him, that was all.

Orlando thought of this sometimes when the events of these years were revolving in his mind, given new meanings by the new light in which he was looking at them, a light which cast long shadows and was not the light of noonday any more. He thought of this man as a kind of excuse for Judith; but it was not the same.

She came quietly up the stairs as he was sitting in his little room above the stables, thinking, what an awful thing. What an awful thing, I had better go back to the island. I had better go back to the island, something seems to have gone wrong here.

She had come noiselessly into his room and was standing looking at him, wearing a fawn dress with a loose spotted tie and shoes with three straps. She asked him what had happened.

He said, 'He ran into the viaduct.'

She had not been in the house when they had taken Leonard home and carried him upstairs. Orlando had left the doctor waiting for her. He had not wanted to tell her himself.

'But he must have been going so fast,' she said.

Orlando nodded.

'Was he in a temper?' she asked.

'Yes,' said Orlando.

'Had you quarrelled?'

'No,' said Orlando. 'He was upset about something. To do with the business.'

She nodded.

'He was in a temper,' she said. 'Poor Leonard.'

He stood up saying, 'I'm sorry.'

At the same time she moved away from him, looking round and saying, 'I've never been here.'

She looked at his armchair, his little writing-table, his bed. Orlando did not know what to do. She walked towards the window and looked out into the stableyard.

'It's nice,' she said.

He had followed her, so that when she turned back to face the room again they were close enough for him to put his arms round her. They stood without moving until she looked up at him and they kissed.

Their kiss became passionate. They had wanted it since they had first seen each other in Leonard's office. In Leonard's office she had coldly smiled, had sniffed. In Leonard's office he had turned his head, had said he would like to meet Noël Coward. What do you do with a thing like that? They kissed. Neither of them was a stranger to the natural consequence. They were in trim, like swordsmen; joined battle, subdued each other, the fawn dress on the floor, beneath the fallen eiderdown.

Afterwards she quickly and silently dressed. He heard her steps on the cobbles of the stableyard. He had not raised his head from his folded arms. The thought of Leonard spread, like a bruise. But he would have done it again, any day.

She thought, he wants me, crossing the stableyard, he wants me and I am justified. Touch and skin and strength and he wants me like Venus and Adonis – looking at the poem in the back of my musty Shakespeare, doing Macbeth with Miss Grierson – he pants for me like that, gasping from his young mouth for me, Judith, my lineaments redeemed, Judith justified. I knew, crushing the spring grass beneath my shining shoes, I knew he would be like that, ardent a word I like; ardent, argent, daybreak, spring, all these for Judith, for Orlando; and so the familiar wide ride up the hill through the trees and at the top Corbett waiting, black butler's coat black tie, to say they are here about the funeral arrangements, oh funerals how desolate, poor Leonard poor poor Leonard.

Orlando had a dream in which he held Agatha in his arms, two years old perhaps and laughing. It was at the Zoo and she was watching the monkeys. Laughter possessed her. Amazed by the monkeys and her own laughter she was helpless, rollicking in his arms in a passion of delight and laughter.

'They're like us,' she cried. 'They're like us.'

And the ridiculousness of it seized her again and her baby's high laugh attracted attention so that other people watching the monkeys turned to look at her and laugh too.

So did Orlando; it was impossible to do anything else in the face of what seemed laughter in the absolute.

Someone gave her a bag of peanuts to give the monkeys and he put her down so that she could feed them. This quietened her; she merely watched them now, and he awoke.

Later in the day he realized that it had not been a dream but a memory. He had once taken Agatha to the Zoo, with Jen the nursery-maid, and she had been seized by uncontrollable mirth in front of the monkeys' cage. He could not remember much more about the afternoon, except that he had thought Agatha was too young to ride on the camel so he had put her in the llama cart with Jen, but Agatha had resented this and afterwards he had let her ride on the camel too, a little guiltily because he was afraid of spoiling her.

He remembered this when he was lying in hospital in 1940, thinking about Judith his wife and Agatha his favourite daughter.

The day after Leonard's death Orlando went to see Conrad.

Conrad had returned from London that morning and was waiting to see him in the library.

Orlando explained what had happened and that it had been the letter from the managing director of Logan Holdings which had made Leonard lose his temper.

Conrad listened in silence, watching Orlando's face attentively. When Orlando had finished speaking Conrad said nothing for some moments. Orlando was feeling tired and wanted to go away from Mount Sorrel.

Eventually Conrad said, 'I always knew that Leonard was a much less stable man than he seemed. It's a sad thing, an unnecessary death. It won't do those two rather difficult sons any good to be without a father either.' After another pause he went on, 'What amazes me is that he should have been so completely taken by surprise. It was not very acute of him to have been quite in the dark as to what was going on, was it? You knew the way their minds were working I suppose?'

'I suppose so,' said Orlando.

'I hope you don't blame yourself in any way. That kind of knock is a hazard of a business career, you know – or of any other career for that matter. Of course his death was an appalling thing to happen, but no one could possibly have foreseen that he would react in such an extraordinarily unbalanced way, or that chance – which was what it was – would turn his accident into a fatal one. But for that chance the whole thing would have blown over in a day or two. He had plenty of other interests.'

'I do blame myself,' said Orlando. 'If I had thought more about it I should certainly have known that Leonard would have minded the whole thing more than anyone else in a similar situation. I knew perfectly well what he felt about Timberwork, and even though I thought some of his feelings were phoney I also knew that with Leonard his phoney feelings were sometimes mixed up with his real feelings.'

'They had become real, yes, he had assumed them,' said Conrad. 'He had assumed attitudes that were not natural to him and they had become part of him even though they still didn't look quite right from the outside. That was one of the reasons for his fundamental insecurity of course. It is always difficult when a man assumes a personality which is not really his own. We all do it to a greater or lesser extent of course.'

Orlando found Conrad too detached.

'I could perfectly well have warned him,' he said abruptly. 'I have decided to go back to the Morbihan, where

I belong. King only meant me to stay a few months and I
have been here nearly two years. I don't think he would
have approved of that.'

Conrad said gently, 'You don't really belong in the
Morbihan, you know.'

Orlando was silent, thinking of King.

'I don't think by any means that you should stay in
Timberwork indefinitely,' went on Conrad. 'There is wider
scope elsewhere.'

Orlando thought, I am not interested in wider scope, I
don't even know what it means, King was right, I shall go
back.

'You see,' said Conrad. 'The life that King lived, and the
life that he may have wanted you to live – although I am not
convinced that he did – was the life of the contemplative,
the recluse, the life of someone who has seen something
of the world and has rejected it. It's a life which has great
attractions. I half would like to live like that myself. I could
do it here if I had the strength of mind to throw off all my
other ties. But it would suit me better than it would suit
you, because you're not a contemplative at all. I've a bit of
it in me, I believe, but you haven't. You're a man of action.
You may smile, but I've never known you theorize about
anything before you do it. You just do it. It's not just a
matter of age, it's a matter of temperament.'

Orlando thought, I like to hear him talk, they have a lot
of charm this family, I shall go tomorrow on the boat from
Southampton, I have not much luggage.

'Under the new arrangement you can reasonably hope
to accumulate some capital,' said Conrad. 'This is essential
if you are to go into politics. Your practical business experience will also be useful to you in politics, or rather it will
make you useful. Because this is the great new issue, you

know, the reformulating of capitalism. The people who tell you it's inevitably decaying and the people who tell you it's as healthy as it was in the last century are equally wrong. Capitalism has got to be modified not abolished. Instead of no capitalists we want new capitalists, men of sense and sensibility who can make peace between capital and labour. The way to achieve this, in terms of practical politics, is through the Conservative Party, not through coalition governments and not through socialism. Coalitions run counter to the spirit of English Parliamentary government and socialism, for all the humanitarianism of some of its ideals, means eventually servility, society servile to the state. Private ownership, collaboration between industry, labour and government – a properly planned economy – But I don't want to make a political speech.'

'Oh, I agree with you,' said Orlando. 'Of course I agree. But I don't feel that I've any part to play in all this. It would be years before I could accumulate the experience to speak with any authority about these things. I haven't even been brought up in England.'

'Do you know, that could be part of your strength?' said Conrad, leaning forward. 'You're unprejudiced. This is such an old society. So much weight of tradition is attached to its institutions, it's difficult if you've been brought up as part of it all – particularly the more privileged part of it all – to see clearly, without prejudice. I've noticed already, many things are more obvious to you than to me, because of your lack of preconceived notions. When we talk about the social system here, for instance. Or even foreign affairs. Isolated though your life in France was, you nevertheless understand the European situation far more easily than many people who have never left this country. France's attitude towards Germany, for instance, which to many of us seems unreasonable and which it is so vital that we should understand.' Conrad stood up and began to walk about the room.

He himself had not realized until that moment how dear to him had become his ambitions for Orlando.

'This is premature,' he said. 'But I don't want you to think of all this as merely something you might become interested in at some far future date. The local seat here is going to be vacant, and I still have a lot of influence among those responsible for the selection of the candidate. It's always been a Conservative seat. I wish it wasn't vacant because I wish that Leonard were alive to fill it, but he's not, and you could probably have it, and you could probably combine it with still working pretty hard for Timberwork.'

Orlando saw himself walking for the first time into the chamber of the House of Commons.

'I am inevitably barred from much that goes on in practical politics by being in the Upper House,' said Conrad. 'A close ally in the Commons would make life a good deal more interesting for me. Who knows? I might be minister for this or that and you my under-secretary in the Commons.' He turned towards Orlando in his perambulations, smiling now. 'I'm not holding out to you any idea of your duty,' he said. 'Or of glory and renown or anything like that. I'm just holding out to you the sheer fun of the thing.'

That's the way to his heart, he thought, beaming down at him. And it was. Orlando laughed aloud.

Conrad took a book out of the bookcase and gave it to Orlando.

'Read this before you write your election address,' he said. 'You've probably read it already but it repays study. Tone it down a bit of course, make it sound safe.'

It was a yellow book called Britain's Industrial Future published a few years previously by the Liberal Party.

Orlando said hesitantly, 'There's one thing I ought to say.'

'Yes?'

'If I stay – I mean if I don't go away – I am not quite certain what will happen about Judith.'

'Judith?'

Orlando looked embarrassed.

'I didn't know,' said Conrad. 'I didn't know there was anything between you and Judith.' He looked serious.

'There wasn't, isn't,' said Orlando, quickly.

Conrad waited for him to go on.

Orlando said awkwardly, 'I thought perhaps you ought to know that there might be something, later on...'

'She is too old for you,' said Conrad.

'I haven't really thought about it,' said Orlando. 'It's just that – well, supposing we became fonder of each other, I shouldn't like you to feel that I had done anything under false pretences.'

Conrad considered this for some moments. Then he said, 'Your private life is of course entirely your own affair. I can't imagine that you would do anything dishonourable. As to Judith, I must honestly say that I don't think she would be the right kind of person for you. Of course I am fond of her, as my sister, but she had a rather different, and more worldly, upbringing than I had, and quite apart from the age difference I should feel happier were you to find in due course someone of more substance as a personality, more stability. But of course one man never knows exactly what another needs in a woman. Let's allow it all to take its course. You're too young to marry anyway.'

Orlando still looked embarrassed, his vague and bewildering thoughts about Judith not having crystallized themselves in the least in terms of matrimony. He was relieved when Henry came in and said to his father, 'Flora says are you coming to have tea with us.'

Conrad held out his hand to Henry, who went to him and stood at his knee.

'Yes I'll come. You'll have some tea, Orlando?'

'Thank you but I must look in at the mill before they leave. I haven't been today.'

Conrad nodded. 'It would be a good thing, then. We've been talking about the future, Henry,' he added, changing his tone of voice because Henry had not yet been told of his uncle's death. 'Can you imagine Orlando as Prime Minister?'

'No,' said Henry. 'I think he should be the chief general. You should be Prime Minister.'

'Good,' said Conrad, looking pleased. 'And what will you be?'

'A jazz trumpeter,' said Henry.

There was snow in February. Jen had come over to Mount Sorrel to look after her aunt who had been ill with bronchitis, and when the time came for her to go home to Radstock where she lived the snow was too deep and the buses were not running so she stayed on over the weekend. She was nearly sixteen and had left school a year ago but had not yet been able to find work. She lived at home helping her mother with the house and the younger children, and the washing which her mother took in to earn a little money until Jen's father could find work again. Jen's uncle Stephen Parker worked in the woods at Mount Sorrel and they had a pleasant cottage in the village and only two children, boys of eight and ten, so that Jen found things much easier there than at home and was secretly rather pleased when the snow prolonged her stay.

When the Parkers asked her to go with them to the wedding on Saturday she refused, saying that she had rather not, that she had not been asked, that she didn't much like parties and would rather stay at home and listen to the wireless.

'Come on, do, it will do you good,' said Mrs Parker. 'I've only to mention you're stopping with us and of course you'll be asked.'

Jen gave her customary little dip of the head and said, 'I'd sooner stay.'

The head movement was a characteristic reaction when she was spoken to by anyone except her immediate family or a child. It was like a startled young horse snatching at the bit and gave an effect at once shy and flirtatious.

'Let her stay,' said her uncle. 'She's quiet, she'd sooner stay.'

She consented, though, to stand with him outside the church, Mrs Parker, who sometimes helped in the kitchen, having been given a seat inside. Jen stood with her uncle in the crowd to see them come out. A weak winter sun cast long shadows from the leafless lime trees across the white churchyard which they bordered, and when the bride appeared, the organ from the opened door sounding out from behind her, she too was white, and her face and her dark hair and the black of the bridegroom's coat and the swept path before them and the dark porch behind were brighter because of the surrounding white, her white dress, the snow on the roof of the porch and over the churchyard, smoothing over the graves. Her dress came just to her ankles and had no train. It was of white satin but trimmed with a wide band of thick white fur, and white fur and diamonds were mingled in her small head-dress. Her face passing them smiling seemed miraculously smooth and glowing. She passed on the arm of her husband followed by a serious little boy wearing a green velvet coat with gold frogging and white velvet trousers and buck-led shoes; and then all the guests came out of the church after them and through the pale sunlight and the snow into the house, leaving a composite impression of velvet and fur and shining top hats and venerable age and youthful well-being, and the two sons were so tall and handsome and who would have thought she was old enough to have sons that age?

'He hardly looks older, does he?'

'He looks young to be the Member.'

'I heard him speak. He knows what he's talking about.'

'They all say he's good down at Timberwork too.'

'Looks like the wife goes with the job,' said Jen's uncle.

'What a thing to say!' The woman standing next to them was shocked.

Jen wished he hadn't said it too.

If it had been her she would have had more children round her, all her brothers and sisters and her three little girl cousins who lived near. The only trouble was, perhaps by the time she got married they might all be too old. But she didn't believe in marrying young, her mother had done it and it had been a mistake.

The tenants sat at long tables in the hall during the recep-tion and Mrs Parker took with her her biggest handbag lined with greaseproof paper and brought it back full of bridge rolls with anchovy paste in them and tomato sandwiches and a chicken leg. Jen was rather shocked. Mrs Parker said that she was perfectly certain Lord Field would have been only too happy for her to fill up her bag as full as she liked if he had known about it. Jen ate the food anyway. Mrs Parker said she was sorry she hadn't been able to bring any champagne but Jen said she didn't much fancy champagne.

Some months later Mrs Parker wrote to Jen and said she had heard they were looking for a nurserymaid at Wood Hill because there was a baby expected and why didn't she apply.

Jen got the job as the result of a compromise between Nanny and Orlando. Judith was away in hospital – she was ill for most of the pregnancy – so Nanny and Orlando interviewed the applicants. Nanny was old, and apart from that had become since Paul and Stephen had been away at school more of a housekeeper than a nanny. She virtually ran the household for Judith and so when she announced that with the arrival of the new baby she would need a nurserymaid to help her Judith agreed, with what Orlando felt to be an insufficient protest.

There were several applicants. Nanny favoured a strapping eighteen-year-old who had been working on a farm, but Orlando thought her too ugly. He preferred a small girl from Bath with gleaming teeth and bouncing fair curls, but Nanny said she looked flighty. They compromised on Jen. She was too shy to say anything much but Orlando liked the way she smiled whenever they mentioned the baby and Nanny said she looked willing to learn; in other words, thought Orlando, easy to bully.

Agatha was born in November 1933, sixteen months after Leonard's death.

Judith took some time to recover. She lay in her white bedroom at Wood Hill and wept, seeing day after day dawn grey and damp, the leaves fallen or falling in the dim soggy woods behind the house. Orlando was busy, with the

House of Commons now as well as Timberwork, and could not spend as much time with her as he would have liked.

'We'll go away. The moment this session is over I'll take you to the sun.'

'It ought to have been a boy,' she said. 'I wanted you to have a son.'

'But I'd just as soon have a daughter. And it's a nice little baby. And there's Paul and Stephen after all.'

'They're not your sons, they're Leonard's. A man ought to have a son. It's very important. It's part of being a success.'

'If you really think I must, perhaps we could have one later.' But she cried again, because she thought she might be getting too old and she had hated being so ill with Agatha. He did not understand this because he did not think about her age, and she never mentioned it. Nor did he understand the tremendous significance which she attached to having a son. Children seemed to him neither here nor there. A birth was rather moving and no doubt it would be delightful to see one's own children growing up; that was all. The idea of sons as a matter of prestige was strange to him. He had not seen Judith weak before. Sometimes she had seemed almost too strong, but that was only a little – and quite pleasurably – frightening: now he was worried. He was also disappointed that when he was nice to her she was not able to respond. He was used to more immediate success.

'I'll take you away,' was all he could think of, 'I'll take you to the sun.'

When the Parliamentary recess came they went to Taormina for a fortnight. After that Judith was herself again.

She introduced him to Emerald Cunard and Sibyl Colefax and the Duff Coopers. She gave little lunches for him to meet Tom Jones and Bernard Shaw and Lady Ottoline

Morrell and the Archbishop of Canterbury, and she took him to stay with the Astors at Cliveden.

Conrad took him to lunch at the Athenaeum and to dine at Grillons. He introduced him to Lord Halifax and Lord Salisbury and Geoffrey Dawson and shooting.

Orlando liked them all and some better than others. He liked shooting better than weekend houseparties because the latter tended to include games he did not care for like croquet or musical chairs; and he found Lady Cunard's parties too crowded and the Archbishop of Canterbury too anxious to please. But by and large all of it was fun. And what was the most fun of all of course was not so much that he liked these new friends as that they liked him. He was so nice, so new, so good-looking, so able – 'An able young man, that,' said Tom Jones to Baldwin at breakfast – so polite, so sensible, so refreshing, so amusing, so modest – for though they accepted him there was no question but that he was still serving some kind of wholly agreeable but nonetheless arduous apprenticeship – and then it was so interesting about his rather mysterious background, and so intriguing about his marriage to Judith and how it was going to work out, and so significant that he should be, not a banker, not a City man, not a chairman of corporations, but a practising manufacturer.

For Timberwork still took up at least as much of his time and energy as politics. He found it perfectly possible, particularly in view of his party's large majority in the House of Commons, to spend a considerable part of each day at his office either in London or Mount Sorrel, and the firm continued to flourish in its new circumstances. Its success, like Orlando's own, was accompanied by a continuous rumble of protest from Graham Harper, now the firm's Chief Designer at a rather high salary.

'I'm only here another month or two, I tell you that, I'm not selling my soul to capitalism. I just don't want to starve, that's all. I'm not going all the way with the thing like you are. You'll be the first to go when the change comes, I warn you. You've backed the wrong horse. I'll tell you another thing, your friend Logan doesn't care tuppence for this firm. He only wants to get rid of the competition, that's all. In a year or two's time he'll close this place, saying it's uneconomic or something, which it probably is anyway, and we'll all be out of a job. Except you, that is. You'll be making those pompous speeches in the House of Commons and living it up in society on your salary as a director of Logan Loganberries or whatever it is and forgetting all about your humble beginnings as a simple factory hand. No, honestly, what a thing to go and do, sell out to the bosses like that. It's just crazy, that's all. In another year or two all this kind of big business mucking about will be put an end to...'

'And in the meantime you and I might as well go on making an honest living.'

'Honest. I like that. Might as well go on making a dishonest living is how I see it, since the whole system's dishonest anyhow. I'm only going to stick it another few months I can tell you, then I'm going to give it up and work full time for the revolution, the time will be ripe then, there'll be some point in my going. I can't tell you the details now, you've put yourself on the other side of the fence good and proper now, but I can tell you things are going to start moving soon. You don't take me seriously do you? But you wait, it's got to come, that's all.'

Orlando didn't take him seriously. But he liked him; and was glad to find that their relationship had not suffered by his marriage. The marriage in fact had improved it. The months before the marriage had been a time of alienation from Graham, the months during which Orlando was being drawn closer to Judith, when his physical relationship with her was becoming increasingly important to him and when he was still uncertain as to where it might lead him, the months during which Flora McLeod the governess gave her notice to Conrad and went quietly back to Argyll, the months which Orlando filled with business and social activity so that he had no time to plan his private life, and which ended one evening when Judith said, 'I've been a widow for six months.' During that time Graham seemed reluctant to talk to Orlando and Orlando sometimes thought, when I have time I must do something about Graham. But when the engagement was announced matters improved. It fitted in with Graham's concept of Orlando as a ruthless capitalist fighting his way to the top and made it possible for them to be friends again. Obscurities vanished, shades of disapproval, or jealousy, were dispersed. Graham felt that he knew where he was. Orlando resumed his habit of looking in from time to time at Graham's unappealing cottage on his way home from work, and Graham would tell him about the coming salvation of the world through political action and Orlando, the practising politician, would answer that he did not believe so much could be expected from politics.

'You're really hoping for some kind of spiritual renewal, and you won't get that from politics. It's not in the nature of political systems to provide for people's souls.'

'It will be. There'll be a change of heart. It's the only way.'

'I don't know why you're not a religious maniac instead of a political one. You might have more hope there.'

'Religion. God died a hundred years ago, didn't you know? Besides, what religion? C. of E. I suppose you mean. Matins, with the Lord in his private pew and us underlings

clustered somewhere at the back in the draught, getting the
fumes of the paraffin stoves that are keeping Mr Orlando
and Lady Judith's arses warm. No bloody fear.'

The font was decorated with daffodils.

The christening was in the Easter holidays so that Paul
and Stephen could be there. They were thirteen and twelve.
Paul had just had his second half at Eton. Stephen was
to follow him there in the autumn. Paul was still smaller
than average and very pale. Nanny had decreed a course of
Radio Malt for the holidays. He said he liked Eton. He was
in the lowest form and was fag to a big boy called Stuart
to whose mother Judith, being a third cousin, had written
saying, 'Please ask Jack to be kind to my poor Pauly who is
such a weakling.' Stuart's resulting initial hostility had been
overcome by Paul's extreme subservience. Stuart laughed at
him but did not bully him.

Stephen was embarrassed by the baby and went red in the
face whenever he looked at her. Paul spent a good deal of
time in the nursery watching her being bathed and dressed.
Sometimes Nanny let him give her her bottle.

'You don't really like her, do you?' Stephen asked him
when they were haphazardly arranging their stamp collec-
tions one wet afternoon.

'Yes I do,' said Paul.

'Why?'

'Because she likes me.'

She smiled at him certainly. But then she smiled at everyone, it being so far her only means of communication.

She smiled at her christening, and did not cry at all.
Nanny said it meant the Devil was still inside her; she had
not cried him out; Jen said, 'There's no devils inside of you
is there my dear,' receiving the baby from Nanny on their

return from the church. She sounded her r's in the Somerset way. Nanny said, 'You may change her nappies and I will take her down to tea,' and went to put rather too much powder on her own nose.

Jen laid Agatha down on the bed with the long skirts of the christening robe spread out carefully in a circle round her so as not to crumple them. The silk was beginning to yellow with age. Judith and Conrad had worn it in their time and so had their father and his two sisters; but the embroidery and the frills of Brussels lace were untarnished.

'Are you pretty?' Jen whispered. 'Pretty?'

Agatha listened.

Jen unfastened the safety pin and found the inner muslin nappy a little dirty.

'There's a clever girl,' she said approvingly, putting a clean nappy underneath Agatha's bottom while she rinsed the small amount of yellowish matter from the first one and dropped it into the bucket for washing.

When she came back to the bed Agatha was making little random kicking movements with her legs and smiling. The nappy was wet.

'Nothing but trouble, are you?' Jen said, pinning on clean nappies and readjusting the long skirts. 'Nothing but a nuisance.' She picked her up and kissed her, inhaling the warm smell from the nape of her neck, and carried her into the day nursery to find Nanny.

'She's still a bit loose,' she reported, conscious of her sense of responsibility. 'Not much but a bit loose.'

'A spot less sugar in the feed,' said Nanny, beginning the descent to the drawing room.

Where they were drinking champagne and eating little cakes.

'Oh, she is rather sweet isn't she?' said Judith dipping her finger into her glass and putting it into the baby's mouth.

Agatha sneezed.

'Although they are rather revolting really at that age,' said Judith to the vicar who demurred though privately agreeing.

Agatha was arranged on the sofa so that Nanny could be given a glass of champagne.

Sir Giles Logan a godfather said 'Ah,' to her with benevolent intent. His christening present had been a block of shares in Logan Holdings. 'Ah,' he said, liking the whole atmosphere.

'Isn't it the little pearl then?' The German princess bent with clashing necklaces wetly to kiss her. 'The little pearl. And she is good yes? She will let her old godmother hold her on her knee?'

Lady Colefax said, 'The Germans are so wonderful with children,' and turned away. Orlando filled her glass sympathetically. He wished Judith had not insisted on the German princess as a godmother. She had said, 'It would be so wonderful if she was musical. Or she might like to spend her school holidays in Silesia…' – 'Two fairly unlikely eventualities,' Orlando had mildly interposed – 'Well, then, she might leave her some of that marvellous jewellery, and anyway a princess is a princess. Besides she's been very kind to me.'

So the German princess crooned on the sofa until Nanny said firmly, 'Someone's falling asleep,' and prepared to take Agatha back to the nursery.

Orlando walked with them to the door.

'Good-bye, baby,' he said, giving her his finger to hold.

Agatha smiled.

'Knows her Pappa already doesn't she?' said Nanny.

Orlando turned away, feeling foolish. But he was glad she had smiled.

In that March, too, the Warings came.

Graham Harper went to Bath, to the dentist, and came out into the sun and wind with a scarf round his jaw, having had his tooth stopped, looking pale and weedy, breathing into his woollen scarf; and stood under the plane trees on the smooth grass in the middle of the Circus, where his dentist practised in a fine Georgian drawing-room disagreeably partitioned into three; he stood with his hair wispily blown from his forehead and looked down Gay Street where the stonework needed cleaning and allowed his eye to be led across to the hills on the other side of Bath, because Bath was planned and so it was permissible and not frivolous to admire it and to let one's eye so be led to the hills, now yellowish green because of the spring. It had been done through private enterprise and speculative builders and nearly two hundred years ago, but still it was town-planning, something with which a good Socialist could sympathize: so he allowed himself to feel affection for Bath, knowing too that his late mother, Bristol born and bred, had considered it effete and snobbish, which gave him another good reason for liking it, since he looked on it as a pious duty to diverge from her in as many ways as possible. He even thought for a moment walking down Gay Street of having tea in the Spa Hotel and watching the three or four aged notabilities whose arrival to spend Easter in Bath was respectfully chronicled in the local paper; but then he noticed the first of the plain vans turning the corner from George Street into Queen Square.

He stood on the pavement and watched them pass, five plain vans with men in black inside them.

Any fool might have seen they were the enemy, with their uniforms and their coarse expressionless faces, Blackshirts, Fascisti, Mosley-ites, enemies; yet the people on the pavements hardly bothered to turn their heads. Impatient and excited, he bought a paper, found a small announcement to the effect that the meeting was to be in the Colston Hall in Bristol and would be addressed by the Leader himself, and resolved to go.

The Leader was, among other things, Guy Waring's Leader, long sought for and found at last.

'Darling Judith,' Penelope had written. 'It would be such fun if we could stay with you for the meeting – we don't seem to have seen either of you for ages – we've become so wrapped up in the Movement our social life seems to have lapsed completely! We're both dying to see your new baby!'

Orlando was away in London, but they came to stay, and the formality of seeing the baby was indeed observed. After tea Judith took Guy and Penelope up to the nursery. Guy looked at the baby with due masculine indifference and walked towards the window, asking Judith about the woods and Conrad's farming. Penelope leant over and saw Agatha's origins: Judith's forehead, Orlando's eyes, Judith's delicate nose, Orlando's wider mouth, Judith's little ears in Orlando's brown hair; a blatant piece of complicity, a shocking giveaway, she might as well have caught them in the act of love, and her heart beat faster as if she had. 'How sweet,' she breathed. 'How pretty.' Meaning how obscene, small babies are obscene, they are too intimate. 'I never know what to say to them at that age,' she said. 'My maternal instincts are underdeveloped,' she laughed.

'Mine are non-existent,' said Judith, leading the way back to the drawing-room. She meant that kindly, but then could not resist adding, 'Orlando dotes on her, though. It's really rather sweet,' and that she said on purpose to annoy.

So Graham saw them walking in through the crowd outside the Colston Hall, the small plump man with his little moustache and the two ladies of fashion looking like ladies of fashion. Graham had never found Judith attractive, although he could recognize her beauty. He would have liked for himself someone four times as fat, golden and brown and warm like a bun in which he could bury his teeth, but he had never found such a creature and liked to think of himself as heartless with women, history being for the time being all against the private life; so that, liking Orlando as he did, he preferred to think of him as heartless too, and merely using Judith as a stepping stone in his climb to power. He refused to believe that she might influence Orlando's opinions in any way, and so was not alarmed on that score, but did resolve to warn Orlando of the danger of his wife's becoming involved with such a set of dangerous lunatics.

For the danger seemed to him evident and electric, even though he himself found the Leader's two-hour speech so boring after the first noisy few minutes that he left. There were enough shouts of acclaim at the beginning to make the thing frightening, and there was the group of Blackshirts at each entrance and the strong singing of 'M-O-S-L-E-Y' as the tall figure marched up the steps on to the platform, turned to face the crowd and raised his right arm in answer to his followers' salute. When the shouts and boos and cheers had died away and the first impact of a powerful personality had faded the speech sounded to Graham much like any other politician's speech – he was not sure whether this left him primarily surprised, relieved, or disappointed – and noticing that a number of people were quietly walking out he got up to do the same.

As he approached the main door, a man in one of the back rows stood up and began to shout, loudly but incoherently, about Hitler. At once four of the Blackshirts moved towards him. Without any apparent effort, they lifted him out of his chair and carried him, limp in a mackintosh, a small man, to the door, which two other Blackshirts held open.

Graham followed. He saw the man's white face turned furiously back towards his captors, heard him say, 'Leave go of me you ...' and saw the strong fist clap into his mouth, jerking back his head. They let him go. A knee under his backside rolled him head first down the steps.

'Hey!' said Graham.

Two ambulance men who had been standing, bored, by their ambulance outside the building, ran eagerly forward to pick the man up from the pavement. A faint reproving murmur came from the crowd which had been waiting for some time for just this kind of thing. The Blackshirts went back into the hall.

Someone said to Graham, 'What happened?'

'They threw him out, that's all,' he said. 'For interrupting.'

He hunched himself into his coat collar and walked away, hating the crowd for being so many and for hoping to see blood. He had seen it. When the fist had met the white face there had been red blood – nose, teeth, tongue? – he did not know. He had seen angry faces at demonstrations in which he had taken part, and heard violent voices, and been roughly pushed and pushed back. This was the first time he had seen, at close quarters, a fist on a face, followed by blood; the first time he had stood within reach of a Fascist thug beating up a victim, and had said, 'Hey!'

History dictated that the working classes should use violence to overthrow their oppressors and to secure a

just and peaceful future. History then required of Graham
Harper, product of the English minor bourgeoisie, product of Clive and Grace Harper and of Bristol Grammar,
not devoted allegiance to a cause, not goodwill for the
poor and scorn for the secure, not paperwork, not conspiracy, but that he should bash someone's face in. History
required his blood. History required him to spill his guts.

From that time Graham became obsessed by the fear that
when history handed him his moment, he would be unable
to match up to it.

'Graham exaggerates,' said Judith.

'He does dramatize things, I know,' said Orlando.

'It's something to do with living alone. Can't you find
him a girl?'

'He can never stand them for more than a week at a time,
that's the trouble.'

'I suppose it's all his mother's fault as usual. Shall I tell
him about my psychiatrist?'

'You're not still going to that fraud?'

'I haven't been lately, no. I don't need him now I've got
you.'

'I should think not. His mother's been dead for years
anyway. Graham's I mean.'

'Oh that doesn't mean a thing. It's all in the first year that
the harm's done. At the breast, don't you know.'

'Good heavens,' said Orlando. 'But this meeting, then,
you didn't think it was alarming?'

'I've never been so bored in my life. I can't imagine how
anyone could take it seriously. I know there were a lot
of people there, but most of them had only come out of
curiosity. If Graham thinks they're going to take over the
government of the country he's out of his mind.'

'Well of course he is a bit out of his mind where politics is concerned. He thinks this is the beginning of the inevitable stand the upper classes must take in defence of capitalism in decay. You know how he talks.'

'People like Graham never know who is upper class. You should have heard the ghastly accents echoing round the room where we went for drinks afterwards. People like Penelope and her friends are always saying they can't wait for Tom Mosley to be in power so that they can get rid of all the frightful people they have to make use of for the time being.'

'That would put Graham's mind quite at rest, I feel sure. They do seem to have got Rothermere's support though.'

'Press lords are such ghastly bores though, aren't they? No but seriously it's all meaningless in England, isn't it? Conrad thinks so I know.'

'Yes, so do I. It's against every English political instinct. He'd have done much better to go on working through one of the recognized parties. I was only interested to know what the meetings were like.'

'Oh of course some people get fearfully excited for one kind of twisted reason or another. Penelope had an orgasm every time he did the Fascist salute.'

Orlando rather liked being shocked by Judith. 'Did she?' he said, smiling. 'Did you?'

But suddenly his smile seemed to her to be fatuous.

She slapped his face.

He stared at her in amazement.

She stared back coldly. Then she sniffed, twisting her nose sideways.

'Why did you hit me?' he asked.

She turned away. 'You don't know much about women, do you?'

'No.'

They did quarrel sometimes. When Judith was angry she hit him, or threw things, or seized him by the hair and kicked him on the legs like a schoolgirl in a tantrum. He held her by the wrists until she calmed down. Afterwards sometimes she showed him blue bruises on her white fore-arms and asked him if he wasn't sorry. He was sorry, but he wished she would not hit him, and would not pretend otherwise, so that their reconciliations were not always perfect, and sometimes they quarrelled again, about methods of quarrelling. Judith thought it was better to 'have it out', Orlando that it was better to avoid a scene. She suspected him of being a moral coward, he was sometimes afraid that she liked violence for its own sake.

When she told him that he did not understand women he was obliged to agree with her. After all he had known so few, having no sisters and never having seen his mother.

'But the girls in France, the sturdy sexy peasant girls with whom you tumbled under the menhirs.'

'Under the what?'

'Those ancient stones, aren't they called menhirs? You told me you were always rolling about with the village girls under them.'

'I didn't tell you that. I said I had my first experience there. And she wasn't a village girl exactly, she was the wife of one of the sardine fishermen. And she wasn't a bit like you.'

'I should think not,' said Judith, sniffing.

'None of the French girls were. And one couldn't really tumble them under the menhirs because they were mostly very proper, especially before they married.'

'You're sentimental about them.'

'Probably. Perhaps you're sentimental about the young men you used to go to dances with when you were eighteen.'

'They were all killed in the war. Everyone's sentimental about them.'

'I suppose so. Poor Judith. Was your life blighted?'

'No, I enjoyed it really. It was all quite dramatic, you see. Our parents were really awfully conventional. Life was fun in a way, but dull, too. Nannies and governesses. And then there was the summer of my coming out, which was quite exciting but also rather terrifying because things were more formal then and grown-up parties did seem most frightfully grand. Also I think one's childhood had been so sheltered that everything was much more surprising than it would be now. One was conscious of being embarrassingly innocent. And then suddenly there was the war, quite unexpectedly it seemed, and everyone volunteering and being fright-fully brave and getting killed and so on. I suppose I wasn't old enough to have really known any of them – perhaps a few of Conrad's friends – but otherwise they were just faces, or people one had danced with. I didn't know them well enough to mind when they died. It was terrible, but exciting. And then my mother died, and Mount Sorrel was turned into a nursing home. Conrad thinks that was when I became hard. He thinks I'm hard, did you know?'

'Rubbish. He couldn't possibly think anything of the kind.'

'Oh yes. And rather immoral. He is quite harsh in his judgements, Conrad, although he doesn't often give them away. He's like my father, religious. My father used to say prayers every morning when Mount Sorrel was a nursing home. The soldiers were terrified of him.'

'Were you?'

'I suppose so, in a way. He was such a distant figure. I don't think I ever liked him, exactly. I really saw so very little of him. I used to meet him in some passage and he

would reprove me for walking too fast, or singing. I think
he thought women were rather disgusting. He was awfully
distant with my mother too. What he cared most about
was the unity of the churches. The house was always full
of churchmen of different denominations trying to unite.
One of them put his hand up my knickers once. He was a
Methodist, I think. I thought he was mad. My father was
a sort of Anglo-Catholic, he liked incense and ceremo-
nies. He was rather impressive taking prayers; frightfully
good-looking, like Conrad only taller and with white hair.
I suppose I did admire him, now that I come to think of it.
He was a very authoritative figure always.'

'Oh yes, authority, that's what you like in a man. You
told me. Was it what your mother liked?'

'She was submissive certainly. Too much so. I think I
thought she was rather feeble really. That's why I wanted to
be a boy. I hated being a girl.'

'Do you still?'

'I suppose so. I've rather stopped worrying. It seems a
bit late to do anything about it.'

'I should be awfully sorry if you did.'

Orlando was pleased that Agatha never seemed to dribble,
or cry. He thought he would like her to be very well-
educated, studying Greek perhaps, with learned tutors; she
should have every opportunity. In the meantime her existence, though it struck him, now that she had smiled at him,
as marvellous, was also as yet elementary: he recognized
that the nursery was no place for a man.

Occasionally he watched the rituals of bathing or feeding, at which Jen officiated with increasing regularity as
the mysteries were imparted to her by Nanny. Jen's hands
were a little clumsy and inept, her movements not expert.

She was slow, because she was always slow and because she especially lingered over any task which could be accompanied by her own conversation with Agatha, a conversation in which the words were of no importance and of which she herself was only half aware: it reminded Orlando of how when he lay in bed in his flat over the stables he used to hear George Johnson talking to the horses as he groomed them.

Jen's deep devotion to Agatha became a quiet and mostly unnoticed undercurrent in the household. It nevertheless amounted to a continuous process, an irreversible imprinting. If nobody afterwards asked, I wonder what became of Jen?, it was perhaps because the devotion concerned was so absolute as to be almost anonymous.

[*]

'The good times are here for Mr Orlando,' wrote Graham in his diary. 'The apt young Member of Parliament, protégé of the powerful Lord Field, with what simple pleasure he accepts his good fortune. How could anyone grudge it to him? Except a disagreeable Left Wing designer rather spotty about the chin (BUGGER those spots). And the money rolls into his lap and he runs it through his fingers and laughs like a child (a new car this week and one really must have a flat in Town, mustn't one, when one is married to a Society beauty). But oh the unassuming charm with which he still wears a simple pair of grey flannel trousers when he comes down to Timberwork, and the ease of manner with which he mucks about all one morning with Desmond and Bill over some carpentering problem, and the nonchalance with which he turns up in one of his old fisherman's jerseys the day the wicked Sir Giles himself is to inspect us. Doesn't it make us all love him?

'Well I spent the day in London with weedy William whom I admire no end and we sent out a whole lot of pamphlets and went to a sort of meeting in Archer Street and of course I want to spend all of my time doing that and I'm just waiting for Cowan to show some signs of being able to take over my job to give it up and join weedy W. and his gang, BUT why does a talk this morning with Mr O. stimulate me more than anything that happened yesterday? No, not more than the meeting, that was good – but why does weedy W. go on so about masturbation and why does he chatter so about Wystan and Christopher and Stephen and then make schoolboy secret society whispers? I think he thinks I'm on to his guilty secret, which is that he's NOT A HOMOSEXUAL AT ALL. I wish he'd come and work in Timberwork for a bit and be ordinary and get some idea of the point of the society he says he wants to create. Better still, I wish he'd go to Russia for a taste of reality. I wish I could go myself but not with weedy William.

'I wish I could keep the personal aspect out of things. What does it matter if w. W.'s a bit of a silly? He's working on the right side. What does it matter that I can't help liking Mr O. in a way? If I am asked to kill him I shall. IF I AM ASKED TO KILL HIM I SHALL.'

Conrad walked up through the woods to talk to Orlando in June, before the birds had stopped singing, before the grass had dried to paler green or brown, before the pause of high summer.

'A perfect English day,' he said to Orlando, walking in through the open French window to the study where Orlando sat at his desk.

'Hot in London though, wasn't it?' said Orlando. 'Another letter from Watkins.'

Conrad took the letter.

'Have you got people staying?' he asked.

'The Graingers and the Hopes. Rather political, I'm afraid. Judith's taken them all to Longleat for tea.'

'While you're conscientiously at work?'

'All my constituency letters come here, that's the trouble, and there's too much for Miss Wright if I leave them till Monday. I'll have to get someone else I think. Perhaps someone in London for a day or two in the middle of the week.'

'Share mine if you like. She's quite efficient and it's not a full-time job because old Jones in the estate office here does quite a lot of my stuff. What's Paul been up to this time?'

'You'd better read it. I don't know what to do about it, and nor does Judith. Watkins doesn't usually exaggerate.'

Conrad read the letter, half-sitting on the edge of Orlando's desk, which had been Leonard's, and put it down beside him in silence, frowning. Birdsong and sun came through the open window.

'It's hard for me to believe,' he said. 'Eton was wonderful for me. A place where one proved oneself, took one's place, was accepted. Why is it so different for him?'

'Perhaps it's that he doesn't want to take his place.'

'No, it's that he can't. He's not a rebel, Paul, it would be much better if he were. Are you going to go and see him?'

'We'll have to,' said Orlando. 'But I feel completely inadequate. I wish you'd come with us.'

So Paul came upon them sitting in his housemaster's room, Judith dressed in some dark colour, darker-haired, white-faced, her scent in the room, her bag, gloves, scarf thrown on one chair, herself in the corner of another. Orlando sat on the arm, head bent, ill at ease. Conrad stared seriously at his own long fingers which he held up so that their tips were touching, his elbows resting on the arms of Mr Watkins' favourite chair. The three figures, not yet looking at him – he stood for a moment silently in the open doorway – appeared to him for that moment with an extraordinary strength and clarity, more than mere people, icons. He thought, they are going to hurt me, with a little shiver.

Judith was the first to see him. She did not move but stared at him directly. 'Oh Pauly, what have you been doing?' she said.

He came into the room.

'It's a fuss about nothing, they didn't understand,' he said easily. 'It was only a business deal that didn't pay off.'

'Did you expect it to?' asked Conrad.

'Oh yes, this chap Brock's frightfully knowledgeable about films. He's made several himself, just amateur ones you know, but frightfully good, and his brother's in the business and knows all about setting up a film and everything and we were going to do it with him, quite professionally and everything, and it was going to be the lowdown on public schools kind of thing, you know, like *The Loom of Youth* only a film, but look how well that did. I mean it's fashionable nowadays, that sort of thing, it was going to be a serious sort of debunking, though, not a joke, and all the people we sent the prospectus to were frightfully keen on the idea, and Brock's brother was going to...'

'Wait,' said Conrad. 'Brock's brother knew about the idea but not about the prospectus, so that you used his name and the name of the film company for which he works fraudulently. You also omitted to mention in your prospectus that you had not obtained the permission of the Eton authorities to make a film here, and that therefore it was extremely unlikely that any such film would ever materialize. Don't you understand that what you have done is to obtain money under false pretences, which is a crime?'

'Well, we'll return it of course. If only one of the investors hadn't complained to the Headmaster we'd have sent it all back by now.'

'But you have spent it.'

'Only a little bit. All the rest is in my bank.'

'A little bit? Mr Watkins tells us that the amount by which you are short, and which presumably your family will have to raise, is £500.'

Paul's face became that of a boy at least five years younger.

'I don't know anything about money,' he said. Suddenly he smiled directly at Orlando, much as he had smiled on the day they had first met, when he had said, 'We are friends, aren't we?' 'I really am hopeless about money,' he said. 'Brock was meant to be doing all that, I was just keeping the money in my bank for the time being because Brock hasn't got a bank account – his father says he can't have one until he's seventeen – and then we were going to start a joint account. Only we quarrelled you see because Brock decided the whole idea was no good and backed out when we'd only sent out hardly any of the prospectuses, so then I went on by myself thinking he'd get over it and come back to being keen on the idea and then in the meantime I found I'd spent some of the money.'

'£500,' said Conrad.

'Apparently that's what it was,' said Paul. 'Isn't it awful? I can't think what I spent it on.'

'Expensive presents for a much younger boy,' said Conrad. 'By name of Ramage.'

'Oh Ramage, yes,' said Paul. 'Ramage has rather expensive tastes. Everyone's always buying him presents.'

'Indeed,' said Conrad, in a tone of comment rather than inquiry.

'We're not getting anywhere,' said Judith. 'Look, Paul, it's no good pretending you don't understand the situation. You know jolly well you've made a complete mess of things. The point is that if we try we can probably stop them sacking you. If we do that, will you pull yourself together and see that it doesn't happen again? Or are you unable to do that?'

Paul bowed his head, accepting what he had anticipated.

'I'll pull myself together,' he said childishly.

'Do you want to stay here?' asked Orlando.

'Of course,' said Paul.

'Do you understand what pulling yourself together involves?' said Conrad, speaking quite gently. 'It means concentrating on your work and really trying to improve at it. It means giving up frivolous friendships, some of which may be quite hard to give up. It means saving up enough money out of your allowance to pay us back most at least of the £500 which we shall advance you to pay off your debt. It means disciplining yourself in every way so as to try to be a decent member of society and a credit to your family.'

'I know,' whispered Paul.

'Good,' said Conrad, rising briskly to his feet, 'let's hope you succeed at it.' He rested his hand for a moment on Paul's shoulder. 'Are we supposed to go over to the Headmaster now?' he asked Judith.

'Yes,' she said. 'Watkins is meeting us there. I'm glad that's all right then, Pauly. Will you walk over with us? Then you'd better leave us at the dreaded doorway.'

Paul walked between Judith and Orlando. For a moment Judith turned to say something to Conrad and Paul murmured to Orlando, 'I hate it here. I want to leave. Don't tell them, though, don't tell them.'

On the way back in the car Judith said to Orlando, 'You were awfully tiresome there, my darling. Why did you keep saying we must wait until the end of the half to decide, just when we were persuading them to keep him?'

'I was in an awkward position,' said Orlando. 'He told me not to tell you so for God's sake don't let him know that I have, but when we were walking over to the Headmaster's house Paul suddenly whispered to me that he hated it and wanted to leave. I didn't know what to do.'

'But when you asked him before he said he wanted to stay,' said Judith. 'How like Paul. He doesn't know what he wants, you see. He's always been like that. He changes his mind from minute to minute. I think he really wants to be told what he wants.'

'The real point is,' said Conrad, 'that being sacked from Eton is a stigma that sticks to you for the rest of your life. He can't be expected fully to realize that at his age but later on he will and he'll be jolly thankful he avoided it. I think he'll settle down again and make a bit of an effort. The last few years are always the best at Eton. It would be an awful pity to miss them.'

'Besides,' said Judith, 'what are the alternatives? Only some minor public school which would be much less toler-ant, or else some cranky progressive place which would turn him into a real freak. No, I'm sure we've done the best thing. But talk to him again in the holidays, darling, and make sure.'

'Dear Paul,' Orlando wrote. 'It was a bit awkward the other day because I didn't know what you felt until just before we went into the Headmaster's room. Also I was hamstrung by the fact that you had told me not to tell. All I could do was to say that I thought we ought to review the whole question of your staying or not again at the end of this half. Perhaps by then you'll have a clearer idea of what you really want? Incidentally I was much impressed by the Head and by Mr Watkins. They both seemed such very tolerant and civilized people and they both spoke of you so nicely although I think you puzzle them rather. They seemed the kind of people one could reasonably co-operate with. Am I wrong about this?

'Of course, we're all a bit worried about your friendships and so on. I feel very inadequate here because of never having been to a boarding school and having very little idea of what life in such institutions must be like. I imagine the atmosphere is such that emotional relationships could become rather intense. Real friendship is so terribly important, one wants to be awfully careful not to abuse it. Also later on good relationships with women are such an important part of a man's happiness that one shouldn't do anything to prevent their developing naturally in due course. You probably find this hard to believe at the moment, but it is so.

'Let's anyway discuss the question of whether or not you stay at Eton really fully as soon as the holidays begin.'

On the first day of the holidays Orlando said to Paul, 'Did you get my letter by the way? The one I wrote after we came down to see you?'

'Oh yes,' said Paul. 'I'm sorry I didn't have time to answer it. Things get so frightfully rushed towards the end of the summer half.'

'How is school these days? Do you think you want to stay there?'

'Oh yes,' said Paul. 'I love it really. I'd be miserable anywhere else.'

'But you did want to leave, didn't you? When we came to see you?'

'Oh, that was just a mood. You know how it is.'

'I see.'

Orlando felt dissatisfied with the conversation but could think of nothing else to say. After all, he thought, Judith probably knew her own son better than anyone else did.

Here is Judith as a helmswoman. 'I am one of the finest helms-women on the Solent,' she told Orlando.

'I knew it the first moment I saw you,' he said enthusiastically, adding, 'What does it mean, though?'

It means she braces herself against the side of the boat as it heels over in a gust of wind, her legs stiff in yellow oilskins, fine-boned bare feet gripping the opposite gunwale, and the boat flumps into a wave and the spray hits her face and runs down her cheeks, and her hair whipped straight and wet blows into her eyes and is flicked back, and she heaves again on the mainsheet and says, 'For Christ's sake get that jib in, can't you?', bending to look under the boom at the nearest boat, muttering, 'I'm not pointing as high as number ten. Can't you get it in any further?'

'Well, not really, no.' Orlando is sitting in the bottom of the boat quite comfortable and dry. 'You look wonderful.'

'Ready about! Lee-oh!' She has swung the tiller over and is perched on the other side of the boat before he has finished adjusting the jib sheets.

'I'm not going to make the mark,' she says, tortured.

'Like a Fury,' he goes on. He peers over the side of the boat for a moment, receives a dollop of spray in his eyes and retreats. 'You'll make it all right.'

But she is suddenly shouting, 'Starboard!' menacingly, 'Starboard! What the bloody hell do you think … Look out! Mind their boom!'

A boat staggers beside them, sails trembling, an inch away, rattling and shivering. They slide past within an inch of touching. Two men in oilskins pull ropes and avoid looking at Judith.

'I had to alter my helm! You'll have to go home! Here,' she holds out a sodden white handkerchief to Orlando. 'Tie it on the rigging. Protest. Stupid fools. Can't think who let them into the club. Number eight used to be old Lord Randle's boat, he sold it at the end of last summer.'

'We're coming up to the buoy.'

'Right. We jibe here. Will you look after my mainsheet?'

Then smoothly running home, the wind behind and the tide with them so that the big green waves heave them forwards. 'You're going to win.'

'I usually do,' smiling at last.

'I want to kiss you where your neck goes into your shirt, that first dry bit, just inside.'

'Do shut up. This is serious.'

The boat she sailed was her own and Conrad's, but Conrad very seldom used it. He had bought it when his wife was alive and after her death had asked Judith to share it with him, and she had raced it for three or four weeks in August ever since. Leonard had never been her crew. He had played tennis instead of sailing. After a time Orlando was lent someone else's boat and raced against her. She won at first because she was practised, but soon Orlando, who had spent much of his early life in sailing boats, began to beat her. They raced every day, taking the boys as crew. Judith took Stephen because he was more efficient but Orlando and Paul still won.

'Oughtn't we to let Mummy win?' Paul said once.

'Certainly not.' Orlando enjoyed beating her. Every time he did she said, 'Well done,' quite stiffly, not meeting his eyes and added, 'We were luffed on the first run,' or 'Stephen got the mainsheet twisted,' or 'She doesn't seem to be going at all well lately. I think she needs her bottom scraping.'

He found this touching and when they went back to their rented house to change he would help her to remove her wet clothes and sometimes made love to her before she had her bath. Often she would say, holding back, 'You want me, don't you?' urgently, and he would say, 'I do,' whole-heartedly, 'I do, I do, I do.'

'They are quite wrapped up in each other, aren't they?' the nannies on the beach said to Jen.

Jen blushed, not having thought about it.

Nanny's sister had died and Nanny had gone to Worthing for the funeral. She was coming back soon because she liked sitting on a deck chair on the beach with all the other nannies and the odd Swiss or German nursery governess, and exchanging news about the families and preventing the children from throwing sand at each other or staying in the water too long; drying the smaller ones and pulling on their jerseys and issuing ginger biscuits after bathing; nodding knowingly when certain things about the parents' marriages or divorces or drinking habits could not be said in front of the children; agreeing about young Mark, how he had always been highly strung, and how it was really a disgrace how little Andrew still wet his bed at seven and what a time he would have when he started boarding school next year, and how Serena was so naughty and jealous of her younger sister and always pinching her, and Rose really terrible about biting her nails, they had tried everything, bitter aloes and gloves at night, but nothing would stop her, and little Caroline was a terrible suck-a-thumb still, and that Torquil not fit to play with the other children at all. All this Nanny liked and was not prepared altogether to forgo, but the decencies had to be observed and for a few days Jen was left in charge.

She had not much to do for the boys except to see to their clothes and make sure they got to bed in time, so every day she wheeled Agatha in her pram down to the beach, and sometimes knitted on a bench by the path behind the bathing huts while Agatha slept in the shade and Jen looked up uneasily as noisy older children passed dragging their tin spades on the stones or shouting at each other or bawling, redfaced, at being taken home too soon. When Agatha was awake she took her down to the water or let her kick on a rug on the sand, not forgetting her spotted bonnet if the sun was shining or her cardigan if it wasn't; and held her in the water, each day a little deeper, until she would lie and kick and laugh until Jen's arms trembled with the strain of holding her, so she carried the fat baby back to the rug to be dried and changed and sometimes lie naked while the nannies said look at her then, the best of the bunch, they'd say, and asked Jen if she'd always been good with babies and Jen blushed and said she was the oldest of seven and they said that was better than any amount of training they'd always thought, and Jen thought, I could manage quite well on my own if only Nanny would leave.

'I think we should do something about the Edens, darling,' Judith said. 'I used to know her quite well at one time, and you could do worse than hitch your wagon to his star.'

'There are so many stars,' said Orlando lazily. 'I can't hitch my wagon to all of them.'

'I don't see why not,' said Judith.

Orlando remembered Agatha stamping her foot. She was perhaps five at the time, or six, and furiously angry. Every part of her being was engaged in this passion.

'You will rot,' she shouted, stamping, staring at Nanny who was the object of her wrath. Nanny trembled with affront. Agatha stared, righteousness in judgement on a sinner.

It was because of Jen and the buns, he remembered. Jen had been found to have been taking buns left over from nursery tea home with her on her days off. Nanny had reprimanded her within Agatha's hearing and then the whole story had come out, of complicity between Jen and Agatha, of the regular parcels of rather stale leftovers which Jen had been taking home every week, because of little Bob. Little Bob was two, Jen's mother's eighth and an acknowledged mistake, but loved of course by Jen, and at second hand by Agatha, who had never seen him but who was knitting a series of woollen squares of different colours and uneven consistency which were to be joined together to make a blanket for him.

In the middle of the unfolding of this story, with shame on Jen's part, reprobation on Nanny's, and defiance on Agatha's, Orlando had walked into the nursery to ask Agatha if she would like to come out into the garden with him. He asked why they were all looking so serious and Nanny told him. This was the cause of Agatha's rage.

'How dare you tell him?' she cried. This was when she stamped her foot and shouted at Nanny, 'You will rot. You will rot in Hell. You will rot in Hell for what you have done today.'

Jen was horrified. 'That's not the way to talk to Nanny,' she gasped, so shocked that she moved away from where she was standing near Agatha and stood closer to Nanny. Both of them looked at Agatha as if she had come from another planet.

He managed to calm them all, discovered that Jen was really afraid that her brother did not have enough to eat, suggested that in that case it would be better if she collected a dozen eggs from the Home Farm on her way home every week and undertook to arrange this, reassured Nanny as to the propriety of her moral attitudes and secured her agreement to Jen's one day taking Agatha to see Bob; so that Agatha thanked him rapturously and Jen blushed until her eyes were full of tears and Nanny was pacified and accepted Agatha's apology.

He could not remember whether Agatha ever did go to Jen's home, or how long the egg arrangement continued; but in hospital, in the war, he remembered the two women staring, momentarily helpless, and Agatha isolated and outraged.

[*]

He wore a black coat and pinstriped trousers for the House of Commons. The business simply of walking in, being recognized by the policemen, walking briskly along the passages, hardly ever failed to raise his spirits. He felt at the heart of things, and would have skipped had he been younger by fifteen years or so; as it was he usually started to hum.

Humming so he walked one day down the long corridor joining the House of Commons to the House of Lords, to lunch, as he often did, with Conrad, and to arrange for Conrad's secretary Barbara to give him one morning's work a week.

He found Conrad sitting rather uncomfortably on one of the leather-seated benches in the central hall dictating to Barbara. He raised a hand to Orlando and went on '... of supporting America whole-heartedly in the East. I think our various efforts have secured the Cabinet's agreement as to the disastrousness of forcing Japan and Germany together and the consequent necessity of recognizing

Germany's legitimate aims in Europe despite the recent gangsterism of her leaders. How are you, Orlando? Then you can add that I'd like to take him up on his invitation this year if I can but I don't know that I can spare the time, only put it in your own inimitably courteous way.' He stood up and put a hand briefly on Orlando's shoulder. 'It would be rather fun to go and see Smuts in South Africa, wouldn't it? If only it didn't take such a long time to get there. You've met Barbara, haven't you? I'll leave you to fix the details with her while I go and see if our table's ready.'

Orlando sat down beside Barbara. He noticed that her smile was friendly and less respectful than when she smiled at Conrad. She had a pale broad face, big greenish dark-lashed eyes and brown bobbed hair which curved forward over her cheeks. She was primly dressed and had long bony hands with short nails: her hands were still occupied in a responsible kind of way with her notebook, but they had a childish look and the fingers of the right one were rather inky in spite of the fact that she was using a pencil for her shorthand.

'How old are you?' asked Orlando.

'Twenty,' she answered.

Orlando thought benevolently, we shan't have her for long, she'll be leaving to get married.

'Could you meet me every Wednesday morning at ten in the Central Lobby of the House of Commons?' he asked.

'Of course,' she said.

Conrad and Orlando went into the dining-room.

'I have arranged Wednesdays with her,' said Orlando.

'Excellent,' said Conrad. 'Nice little thing, isn't she? And quick, I think you'll find. What would you like to eat? Shall we have a glass of wine?'

Orlando suspected Conrad of intermittent melancholy and loneliness. He had many friends, but none of them were intimate, and though he received a great many invitations he was not a gregarious person nor did social life in itself interest him. Judith at one time tried quite hard to persuade him to marry again, for his own sake, for Henry's, for Mount Sorrel's, but no one could more resolutely not pursue subjects of conversation than Conrad, and Judith had admitted defeat.

'Doesn't it just show you,' she said to Orlando once, 'what a difficult man Conrad is? I'm his sister, I saw quite a bit of him during the time that he was married, and do you know I honestly don't know whether he loved Alexandra so much that he could never marry again, or whether he found married life an awful bore and decided that once was enough. He's so formal, one never knows that kind of thing about him. It might even be that he thinks he's going to meet her in heaven. I just have no idea.'

Orlando had no idea either, but was certain that Conrad would have had no difficulty in finding a wife had he wanted one, certain too that when on some evenings, looking in unexpectedly at Mount Sorrel to see Conrad on this or that small point to do with Timberwork or politics or the Mount Sorrel estate, he found him at his desk or in the garden alone, evidently pleased to see Orlando yet unable to talk easily, to meet his eyes, to throw off, it seemed, the despondency in which the unexpected visit had caught him, certain that on these occasions it was loneliness that made Conrad look almost ashamed, and some kind of boredom and gloom which made it hard for him to talk. These occasions were not frequent, and they occurred at Mount Sorrel rather than in London.

In London he was nearly always cheerful and alert.

He might visit South Africa. He might visit Germany '… to see for myself. Why don't you come? Not that I believe one does see much however unofficially one tries to do it. There's a woman called Doctor Gartner who will lay the whole thing on for one in a sort of semi-official way, and arrange for one to see Hitler and all the rest of it. I must find out more about her. She seemed a nice reasonable kind of woman. Of course as you know I was in the army of occupation after the war and I haven't got this wild anti-German thing that some people who've never been there have. They were a civil, sensible kind of people, we found. They'd had a ghastly time too. The last thing they wanted then was another war. Hideous language of course.

'… Judith's too thin. Can't you get her to slow down her pace a bit? I think she'll wear herself out.

'… I'm glad to hear Paul's improving. He still seems to get appalling marks in everything except English though. I wonder if he ought to go to university at all? He certainly should go to Oxford if Stephen goes to Cambridge, but perhaps it would be better for him to miss it altogether if he's only going to idle about and get into trouble. He could come to London and we might find him something in publishing.

'… It's all another bee in Winston's bonnet. He's an odd man, you know, awfully unreliable, wildly wrong over India, yet one can't help liking him. We ought to move towards rearmament of course, but not at such a speed as to panic the electorate into voting for a socialist government. That would be the worst of all possible evils.

'… That was a good speech of yours the other day. I'm glad social problems are becoming your subject, as well as commerce. There's a lot to be done there still, though it's all improving at a great rate. You got a nice little bit of support from Chamberlain, didn't you? He's good on all that sort of thing. Pity he's such an uncongenial little man.

'... You think young Graham Harper's all right, do you, in spite of his politics? I know he's a good designer and puts in an extraordinary number of hours at the thing but I wish he'd stop messing about with all those Bolshie politics. It can't do any good in the works. I suppose that most of them have too much sense to take him seriously, haven't they?

'... Logan told me at the time of the takeover that he'd have you on his main board in two years' time. I'm glad he didn't wait so long. It will mean more London and less country, I suppose? Will you have to get a bigger flat? I don't see Judith spending much time on her own at Wood Hill.

'... They want me to take on some kind of job – this is just absolutely between you and me – if there's a change in the Premiership, which there will be pretty soon, I've no doubt. I can't make up my mind, quite honestly. I don't really want to make a career of politics. It would take me away from Mount Sorrel too much for one thing. The absurd thing is that that makes them keener to persuade me. One gets a reputation for detachment. But they're wrong, of course. To be really good at politics you've got to be wholly involved in the game. Getting and keeping power, that's all most of them think about and that's as it should be. It makes you a professional, you know the rules by heart and keep to them. I'm an amateur, I'm afraid. Coffee?'

The arrangement with Barbara was a success. Orlando enjoyed their weekly meetings, partly because she was efficient and partly because she was much prettier than Miss Wright at Timberwork.

Once Conrad said, 'I told Barbara you'd spoken well of her and she positively blushed with pleasure.'

Orlando began to think that she liked him. Once, when he had rather more correspondence than usual to deal with, he interrupted their work to say, 'Let's just go round the corner and have something to eat,' and after that he several times gave her lunch, taking her to a little quiet restaurant by Westminster Bridge. She talked a good deal at these lunches, though she never failed to resume her role as the respectful secretary on their return to work. He found her conversation restful, though on the whimsical side. She hated London, she said, and was not interested in politics. She wanted to live in the country in a cottage with hollyhocks in the front garden and a field at the back with lambs in it. She giggled. 'No, really I do. You don't believe me. London's so dirty.'

'You'd be bored.'

'I wouldn't. I love gardening. And sketching. And then my mother could come and live with me. I've asked Lord Field if I couldn't come to Somerset and work for him there but he says he only needs me in London. I could do that, though, couldn't I, be someone's secretary on their estate? That's what I'd really like to do.'

'Wait until I've made my fortune. I'll buy a few thousand acres somewhere.'

'I thought you'd made it already.'

'Not enough to buy an estate in the country. But perhaps you'll be married by that time.'

'I'd only marry someone who lived in the country, in a cottage with hollyhocks, and I don't know anyone like that. I only know people who work in London in boring offices. And I wouldn't like to live in the suburbs either. My sister does that. She's married to an accountant. He's very boring. My father was an accountant too but he wasn't boring at all. That's probably why he never made any money. He played the cello but I don't think he was much good at that either.' That thoroughly agreeable smile again. She wore no lipstick. She seemed to remind him of someone, though he could not remember who it was.

One day when he said, 'What about some lunch?' she said, 'I want to show you something,' and pulled from the thin dispatch case in which she carried her papers and note-books several pen and wash sketches of the Lake District which she had done the summer before when she went for a holiday there with a group of friends.

'But they're very good,' he said.

'Don't sound so surprised,' she said. 'I told you I liked sketching.'

He thought she had probably carried them about with her for some time, waiting for a suitable occasion on which to show them to him.

One Tuesday afternoon Conrad telephoned Orlando in his office in the Logan building to say that Barbara had some work to finish for him in the morning and that perhaps it would be easier for Orlando to come to Conrad's rooms in Lord North Street in the middle of the morning so as to give Barbara what work he had for her to do there. He went to Lord North Street. He and Barbara were alone. At the end of the morning he said, 'I can't offer you lunch today, I'm afraid. I've got something boring to do in the City instead.'

'That's all right.' She smiled, and he kissed her. He had not exactly meant to, but she seemed unembarrassed. He kissed her again, confirming what he had imagined about her mouth.

Then he put his hand on her cheek and said, 'I'm sorry,' not meaning exactly that he was sorry but meaning rather something to the effect that she was not to take him seriously, which she seemed to understand, nodding and saying again, 'That's all right.' He kissed her on the forehead then and left.

He was rather formal for the next few Wednesdays, but she seemed so far from presuming on anything that he soon slipped back into the habit of the occasional lunch. Once he was thinking what to say in a letter and she was looking at him, waiting for him to go on dictating, when he suddenly became aware that her eyes were full of tears. He looked at her in alarm. She lowered her gaze, and he finished the letter quickly. She seemed to recover, and he told himself it was probably nothing to do with him. He thought he would be careful all the same because he did not want to upset her. The annoying thing was, her look made him want to kiss her again.

It was at the Opening of Parliament that Judith met Barbara. Conrad had given Barbara a seat to watch the procession and afterwards she came back to Lord North Street to hand round sandwiches because he had asked a few people there, it being within walking distance of Westminster.

Judith saw her, darkly dressed, deferential, dowdy. Later she saw her holding a plate of smoked salmon sandwiches in front of Orlando and laughing. Judith approached.

'This must be Deirdre,' she said. 'I've heard so much about you.'

'Barbara,' said Orlando. 'My wife.'

'How stupid of me. You look like Deirdre, though. You must be Irish, aren't you, with those wonderful eyes?'

'Well, Orlando?' A bluff imperious peer jovially demanding his attention; beef it was, beef prices; he had some healthy herd of beasts in Argyll glistening with well-being as he glistened himself in his robes. Orlando left Judith and

Barbara in conversation, unwillingly because it seemed curiously unsuitable.

On the way home Judith said, 'She's rather sweet, your secretary. Keen on you, too, I noticed.'

Orlando felt that he sounded constrained when he said, 'Yes, quite sweet.' He did not know why he should not want to talk about Barbara to Judith. He put his hand on hers and said, 'You were looking very nice. Everyone said so.' But she had noticed the constraint, and Barbara's eyes, and the expression in Barbara's eyes when she looked at Orlando, and a few days later she walked into the library at Mount Sorrel and said to Conrad, 'You must get rid of Deirdre.'

Conrad was in an armchair reading Herodotus and intermittently dozing. His legs were stretched out in front of him and his feet rested on a leather stool.

'It's a funny thing about your shoes,' said Judith. 'No one else can ever get them as clean.'

'It's a secret of the household,' said Conrad, contemplating his shoes with equanimity. 'I believe they clean them with saddle soap before they polish them. It's something Alexandra taught March. The old Field Marshal was very particular about his shoes.'

Judith stood looking down at him. She was wearing riding clothes.

'Forgive my not getting up,' said Conrad.

Judith smiled and sat down on the sofa.

'I want you to get rid of Deirdre,' she said.

'Who is Deirdre?'

'The secretary. Madge or whatever her name is.'

'Do you mean Barbara?'

'Yes, Barbara.'

'But why on earth?'

'You must either get rid of her or tell Orlando that you need her on Wednesdays and he must find someone else. But preferably get rid of her.'

Conrad frowned and removed his feet from the stool.

'What are you talking about, Judith?'

'She is in love with Orlando.'

'Oh nonsense. She's a thoroughly sensible nice girl who knows her place. She wouldn't dream of causing any trouble.'

'She's in love with Orlando and he knows it.'

'Surely you're dramatizing? Besides, Orlando is devoted to you. You must know that.'

'He may be devoted to me but he is extremely susceptible to flattery. You can find another secretary, can't you? It can't make any difference to you.'

'It does make a difference to me. She's a very efficient secretary and besides I like her. I don't want to get rid of her.'

'Then I shall have to resort to other methods,' said Judith.

'What on earth do you mean? Besides, I know Orlando is younger than you and therefore you may think you know better than he does in some particulars, but are you sure this is the right way to treat him?'

'I'm not treating him, I'm treating her. And it is the right way to treat the Barbaras of this world.'

Conrad sighed. 'It seems a bit high-handed to me. Would you like me to sound him about it, discreetly? I'm sure you'd find you'd been worrying needlessly.'

'No, if you're not prepared to get rid of her I'll deal with it in my own way.'

'I don't see that you need rush anything. Give me a little time to think it over.'

'I know what that means.'

'It means what I say, that I'd like time to think it over. I'm sure we can arrive at some compromise.'

'I haven't your faith in compromise,' said Judith, standing up and moving towards the door. 'See you for lunch tomorrow, you're helping us out with the Severn bore. Don't worry. I should probably feel the same in your position. I don't blame you at all.'

'Good of you,' said Conrad, reaching for his book and putting his feet up on the stool again.

One day Barbara was offered a job by Lord Randle, at nearly twice her existing salary, as secretary and bookkeeper on his Hampshire estate. A small cottage went with the job, with a garden going down to the river Test.

'It was so wonderful of your wife to mention it to Lord Randle,' she said to Orlando. (Here the plan had gone slightly awry because Lord Randle, who was seventy-six after all, though gallant as ever with the ladies, had forgotten that he was not supposed to mention Judith's name during his interview with Barbara.)

Of course Orlando asked Judith why she had done it and she said she had done it to help Barbara and Orlando did not believe her.

'Well, it does help her, doesn't it?' said Judith. 'It's what she told me she wanted. Why did she accept otherwise?'

Orlando had asked Barbara that question and she had answered, 'Because it's what I've always wanted. I mean, isn't it? And besides, well, now is a good time altogether for me to find a new job.'

'Judith, I think you sometimes have a way of manipulating people for your own ends,' said Orlando rather heavily. 'I shouldn't like ever to feel that you were trying to manipulate me.'

Judith turned away irritably. 'What does it matter? You'll never see her again.'

'What makes you think that?'

'What do you mean?'

Judith's sharpness elicited a more provocative reply than he had intended.

'I have asked her to lunch with me on Wednesday as usual.'

He expected that 'as usual' to make her hit him, but she didn't. She said quietly, 'I see,' and neither of them referred to Barbara or the proposed lunch again until after it was over.

The lunch was rather a sentimental occasion. He put his hand over Barbara's and talked of her future, her prospects, her hopes of happiness. They did not mention Judith. She told him about her sister's baby and he talked about Agatha. She laughed at him for not knowing whether Agatha had her rest before or after lunch: he did not know why this should amuse her. He drove her to Temple underground station, said good-bye, and then while they were still sitting in the car he kissed her passionately. She responded passionately. He wished he need not let her go but did, and then thought that it was just as well and that no doubt Judith was quite right, only she might have done it in a more subtle way. But then Judith was never subtle although she probably thought she was. It made him smile to think of her, and to think of Barbara too. He felt generous and thought of buying Judith a present.

When he went back to their flat in Hyde Park Gate that evening he had only had time to buy her some flowers from a barrow on the corner of the street. She was sitting at a little desk by the window writing letters when he came in. Straight-backed, she looked coldly at the pink roses.

'So you had an enjoyable lunch?' she said.

'Yes, thank you,' he said. 'How have you been getting on today?' He kissed her on the cheek, putting the roses on the desk in front of her.

'Quite well, thank you,' she said, addressing an envelope.

He sat on the sofa and looked at her, smiling.

'You look very stern and businesslike,' he said. 'Tell me what you've been up to. Was it your Conservative ladies lunch or is that tomorrow?'

'I had lunch with an old friend of mine.'

'Who was that?'

'Tom Marling. I don't think you've met him.

'No, I don't think I have. Tell me about him.'

'I don't think you'd like him particularly. He was my lover before I married Leonard. He was never very amusing but always good in bed. He hasn't changed.'

Orlando said nothing. Judith folded her letter carefully and put it into the envelope.

Orlando said, 'Why are you teasing me?'

She looked at him with intense bitterness and said, 'I am Judith. I am not to be trifled with.'

He wanted to laugh. She looked so absurd. But she meant it.

Afterwards he did not remember the details of the time that followed, only that it was bad. Nights of too much talking, days of indigestion. 'Why did you have to go and spoil everything, Judith?' Because she was rather pleased with herself about it. She thought it a fine passionate gesture, like Sarah Duchess of Marlborough cutting off her hair after a quarrel with the great Duke. Orlando could not make her understand that it did not appear to him in that light at all. For some days indeed it seemed to him that he could not make her understand anything. But in the end

of course they were reconciled, and went for a short holiday in Paris. It was a success. Judith enjoyed her superior
knowledge of sophisticated Parisian life but was proud of
Orlando's perfect French. She was thoroughly affectionate
and said that she would like to have another child, a son
this time.

Back at Mount Sorrel they went to Church as usual on
Sunday. Orlando prayed, forgive me my trespasses as I
forgive them that trespass against me, and thought with a
kind of peaceful sadness how people who love each other
inevitably hurt each other. At the back of his mind there
was just present, shunned by his conscious thoughts, a small
awareness that he could be said to have received a sanction
for behaving less well himself another time, should another
time materialize.

'Mr Orlando is a perfect gent,' wrote Graham Harper in
his diary. 'In other words a perfect shit. I wonder why I
like him? He gives the glad eye to balding Bertha on the
switchboard while Lady Judith's little tummy is swelling up
again – she came in to bring him some papers he'd left
at home, all dressed up to drive to Town, painted to the
eyebrows as usual. I'd rather have balding Bertha myself, at
least she's got a decent figure. The smelly cat from next door
is kneading my knees. Rally tomorrow, Trafalgar Square.
I'll stand among those white faces, they'll wear the same
clothes, white choker and worn boots, boots with holes in,
I'll feel a phoney because I haven't got holes in my boots,
then I'll go with the others for coffee in the committee room
and feel a phoney because I haven't got an Oxford accent.
I'll try to put on a West Country working class accent
but there'll be a nasty touch of Bristol Grammar breaking
through, I'm no mimic. And there's Mr Orlando, no more

upper class than I am and a bastard at that I imagine. Whose son was he I wonder? Some student's, I suppose, since the old guardian was a don. Student and tobacconist's daughter, but he thinks he's the Son of God secretly. Perhaps he is. Member of Parliament, director of companies, husband of Lady Judith, brother-in-law of Lord Field, Son of God, what more can he want? I hope I miss the crucifixion though, I hate that sort of thing, I'll take a day off the day of the crucifixion.

'He's a man of action, Mr Orlando, in other words a creature of instinct, in other words indistinguishable from a madman. Men of action don't reason, they haven't time, they act it all out, like a dream, they're someone else's dream. The thinkers think and while they sleep the men of action act out their thoughts in a dream and this is mankind, nothing is not associated. In Germany they had some bad thoughts and now they're having bad dreams. I can't think or act, just as I'm neither upper nor lower class. I'm the offspring of a class which ought to have been sterilized, on grounds of moral hygiene. Poor old Graham, Mr Orlando says to Lady Judith, bit unbalanced, what he needs is a girl. Oh, Mr O. you wait, it'll all catch up with you one day, this life of action.'

Agatha did not like Jen's father.

They did go, one day in winter, rather cold, on the bus to Radstock, Nanny not at all approving, and found little Bob playing in the yard behind the house and the father rheumy-eyed in his chair by the fire, minding little Bob while Mum was out delivering the day's washing.

'I done pee-pees in my train,' said little Bob, and showed them how, pulling his penis out of the leg of his shorts and going 'Psss ...' into a cardboard box, his train.

'Dirty.' Jen smacked his hand briskly and led him into the kitchen to see what they had brought him. 'Lovely eggs,' she said. 'What do you say?'

'Thank you,' said little Bob.

'Have you been a good boy while I've been away?'

'Yes,' said little Bob. 'Kiss it better,' holding out his finger which was blistered.

'He's forever at the stove putting his finger into things,' said his father from the corner. 'I can't have my eye on him all the time, can I? It isn't a man's job, baby-minding. Come here then, little Miss Agatha, let's have a look at you. So you're the one we hear so much about. You've pretty golden hair, haven't you? I won't hurt you, don't shrink away. There, that's a soft little cheek, isn't it? Would you like a sweetie? You would, wouldn't you? And I'd like to give you one. But I can't. That's what they've done to me, you see, they've deprived me forever of the joy of giving. Have you any idea of what that means, little Miss? You haven't, have you? Your father's a lucky man, because he can send eggs to the likes of me. Deprived forever of the joy of giving.' He nodded several times.

'The eggs are for little Bob, Dad,' said Jen. 'I'll take him over to play in the field now, with Miss Agatha, until Mum gets back. Are you getting the tea then today?'

'My back's playing up. It's this cold wind we've been having.'

Over the road in the field she liked little Bob better. Whatever Jen or Agatha said he laughed, and then he jumped in circles or rolled down the hill, until his face was red with warmth and excitement and he began to talk rubbish because he was pleased to be with them. But at tea Jen nagged at him, wanting him to show at his best in front of Agatha. Jen's mother was immensely fat. She sat heavily on her chair, which creaked each time her full weight bore down upon it as she lifted her elbows from the table and raised her cup of tea to her lips.

'She's a look of Princess Margaret Rose, hasn't she? Fairer, of course.'

'Oh Mum. Mum thinks of nothing but the little Princesses, do you Mum?'

'I've always liked the Royal Family. Nice people, I've always thought. Did you see the photographs of them in the garden with the Queen and the dogs, the little Princesses I mean? One of those women's magazines it was, I brought it home Wednesday from the Vicarage, they had it up there when I took the washing. She's in a state up there, that maid's left her, that Bertha, without a word of warning, gone off with one of the men from the pit up there, married too and wife six months gone, she's no one to help her, Mrs Males I mean, and the boys home from school any day now. I'd have done it myself if I could have left the kids with Dad for a week or two.'

'You'd never,' he mumbled from his chair by the fire where he was drinking his tea. The fire was small and he preferred not to leave it. He had a mug of tea in one hand and a thick slice of bread and margarine in the other.

She did not answer, lifting her teacup again, tired. She was kind, that Agatha could see. 'Give anything for a smoke,' she said. She put down her cup and fished in the pocket of her overall for a toffee which she gave to Agatha. 'There then,' she said smiling.

'Where d'you get that then?' the husband asked.

'Mrs Males gave them me,' she answered. 'He's a terror for sweets,' she said to Agatha. 'It's since he gave up tobacco. Catch,' she said, and threw him one.

Agatha smiled, because it seemed to be expected. She thought it horrible that a grown man should be a terror for sweets.

On the way home in the bus she said to Jen, 'What did he mean about the joy of giving?'

Jen gave her typical little jerk of the head. 'It's something the social worker told him,' she said.

'I see,' said Agatha, mystified.

It stayed in her mind as a painful episode, the visit. She was not quite sure why, because nothing terrible had happened. She went on knitting her squares for little Bob's blanket, and remembered to ask after the family whenever Jen had been home for her day off, but she liked Jen better when she was her Jen, at Wood Hill, giving her her bath or walking with her in the garden, not among her own family in the little house that did not smell quite right. She did not know why she should have felt an alien in that house, but it was that that distressed her, that feeling of separation, of recoil on her own part.

'One day little Bob will come and live with us,' she said. 'And you can look after him as well as me and he can have the room next to mine and nice clothes and so on.'

'Whatever would Nanny say?' said Jen, laughing at the idea.

Nanny of course would never allow it.

Once, before he met Judith, Penelope told Orlando that she had sat next to her at the hairdresser. (Orlando was talking of presenting his letter of introduction to Leonard.) Judith was waiting to have her hair combed out, and was looking at a magazine. She sneezed, said quietly, 'Bless you, Lady Judith,' and went on looking at the magazine.

'That shows you the sort of person she is,' said Penelope.

It didn't, but he thought it very funny.

'It doesn't mean a thing, you know. It never gets any bigger.'
Penelope and Judith by the swimming pool at Eden Rock.

Judith had said, 'Let's go down to the Riviera for a day or
two. I'm sick of London.' And there had been the Warings
by the pool, Guy paunchy, Penelope painting her toe-nails,
and opposite them an American blonde with a beautiful
figure and a forty-five-year-old face and a boy in atten-
dance who could have been her son but it was not likely.

Judith was pretending to believe it nevertheless, in order
to annoy Penelope who liked to show that she was wise
to anything. And the boy walking round the pool with an
elderly Italian man of courtly demeanour (equivocal again –
'who whom there, one wonders,' offered Judith as a red
herring) was overheard, raising his voice a little petulantly,
to say, 'She's really too absurd about her bosom.' What did
that indicate, the lover or the son? And then the splendour
of his equipment for the former role caught their attention,
revealed as it was, if not positively displayed, by his choice
of minuscule swimwear.

'Too marvellous,' Penelope said, the smell of her nail-
varnish mingling in the air with the salt and the suntan oil.
'No wonder he wants everyone to see.'

'It doesn't mean a thing, you know,' said Judith gently.
'It never gets any bigger. There was Charlie Scrimgeour,
who was excused shorts at Eton. He was no better than
anyone else when it came to the test.'

'What a let-down,' said Penelope, calmly, dabbing at her
toe-nails.

Orlando raised his head from his folded arms and saw
Penelope's little round face wrapped in concentration on
her task. Over her bent curls Judith sent him a satirical

look. Excused shorts, he thought, putting his head back on his arms and submitting himself to the sun again, excused shorts. Bless you, Lady Judith.

When she was pregnant with Imogen in the early spring of 1936 she was very calm. She was not ill this time and lived mostly at Wood Hill. 'Isn't it unlike me?' she said. 'Aren't I the picture of domestic contentment?' sitting in front of the fire sewing, with Agatha, who was three then, settled with her own little table and chair, drawing and talking, the hour after tea, between five and six.

She had taken up embroidery and made four chair seats that winter, for the long-backed chairs that stood in the hall. She supervised the cooking with more attention than usual but did not seem to need to entertain on her usual scale. 'I've put off the Fortescues. I couldn't be bothered with them. It's so much nicer when it's just us.' Conrad, now Leader of the House of Lords and more and more involved in politics, had to be away for his son's half-term holiday from school, so Judith had Henry and two of his schoolfriends to stay. There was snow, and Judith asked all the neighbouring children whose names she could remember to toboggan on the long hill in front of the house, and when it began to get dark she lit a great bonfire which the gardeners had prepared and gave the children sausages and buns and hot chocolate, and some of them went on sliding down the hill in the dark, and having not enough toboggans between them they took trays from the house and sat on them with their arms round their knees and went spinning in circles down the tracks they had been making all afternoon which became more and more slippery as the night frost set in again.

Henry was ten and at his preparatory school, competent, reserved, kind to Agatha, who admired him. Orlando

liked him, but Judith found him unresponsive. She wrote
often at this time to Paul and Stephen at Eton. They were
not at all used to it, but it was part of the new regularity of
her life. Most mornings at her desk she would add a paragraph to one or other. 'Agatha has got a cold. She caught
it from Jen who gets them from her family when she goes
home. This is one of my little irritations. But I haven't
many I must admit. Orlando says Hoare ought to lie about
his silly agreement with Laval over Abyssinia and pretend
it was all a mistake and back out of it but he doesn't think
he will. He thinks Baldwin will sacrifice Hoare. Conrad
says the moral force of the government will suffer if Hoare
stays – and you know what an authority on moral forces
Conrad is. Sam Hoare is one of his best friends too, so
everyone feels that strengthens his argument. So poor old
Sam, who was only trying to prevent Musso being pushed
into the arms of Hitler. Talking of which Penelope swears
she'll take me to see him (Hitler I mean) – she says he has
the most beautiful hands – I always think that's a bit of a
last resort, don't you, like saying someone's really terribly
kind – it implies they've nothing else to offer. I do hope
you're working, darling, and being less frivolous' (this
was to Paul). 'You can see how your country's going to
need you, can't you? I mean you'd be such a good Prime
Minister, I expect. I do want to be able to be proud of you
and I'm sorry I haven't written more often but I *am interested.* Everyone says how wise Orlando is and what a gift
he has for solving problems – he's on so many committees
now in the H. of C. and chairman of two – and also Jack
whose PPS he is told me definitely he'd be a junior minister v. soon. So do work darling and follow his example and
don't write asking me for money all the time because it
does worry me.'

She grew quite plump all over, which suited her in a way although it drew attention to the fact which her slightness usually concealed of her being a very tall woman.

'I've got so fat this time, I look a nightmare,' she said contentedly. 'I don't look at all like someone it's nice to come home to.'

'That's exactly what you do look like,' said Orlando, putting his arms round her. 'I like it very much.'

He was away from her a good deal because the House of Commons kept him in London and so did the meetings of Logan Holdings. Sir Giles Logan was drawing him more and more into the affairs of the parent company so that he had no time for more than a day a week at Timberwork. Judith, who was usually restless after a day or two without him at Wood Hill, was reading Trollope – 'You're just like Phineas Finn and of course Conrad is the Duke of Omnium' and doing her embroidery, and taking Agatha for walks, and even bothering to go to an occasional meeting of the village Women's Institute. So his relationship with her became less disturbing, and his business and political work more seriously absorbing, and he thought, We are growing up.

'I have a suspicion that Mr Orlando is preparing to ditch us,' wrote Graham Harper in his diary. 'He spends too much time with the wicked Sir Giles plotting capitalist plots. They'll close us down before long, I'm sure of it, and all my friends here for whom he cares not a jot although they like him better than they like me, such being the way life's little ironies run, will be out of jobs and on the dole. He's too often in his City suit these days. Where are the baggy corduroys and the fisherman's jerseys from the old days with the Quiberon sardine fleet? Lady Judith's given them away for jumble no doubt, it's spats and a cigarette holder and a bit of a paunch already though he's only the same age as I am. And I told him the problem with the production hold-ups and the tiffs between Geoffrey and Tom and he exercised his authority and solved it all quite neatly and left them happy, with Geoffrey in charge and Tom's face saved. Oh wise Mr Orlando, the sensible fellow, the sunny sensible fellow, what more do we need?'

'The truth is, Orlando,' said Sir Giles Logan speaking confidentially in the City Universities Club, 'that Timberwork is no longer an economic proposition in its present form.'

Orlando looked at his plate of steak and kidney pie and said nothing. He knew all Sir Giles's arguments in advance and he knew how convincing they were and he knew that he was going to oppose them. So for the time being he listened quietly.

He did not like Sir Giles particularly, but he recognized and admired his shrewdness, and found him easy to deal with on a straightforward basis of recognition of interests involved. Sir Giles suffered unfortunately from high blood pressure, which gave him a red face, and from the exclusivity of his interest in his business, which made him a dull companion. In the City he was said to be no fool. He lived uninterestingly in a suburb with a homely wife who played bridge in the afternoons and made him Ovaltine at bedtime.

'Hardman Bowles are doing very well,' said Sir Giles. 'I suppose you want a glass of red wine, do you? I'll have Malvern water myself. They're doing fantastic business, as you know. Bullet-proof steel. Flooded with orders. Business is not likely to drop off either. If you ask me, and however much they may like to keep quiet about it, there's going to be as much as we can cope with in the way of Government business for the next few years, and they're bound to step up the pace, aren't they? There's this latest development in the Rhineland – you know more about it all than I do I don't doubt.'

'I know very little about it,' said Orlando. 'But nothing that makes me inordinately alarmed.'

'That's as may be,' said Sir Giles. 'But there's no doubt in my mind that any government's programme for the next few years is going to include a measure of rearmament, and that means business for Hardman Bowles. And in the last resort – the worst resort if you like – there'll be even more business for Hardman Bowles.'

'There's not going to be a war,' said Orlando.

'Let's hope you're right,' said Sir Giles. 'All I'm saying is that I can see no reason at all why Hardman Bowles should not continue to increase its turnover and its profits and every reason why it should.'

'Hardman Bowles is not part of Logan Holdings.'

'Not yet. Perhaps it never will be. That's another matter. But as you know I've been a director for some time. Old Hardman is going next month – at last – and they've asked me to take over as Chairman. I haven't all that much time to give to the thing and there are one or two of the directors with whom I don't necessarily agree. I should like to have someone else I could trust on the board, and I don't suppose there would be very much difficulty if I were to suggest someone – particularly someone of your standing.'

'But I should have to resign if I should ever get office,' said Orlando. 'One never knows about these things but I rather think that if I were to be offered office within the next couple of years I should accept in spite of the financial sacrifice.'

'Then there's all the more reason to do it quickly,' said Sir Giles. 'Let's centralize Timberwork, rationalize Logan Holdings, get you on to the board of Hardman Bowles – which incidentally will make you eligible for a certain number of preference shares which will stand you in good stead if and when you do have to give up your director's fees – and with any luck you'll have time to help me draw Hardman Bowles into Logan Holdings before you get your Ministry or whatever it may be.'

Orlando smiled. 'Simple,' he said.

'Simple and sensible,' said Sir Giles, smiling back.

'I'd like some time to think it over.'

'Of course. Telephone me in a day or two.'

Angela Payne. Not even a very pretty name. And after he had seen buildings crumble and streets of flame he could hardly even remember what she looked like. Certainly he felt no nostalgia for her somewhat muscular embrace. He had wanted her to like him, that was all.

She became quite a famous war correspondent. But at the time when he knew her she was a bouncy pushing girl working for a society gossip column. He met her at a party. She was impressed by him. He thought she overestimated his value – social, political and financial – but he was flattered nonetheless. Sex was a casual business with her. Besides, he made it clear from the beginning that he was devoted to his wife. There was perhaps a week or two of danger, a week or two when he spent too much time with her, a week or two when the fresh success of it all was a bit intoxicating, when he thought, I wonder if this is going to be important. But it wasn't. He began to think that she liked introductions to celebrities better than love-making. The thing ended when she went off to Spain with her camera. He saw her after she came back but they were never lovers again. If Judith had never found out about it, he would hardly have remembered the episode a year or two later. At least, that's what he told himself. Judith said it had toughened the fibres of his being. He told himself she used to want him to be tough anyway.

'If you hadn't been under the influence of a heartless woman you could never have agreed to closing down Timberwork. A year ago you would never have done a thing like that.'

'I was never remotely under her influence.'

'At the time when I was most like a wife. At the time when I was being so quiet and domesticated and homemaking and all that nonsense. Never again. I'll never try to be a good wife again. How am I expected to be a good wife if I am married to a liar and a cheat? I'll never let you make a fool of me again, never, never, never, never, never.'

Judith. He had seen towers crumble and streets of flame. It had only seemed like justice in the end.

The closing down of Timberwork was phased to cover a year. Most of the employees found work locally. A few went to work in the main Logan factory in Epping, moving their families with them, and a few went on the dole.

Conrad spoke to the men at a factory meeting. He explained to them at some length the economic realities of the situation. He explained to them the measures which the management were taking to give the men time and opportunity to find other employment, and he spoke of his own and Orlando's personal regret at the coming to an end of something which had meant so much to them both.

'You can't stop progress,' he said. 'A healthy and prosperous industry is of immense importance to this country and so to all of us, since we all have a personal stake in peace and prosperity. None of us should want to live in the past. But what we should be able to do is to preserve what is best and most valuable in what has been handed on to us by our forefathers, and there is one thing which all of us here have in common and of which Timberwork has been an important part – but by no means the only part – and that is the fact that, whether we are conscious of it or not, Mount Sorrel is our community, it is where we belong, and it is a whole community and a good one. That is why, in the period of adjustment which is to come, none of us will be alone, because that is the point of a small community like ours. Some of you may choose to make a break and take your families to Epping where secure jobs are offered you. Most of you will probably stay because you are Mount Sorrel people. Bill Coade here is going to be chief personnel resettlement officer, and will be working with your Managing Director over the next few months. You've been told about that and you've been told about the final bonuses. All I want to do is to remind you of something which is so unconscious in all of us that we perhaps need reminding of it from time to time, and it is just this, that we are a part of a living and functioning community and that we all have an equal interest in preserving it.'

His sincerity was obvious and they cheered him accordingly.

Evensong.

'Lord, now lettest Thou Thy servant depart in peace.

Faint smell of damp stone and the yellow light through the stained glass window in memory of his wife falling on Conrad's head bent in prayer.

'Oh Lord God,' in his clear voice, taking the service on the first Sunday in the month when the Vicar had to go to the remote hamlet in the Mendips whose few inhabitants were also part of his flock. 'Oh Lord God,' Conrad with the yellow light on his head, no more than a dozen in his congregation, on an evening of cold sunshine and half promised spring. 'Oh Lord God, when Thou givest to Thy servants to endeavour any great matter, grant us also to know that it is not the beginning but the continuing of the same until it be thoroughly finished, which yieldeth the true glory.'

Afterwards he will explain to Agatha that this was Sir Francis Drake's prayer after the attack on the Spanish ships in Cadiz which helped to delay the Spanish Armada. 'He burned the seasoned wood which the Spaniards were going to make into water barrels to take with them on their voyage to England.'

Take her, Orlando said to Conrad in his thoughts. Teach her the things you know and which I have never known. From the bomb damage to which I have brought her, be her resurrection and her life.

Imogen was born in May 1936, and Judith as usual was in a state of nervous disequilibrium for some months after the birth. Her disappointment at again failing to provide Orlando with an heir was made worse by the fact that this was also the year of her fortieth birthday.

Agatha was three. She sat on a rug on the lawn next to Jen who had put down her knitting to make a daisy chain.

'Why does it break? Why?'

'Because the stalks are thin.'

'Why are they thin?'

'All daisy stalks are thin.'

'Why all daisy stalks are thin?'

'Would you like a real long daisy chain to hang round your neck and all the way down to your tummy?'

'Yes.'

'Then don't say "why" again once until I've finished it.'

'Why?'

'Because it irritates me.'

'You must be nice to me though.'

'I will be nice to you if you don't say "why".'

'OK.'

'Who taught you to say "OK"?'

'Henry did. And I can say "beg your pardon".'

'Who taught you that?'

'The butcher's boy did.'

Graham Harper walked down the steps towards them. He had come to look for Orlando.

'He's expected back from London any minute,' Jen told him. 'Lady Judith's not coming back until tomorrow.'

'I know.' He would not have come if he had thought there was a chance of running into Judith. She made him feel ill at ease.

'How's your father, Jen?'

Jen had grown a little fatter. It suited her. Her cheeks had a light down on them, bleached by the sun so that you only noticed it from certain angles. She bobbed her head at Graham and answered that her father was very well, thank you.

'Still over at Harringtons?'

'It didn't work out very well,' said Jen.

'You don't mean he's out of a job again?'

Jen nodded. 'Geoff and Peter are doing well now though,' she said defensively. 'And Mary's gone into service over at Bath.'

'Why doesn't he come to Spain with me?' said Graham. 'Will you give him a message from me? Tell him if he wants something really worthwhile to do why doesn't he come to Spain with me and fight for the working classes? Tell him I can arrange everything if he wants to come, all expenses paid and all that, I'm in touch with the people organizing it and I'm going myself in a month or two. Wouldn't he like a bit of action after so much sitting about waiting for a job?'

Jen blushed.

'I think fighting is wrong,' she said.

'Of course it's wrong, unless it's the only alternative to something even more wrong which is an international Fascist conspiracy taking over the government of a democratic country. Will you tell him, Jen? Tell him that if he's interested at all, or wants to know anything more about it, he can come and see me any evening. I'm always in. Will you remember to do that?'

'I'll tell him,' she said rather distantly. She didn't much care for Graham. She thought him rather rude, and didn't fancy the way he talked so much. She was glad to be relieved of the need for further conversation by the sound of the Bentley's horn in the drive. Agatha ran to meet Orlando, who drove up to the house with a fluster of gravel and his hand on the horn hoping to make her shriek with excitement, which she did.

He picked her up and carried her down to where Graham was waiting for him. They talked about one or two minor matters concerning Timberwork. Graham had no intention of talking to Orlando about Spain until his decision was irrevocable.

'It has come and they haven't recognized it,' he wrote. 'This is the real confrontation. Or at least for me it is, for I have had to come back in spite of everything to the necessity for seeing things in personal terms. As long as one knows which area of one's reasoning is the personal one, there's no need for confusion. And there is something personal for me in Spain. I believe the Fascists are showing their hand at last, and I believe those workers who resisted them when no one thought they would last out for more than a day or two have set an example which will be followed by thousands of others, but most of all I must admit I believe something is happening for *me*. Coffee parties are over, there's a new feeling even when exactly the same gathering turns into an Arms for Spain meeting. And I can go and do all that I have ever wanted to do which is to achieve anonymity. I can march behind another man, shooting when he shoots. Like Orlando I can lose myself in action. But the action will not be mine, it will be history's, that's why I can count on anonymity.'

'I wonder why you won't compromise, Judith,' said Orlando.

He was lying on his bed with his eyes shut. It was three o'clock in the morning. They were both very tired.

'Compromise is for business,' said Judith, speaking quietly because her throat was sore. 'You can't have the same values in your private life as you have in business or in politics.'

'I know that,' said Orlando.

'Perhaps you behave better in business.'

'No, I don't.'

'At least you seem to be cleverer at it. You haven't managed your marriage nearly as well as your business life.'

'No.'

'Why is that, do you suppose?'

'I suppose because it's a man's world. I don't understand women as you've often told me.'

'I suppose men expect each other to lie and cheat?'

'Perhaps.'

She put her hands over her face, sitting on the bed.

'I love you,' he said.

'That doesn't mean anything,' she said in her tired hoarse voice. 'Because you can go straight from me to someone else and say the same thing.'

'Let's go to sleep.'

'Yes.'

'Lie down, Judith.'

She lay down.

'She's sorry for you, of course. Tied to a wife who bores you.'

'She doesn't think that at all.'

'You must have told her you were tired of me or she wouldn't have got involved with you.'

'She doesn't think like that. I told you. I never said anything nasty about you. I never have.'

'Don't lie.'

'Let's go to sleep.'

She threw off the bedclothes in a convulsion of anger.

'You can go to sleep, you've nothing to worry about, nothing to keep you awake, night after night ...' Long deep sobs again.

He put his arms round her.

'My darling, we need sleep. Please sleep now. I'm sorry about everything. Please try. Please try, Judith.' And please stop crying. And please stop suffering.

'Why should I when you've never tried to do anything difficult for me, or for us, for our marriage? Why should I be the one to try?'

'Please, Judith.'

She looked at him. They looked intently into each other's eyes. She said, 'I am trying, Orlo.' It was true. He could see it in her eyes. But she hadn't the training.

'You don't allow for the extra, Orlando, said Graham. 'The trouble with you is that you don't allow for the extra.'

'I don't understand what you mean.'

Orlando was in his City office, that is to say the office of Logan Holdings in Old Jewry, where he now spent several mornings a week. Graham had come to see him there in answer to a note which Orlando had left in his cottage asking him to come and see him at Wood Hill. Graham had not been at home much during the last few weeks and when he had been there he had avoided Orlando because he did not yet want to explain to him why he was making no attempt either to find another job or to follow up the various efforts Orlando had made on his behalf to make sure that he would be taken on as a designer by Logan Furniture should he so wish. He called on him in Old Jewry because he was spending the day in London and because that morning he had received confirmation that he was expected to leave the following Wednesday from Southampton with a group of volunteers for the International Brigade.

'You don't allow for people doing what can't be expected of them. It can't be expected of them but they're always doing it.'

'Doing what?'

'More. Something extra. You always allow for human beings being average. You never allow for their reserves.'

In the dull little room which had nevertheless a certain long-standing City sobriety about it, Graham looked more than ever bedraggled. Orlando wondered whether his clothes had always looked as dirty as they did today.

Certainly he must have slept in his shirt. His knitted tie was crooked and had gone rather string-like round the knot. His suit and his shoes needed cleaning and his trousers looked as if he had shrunk since putting them on. Orlando, neat, busy, and rather tired, looked at him with irritation. Of course his hair needed cutting as usual. It would also have benefited from a wash. So would his hands for that matter, which were lighting a cigarette.

'You aren't fit enough,' said Orlando. 'Why wait until the cold weather has started? There's snow, I hear.'

'They wouldn't take me earlier,' said Graham. 'Maybe they're running out of volunteers.'

'I think you're being a bloody fool.'

'I didn't expect you to think anything else.'

'How can you be so simple as to see the thing in terms of black and white like that? One side's no better than the other.'

'It is sometimes necessary to over-simplify,' said Graham.

'I'll tell you something about this war,' said Orlando. 'In terms of the real issues, in terms of history, which you're always going on about, this war will be seen in a few years' time to be totally irrelevant. If you think it's the French Revolution all over again or some such rubbish you're going to be totally disillusioned.'

'"Bliss was it in that dawn to be alive,"' said Graham. 'Do I look as if that's how I feel?'

'God knows,' said Orlando. 'You always just look half-starved to me.'

Graham laughed, flicking his ash on to the Turkey carpet.

'Well,' he said. 'I daresay you'll be Prime Minister by the time I come back. Or King perhaps. I shouldn't think this weedy little new fellow's going to last long, he looks worried to death already. They'll give you the job, after a public plebiscite – another broadcast talk like that last one you did and you'll be there. Hope you'll set a better moral tone than poor old Ed.'

'Graham, do shut up,' said Orlando. 'Seriously, I wish you wouldn't go. There's just no point. It will be uncomfortable, boring, possibly even a little dangerous, and certainly the worst way to see Spain for the first time. You'll meet some terrible people too.'

'I know,' said Graham. 'Well, I must be off. I've got a bayonet practice in St Pancras Town Hall.' He laughed, high-pitched. 'You'll see what I mean. Honest you will. About the aspects you ignore.'

'You've changed since I first knew you,' said Orlando. 'I can't quite put my finger on it but you have.'

'It's the process of maturation,' said Graham. 'You wait. By the time I come back I'll be positively balanced.'

'Then we'll go into partnership together,' said Orlando.

'OK,' said Graham.

Judith at her desk in the white drawing-room, writing to Paul.

'The baby is very well and putting on weight. Nanny says she's the easiest of any of you. Agatha loves her and doesn't seem to have thought of being jealous. She's very helpful when Nanny's bathing her. We've definitely decided on Imogen for her name but I don't love her I don't love her I don't love her she means nothing to me at all...' She tore up the piece of paper and threw it into the waste-paper basket.

'Dear Paul,' she began on another sheet.

I won't eat anything at all for lunch. Why did I eat two pieces of toast. I'm always hungry that's the trouble. I feel distended, it's wind or flatulence, is that what flatulence is? There must be something wrong with me. I know my tummy went down much quicker than this after I had Agatha. Oh God why am I so ugly? I hate being fat more than anything in the world, I can feel the roll of fat round my waist and it disgusts me, it makes me so tired too, I know being fat makes one sleepy, I never used to feel sleepy in the mornings like this. She opens some door, I don't know, it's Kinnerton Street, some mews door she opens and breaks into smiles, and he comes in and shuts the door quickly and puts his arms round her and kisses her and she ... I will have someone of my own, I will go to London next week, Johnny Barwick has always wanted me I know, I will ... I'm so ugly, I'm old old old, I will go on a cure and get really thin, I will have my hair done, there will be someone, I will come in and he will say oh Judith how beautiful you are, I love you I love you, Judith, I love you. Orlando, I want to leave you because I have found someone else who loves me very much. I will get Max Beaverbrook to sack her. Dear Max, there is a girl called Angela Payne on your staff who accepts bribes and is a morphia addict. Oh God please let her be killed in Spain. I never really liked her, Judith, it was a mistake, I told her I didn't like her, I told her I despised her. I will do exercises. Why doesn't Nanny make me do exercises, the doctor told her to remind me? I'm so tired, I will go to London tomorrow. Dear Orlando, I have gone away. I think it's partly constipation. My father had flatulence when he had duodenal ulcers. Oh God, I wish I believed in God. I hate everything. Someone will say I love you, Judith, I love you I love you.

'Dear Paul, The baby is very good ...'

Orlando had time to support Sir Giles Logan in the absorption of Hardman Bowles by Logan Holdings before he himself resigned his directorship in order to become

Financial Secretary to the Treasury. His shareholding in both Hardman Bowles and Logan Holdings was by that time considerable, so that the financial loss involved in giving up his directorships was small. He found his new work absorbing and enormously enjoyable. The possession of office lent him authority.

'I think it is Saturday,' wrote Graham in Spain. 'They will be shooting at Mount Sorrel. Some of the men who lost their jobs when Timberwork was closed are glad enough to earn a bit of pocket money as beaters even though Drummond the head gamekeeper keeps them at it pretty hard all day. We could do with Drummond out here, and a few of his beaters too, to round up the Falange and drive them towards us, presenting themselves nicely so that we could get a decent bag. I wish we had a break for lunch. I'd even be quite glad to see Lady J. for once if she were to come tripping over this snowy hillside in her tweeds and ribbed stockings and elegant brogues, followed by the servants with the hampers of food. They'll be somewhere in the woods no doubt, or in that little dolls' house by the lake, seven or eight local neighbours, that boring colonel they can't stand but who's such a good shot, and that little red-faced Lord with the Hitler moustache who owns some of the best pheasant shooting in Wiltshire. I only went once. Mr O. asked me – I told him I had a good eye for coconuts, I have too, I always win prizes at fairs – but I didn't shoot a pheasant and I haven't shot a Spaniard yet either. Our Lord was very gracious to me but they didn't ask me again. "I think we'll have no talking here," he'd say, starting to walk slowly across a field of turnips or some such, followed by his loader with another gun and his old dog Janet, too blind to be much use now but she wouldn't miss it for worlds, Janet, she used to be one of the best gun dogs in the business, now they just bring her along for the walk, good old Janet. There's Hector, her boisterous yellow son but he hasn't her nose, hasn't Hector. The Colonel's lady brings two awful spaniels and tramps along behind her husband, with inappropriate cries of "Your bird, Arthur, oh Good Shot!" and "Wally, Louisa, come here, sir, to heel, drop it!" Everyone agrees in finding her perfectly awful. "Church, Wally, Church," she says. "It's the only thing that will make him sit, we always say it when we're going to Church."

'"Those dogs of yours need a bit more training don't they?" says Lady J. down her nose offering the beaters the leftovers from Mr O.'s retriever's plum pudding, or something of the sort. Oh that's the life all right. "We'll take the Henry plantation after lunch," says Our Lord. "The wind's right." (Mixed conifers and softwoods planted to celebrate the Young Master's birth – there's the Alexandra plantation next to it, poignant in spring the pale green of the young larches planted in honour of the late lamented bride.) And I'd rather be there I daresay than here on a freezing hill God knows where with a group of ill assorted companions most of whose language I can't understand (that goes for the mad Irishman too). Or would I? I don't know. The present doesn't mean much to me. In prospect this was good, maybe in retrospect it will be good again. At the present moment it's bloody Hell, but then so are a lot of things. Come to think of it, I hated that day's shooting too, at the time. It was cold too, though not as cold as this. My fingers can hardly hold my stubby pencil which is soon coming to an end anyway. Perhaps the enemy who we've been watching for days, so near, so ridiculously doing exactly the same as we are, that is to say trying to keep from freezing or starving, will make a move tonight. I'll have no pencil left to write about that.

'My watch says 2.0. If the time's the same in England the lunch break will be over, the servants will be packing up, Lady J. will be trying to make up her mind whether to walk with the guns or not and expecting to be persuaded. Our Lord will be ready before anyone else, looking at his watch, waiting to issue his quiet words of command. They're a sight better organized than we are. Good shooting, Mr O.'

The wind blew across the sierra, flustering the snow across the shallow trenches where they sat. On the way up the hill they had passed a group of women coming down. Most were carrying children, or leading them by the hand. They did not look into the faces of the men as they passed on the narrow road. They were dressed in black and followed each other in silence, their faces without expression. Had all their men been killed, Graham wondered, or was that the way they looked when they went to the village shop to buy bread or to the communal washplace with their sheets? He did not know, he was a foreigner. Standing still for a moment to allow one of them to pass he saw her worn forbearing look above the head of the baby she carried in her black shawl, its face turned in to her shoulder, a girl of six or so following, holding her skirt, and they were the women of Thebes fleeing before the plague, bit parts in the most ancient drama in the world. Just the thing for *Picture Post*, he thought, if only I had a camera – Christ, isn't life corny? – the thin snow flakes driving past their black bent heads on the road downhill marked by marching men, and in her hand as well as the edge of her shawl she carries showing between her fingers, oh yes, earth, I have heard of this, they carry a handful of Catalonian earth when they go into exile. This is the real thing, there will be fighting soon.

So he had walked on up the hill, slowly against the snow, with his heavy soldier's accoutrements, a shabby collection in need of replenishing, a tin mug clinking somewhere against a buckle, and the excitement he felt, for the first time for weeks now, was not because of the fighting but because of the earth held in the women's hands.

For some time the fighting did not come. When he had written 'good shooting, Mr O.' with the last of his stubby pencil he closed his notebook and packed it away in his rucksack, irritated by the sight of the stiff red fingers emerging from his damp mittens, and hearing what seemed to him the cold sound of ice in the wind and the red-bearded Irishman's interminable voice, 'And all laid out there like a tart, you'd say. "Holy Mother of God," she says, "it's nothing but a fucking virgin I am, you know," she says like that ... And Holy Mother of God, thought Graham, send a little bullet just to shut him up for an hour or two, just to ... And it came. With a mild distant crack and a groan from the Irishman, then a shout; and then they were coming across the hill and Graham was on his feet in answer to a command trying to remember the drill he had been taught in the draughty gymnasium in Barcelona and running across the hillside with his rifle held ready and thinking, here we go, thank goodness for that, and listening for orders and firing once and running and then a man quite close, dark, a smile on his face from his pleasure in his action, and so they raised their rifles and shot at each other, and running on Graham thought, I wonder what became of him, and found his leg would stand no weight and putting down his hand and finding it red thought, thank God I'll be able to go home, and noticed his wet shoulder and feeling with his other hand found his neck wound. At the same time he realized he had sunk to the ground and a feeling of mystification began to overcome him. A strange warmth and a strange mystification.

He heard the sound of men running, heavy feet occasionally stumbling, and thought, wait. He heard the
cracking sound of rifle fire retreating. He thought, wait,
hearing the feet. They did not wait. They were the survivors. In his mystification it did not occur to him that he
was not.

All of his being was fully absorbed in the action in which
he was involved. He had no time to call the action dying.

King walked through the empty house at Wood Hill,
looking for Graham Harper, his long strides carrying him
quickly through room after room. He did not ask why
there was no furniture but he came down the stairs frowning, saying, she has no blankets, and Orlando remembered
that Agatha was upstairs in one of the bedrooms. You
haven't allowed for the extra, said Orlando, she needs extra
blankets.

It was after Graham's death that Orlando began to
remember his dreams. Not all of them were of the same
kind but the ones which he remembered and which recurred
had a certain shape about them, as if some aspect of himself
were making pictures on the walls of his cave.

'A pointless tragedy,' said Conrad. 'I liked him.'

He was leaning back in his armchair in the library at Mount
Sorrel, his feet in their well polished shoes on the stool in
front of him, a whisky and soda on the table by his side.

Orlando stood a little way away, looking out of the
window.

'I tried to dissuade him,' he said.

'No one could have stopped him,' said Conrad. 'He was
just the kind of fool that particular war was made for.'

'I sometimes thought he didn't altogether believe all that stuff he used to talk about. Especially in the last few months. But perhaps he did.'

'I hope so, since he died for it,' said Conrad. 'But perhaps he was too intelligent. A rotten business. Of course, I don't know that he'd ever have been a happy man.'

Orlando shook his head, turning back into the room.

'The P.M. will definitely go after the Coronation,' said Conrad. 'He told me last night. Neville Chamberlain will have the job at last.'

'It won't be an exciting Government,' said Orlando.

'Quite an efficient one, I think,' said Conrad. 'After all,' he added encouragingly, 'we shall both be in it.'

Judith's Coronation hat was a white satin cloche with a wispy silk pom-pom over her left ear: she also wore a long white satin dress with a beaded bodice and long white gloves and satin buckled shoes. In this outfit she searched for Paul and Stephen in Westminster Hall. She and Orlando had sat in the Abbey; the two boys had been in a stand outside Westminster Hall to watch the procession.

Against the crowd she thought, I am fighting for my life, smiling to friends, 'How lovely to see you, I thought it would never end, I was dying to pee, oh well we all know the English do that sort of thing better than anyone else, I thought he was going to pass out, isn't she too wonderful one must admit, darling you look divine, have you seen my hopeless boys, look at you in those heavenly robes, can't you wear them all the time, heavens how extraordinary Maud looks, oh there you are at last, what have you done to your tie, Pauly?' And she was sweeping them out with her, on to somewhere else, to get to the car, to hurry because the crowds would make them late, and all the time the feeling that she must summon up her strength to show them all, to show Orlando then; and in the meantime smiling and chattering and turning her head from side to side, a fine white peahen among the birds of her feather.

He had given her a dress to wear that night, dark blue low cut satin with sequins from Schiaparelli, and he told her that she looked very beautiful in it and she agreed.

'It's because it makes my hair look a bit blue too and that makes my face look whiter,' she said in front of the glass. 'I look thoroughly artificial. Artifice is a thing I like, don't you?'

'I like it in you,' said Orlando. 'If that's what it is.'

He put his arms round her waist, carefully, from behind. 'I shall feel very proud of you.' He kissed the back of her neck. 'You do love me, don't you? And all that horrid business is over?'

'Of course,' she said, looking with attention at her mouth in the mirror.

'I know we said we wouldn't talk about it,' said Orlando. 'But you have forgiven me, haven't you? I know I don't deserve it.'

She did not speak, staring into her own eyes.

'Because I do love you and you make me very happy,' he said. 'That's to say, when you're nice to me you make me very happy.'

'Then I must always be nice to you.'

'Yes.'

'Because your happiness is the most important thing in the world,' she went on.

'Yes,' he said, laughing and squeezing her round the waist slightly before he turned away towards his hairbrushes.

She said nothing more, running jewels through her fingers wondering which to wear, and he was satisfied and said, 'My new Ministry is quite an important one at this particular juncture.'

'You sound like Leonard,' she said, startled.

'I think Leonard would be quite proud of me.'

'Would you like him to be proud of you?' asked Judith.

'Of course,' said Orlando. 'He was my patron.'

'You don't resent him any more then,' said Judith.

'I never resented him,' said Orlando. 'It was he who resented me.'

'I don't think that's quite true,' said Judith. 'I think you have stopped resenting him because you have surpassed him.'

He had not particularly thought of it, one way or the other, but as soon as she said it he recognized its truth. He had surpassed Leonard in every way. He could not help feeling pleased to hear her say so. After all, she had been Leonard's wife.

So they walked side by side up the staircase at Londonderry House, and a certain sense of occasion, of anticipation, of being bathed and perfumed and jewelled and dressed in their best clothes, a certain awareness that important assumptions as to their being where they belonged were theirs to make, lent them a sort of gloss, an excellence of physical tone, a tightening of stomach muscles, a briskness of blood circulation, a brightening of eyes, for that particular moment, mounting the stairs at Londonderry House.

And I belong, Orlando knew, it is that that marks how far I have surpassed Leonard, and that is the difference between now and a few years ago. It is like the difference between falling in love and being married.

'It's not a joke any more, is it?'

He was no longer surprised by Conrad's percipience, and merely shook his head, smiling at Conrad for his splendour, the orders on his chest, and the turned heads that followed his progress through the crowd.

'You're looking very grand,' he said.

'I'm planning to slip away almost at once. Can we meet tomorrow morning? We're having a certain amount of trouble over this Palestine thing. You could help enormously in the Commons. We'll have to modify our agreement with the Jews a little, there's no doubt of that, but it will be a longish business and take some planning. Can we discuss it at leisure?'

'Of course. I'll come to Lord North Street. It's not one of my subjects, but I'll certainly help smooth things over if I can.'

'Did Paul and Stephen get a good view? I didn't see them afterwards.'

'I think they enjoyed it. Paul brought a note from Watkins. He wants to see us again.'

But a kiss in the air over his right ear announced Penelope Waring and Conrad moved away. She was the kind of woman for whom he didn't care.

'You still get asked?' said Orlando. 'I thought you might have been dropped.'

'What a foul thing to say,' said Penelope. 'Why should I have been dropped? If you mean for my thoroughly sensible political views I never heard anything more absurd. If you aren't more polite I'll tell you some of the nasty things I've been hearing about you this week. People have started being malicious about you, did you know? It shows you must be getting somewhere at last.'

Annoyed, he noticed that her complexion was beginning to look rather coarse. At the same moment she said, 'You're getting much fatter round the chin. Jowly.'

He burst out laughing and said, 'Go away.'

She did, because a bore began to talk to him.

'I know some of our own side aren't really behind it,' this Williams was saying as Penelope, raising her eyebrows at Orlando, disappeared into the crowd. 'That's why I wanted you to know, and it's not because it's a National Government mind, because I don't set much store by that either as you well know, a euphemism for a Conservative government I've called it before now, but I'll not be one of those who try to undermine any effort made by anybody other than the Labour Party to improve the employment situation or to relieve hardship among the unemployed, and anything you do in that direction will always have my support. That's what I wanted to let you know; anything you do will have my support.'

'I knew I could count on you,' said Orlando, putting his hand on the other man's shoulder for a moment and being already quite willingly distracted by the strident tones which reached him from some way away, cutting across Williams' reiterations, 'The 23rd, Orlando. For the week-end. I've fixed it with Judith. Lunch on Saturday.'

He nodded and smiled, agreeing. He knew that Judith would have found out who else would be there and that it would be worth going.

The daunted Williams having disappeared, he was momentarily at the mercy of a saturnine figure whose name and function had escaped him and who said several times in a secretive manner, 'You are one of us, aren't you?' The phrase came up in the middle of quite banal observations about their immediate surroundings and Orlando, searching his memory, could only return evasive answers and was finally reduced to paying an inane compliment to the wife of a colleague whom he regarded as wet and with whom he did not want to become more closely associated, whereupon she asked him to dinner – 'Such an interesting journalist just back from Berlin' – and thinking, God save me from another of those, he replied that just that particular day was unfortunately no good at all and before she had time to mention another he was swept away by a tiny creature all covered with feathers who said, 'Darling, Harold and the Archbishop are being so unutterably silly together, do come and save them from themselves.'

On the way home he asked Judith who the dark man could have been and she said, 'Oxford Group, I should think. Or Communist, or Jew, or homosexual.'

'Why should he assume I was any of those things?'

'Rosicrucian, then. Or transvestite. One of us. I don't know. What are you one of?'

'I don't belong to any group. Except the group that believes in keeping the ship of State afloat. In foreign politics I suppose I am becoming known as an appeaser.'

'Perhaps he was an adulterer,' said Judith.

'Very likely,' said Orlando. 'But I don't think it was that he was referring to. I think perhaps your first guess was the best.'

'You know Imogen isn't your child, don't you?'

'Your friend Betty's become a very keen Oxford Grouper. Didn't she give all her money to it or something?'

'Only ten thousand pounds,' said Judith, beginning to cry.

He put his hand over hers. 'Darling, not in front of Manners.' Manners was their chauffeur, from whom they were separated by a glass panel. 'I think you're a little drunk but don't worry.'

He had noticed once or twice before that Judith could leave a party apparently completely sober and only let it appear when they were alone that she was nothing of the kind. He put this down to some kind of training and admired her for it.

'Never mind,' he said. 'We'll have you in bed in no time.' And when they were home he put her to bed, kindly and efficiently, and she staggered and cried and said only once more, 'She isn't, you know, she isn't your daughter'; but then she fell asleep, and in the morning neither referred again to that particular remark.

Agatha and Imogen had Coronation mugs. Agatha was allowed to use hers at once but Imogen's was put away until she was older because Nanny said she would break it by banging it on the tray of her high chair, or throwing it on the floor.

Jen said to Agatha, when Agatha was in the bath, 'My father doesn't hold with the Coronation.'

'Oh dear,' said Agatha. 'I suppose he wouldn't. Does he still think Edward VIII was got rid of because he was on the side of the working classes?'

Jen nodded, pursing her lips.

'I wish he could talk to Uncle Conrad, just for a moment,' said Agatha. 'Uncle Conrad would make him understand everything. He can't still want that horrid woman to be queen when Queen Elizabeth's so much prettier and everything?'

'I don't know,' said Jen. 'It takes a lot to make him change his mind.'

'Uncle Conrad could, though, couldn't he?'

'He's so suspicious. Have you washed your neck? He never believes anybody.'

'He'd have to believe Uncle Conrad. Everybody does. Why don't you get him to come here by chance one day when Uncle Conrad's coming to lunch and then I'll tell

Uncle Conrad he must explain. Do that, Jen. Will you really? Can't I have a last swim?'

'You won't have time for a story.'

'I don't want a story tonight. I'm going to go straight to sleep so as to be in really good shape for tomorrow.'

'Whatever for?' asked Jen astonished.

'I'm going riding, early, with Henry. It's his half-term and he's coming to pick me up with Mr Johnson and Browny and I'm going all the way with them and some of it off the leading rein, Mr Johnson promised, to show Henry. They rang up this evening when I was downstairs and Mummy nearly said no because she's got a bad headache but then she said yes and I know Mr Johnson will let me go a bit of the way without the leading rein because he said before he would when Henry came home from school.'

'I'd better get your shoes cleaned then,' said Jen, wrapping her in a towel as she stepped out of the bath.

'Yes please. D'you think we ought to brush my riding hat? Oh Pappa, I'm riding with Henry tomorrow.'

Orlando had looked round the bathroom door.

'I thought you'd be in bed by now,' he said. 'I've come to say good night.'

'I am in bed,' said Agatha, struggling into her dressing-gown.

'Teeth, Miss Agatha.'

'I'm not even having a story,' said Agatha through the toothpaste

'That's a pity, I'd thought of rather a good one to tell you.'

'Probably that would be all right. Told stories are much less tiring than read ones because I don't have to look at the pictures.'

He had no feeling yet for Imogen. She was too young. Agatha had been his first child: he had hardly looked at a baby before. She had seemed miraculous but that was in the time of miracles. Besides he had less time now for domestic life. Imogen had hardly had a chance to make her presence felt.

He brushed Agatha's dark gold hair which was cut in a long bob (once Nanny took her to have her hair cut and they short-bobbed it and Judith was very angry) and told her a story about a hippopotamus which made her laugh; then she got hiccups, and he tried to make her drink water backwards; at last the hiccups stopped and he finished the story and went downstairs to have dinner with Judith.

Orlando had a broad chin – Agatha had inherited it – but Judith's chin was pointed and a little too long. It looked feminine in Paul, in whom it was reproduced; but his fair pale face was handsome though at seventeen rather spotty.

'So this time they have really had enough of you,' Orlando said to him.

'Yes,' he said, looking out of the window.

'What do you expect us to do about it?'

'Nothing,' said Paul.

'We can't talk them out of it again, you know,' said Orlando. 'We've used up all our efforts and influence. You must realize that?'

'Yes,' said Paul.

'What are you planning to do?'

'I don't know.'

'You do realize you've got to do something?' said Orlando impatiently. 'You can't just live here, you know. I've given you all the benefits and opportunities of life here and you haven't shown yourself exactly grateful, have you? You'll have to do something to support yourself now.'

'Mummy wants me to go into the Army.'

'I've explained to her that I think it quite unsuitable. She thinks she can persuade one of her military friends to take you on but whoever it is they're bound to ask for some kind of report from your school, and they're not likely to get an encouraging one.'

'She seemed to think Colonel Barwick...'

'I've advised her not to mention it to Colonel Barwick.'

There was a pause.

'Is there nothing you want to do, nothing you're interested in, except your personal pleasures?'

'No,' said Paul rather quickly.

'I want to help you, you know,' said Orlando.

'Thank you,' said Paul.

Orlando sighed, and reached out for a letter which was lying on his desk. (He was sitting at his desk in the study at Wood Hill. Paul was facing him, rather as he had faced Leonard on the day Orlando had first met him, when Leonard had suggested that the garden boy should bowl him a few cricket balls, the day Orlando had left his new hat on the train.)

'I can offer you two alternatives. I don't suggest that either of them are permanent solutions, although both could lead to a career in industry if you found you were interested. I think that both would be good experience for you for a few months, if not necessarily a hundred per cent pleasurable experience. One is to work on the floor of the factory at Hardman Bowles in Birmingham – that's the one I'd choose myself I think because it would be quite unlike anything you've ever done before and a fascinating experience if you could stick it – and the other is as clerk in the accounts department of Logan Furniture at Epping. At the end of a few months there you could decide whether you would like to study to be a chartered accountant in a City firm which I could arrange and which is an extremely useful background for a business career.'

Paul was no longer looking out of the window. For a moment his very light blue eyes met Orlando's, then he looked down at the floor.

'Hardman Bowles is an armament firm, isn't it?' he asked.

'Yes,' said Orlando.

'Then I'll do the other, if that's all right.'

'If that's what you want,' said Orlando. 'You can start after the holidays. We'll do something about finding you lodgings.'

'May I go now? I'm having a driving lesson at five.'

Orlando nodded.

Paul went quietly out of the room. He walked towards the stables with his hands, which were trembling, in the pockets of his grey flannel trousers. On the way he met Stephen, who was carrying a gun with which he had been practising target shots.

'How did it go?' asked Stephen.

'Bloody,' said Paul.

'Bad luck,' said Stephen. 'I thought he might have been decent about it.'

'I'm going to work as a clerk in Epping.'

'Good Lord,' said Stephen.

'It was that or making bombs.'

'Making bombs?'

'In his bloody armament factory in Birmingham. I said I'd rather die.'

'Better than being a clerk in Epping I should think,' said Stephen.

'I'd rather die than make bombs for him and his friends to make wars with.'

'Is that what you told him?'

'More or less.'

'He's always making speeches about not making wars.'

'Not above making a packet out of the manufacture of bombs though, is he?'

'So he wasn't decent.'

'No.'

'And all that about him doing the talking because of being near us in age and able to understand?'

'That was just Mummy's wishful thinking. She's besotted.

'He's got a bit pompous lately, that's all. He'll recover when he's got used to hearing himself called Minister.'

'It's all very well for you. You never get annoyed.'

'Don't be too fed up with him. He's all right really.'

'Not any more he's not.'

Paul walked on towards his driving lesson, and Stephen went back to the house. When Agatha found him later in the gun-room and asked, 'Where's Paul?' Stephen answered, 'In one of his moods.'

'Oh,' said Agatha. 'I'd better leave him alone for a bit then. Can I stay and watch you clean your gun?'

'If you like.'

Although she liked Paul better to talk to, she enjoyed watching Stephen when he was doing certain things, like cleaning his gun or mending his bicycle. He never spoke as he worked but occasionally whistled through his teeth.

'Let us distinguish in the first place,' orated Orlando, 'between the moral issue and the political one, and let us acknowledge that the two are necessarily separate though by no means self-contained spheres. Morally speaking

there are features of the present regime in Germany which
the vast majority of people in this country in their hearts
deplore. We ourselves have long preferred a democratic
to an absolutist rule. We have believed in tolerance for
minorities. Anti-semitism, unfortunately a universal and
recurrent disease, has not struck seriously in England for
many generations. Nor can we feel at ease about the treat-
ment by the Nazi party of the Christian churches, nor about
their attitude as far as it is known in this country towards
their political prisoners. Stories of varying credibility and
authenticity have reached us about detention centres, about
pressures put upon intellectuals and leaders of opinion,
about brutality in the execution of justice. None of this can
strike anything but coldness into the heart of the average
Englishman, nor arouse in him any emotion other than
opprobrium. It is, however, nothing to do with politics.

'What then is "to do with politics"?

'Ladies and gentlemen, the avoidance of violence is to do
with politics. Flexibility is to do with politics. Conciliation
is to do with politics. The recognition of rival interests is to
do with politics. Because politics is the art of conducting
human affairs by discussion, by negotiation, by reconcili-
ation of opposing views, so as to avoid the breakdown of
relations, whether nationally or internationally. It is therefore one of the most important, as well as one of the most
underrated, of human arts.

'The present European situation comes within the sphere
of politics. What then is the political solution? Ladies and
gentlemen, peaceful adjustment is the political solution.

'The Imperial Conference has recently demonstrated
beyond any shadow of doubt that our friends in the
Dominions are strongly opposed to any policies of ours
likely to lead to large-scale military commitments in

Europe. They have faith, as I believe the vast majority of the public in this country also has faith, in the power of negotiation, of round-table conference, of adjustment. Our policy should be to state our case – from a position of strength by all means – let us argue from a position of strength but let us argue – and having stated our case let us listen to other cases, in order to recognize such claims as can reasonably be accommodated. This recognition must be not a moral one but a practical one.

'The one solution which must still be unthinkable to all reasonable men is the solution of 1914, with all the unknown but only too imaginable horrors that must follow from an outbreak of war on such a scale after twenty years of advance in our knowledge of gas and explosives. All reasonable men must surely favour the alternative solution, the political solution. All reasonable men must surely give their support to those of their representatives who are seeking by well tried political methods the object of all political action, peaceful adjustment. And this must resolutely and avowedly be the policy of this Government.'

The audience clapped and cheered, some of them drumming their feet on the floor of the hall.

Orlando acknowledged their acclaim with a cheerful wave, thinking, that should get the weekend press all right.

'I read your speech,' said Diana.

She often wore a beret on one side of her head, over her sleek black hair with its smart strict cut. Sometimes she wore a matching scarf, one end of which would be flicked over her right shoulder. She had a smooth slightly oily skin which could look sallow when she was not well. Usually she was well, and there was a pinkish flush under the olive of her cheek and a brightness in her dark sometimes insolent glance. She wore rather tight woollen jerseys, usually striped, and the latest kind of American uplift brassière.

When she first appeared in the office of Logan Enterprises as Sir Giles Logan's personal secretary (her shorthand and typing were of an alarming accuracy and speed) Orlando immediately felt an impulse to remove the striped jersey and the uplift brassière. It very soon became clear that any such action would be perfectly acceptable to Diana, and a week or two of her dark glances, a week or two of her seeming always to have lost some particular file that could only be in his office, a week or two of the tilted beret and the little flicked scarf, and it ended in her bed-sitting room in Bayswater, her voice with its perfect enunciation but curiously coarse timbre saying breathlessly, 'I didn't think it would come to this, I really didn't.'

'Why not?' He was pulling off the striped jersey.

'I thought it was just a joke. It usually is with me.'

'It isn't with me.'

'No, I can see that,' she said rather nervously.

He had disclosed and touched her breasts, smoother and more olive even than the rest of her, with large protruding nipples the colour of ripe figs, and all her body dark and smelling of sweat and musk and some kind of herb soap she used. She did not shave under her arms. Her teeth were white and her tongue was red and glistening.

She aroused in him the extremes of physical passion. He never liked her.

'I read your speech,' she said.

It was towards the end of the summer recess. Judith was staying with friends in Antibes. Orlando's affair with Diana was in its third month. She was making tea.

'It was all over the papers. Didn't you feel proud?'

'In a way.'

'I suppose you're used to it. My family have always been Conservative. A lot of people are round us even though we're near Coventry and all that big industrial development there. You like the milk in afterwards, don't you? And no sugar, that I can remember at last.'

She handed him his cup of tea and took hers over to the sofa. Putting it down on a little table beside her she stretched herself slowly, then tucked her feet up underneath her on the sofa and smiled at him, showing her fine white teeth. He smiled back.

'Your wife is lucky being by the sea,' she said. 'Does she like swimming?'

'Yes,' said Orlando, who would have preferred that Diana should never speak of Judith.

'I like swimming too. I won a prize for it at school, would you believe it? How old is she?'

'Who?'

'Your wife.'

'I don't remember.'

'I know she's a lot older than you so you don't have to be so secretive. You're very loyal, aren't you?'

'Let's not talk about it.'

'I can't help being curious you see. I'm sorry. Only if you were really happily married you wouldn't need me, would you?'

He looked at her in surprise. Then he smiled. 'Women are very romantic,' he said. 'I am happily married and I do need you. Do you mind?'

'No,' she said. But he could see she did. She would have preferred him to have said that his wife did not understand him or was no good in bed. Neither of those things was true and he was not prepared to say they were.

'Diana,' he said, making an effort to understand her feelings and an offer he very briefly hoped she might accept, 'if you would rather, we could finish all this. I'd be very sad, but ...'

She stretched herself again with an easy smile. 'Oh you,' she said. 'You'd get your own way with anybody, wouldn't you?' Which he took with relief to mean that she was satisfied with the situation.

When he went home to Wood Hill that weekend he found the evenings lonely without Judith and he wrote to her saying that he found after all he could get away the following weekend and would join her in Antibes.

Judith in Antibes. Wearing white floppy beach pyjamas with a blue spotted necktie and a wavy-brimmed Mexican straw hat. Cigarette holder. Dark glasses.

'I simply refuse to dine with Willie without having my face done. He's such a cat. I've got to get to the Carlton somehow. No, of course my maid can't do it. I need mud. That's not mud on the beach, Shanks, that's tar. What a foully malicious suggestion. Shanks has just suggested that I should put tar on my face. Isn't he a rotten brute? No, Orlo, I utterly refuse to let you spend any of your precious time here driving me about when you could be lying on the beach getting all golden brown so that all the old queens will make passes at you, and I shall get terribly jealous. Why don't I ring up for a taxi? Oh well, if you insist then, we could buy some presents for the children, couldn't we? Doesn't anyone else want to come? Oh do come, someone.'

No one came.

In the car Judith said, 'My face won't really look any different, will it? It's an awful waste of money.'

'Not if it makes you feel better.'

'I seem to be always doing things to make me feel better.'

'We all need a lot of bolstering up.'

'They don't always work with me, the things I do. Do they with you?'

'Not always.

'I've been realizing while I've been here that I'm not in awfully good shape at the moment. I never have been really since Imogen was born and then there was all that difficult time. I know it's a long time ago but I seem to be rather neurotic these days somehow. Do you think ...? I mean, everything is all right between us, isn't it?'

'Of course,' said Orlando, putting his hand over hers as he drove along the corniche in the sun, above the startling blue sea.

'I sometimes think we used to be more friendly. You're so often away and I can't help feeling that you don't need me any more. I don't know why but I don't seem to feel much use at the moment.'

'Of course I need you. I don't know what I'd do without you in the constituency.'

'I don't think that's what I mean exactly. We do love each other, don't we?'

'Of course we do.'

'We're not very often alone though are we? I mean we don't seem to like doing things together any more.'

'This doesn't sound at all like you,' he said smiling. 'It's you that likes to do everything in a group of your friends.'

'Yes but all this social life, it's rather empty isn't it?'

'It's something you do very well, and it's fun for you, and stimulating. I don't think it's all that empty.'

'You don't feel any of this then, what I'm trying to say?'

'I don't think so. I'm happy, my life is full and interesting, I'm very fond of you. I don't quite know what it is you are trying to say.'

'Nor do I exactly. Do you think I ought to go and see that psychiatrist I used to go to when I get back to London?'

'Yes, I certainly should if you think he can help you.'

'I wish you could stay a little longer.'

'So do I. But I'm afraid it's quite impossible. I've got so much on in London at the moment.'

The salt cold wind blew over the island; King turned from his half-finished tower, threw up his arms, fell dead; the wind blew through the house on the island, where Sid peeled potatoes into a bucket by the fire; it blew through Wood Hill, through the white empty rooms and up the white bare stairs; and Orlando in his narrow bed suddenly moved, lifting his hands to the pain across his eyes.

'Then we must sack them,' said Orlando. 'And if no one's prepared to do it, I will sack them myself. There's no alternative.'

'It's insecurity,' said Sir Giles. 'People don't buy bedroom suites when they think there's going to be a war. They're not sure what's going to happen. They think they'll wait and see.'

'There's not going to be a war,' said Orlando.

'We could hang on another month or two and see how the figures look then.'

'We'd much better do it now. If we wait until later we may have to be more drastic. We can always take them on again if things improve. I'll see the Union boys.'

Sir Giles nodded. 'I think it's probably the right thing to do.'

'Of course it is. A few months' retrenchment, a year even, and then we can be ready to go ahead when things have settled down. It's better than being over-extended.'

'You don't think we're over-simplifying? We have to think of the effect on the shares.'

Orlando shook his head.

'It won't be anything much. A firm management gives confidence. A good half-yearly report will pull the share prices up again.'

'If we can produce a good half-yearly report.'

'We'll do that, don't worry,' said Orlando.

'Orlando, Robin Barwick wants to marry me.'

'You are married already, Judith.'

'He is in love with me.'

'Do you love him?'

'Well not exactly, but he makes me feel that he needs me and that I could make him happy.'

'And I don't?'

'I tried to talk to you in France. I tried to tell you. It cost me an awful lot that, and you seemed hardly to be listening. I tried to tell you I needed help.'

'How can I help you then?'

'Don't ask in that tone of voice. How can I possibly answer? Besides I don't know. It's probably too late.'

'I think you would find life very boring with Robin Barwick.'

'Perhaps.'

'Was it exactly loyal to me to get into a situation such as to allow him to propose marriage to you?'

'Oh, Orlando, for heaven's sake, are you always exactly loyal to me?'

'Yes, I believe so.'

'And do you always resist the temptation to encourage people to become fond of you so as to feed your own ego? Do you never exploit people?'

'This is your psychiatrist again. He sounds a terrible prig, that man.'

'Well, do you?'

'I don't know what that means. Of course I enjoy stimulating relationships. All men do.'

'Not women?'

'It's different for women.'

'I am really astonished at how much I can dislike you sometimes.'

'Isn't it time you went to change?'

'Why?'

'We are dining with Sibyl Colefax.'

'I don't think I'll come. I've got a headache.'

'It's rather late to say that. I don't think she'll be very pleased if you cancel now. Besides you know it will amuse you really. Come on, Judith, let's make peace. Go and change. Pax, as Agatha says.'

'It's a game then, to you?'

'I can't take it very seriously somehow. Robin Barwick indeed. Go on, Judith, go and change.'

'Hitler is preparing to go into Austria,' said Orlando. 'Whatever happens we must have signed some sort of agreement with Italy before he does it. It's no use waiting for the Italians to withdraw their troops from Spain. We must start talks now.'

'Anthony doesn't agree.'

'The P.M. does though. You must exert your influence, Conrad, and get them to see eye to eye.'

'Of course I'm doing all I can. But I feel very uneasy about it. I've a nasty feeling we're going to lose Eden.'

'You mean he'll resign?'

'I think he might this time.'

'Then you must succeed him.'

'No, no, of course it must be Halifax. But let's hope it won't come to that. It will be very serious if it does.'

'I think you take too gloomy a view. If the Germans can peaceably achieve what they want in central Europe, and we and the French can make them some kind of offer in Africa, what more do they want? They'll have their security then. I heard it on very good authority only the other day that the German General Staff are scared stiff of war with this country and would never let Hitler push them into it.'

'I hope you're right,' said Conrad.

'Of course I'm right,' said Orlando.

'Of course you're quite right,' said the plumpish man. 'Life's for living, sort of thing? I must say I wish I had your opportunities though. My wife hardly ever comes down from Scotland nowadays and when she does somehow it seems to be a question of dinner with relations, don't you know, or taking some old aunt to the theatre. And really the House takes up so much of one's time these days, with all these wretched debates on foreign affairs. I must say I wish I knew someone to spend a bit of time with, you know, some nice girl or something. To be quite frank, just between ourselves – I've had too much to drink, too, blast it, waiting for that bloody division bell to ring – but anyway my wife as I say, it's not exactly that she's past it, but she seems to have lost all interest in that sort of thing, do you know what I mean? And I don't like to, well, you know, force it on her exactly but of course one does miss it rather, don't you know? Not that I'd necessarily want anything of that sort, it's more a bit of companionship I'm looking for, you know what I mean? Someone to take out to dinner occasionally, that sort of thing.'

'I might be able to introduce you to someone.'

'Really? Oh I say that would be most frightfully decent of you. Could you really?'

'Yes, I think so. I'd have to ask her first. I'll let you know.'

'Will you really? Tnat's jolly nice of you. I knew you were the chap to ask. You'll let me know if there's anything I can do for you in return, won't you?'

'I don't understand,' said Diana. 'Who is this man?'

'A perfectly nice Scottish M.P. lonely in London because his family stay in Scotland most of the time. Quite good-looking though a bit fat, thoroughly kind and well-meaning. You'll like him.'

'And what am I meant to do for him?'

'Only allow him to take you out to dinner if he rings you up.'

'Nothing more?'

'Nothing that you don't want to do.'

'But why?'

'He told me he was lonely and I thought it would be a nice thing to do. Also I'm going to be very busy the next couple of months with this new bill I've got to try and see through, and I don't want you to be lonely either. But don't do it if you don't want to.'

'I'll see,' said Diana.

'This is something for you because I've never really given you a present. I want you to get yourself some clothes you really want and you'll choose them much better yourself.'

'Oh, no, I – please –' Her eyes filled with tears. 'I'm not –'

He put his arms round her. 'Listen, I want you to have it because of the happiness you've given me and because I'm very fond of you. But if you don't want it throw it away.'

He kissed her as she stood unresisting in his embrace.

Then she said, 'Please go,' and he left.

She did not come into the office for a few days and when he asked one of the other girls about her they said she had sent in her notice, but his friend Macdonald told him that she was well and happy and had found a job in an advertising agency. He noticed from his next month's bank statement that his cheque had been cashed. It was for £200.

'A most awkward thing,' said Conrad. 'Either awkward or ridiculous, I'm not quite sure which. Perhaps both.'

'Yes?' said Orlando, thinking that it was probably the first time in his life that he had seen Conrad embarrassed.

'You know how these things get around, the odd little sources of information one has. A certain editor of a certain scandalous news sheet who is running a perpetual and pointless little campaign against a figment of his own imagination called the Cliveden Set, thinks he has some information about you which will make things awkward for you and help to denigrate the group to which you belong – something about a secretary, a baseless piece of nonsense no doubt.' Conrad looked with attention at his own hands, the fingers of which were touching as in prayer.

'Quite baseless,' said Orlando.

'I knew it would be of course,' said Conrad, still looking at his hands. 'But I understand they're planning to use it next week.'

'Your particular source of information,' said Orlando, 'might perhaps be told that before they do such a thing they ought to make quite sure that they are not muddling me up with Macdonald, Willie Macdonald who sits for Perth.'

'Ah,' said Conrad.

'They're a bit haphazard in their methods, these muck-rakers,' said Orlando.

'Yes,' said Conrad.

The next issue of the *Week* carried no mention of Orlando's name.

'Shanks Pendleton says there's going to be a war,' said Judith.

'Shanks Pendleton knows nothing about it,' said Orlando.

'He says that after Austria Hitler will move into Czechoslovakia.'

'Czechoslovakia has three million Germans within her borders. Her position doesn't seem very strong in any sense. She's also drawing closer all the time to Russia, which is not in our interest. What we should try to do is to suggest a practical and peaceful solution before Hitler imposes one by force.'

'Shanks thinks the Germans will be making gas attacks on London from the air by the end of the year.'

'You don't think you are seeing too much of Shanks Pendleton?'

'Everyone sees too much of Shanks Pendleton. I find him quite cosy though.'

'He's not advising you about doing up the dining-room I hope?'

'He's suggested one or two things. I think he has very good taste.'

'I don't see why we have to do up the dining-room again. It's going to be very expensive.'

'It's so boring as it is.'

'I suppose it's all right if it amuses you.'

'You have quite a little way of taking the fun out of things, haven't you?'

'And Shanks Pendleton puts it back again?'

'No. I wish he did. Listen, if we're really going to agree to Paul's having a year at the Sorbonne at least he can find us a French governess for Agatha, don't you agree?'

'I don't know that I do. I can teach Agatha French. I think she could perfectly well have a few years at the village school. It worked excellently with Henry. Then we can get a governess to bring her up to the standard for boarding school. By that time we may be a bit better off. Logan Furniture shares are still right down.'

'Yes but all your other things are doing all right.'

'Logan Furniture still constitutes a large part of Logan Holdings. If it doesn't pick up we may have to liquidate it. That obviously means a bad year or two for the holding company.'

'Liquidate it? But I thought you'd taken stern measures and it was all going to be all right.'

'We seem to have miscalculated somewhere. The orders just aren't coming in. There seems to have been a falling off of confidence all round. Giles Logan made a rather silly speech at the shareholders' meeting.'

'We're hardly broke though. I don't see why Agatha should have to go to the village school and pick up a lower-class accent. I suppose we can't afford to send Stephen to Cambridge either?'

'Of course we can. Leonard left quite enough to provide for his sons' education.'

'You know perfectly well you'll never teach her French. You aren't at home enough. You won't have time.'

'Let's leave it a bit then, and wait and see.'

'Which means you're determined to have it your own way.'

'I should like to turn the Timberwork mill back into a sawmill and to pull down all except the original building,' said Conrad. 'It's a mess down there at the moment. Have you seen it lately?'

Orlando shook his head.

'The glass is all broken,' said Conrad. 'Boys throwing stones I suppose. And someone's stolen the lead off the roof of the design office. No one noticed until it was too late to do anything about it. Pirbright thinks he knows the culprit but doubts if he'll be able to prove anything now. It's sad to see it so desolate down there. It would be better to make what use of it we can and pull down what we don't need. The only thing is that I don't know when we'll be able to do it because the demolition work won't be cheap. There's nothing much in there that one can sell – a door or two maybe.'

'Perhaps you need only do enough to tidy it up and make it safe,' said Orlando. 'And let the rest fall down.'

'It's not easy to make it safe,' said Conrad. 'There are so many dangerous places for children to play, what with the disused mines and the quarries; I'm surprised there aren't more accidents. Tell me, now that we have a moment to talk, how do you feel about the present situation? I hardly seem to have seen you this last week or two.'

'Logan Furniture you mean? I'm afraid it's a question of cutting our losses. We shall be all right. The best thing we ever did was bringing Hardman Bowles into Logan Holdings.'

'I meant the international situation.'

'I see, I'm sorry. Oh, I'm behind the P.M., that's all. He seems to be being quite businesslike about it.'

'You're not worried?'

'Of course I'm worried. I'm not a complete fool. It's a worrying situation.'

'I mean, you're not worried about our policy?'

'You mean that you are. What do you think we ought to do?'

'I don't think we're on the right lines any more. I've been worried for some time.'

'I know. But what's the alternative?'

'A stronger line.'

'And the risk of war?'

'And the risk of war.'

'This is rather a change of face, for you.'

'I know. But it came to me rather strongly in the night last night that if we don't take a firmer stand over the dismemberment of Czechoslovakia I ought not to go on. It came to me forcibly that there are things which have to be fought and that appeasement is not always misunderstood when it is called weakness. There can be a kind of moral weakness which is hard to differentiate from a helpful spirit of compromise and which we are in danger of falling into.'

'But in terms of hard politics this means running the risk of a war for which we are not prepared, militarily or in the air.'

'It is hard to tell, even with the statistics one is given by the experts, how prepared or unprepared we arc. Certainly two or three years ago we were unprepared and certainly the fault lies in our not having recognized the danger much earlier, prepared the public for it and rearmed. Whether we should ever have taken public opinion with us is another matter. Baldwin thought he couldn't do it. Neither you nor I were in a position to try.'

'So that what we have to work with now is a situation we did not make. That being so we have every reason to try to reach a reasonable solution without war.'

'It has now become clear that no reasonable solution can be reached with the Nazis by the methods we have been using. We may be guilty of a tremendous failure of understanding.'

'I think you've come to this conclusion rather late in the day. What good will it do now? What possible useful purpose can be served by your resigning at this stage?'

'Not much, except to reveal for what it is worth the conclusion I've come to. It's just a personal thing. It would be wrong to go on in an administration with whose policy I no longer agree.'

'So you will sacrifice your political career?'

'It will be no great sacrifice.'

'It would be for me. You can afford to be detached. You have so much else. You have your seat in the House of Lords whatever happens, you have Mount Sorrel, your charitable works, and all the rest of it. I have staked much more on political life. Business is going bad on me, and besides I have had enough of it, I have done it all, I don't want to be an American-style tycoon. I have channelled everything into my political ambitions and I can't afford to throw them over. It is nearly always a mistake to resign on a so-called matter of principle. I want everything there is to be had out of politics and I can't afford to treat the thing lightly. I've got to be there. All the time.'

'You didn't use to be so single-minded.'

'You didn't use to be so half-hearted.'

'So we shall diverge. I shall be very sorry.'

'Of course, so shall I.'

'I wish I could feel we understood each other better. I wish I could make you see how it seems to me that we have become shortsighted, small-minded, unworthy of our past.'

'I know the arguments. But I think you are indulging yourself. You are giving in to the refinements of your conscience instead of dealing with realities. But we shall win. After Czechoslovakia Hitler will be satisfied, we shall get on to terms with him. In a few years' time Germany won't be our main problem any more. It will be Russia. But you will have shrugged off your responsibilities by then and retreated into your patrician solitude, away from the sordid market-place.'

'I am sorriest about our divergence. I could never have foreseen it. I hope it won't affect our personal relations. It certainly won't on my side.'

'Nor on mine, of course,' said Orlando, stiffly.

'Madame Souris a une maison,' said Agatha. 'May I colour in the pictures?'

'Later. Go on reading.'

'Madame Souris ... Mummy, I can speak French.'

'How lovely my darling. I've refused Conrad's invitation for tomorrow, Orlando. I thought it would be better.'

'But you had already accepted.'

'I retracted,' said Judith. 'With all this publicity I really think we'd better not go there for the time being.'

'Perhaps you're right.'

'Besides I am so cross with him. It's so like him to take such a high moral tone when I bet he's only done it with an eye to his own advantage like anyone else.'

'It won't be to his own advantage. Not at this particular stage. It's merely a pointless and irrelevant gesture.'

'That's what I told him. At least I told him he was a bloody fool which comes to the same thing. Hurry up with that won't you because you know we've got all these people coming to dinner. Good night my little darling. Bonne nuit. Dors bien.'

Crowded on his accustomed bench with slightly sweating hands, seriously listening to the harsh voice droning on with what seems to be a story of failure, and men with faces which reveal their uneasy stomachs. Bombs on London, they are thinking, ruin, death, German supremacy in the air, Guernica, destruction, disaster, finish, oh yes we must, no never I'll go to America, I'll thunder against the enemy, I'll toss hand grenades and win glory, I want to go home, this is tension, crowded benches, a historic occasion, we are assisting at an historic occasion, oh love oh death, I want a cup of tea some bicarbonate of soda. And the piece of paper passed down from Lord Halifax in the peers gallery and Hoare passes it to Orlando who passes it to Sir John Simon who passes it to Chamberlain and there is to be a conference, Hitler has agreed, and there is shouting and stamping and Orlando rises with the others to his feet thinking I knew they'd see sense, I never doubted it, what a triumph this is going to be for our side, and the man remaining seated next to him says, 'Bad show, oh bad show,' and Orlando thinks, fool.

'Why do you make a face when I say I'm going to ride with Henry? Why, Mummy?'

'Isn't there anything else you like doing? Why do you have to ride with Henry so often?'

'You never used to mind. It's because you've quarrelled with Uncle Conrad isn't it? Why should that make any difference to Henry and me, why, Mummy?'

'Don't be so aggressive, Agatha. Uncle Conrad has been foolish and obstinate in a way you can't possibly understand, and he's not helping Daddy in his career.'

'Henry thinks Uncle Conrad is quite right. He says there must be a war because Hitler is wicked.'

'Henry is a silly little boy who doesn't know anything about it.'

'Whatever Henry says or does he is my friend for ever and ever.'

'All right, Agatha. Let's not discuss it any more.'

'No, let's not.'

'But if you get cheeky and rude I shall have to get a holiday governess. Now run along because I've got a bad headache and the doctor is coming.'

Judith seemed to be always a little ill; nerves, the doctor said, a tonic, over-tired, he said, more rest, a little holiday; and this was the busiest year of Orlando's life.

He was driven from meeting to meeting in the black Bentley; he spoke in the provinces, he addressed the House; he introduced a new Bill, opened a new power station, became the youngest member of the Cabinet; he argued with Giles Logan about the policies of Logan Holdings, in which he was still a major shareholder; he supported his Prime Minister and opposed his brother-in-law; he expected to be listened to when he expressed his views, and was, he expected to be spoken of as a future Prime Minister, and was; he telephoned, received messages, dictated to secretaries, looked in his desk diary for the list of his day's engagements; he lunched, he dined, found time for a little shooting, took a briefcase full of papers to work on when he stayed away with Judith for the weekend; he smoked cigars, avoided bridge, read Agatha Christie or P. G. Wodehouse before going to sleep at night; was bored by Paul and Stephen, wished he had more time to spend with Agatha, was amiable to Imogen; he would have liked Judith to settle down and be less irritable, meant to take her for a holiday some time to get her back to being her old self; admiration he took for granted wherever he went but had no time for other women at the moment and wished Judith would believe him; and the meetings multiplied and the speeches repeated themselves and he ran through his papers in the back of the Bentley and thought, war is unthinkable, it makes no sense.

Nanny had retired arthritically, critically, into a cottage in the village. Jen, having assumed full powers, took the children to Bem-bridge for their summer holidays.

Orlando and Judith went to join them for a few days in the middle of August. The news of the Russo-German pact reached them while they were there, and Orlando went back to London for an emergency meeting of Parliament. Before he left they discussed whether to cut short the holiday and take the children home.

'If there's war we may not be allowed to cross the Solent,' said Judith. 'Billy Vandervell says it will be mined.'

'Stay here,' said Orlando. 'I will telephone you if you need to come home.'

'Will there be war, do you think?'

'I'm afraid so.'

'It means the end of everything, doesn't it?' said Judith.

'I'm afraid so,' said Orlando again.

'The end of civilization as we've known it,' said Judith in a curiously detached tone of voice.

He looked at her. There was a slight flush on her cheeks. She sniffed, perhaps defiantly. He realized that he had no idea what she was thinking.

'I'd better go,' he said. 'I'll let you know what's happening as soon as I can.'

There was no wireless in their rented house and so Judith took the boys, Jen and the two little girls into the house next door to listen to the Prime Minister's broadcast. It was a road of semidetached Victorian houses, most of which were either let in the summer or turned into boarding houses. The house next door belonged to a retired grocer who had the palsy and was more or less bed-ridden. His wife had done the cooking for Judith and her family every summer for years, by tradition greeting them with fish and chips on the first evening of their arrival. In the garden behind her house there was an old apple tree which bore a great quantity of little sweet Beauty of Bath apples, which the children would steal, squeezing through the privet hedge from the next-door garden. Inside, her house smelt of the wax polish with which she cleaned the variegated linoleum of the hall floor. Each side of the front door was a narrow strip of stained glass. Outside the front door hung a striped canvas curtain. It was tied back so that they could walk in, and up the stairs into the bedroom, where Mr Grainger lay beneath a clean white lace bedspread, his wireless beside him. Judith sat on the edge of an armchair, Mrs Grainger on the end of the bed. Paul and Stephen stood, awkwardly large, behind Judith's chair, and Jen and the two small children sat on the floor.

It was eleven o'clock. Agatha saw Jen assuming the expression she wore in Church, and tried to look the same.

Judith jumped up saying, 'It's the end of everything.'

Mr Grainger tried to speak of his son, but his large trembling hands plucking at the white bedspread seemed to engage all his attention and he became silent.

Judith led the way out of the room. For some reason which no one knew, she was smiling triumphantly.

He had known for the last few months that war could probably no longer be avoided; he had known that he himself had miscalculated and misunderstood; and his chief feeling had been one of almost uncontrollable irritation, because however one looked at it war was obviously a disaster and because human beings were supposed to be reasonable creatures and yet had failed to avoid the disaster. He felt himself

to be quite extraordinarily out of sympathy not only with
events but with most of the people with whom he came into
contact in the oddly inactive months which followed the
outbreak of war. He got up in the morning, dressed, had
breakfast, went to the House of Commons; he avoided his
closest colleagues, spoke only once, not very convincingly,
in support of the Government's policy, went home to Wood
Hill; he felt a curious lack of communication with Judith; he
went back to a blacked out London where nothing seemed
to be happening; and all the time he felt this irritation, a kind
of disgust. We shall all be bombed to death, he thought, for
no good reason, it is all an unutterable folly.

Conrad came to see him one weekend at Wood Hill
about the allocation of evacuees in the village. He had
arranged for a boys' boarding school from the East Coast
to take over Mount Sorrel itself and he and Henry were
moving into Orlando's old flat in the stables. They had
knocked through the wall into what used to be the chauffeur's flat and had incorporated that into their own, the
chauffeur having gone to join the Army; and the butler and
his wife were looking after them from their own cottage in
the stable yard. Conrad was full of enthusiasm for the new
arrangement. 'Such charming rooms. It's a little like being
back in an Oxford college. Your life must have been very
pleasant there.'

'I suppose it was,' said Orlando.

'Now, about the evacuees,' said Conrad. He had a new
almost hearty tone of voice which he used for talking
to Orlando, as if to say, 'Come on now, let's be friends.'
It embarrassed Orlando and made him feel stiff and
unresponsive.

'They seem to have caused a bit of an upheaval, don't
they?' said Conrad.

'They're verminous apparently. And their mothers spend all their time in the pub.'

'I'm wondering if there isn't anything we can do to relieve the situation.'

'I believe they're already beginning to go back to London,' said Orlando indifferently.

He turned away from Conrad and looked towards the French window. Immediately a figure was framed in it. A small man with long untidy hair stood outside wearing a dirty mackintosh and carrying a large cardboard box tied up with a piece of rope.

His appearance was so unexpected that Orlando stared at him in silence. The man stared back, then rather hesitantly lifted his hand and knocked.

'Who on earth is that?' said Conrad.

'I've no idea,' said Orlando, opening the window. But as soon as the man outside began to speak Orlando said in astonishment, 'Sid? Sid. I had no idea. I hardly recognized you for a moment. It was so unexpected. Come in. How are you?' He was suddenly extraordinarily glad to see him. 'How wonderful to see you. Come in. This is Lord Field. This is Sid who lived with us on the island. Here, take off your coat. What's been happening to you? I always meant to come and see you. How nice to see you, Sid. Sit down. Have a drink.' It seemed to him suddenly that for all these last few months – or perhaps even for years – it was Sid whom he had been missing, Sid who alone could restore his lost sense of reality.

'Sid,' he said again. 'How wonderful to see you.'

Sid sat down. He showed no signs of surprise at the circumstances or surroundings in which he had found Orlando, nor indeed of pleasure at having so found him. The remembered familiarity of this attitude and of the way

in which he bent down to ease his heels out of his shoes
made Orlando laugh with pleasure.

'Where have you come from, Sid?' he asked.

'I was on this old boat,' said Sid. 'I came from Le Havre
via Jersey, it was the only boat I could get, and there it was
in the papers, in Jersey, we stopped half a day there and I
read your name in the paper, making a speech in Parliament.
I thought there wasn't likely to be another Orlando King so
I phoned up Parliament when we got to Southampton and
they told me your address.'

'You mean you've only just arrived in England?'

'Yesterday. Slept on the road. Had to get out of France.
Didn't want to find myself manning the Maginot Line. I'm
on my way back to Australia.'

His accent was a mixture of French and Australian, so
that he said 'Australia' with a French 'r' and an Australian
'a'. It was not a particularly attractive mixture.

Conrad began to question him politely about his journey
and Orlando went to call Judith.

'It's Sid. You remember, I've told you about him. He's
just arrived. Of course he must stay, mustn't he? This is my
wife Judith. This is Sid.'

'Cripes,' said Sid.

[*]

'A man called Leonard Gardner.'

It was of course the explanation of everything.

As if he had said, 'What has gone wrong, Sid?'

And after that nothing was ever the same again. Even the
past was a different story.

He thought, holding his hands over his eyes, in the middle
of my life, in the middle of my journey, as it happened to

Dante, does it happen to everybody then, some kind of revelation or else the death of the soul?

They sat round the fire after lunch. Orlando had persuaded Conrad to stay because he could see that Judith had taken an instant dislike to Sid.

It was the first time Conrad had eaten at Wood Hill since his resignation from the Government. Judith was not pleased, even now, that Orlando had asked him. He nevertheless helped the situation, as Orlando had hoped that he would, by asking Sid with evident interest about the present situation in France, and about the Morbihan, and a little about King. Orlando as yet felt unwilling to talk about King and was glad of Conrad's more general conversation. Sid answered questions briefly and asked none. He ate solidly, accepting second helpings of everything, and after lunch, in front of the fire, with a glass of brandy beside him, he slipped his feet out of his shoes altogether, and said to Orlando, 'Nice place you've got here.'

'I suppose,' said Judith, looking at his socks, which smelt rather, 'you know who Orlando's parents were.'

'He never told you, did he?' said Sid to Orlando. 'He was going to, but then he died. He gave you a letter of introduction to your father, but he couldn't bring himself to tell you who he was. He was going to tell you when you came back.'

'A letter of introduction?'

'Yes. It was one of those letters he gave you when you first came to England, you remember. I don't know if you followed it up. It was to a man called Leonard Gardner.'

He looked round. All three of them were staring at him blankly.

He said rather hesitantly, 'I never met him myself.'

'He gave me a letter...?' said Orlando.

'He gave you several letters and one was to this Leonard Gardner who was your father. Or so King told me.'

'It's impossible,' said Orlando.

'It's what he told me. That's all I know. Do you know him then?'

'Yes, I – that is, I did know him.' Orlando put his head in his hands, thinking of the look on Leonard's face just before he died. 'He was – well, I don't know – he was Judith's first husband for one thing.'

No one spoke.

Then Sid whistled.

'Jesus,' he said. 'Jesus. You mean you've gone and married your own mother?'

Judith jumped to her feet, knocking over a small table which was beside her chair. An ash tray broke. She stared at Sid.

'I suppose you really think,' she said in a voice which creaked with her scorn, 'that I look old enough to be Orlando's mother?'

Sid looked up at her hopelessly.

'Could be,' he said.

'Get him out,' said Judith.

She turned to Orlando.

'How dare you bring him here?' she said. 'He's mad, don't you see? How dare you?' Her upper lip trembled so violently that she put her hand up to it. 'Get him out,' she said with her hand across her mouth. 'Get him out of here. He stinks. Do you hear me? Why should I sit in a room and listen to a man with stinking feet telling malicious lies? We must get the police and have him taken away. He shouldn't be allowed to go about saying that sort of thing.'

'Judith please ...'

'Shut up.' Suddenly she turned on Conrad. 'You put him up to it, didn't you? You've been trying to blacken Orlando's name, haven't you? I know. You've been trying to ruin him so that I shall suffer. I know you have, you haven't fooled me. I know. You think I'm immoral, don't you? You're trying to ruin me because I'm an adulteress. I know the way your mind works. You can't fool me.'

'Judith, please, come upstairs now. You must take one of those pills the doctor gave you. It's a shock for all of us.' Orlando began to lead her from the room.

'You've got to get him out of here,' she said. 'I'm not going until you've asked him to leave. I know perfectly well Conrad's behind this. He's been against me ever since the first time I was unfaithful to Leonard.'

'Yes, all right, come upstairs now, please come upstairs.'

Conrad began to telephone for the doctor.

'Jesus,' said Sid again.

'Please eat something. Just a spoonful. Look, it's good. I'll eat some first.'

'It is poisoned.'

'But I've just eaten some. Look. With the same spoon.'

'You will put the stuff in afterwards.'

'But you can watch me. One spoonful please. You'll get so thin.'

'It's got something in it.'

'Let Nurse give it to you then. I'll go out of the room altogether.'

'She is in Conrad's pay.'

'Conrad wants you to get better.'

'He is trying to kill me.'

'Just one spoonful, please.'

'Is she in the house?'

'Who? The nurse? Of course, she's just here.'

'I know she's in the house. I went downstairs and her gloves were in the hall. You all think you can fool me but you can't, I know perfectly well what you're up to.'

'Whose gloves, Judith? I don't understand you.'

'Hers. The woman's. I know she is in the house.'

'What woman?'

'Your woman. I know she's here. I don't know whether it's Angela Payne or someone else but I know perfectly well she's here. You think I don't know anything, don't you? Perhaps it's the other woman, the secretary. Oh yes, I know all about her. Robin Barwick told me. It's common knowledge.'

'Judith, please eat just one spoonful of soup.'

'You want me to die, don't you?'

'I want you to get better. Conrad wants you to get better too.'

'You are working together. I know. Conrad is mad like my father. He thinks women are wicked. He wants to kill me because he thinks I am evil. And you are helping him because you want to get me out of the way so that you can marry your mistress. I know all this quite well. I have told the police. They'll get you. You'll be hanged. You know that? Hanged.'

'One spoonful. Please.'

'Why don't the police do anything? I asked for protection. I asked for police protection. I went to see Pirbright. Why hasn't he done what I told him? I suppose he's afraid of Conrad. That's why I wrote to the Chief Constable.'

'Darling, the doctor is here.'

'Would you tell him I don't need to see him today? I'm perfectly well. Besides he's a fool. He doesn't know what he's talking about. Please ask him to leave.'

'Now then, Lady Judith, let's see how things are going today, shall we? Eating a little something? Good, good. I've brought my friend Mr Whitehead with me. He's come all the way from London. Steady now, steady. Oh dear, that was a waste of good soup, wasn't it? Don't bother about that, Nurse. Just hold the arm there, would you? That's the way. Just a little injection to make you feel nice and comfortable and then we'll see what Mr Whitehead has to suggest, shall we?'

As she turned off the main road she began to run again, past the cottage, where a dog barked, rattling its chain, and on towards the viaduct under the beech trees whose branches met above the road so that it was dark and green and damp as she ran. I am Judith, running. I am Judith. But a train was rumbling towards the viaduct. She ran faster than ever. Running is something I can do. I am fleet. I am fleet of foot. She reached the viaduct as the train began to cross it, and leant against the wall, the sound of the train above her. They can't see me, they are in the train looking out of the windows but I have escaped. They can't stop me, I am Judith, they will be sorry then.

When the train had rattled away into silence, she walked away from the viaduct towards the old Timberwork mill. The main building stood as solid as ever, though most of the glass in its windows was broken. Unwilling to cross the open space in front of it, she walked round to the back, keeping close to the bushes, and then approached the half-fallen design office across the rubble of the ruined canteen and a few piles of timber which had been left in the yard. Conrad's plan for making better use of the mill had not yet been implemented; he had neither the men nor the timber to need another sawmill on the estate. Half of the buildings had been pulled down and half allowed to fall down. As she walked towards what used to be Graham Harper's office she thought she heard a sound, and stood still, listening. Of course they are watching for me, they are in there watching, they have been told. Graham will telephone Orlando, he was always trying to turn Orlando against me. I can't move. Listen. They aren't looking out of the window, I should be able to see them. A noise again, someone must be there. Of course, he's on the floor, I know, with one of the girls, Graham's in there, I can hear him, told to watch me and writhing on the floor with the girl from the accounts, I remember her, if I go in I shall see them moving there on the floor among the sawdust like animals, that's what it is, he's in there, filthy oh God how filthy.

With a sudden clutter of small stones falling she scrambled across a pile of rubble and ran for the woods; and along the muddy track deep into the damp surrounding trees, it being autumn and the time of old man's beard and cobwebs outlined with raindrops, until the sound of the stream drowned the imagined footsteps that followed her; and by the stream paused, leaning on a thin tall elm tree and feeling in her pocket for the razor blade she had brought with her. I could never cut my throat oh no some people would but imagine what it would look like, just imagine. Faces leaning over and my face by the water oh how beautiful they say my long white neck how beautiful my eyes closed as if in sleep how beautiful how sad and what a dagger thrust to the heart to make them sorry, oh no I'll have no blood at all near my face. And this hand now out of my pocket and straight like that to dash across my wrist, how deep and hurting not at all, and change hands and down hard across the other wrist oh I am brave I have always been brave Lady Judith is very brave, sailing in high winds and laughing, Lady Judith is very brave. Not to look down at the blood but walk a little way away from the stream, along the path, it runs down my hands, warm, a warm flood in the palms of my hands, walk towards the road a little so that they see me sooner, are sorry sooner, so they are sorry sooner.

'People come to me all the time looking for redemption.'

Orlando wondered what it meant.

They took her to Wimbledon. He had said, 'Let it be the most expensive.'

The Belgian who lived in the cottage on the corner, encountering Judith in the early evening swaying with outstretched streaming arms towards him down the damp road under the beeches whose branches met, had applied tourniquets, wrapped her in blankets and forced her to drink hot tea. If he had not taken a course in First Aid run by the local Boys' Brigade at the time of Munich she would certainly have died. As it was, when she came out of hospital they took her to a house near Wimbledon Common, in a garden, with flowers in the rooms.

Orlando visited her every day during the week, bringing presents, and books to read, and letters from the children. At weekends he went to Wood Hill to be with the children. Judith spoke little and sat with resentful eyes in a chintz-covered armchair wearing familiar clothes which were too big for her now.

One day the superintending doctor asked to see Orlando and suggested that for the time being it might be better if he discontinued his visits.

'It's a very common thing in these cases,' he said, quite as if scrupulous cleanliness and thin-rimmed glasses could immunize against emotion. 'The nearest relative is often the one on whom the paranoic fantasies become fixed. We do notice a marked improvement on Saturdays and Sundays when you are not visiting and we feel that a period with no outside pressures at all might have a favourable result. Of course I shall keep in close touch with you and I hope you will feel free to telephone me at any time.'

'I haven't meant to exert pressure,' said Orlando.

'Of course not,' said the doctor. 'But you're bound to represent to her the life with which she felt unable to cope.'

'Yes,' said Orlando.

'There is an aspect of these cases,' the doctor said more hesitantly, 'which is rather hard to describe without being perhaps rather – that is to say, the close relatives sometimes feel a certain responsibility for what has happened, and the pressure which the patient feels from the visiting relative is a result of this. But people in this condition are ill, that's the point. It's nobody's fault, nobody should feel guilty. And when people are ill in this way they are not in a position to forgive either real or imagined injuries. They can't give forgiveness any more than they can give anything else, that's one of the symptoms of the disease.'

'You mean she has felt that I have been putting pressure on her to forgive me for …?'

'For nothing.' He had ascetic good looks, with his hygienic haircut. He is an intelligent man, thought Orlando with relief. He had not noticed this quality in their previous meetings because the doctor had then spoken only in the language of his profession, which was more or less incomprehensible to Orlando.

'For nothing,' said the doctor again, seriously. 'I don't believe in sin. I only believe in guilt, which I see all the time.

People come to me all the time looking for redemption, for absolution from their sins. I can't give it to them. At least, not in the way they want.'

'Perhaps if you believed in sin you would be able to absolve them,' said Orlando, interested.

'Then I should be in another business,' said the doctor.

'You must write to me,' said Orlando. 'And tell me when a visit from me would be of positive benefit to my wife rather than something to do with my own guilt.'

The doctor looked momentarily surprised. Then he smiled.

'All right,' he said.

'And in the meantime... ' said Orlando, standing up.

'We will look after her,' said the doctor.

He walked in darkness across the rooftops acknowledging his guilt.

When he resigned from the Government and from his seat in Parliament he gave as his reason that he wanted to be on active service in the fighting forces. One or two people said, 'He's as shrewd as ever, getting out before he's kicked out,' or 'It's his wife. She's very ill,' or 'He won't be passed fit, with that limp.'

He was not passed fit, because on his left foot he had hammer toes, which made him walk with a slight limp. He had not, on the other hand, felt fit for political life either. In the end he volunteered to be an ARP warden and was accepted for training in the Kensington area.

He went home to Wood Hill at weekends. Sometimes he rang up the nursing home and asked how Judith was progressing; they did not suggest that he should start visiting again. When he was on duty he liked to walk about rather than sit in the ARP post drinking tea. He wandered about the blacked-out streets, up fire escapes, over rooftops, in his tin hat and overalls, and the others in his group accepted him as the anti-social one, without resentment. 'His wife is very ill,' someone knew.

I have killed my father, he thought, and driven my wife mad. I have helped to lead my country to its destruction. Yet I never meant any harm. Sometimes self-pity would seize him at the injustice of it, and he would lean on some area railing in Queens Gate or Princes Gardens and let tears slide in the darkness down his cheeks; and sometimes then anger against fate would drive out the self-pity and he would suddenly run in a kind of fury along the pavements, bumping into returning diners-out who looked after him in surprise and called out, 'Is there a raid?'

But there was never a raid. The searchlights scanned the soft dark sky and found it empty, night after night. He walked the streets and thought, why don't they come, why can't they finish the thing?

Self-pity or anger were rare states of mind. More common was mere dull pain; also there were times when his nightly dreams were too clear to be evaded in his waking hours. Judith danced, dressed in green, King walked through the empty house, men in tail coats waited for Judith like the chorus in a musical comedy and she came towards them singing with the blood gushing from her wrists, King built his tower with the wind blowing through his hair and his face turned away from Orlando, the same wind blew through Wood Hill, upsetting Judith's vase of pampas grass, blowing open the door of Agatha's bedroom where she lay on the bare floor; and King turned, and threw up his hands, and died. And Orlando walked the streets and thought, I am very unhappy. Sometimes his unhappiness seemed to him so extraordinary that he could only stare at it, as if it were some rare liquid stirring slowly in a glass jar.

Then he would sit on a rooftop, or the steps of a fire-escape, and stare, until he remembered that it was time to report back to the post.

He saw Conrad at weekends, and occasionally in London he would have lunch or dinner with a friend or former colleague, but for the most part these were months with little conversation: there seemed to be nothing to say.

At last the bombs came. At first they were not very near. There were nights when the sky over the East End was copper-coloured, nights when the white flares falling towards the river could be seen from the highest roof in his area, when the silent searchlights wheeled faster across the sky and the sound of aeroplanes grew nearer after the suburban guns had opened fire. One early evening there was an incident only a street or two away. A few incendiaries fell into the street where he was walking. A passer-by helped him to douse them in sand saying, 'Looks as if it's our turn tonight.' But it wasn't, not until the next night.

When it became clear that big raids were particularly likely on Saturdays and Sundays, Orlando took to spending most of his weekends in London rather than going down to Wood Hill. He made a will leaving everything to Conrad, including the guardianship of his children, and left it in his desk at Wood Hill.

After a time he began to notice a kind of elation in himself. This was the first period of intensive bombing and Orlando, feeling that London was in a state of siege, felt also that it would never surrender.

He felt the stirrings of an unfamiliar emotion, which he eventually recognized with some embarrassment as patriotism. He had not felt it when France, the country of his youth, had fallen, he had not felt it when Churchill had spoken on the wireless about the air battles over the South

of England, but when in an unfamiliar light he saw German
bombers coming in low over London he had to recognize
uneasily in himself the awakening of love for his country. Britain Can Take It, said the posters. In his present
state of mind it was as if, in love, he saw the name of his
beloved scratched on the walls as if he had woken up one
morning to find himself seriously in love with Veronica
Lake, or Vera Lynn. Fastidiousness obliged him to keep
the depth of his emotion secret. One effect of it, however,
was to make the evenings when nothing happened in his
sector less boring because his feeling of common purpose
had made him abandon his reserve with the other people
working in his sector. He spent some time arguing with the
intellectual, more time gossiping with the actress: she was
a jolly creature of fifty-five with a deep voice and close-
cropped hair who had been dressed up as a man in many
West End farces. She had joined the ARP for something to
do after she had evacuated her three Yorkshire terriers to
the country. They were called Pip, Squeak and Wilfred and
she had sent them to live with her sister on Box Hill. She
had not gone herself because her sister got on her nerves
and besides she was always hoping for a part. 'Call me
Edie,' she said quite soon to Orlando, because her name
was Edith Terry. 'I pretend to be a relation of Ellen's but
it's never done me any good.'

Several times they were called out to help in the sector
next to theirs which seemed busier than their own. Orlando
became used to seeing gaps where houses had been and
rescue workers digging for survivors in piles of rubble. The
smell of smoke and plaster and leaking gas became disagreeably familiar.

One night there was an incident in their own sector when
a parachute mine fell on a hotel. There were a good many

casualties and after the fire-engines and ambulances had left the rescue workers were still digging. Orlando, tired, was on his way back to the post when he stopped to watch a group of them. There was an odd-looking figure sitting beside the heap of rubble where the men were working. Orlando wondered if she was all right and went closer. She was a woman of sixty-five or so wearing a man's camel-hair dressing-gown and a flowered hat. 'It's all right,' she was saying. 'That's our own guns going now. Don't worry.'

He thought she must be suffering from shock, but as he approached he heard a sound from beneath the rubble. A faint ladylike voice said, 'I do hate it so.'

'They'll have you out in no time now. Don't worry. Whoops!' There was a thump as a bomb fell a few streets away. 'It's all right, Mrs Smalley, love. It's only the guns in Hyde Park.' The flowered hat was slightly lopsided. 'That's Mrs Smalley down there, one of my ladies,' she said to Orlando.

He looked down into the hole and saw that the men were beginning to sink a shaft into the rubble. It looked as though they had some way to go. He joined the line of rescue men who were passing out baskets of rubble to be emptied.

'It's my legs,' came Mrs Smalley's weak voice. 'I know they're broken.'

'All right, Mrs Smalley, love. My friend in Battersea was just the same and she's right as rain now.'

One of the men jerked a thumb in her direction, look-ing at Orlando and grinning, but she was not in the way and might be affording some consolation, so no one asked her to move. The raiders seemed to have retreated now so Orlando went on passing the heavy baskets along the line. It was not strictly speaking part of his job to help the rescue workers, but he thought that probably his own work was over for the night. His back began to ache and he realized that his feet were very wet.

Suddenly there was a tremendous explosion quite close to them followed almost immediately by the roar of flames and the crackle of falling masonry.

Orlando was thrown to the ground. When he stood up he saw that some little way away the whole street seemed to be on fire. Leaving the rescue men to their work he ran towards it. 'All right, Mrs Smalley, love,' quavered the voice behind him.

'Delayed action bomb,' he said aloud. 'Christ, look at that.'

The flames were huge. As he looked the whole front of a house leant forward, crumbled and collapsed.

A man ran out of one of the nearer houses into which the fire was spreading fast. He was carrying a girl over his shoulder, her head hanging down, either hurt or overcome by the fumes.

'Two more in there,' he shouted as he passed. 'Upstairs.'

Orlando put his arm over his face and ran into the house. The heat and smell were intense, but the staircase seemed to be still standing. He made his way towards it. The noise of the flames themselves was so loud that he did not hear the roof falling in. It fell on his head with a force which seemed tremendous but left him still standing, half submerged in plaster.

It was difficult to breathe. Retching and spitting out plaster he began to dig furiously with his gloved hands. His face felt as if it had been burnt. Actually it had been cut by splinters of glass. As he dug he felt his eyes suffusing with tears or blood: it was more and more difficult to see. He dragged himself upwards on his elbows until he could stand. Then he ran, gasping and coughing, and in the doorway fell into the arms of a fireman.

They had made the sign of the Cross on his forehead. He was grateful, and thought some Kensington Vicar was welcome to think his soul was saved, but it did not frighten him. Knowing what he suddenly did know about flesh and blood was not frightening although it was deeply serious.

It was important that he should keep alert and listen carefully for instructions: 'drink this', 'don't touch the bandage', 'swallow this', 'a little prick now, and then you will go to sleep', 'try not to move your head', 'does this hurt? And this?', 'your bell is in your hand, press it if the pain gets worse'.

At first he was bad at recognizing pain. It was something of which he had little experience. He would ask to have a blanket taken off his bed. 'It's so hot in here.' He was sinking into a bath so hot that heat could have no further extreme and yet new waves of heat lapped him again and again until he was pouring with sweat. It was only when he remembered the phrase 'sweating with pain', that he rang the bell when the heat began and said 'Pain' and they gave him an injection and he fell into a kind of swoon.

He could not see them because he had a bandage across his eyes but their authority and understanding seemed absolute. To explain the seeming mystery of their concern he tried to remind himself that it was their job, that they were paid for it. They are the members of the tribe whose allotted task is to look after the sick, he told himself.

'Aren't you tired?' he asked the Sister.

'I wouldn't say no to a fortnight on the Riviera. But we survive, don't we, Nurse? There we are. Nurse will just do your pillows and then you've got a visitor.'

It was Edie Terry, a little embarrassed. She told him the gossip from the post.

'Did they get Mrs Smalley out?' he asked.

She said she would find out.

He was touched that she had come but very tired when she left.

On the fourth day the pain seemed less.

'Bit better tonight, aren't you?' said the young nurse who took his temperature.

'Why did they put a cross on my forehead?' he asked.

'A cross on your forehead? Whatever do you mean?'

'I think it was before they brought me here. I'm not sure, but I remember lying somewhere hard and feeling someone making a mark on my forehead. There was a smell of plaster still, I think it was near where it happened.'

'It was probably before the doctor came. Sometimes the mobile unit writes an M on the forehead of the cases who need morphia so the doctor can give it to them as soon as he comes.'

'What do they write it with?'

'Blue chalk I think. There we are. Night Sister will be along in a minute.'

I wish I knew the others, he thought, my brothers with M written on their foreheads.

That night he slept for several hours without being woken by pain. In the morning he thought he noticed a different tone in the voices which spoke to him. The doctor only said, 'Yes, we'll carry on like this. You're doing fine,' but he stayed to talk about Somerset: he had a great-aunt who lived in Bath. The two young nurses who came to make his bed giggled as they told him how one of them had broken two thermometers that morning. Sister told him she had always loved music. She had a sharp voice and efficient hands, and suddenly she started talking about the proms. 'I've always loved music,' she said. The staff nurse who came to settle his pillows after lunch told him about her husband who was in the Navy. He wanted to be a teacher after the war. He had done half his training. He wanted to teach maladjusted children. For the first time Orlando wondered if he was going to die. He felt better, but then he did not understand illness. It would perhaps explain why today they all stopped to talk to him, almost with tenderness. It was only when the cheerful young auxiliary nurse who came on duty at tea time said to him, 'So you've made it,' that he understood. He was not going to die. This was the first day that they had known it. In their voices they had been accepting him back into the tribe.

That evening Conrad came to see him.

'We'll have you out in no time,' he said. 'Are you well enough looked after? What can I bring you?'

Orlando could only smile and say he was well looked after. Conrad said he would get in touch with the doctor and find out how soon he could be moved.

The next morning Orlando asked where the window was. When he had been told, he lay on his side facing it. He could move his legs. He could move his arms. 'Tomorrow you shall have a bath,' they said.

The fleshiness of flesh and the bloodiness of blood, he thought, I am leaving that knowledge behind, it is not particularly suitable. But Man had made an extraordinary structure, on that given data, it suddenly occurred to him, on the insubstantial basis of this flesh and blood, this physical life and death. Lying with his face towards the window it was almost as if he could see it outside, a building of fantastic beauty and artificiality, the home of such logical absurdities as beauty and truth, human goodness and human love, made by Man for his tribe, out of his need to mythologize, and with no spirit in it but the spirit of Man.

The extraordinary beauty, complexity and desirability of this structure outside the window overwhelmed him. He longed to walk into it, look round it, examine it minutely, even add to it. Really it is crazy, he thought. A crazy building, he thought, dazzled.

He slept, and woke with a kind of prayer in his head, which if he had formulated it might have been: Oh Man, who made God, let me be received into the arms of my tribe, let me be made one with my species.

There followed two or three days of intense happiness.

'Your friends the Warings have been interned under 18B,' said Conrad. 'I thought you'd be interested, so I found out what conditions were like and apparently they're quite comfortable. They've been moved so as to be together and they've got a couple of rooms in Holloway. They can even have people to lunch, I believe.'

'I must go and see them,' said Orlando. 'Poor things. What will they find to talk about? To each other I mean.'

He was sitting up in bed and the bandage had been taken away from his eyes. His head and face were still scarred and bruised, and he was wearing dark glasses. He could see a deeper shadow among the shadows beyond his white-ish blankets and this he took to be Conrad.

'They want to move me to an eye hospital which has been evacuated somewhere in Surrey,' he said. 'They don't know how long it will be but they think they can improve the sight in one eye. They can also teach me how to get about and so on in case it doesn't improve. I'd like you to do something for me, Conrad. I don't know whether it's too much to ask, but I'd like you to take over the guardianship of Agatha and Imogen.'

'I will certainly look after them for you.'

'I'd like you to be their legal guardian and have absolute control over my money and property. When I can be independent, get about and so on, I want to go back to the island. After the war that is. If Judith is better I will come back for her and the children when I have made it ready for them.'

'I see,' said Conrad. 'And politics?'

'All that was a mistake,' said Orlando.

'That seems a little sweeping,' said Conrad, mildly.

Orlando laughed. 'It does, doesn't it? It's really impossible to explain. Perhaps I'll try and write to you or something. I'd like you to bring up my children because you would do it so much better than I could. You'd teach them things I know nothing about, like right and wrong, and tradition. I'm only afraid it's too much to ask.'

'Of course it's not. Nothing could give me more pleasure. But I will only do it until you are fit again.'

'I want you to be their legal guardian and have my power of attorney,' insisted Orlando.

'If it would set your mind at rest I will arrange it,' said Conrad.

'Thank you. I knew you would.'

'You must let me do anything I possibly can. I hope you understand how often you are in my thoughts and in my prayers. If you think of anything, however small, that I can do get them to let me know. I've given them all my particulars.'

In my thoughts and in my prayers. After he had gone Orlando thought, he is a mystery to me still, he is as mysterious and as impressive as when I first saw him at Mount Sorrel, standing with Henry looking up at the picture of his dead wife. I have admired him without understanding him. In his prayers. He means it, he prays for me, he and his God in their mysterious colloquies mention my name.

Orlando moved himself carefully a little further down the
bed, and leant his head, which still ached, more comfortably
on the pillows. He would try to write to Conrad. Should he
use Conrad's own language? I want you to share in my joy,
he could write.

But there was too much to say. I have misunderstood
everything, he wanted to tell him. King tried to tell me, he
spoke to me of love, good and evil, guilt, right attitudes and
wrong attitudes, the true and the false, and I ignored it all
and took the world on its own terms. Ambitious and yet
not ambitious enough, expecting too little of people and
events, smug I became, fat, lax and unloving, using only
the language of the world of affairs and never the language
King tried to teach me. But with what joy I shall go back
and learn his language now. Sid must come. I will write to
Sid in Australia. Poor Sid, how hurriedly he left, we were
not at all kind to him, he must come back to the island, and
grow his vegetables again. And I will finish King's tower,
Agatha could sleep there sometimes; and Judith will be
better, her flat little bottom in trousers, look how good she
is in boats, and I will show her about love, we have neither
of us understood it, we have expected too little of it, how ill
we have used each other, not understanding about love and
concern, that old charwoman saying Mrs Smalley love into
a heap of stones knew more than we did, but I will show
her, we will find out about it together. First I will make it
ready for them and then I will come back for them, and
when we have made it strong there Paul and Stephen can
come and be cured. I'll take her there first in the spring –
delight of not redecorating the dining-room with Shanks
Pendleton – I'll take her there in the time of cornflowers
and wild carnations, feed her on palourdes, oysters, artichokes, asparagus, build out another room for books, buy

another boat, smell the salt soft wind, take off my shirt in the sun, working on the tower.

A thermometer was slipped under his tongue and fingers held his wrist.

'You're looking cheerful tonight,' said the nurse.

When she had taken out the thermometer he said, 'After the war I shall go back to the island.'

Orlando At The Brazen Threshold

He was Lucifer: his hair was serpents, flames and horns: his victims plunged into his great mouth, his ears engulfed them, his webbed wings beat them senseless: between his loins the most awful of his orifices sucked howling offenders into his blue and yellow belly; two he held helpless in his scaly hands, his taloned feet gripped more like squealing rats between an eagle's claws.

Some mornings Orlando rose like Lucifer with attendant devils. He recognized himself in the mirror from a painting he had seen on a church wall.

He stood on the terrace facing immeasurable distance. Swifts dashed past him, so close that the sound of their wings was like flags unfurling: semaphore, a message trying to get through. Fear of death assailed him.

Agatha arrived in April. He found her difficult to talk to. He did not tell her about King's diary.

King had written, 'I cannot live like this, my being founders, I don't know who I am because there is no one to name me, but if I were to dissolve into the nothingness that presses in on me my dissolution would not free me from myself.'

Orlando thought, It is the same. Agatha cannot guess it of me any more than I guessed it of King, nor can I tell her what King could not tell me. How can one tell someone Nothing?

King had written, 'Immeasurable pain, last night my dreaming soul was king again.'

Agatha was seventeen. (It was 1951.) She walked out into the sun but did not find it warm. She had thought the Tuscan spring would have been earlier. Across the rough cut grass was the little stone shrine, with its agreeable shape and its vacant plinth; and the stone walls on whose angle it was set led equally to the right or to the left beside wide grassy paths which had been roads when this group of buildings amounted to a village. Left led to the lower level of the priest's house: that way you ducked under the overhanging branches of the pear tree and went into the old kitchen, the floor of which had a hole in it. There was a pile of outworn shoes in what used to be the fireplace: work had not started there yet. If you took the right-hand path at the shrine you climbed more steeply, turned left under close growing bushes of scrubby alder laced with vines from the priest's ruined garden, and found yourself in a grassy space on the other side of his house, the chapel side in fact, with the small stone belfry on the roof and the flourishing vine in the angle between the door to the chapel and the wall of the house. In this space was the stone well, and beyond it the plain church shape of the tower house, which you passed, at the tower end, to find the promontory beyond.

This grassed terrace, sheltered on the right, or western, side by the four fine ilex trees which gave the place its name, Lecceto, or ilex grove, overlooked a distance of wooded hills and terraced slopes which ended only where it faded into the sky, which might be nearer or further according to the season but was never less than very many miles, and though there were farmhouses to be seen – a big one on the hill in the middle distance, three tall cypresses beside it – and the town of Radda-in-Chianti was well disposed on a further hill, yet Agatha at first found this immensity too vast, and was happier to look left into the mild ravine where sweet corn and fruit trees grew or right into the less steeply cut valley where the vineyard was and the willows which surrounded the spring and where one later evening she first saw, startling against the evening trees, a golden oriole dash the length of the little valley towards the open sky.

'What have you been doing then, all this time?' he asked her.

She seemed to him a character of paper thinness, an existence so slender as to be almost invisible. He supposed this was youth, a condition to which in his present frame of mind he could not find himself sympathetic.

'Nothing much really,' said Agatha, conscious of her inadequacies. 'I mean, school and things.'

'And the holidays at Mount Sorrel, did you enjoy those?'

'Oh of course. I mean, it's my home. I love it.'

'And you get on well with your Uncle Conrad?'

'Oh yes.'

'Does he talk to you a lot?'

'Talk to us? I suppose so.' She smiled. 'It's more like lecturing.'

'What does he lecture you about?'

'Morals. Life. Politics. He thinks I'm opinionated and Imogen's frivolous.'

'And are you?'

'Yes, certainly. Uncle Conrad is always right.'

'He annoys you then. You never told me that.'

She looked embarrassed. 'It never came up exactly. Besides, he doesn't always annoy me.'

Orlando was slightly shocked. 'He's taken an immense amount of trouble over you two. Choosing your schools, being at home as much as he could during the holidays – all sorts of things you probably never knew about. I've got a mass of letters he's written me over the last ten years about you both.'

'Oh I know.' She was blushing with shame. 'I didn't mean to sound ungrateful, I mean I'm not ungrateful anyway.'

'I suppose one isn't grateful to the people who bring one up. When my dear old benefactor and adopted father died I forgot about him for years. It was not until much later that I began to think I ought to have been grateful. In fact it wasn't until this year that I began to know him.'

'He sounds nice,' said Agatha cautiously.

'He was tremendously nice. I didn't realize until recently that much of the time when we were living on the island he was really pretty unhappy.'

He paused before the impossibility of telling a young girl he hardly knew about King. She did not know how to encourage him although she would have liked to.

'Conrad was the person I most admired in the world at the time of my accident,' said Orlando, leaving King unexplained. 'I made him your guardian because I felt quite unable to bring you up myself and I thought he would do it far better. Apart from the fact that I thought I was going to die.'

'It can't be all that difficult to bring someone up,' said Agatha. 'I mean you just have to be there really, don't you?'

She had said this rather quickly in order to avoid consideration of his possible death, either ten years ago or now – because it was still, so she understood it, likely to happen any minute. She wanted to avoid the subject because it embarrassed her. Might she have to say, 'I'm

glad you didn't,' 'I hope you won't for a bit'? How did
one talk about such a subject? Nor was she certain that
there was not some slight pressure from him, some implication that she ought to pity him, and this she was not
prepared to do. She was aware of having no grasp at all of
what death was – which was partly why it was so difficult
to talk about – at the same time no one could deny that it
was natural, and in that case she felt that nothing could
persuade her that it was not also right.

Her haste had led her into saying something which might
have sounded rude. Her father had certainly not been there
during the last ten years of her upbringing and she supposed
he might have taken her remark as a reproach.

'Anyway,' she said in the dry tone of voice she used when
she was embarrassed and which had led her headmistress
to remark in her report, *Agatha must beware of sarcasm*,
'I feel very well-brought-up.' He had had a terrace made
in front of the farmhouse in which he was living until the
work on the priest's house and the tower house should be
finished (he had not yet been able to decide into which of
them he would eventually move). Behind the terrace was an
open arch where once there had been cow stalls, and in the
shelter of the arch they could sit in the spring sunshine for
breakfast.

There were two of these farmhouses side by side along
the track which led to the top of the hill, a few yards only
from each other and from the stone shrine where the track
divided. They had both been empty for no more than a few
years when Orlando bought them and so had been in better
condition than the houses on the top of the hill, which had
been empty for fifty years. Orlando had made one habitable for himself and the other for a family of peasants who
looked after the land and his own needs.

Alert to Orlando, drinking coffee beside her, Agatha was writing a letter in her mind to Paul, her half-brother. 'He seems so suspicious. We talked a bit more naturally today but I didn't manage it very well. I suppose I'm shy of him. It's rather an odd situation, having seen so little of him for so long and then being quite alone with him. I wish Imogen could have come too.'

'What else,' said Orlando, unwilling for the conversation to lapse into another long silence. 'What else did you do at school?'

'We did *As You Like It* last term.' Agatha suddenly felt quite desperate. What did he expect her to have done? She had grown up, that was all, she was an age older than she had been a year ago, she had discovered that ghastly thing about Jane Stapleton, had been defeated and misunderstood by authority in the shape of Miss Clayton, whose side Uncle Conrad predictably had taken, she had read Proust, and knew the Mount Sorrel woods with true knowledge in all seasons, and would be a doctor in spite of all the opposition in the world, and lead people to a better understanding of what the whole point of everything was if only they would see it, and at the same time she had to wait – he must know this surely, he must remember? – until Youth and Innocence, twin pests, at last should let her out of their clutches, or else until the end of the world, for that she cloudily felt to be imminent, a terrible test no more than a year or two away for which she had to be always preparing herself. Impatience rose. 'I was Rosalind.' She jumped up, ran to lean affectedly against the shrine, hand on hip, and began to prattle: 'Leander, he would have lived many a fair year, though Hero had turned nun, if it had not been for a hot midsummer night, for, good youth, he went but forth to wash him in the Hellespont, and being taken with the cramp was drowned; and the foolish coroners of that age found it was "Hero of Sestos". But these are all lies; men have died from time to time, and worms have eaten them, but not for love.'

He saw that it had been a triumph. Her mockery of herself Agatha was for the moment superimposed upon Rosalind's mockery of herself Rosalind, but the ease with which her agreeable voice had risen to the poetry of the last phrase made him understand that it had been a triumph, something that people would remember, Agatha as Rosalind in the school play, her last summer term.

'I see,' he said.

She had come back to finish her coffee. '... And so on,' she said, but happily.

'Perhaps you should go on the stage.'

'Gosh no.'

If I could die, King had written, affirming thus the Nothingness I know to be the All – that would be an action at least; and I know the region into which that dying would take me, while it lasted. It is like a glass dome whose vast emptiness echoes with the sound of my own breathing, half my life is spent under the dome. Most mornings when I wake I find myself there, those early mornings in the waste-land of the wide glass dome immobilized by dread. I *must* get out of bed as soon as I wake up. I *must* not submit myself to those mornings.

I must not submit myself to those mornings, Orlando thought.

Some kind of flower, the lateness of the spring notwithstanding, grew beneath the tangled mass of brambles covering the wall by the path which led round the vineyard to the road, perhaps a crocus, or perhaps, on second thoughts, only a piece of paper.

Approaching to peer through the thickness of the bushes Agatha was stopped short by a loud hissing immediately at her feet. She looked down towards the grassy overhung foot of the wall, and seeing between the bramble branches a brownish sheen of moving skin was seized with violent terror and ran half the way back to the house: snake.

She had been told that they had disappeared since the land had been brought under cultivation again.

When her panic had subsided she took a stick and went back to see it. If it was an adder there would be smudged thumb marks alternating down its brown back. There were, and it was still hissing furiously, and trying to force itself sideways into a small crack in the stone wall, afraid.

'It's rather beautiful,' she said aloud but was still too frightened to go close enough to see its head.

There are *snakes*, she thought, recounting the incident in advance in some letter or other.

It lurked then in the curve of the wall above the vineyard, in the long grass between the entangled clematis and bramble, blackberries and old man's beard, columbine, convolvulus, wild rose, and the grass would be long and green sometimes, and sometimes burnt dry and brown, and then the snake would slide out on to the warm path to sun itself, containing its venom: oh yes, she could affirm it. There is nothing, she thought, nothing I cannot embrace; and if a unicorn should step out of the forest, make his delicate approach along the stony path towards us, the serpent might strike, might bring him dying to his knees; and even that I can embrace.

[*]

Past the snake undaunted though in extraordinary leather leggings strode Miss Theodora Bates to announce to the uneasy Agatha in tones of the jolliest camaraderie, 'I'm your father's tutelary deity. He's told you about me, I'm sure.'

He hadn't. He had told her very little, through being out of the habit of easy communication.

In her drily embarrassed tone, Agatha said, 'I've never quite known what tutelary deity is.'

'Nor have I, no idea. *Un po' di caffè per favore, Nella. Dov'è il signore stammattina allora?*' She spoke the Italian words as if they were English, only raising her voice slightly to mark the difference.

She was already on the terrace. 'Strode across the hills and broke them,' Agatha remembered from an Eliot poem. 'Miss Nancy Ellicot, Strode across the hills and broke them.' Not the sort of person she liked at all. But Nella was extending the warmest of welcomes.

'Marvellous-looking, isn't she?' Theodora settled into the chair placed for her by Nella. 'Wonderful natural dignity they have, these native Tuscans. Your father's lucky, there aren't all that many of them left. They can only scrape a living on these small farms and they get no help from the government. They're all leaving and going to the towns. You get these wretched Southerners who have taken their places. I've got a family of them who do a bit of work for me. They come from somewhere right down below Naples there, quite a different type, you can't trust them an inch. What's more the ne'er-do-well son's already talking of going to work in a factory in Poggibonsi. Even in one generation they're beginning to leave the land. Too bad, isn't it?'

'Yes,' said Agatha, not encouragingly.

'It'll change the landscape completely, of course, if it goes on this way,' continued Miss Bates cheerily. 'Terraces that have been cultivated since Etruscan times going back to the wild, too sad. I don't see this family going though, do you? That Giuseppe seems a good boy. Not mad about the bright lights. Not too bright himself either. That's just as well no doubt. Divine coffee. Does Nella still use that espresso pot, I wonder? I must warn her about them. Mine exploded the other day and now I'm told they always do it. Shot into the air without any warning at all. Had to have the whole kitchen repainted.'

'Oh dear,' said Agatha.

Her effort to sound concerned was half-hearted and wholly unsuccessful. In the short time that she had known them she had seemed to see Nella and her family as truly good. She was now immediately divided between her displeasure at the patronizing way in which Miss Bates spoke of them and her uncomfortable feeling that perhaps her own attitude towards them was, if not patronizing, then probably sentimental. Since she knew only a word or two of their language, and they knew none at all of hers, their mutual friendliness had as yet achieved little, and because Nella was so handsome and strong and maternal, and because the whole family worked in the fields all day and could sometimes be heard singing at night, and because the son leading two white oxen along the path smiled so beautifully, and because the grandmother bending over her young plants in the vegetable patch looked a thousand years old, she had ignorantly idealized them. How could she know what they were really like? Suddenly it seemed insolent to have any opinion at all about what was foreign. Perhaps the whole family was ignorant and stupid, secretly discontented, cheating Orlando, laughing

at him behind his back, perhaps when she heard them singing in the evenings they were all drunk, and the men were
about to wreak their passions upon the women in scenes of
bucolic frenzy while the crazed old grandmother muttered
black magic from her filthy mattress under the stairs. More
probably the truth lay between extremes; but whatever it
was, she would doubtless never know it, never get it right.
A feeling of flat depression overcame Agatha in the presence of Miss Theodora Bates.

'I'm afraid my father had to go to Siena,' she remembered to say. 'With Signor Rossi. It was something to do
with taxes.'

'I hope he's saying the right things. You can't be too careful with these tax people. If you declare your income as
more than a quarter of what it is they think you're out of
your mind, it puts them into the most terrible difficulties.
But I suppose he'll be all right if he does what Rossi tells
him. I'd have gone with him myself if I'd known.'

Her concern had a proprietary tone about it. Agatha
remembered now that it had been she who had been
responsible for Orlando's coming to Tuscany at all. She
had been a friend of a friend – or had it been something
to do with Uncle Conrad? – Agatha could only remember
that when Orlando's return to the Breton island where he
had been brought up had turned out to be a disaster – he
went too soon after the war, there was not enough food,
everyone he had known before 1931 had moved away
or died, the house was a ruin – somehow or other Miss
Bates had redeemed the situation by introducing him to
Tuscany, finding him his village, organizing the work of
restoration. He had stayed in her house, perhaps for as
much as a year – certainly he could never have achieved
what he had without her.

'It's been a great success, this place,' said Agatha, mindful of all this.

'He couldn't have managed it without me, though I say it myself,' said Miss Bates comfortably. 'Not but what I was delighted to do it. I like nothing better than interfering in other people's lives.'

Agatha smiled insincerely, but luckily Miss Bates seemed to think comment unnecessary.

'I'm the other side of Radda there, near the Siena-Florence road. A good deal more civilized. Come and see me any time you like. You may be a bit lonely here. Not that I know many young people. I see a bit of Florentine life. The Consul and his wife are awfully nice people. They come and dine with me in the wilds every now and then and we all agree about how glad we are not to be living in England in the age of Sir Stafford Cripps; and then there's William Holmes of course, charming man, great gardening chum of mine, and his nice young secretary. Anyway tell your father I'll come over tomorrow and we'll make a plan. I must be off. I've got the swimming pool expert coming. Not that I care for swimming myself, look a sight in a bathing suit too, you can imagine, but one's friends seem to like it. Tell him I'll be over about this time tomorrow then. Come on, dogs. Oh fool that I am, I didn't bring them. They're in season and I wasn't sure that brute of Giuseppe's wouldn't be about somewhere. Well, that's a pleasure in store for you, meeting my little dears. Don't bother to come with me. *Arrivederla*, Nella. *A domani. Vengo alla stessa ora vedere il signore. Ciao*, Agatha.'

'*Ciao*,' said Agatha, too loud because of the effort it caused her to use what seemed to her so unnatural a form of farewell. She blushed because of the loudness, then lingered

awkwardly on the edge of the terrace until Miss Bates had
rounded the corner of the house.

When Orlando went back to the island in Brittany where he
had spent his childhood with his guardian, old King, he found
everything very much changed since he had left it in 1931.

He went back in 1946, when travel was difficult. Only
his persistence and Conrad's help overcame all the obstacles to his becoming a foreign resident. He had hoped much
of the return, and his expectations were disappointed. The
house in which he had lived with King was a ruin. No one
had lived there since King had died. Sid, who had lived in
the other house on the island and had been King's factotum
and friend, had looked after things to some extent until the
outbreak of war, but then he too had left, and five years in
the damp sea-air of the Morbihan had done little good to the
two houses. Orlando had moved into Sid's house, and had
set about trying to restore the larger one, but the difficulties
were insuperable. Too much of France needed rebuilding,
and though some of the local inhabitants remembered him
they were powerless to help him. It was even difficult to
find food, let alone labour or building materials.

He had written to Sid, suggesting that he might come
back to the island to help him, and months later he received
an answer from somewhere in the Far East: 'So you're going
back to the old place. I wonder how you'll like it without
King. It's a bloody desolate little damp old island at times.
Not that I minded too much. But it might be different for
you after that toffee-nosed set-up you had in England,
Member of Parliament and lady wife and all. Still it's up
to you. I'm really sorry to hear she died. She seemed a bit
highly strung the time I met her. You know what I've done?
Signed on for another seven years, still a private. I'll be
retiring age after that. The thing with the Army, you never

have to think for yourself. And there's always some real old time-wasting task to put your hand to. Irresponsibility. Anonymity. Lawrence of Arabia and me. Always thought we had a lot in common. You thought I was irresponsible and anonymous before? You should see me now.'

He did not hear from him again until three years later when a brief note reached him in Italy. 'I forgot to tell you I left some stuff of King's in the bank in Vannes. It was papers mostly. I didn't like to put it in store with the furniture so I put it into the safe deposit at the Crédit Lyonnais. Don't know if it's of any interest.' So eventually King's diaries came into his possession.

By that time he had left the island, saved indirectly by a Christmas card from Theodora Bates.

Theodora Bates had spent the war in Italy. She had always loved it – her father had once been British Ambassador in Rome – and she was so delighted by the apparent benefits of Mussolini's rule when she went on a visit to friends in Florence in the early 'thirties that she decided to go and live there, Tuscany being, she said, as good a place to breed pugs as any. It wasn't of course, but she had discovered round about the age of six that overplaying one's natural role was one form of self-defence.

Her faith in Fascism did not survive Italy's entry into the war and the disagreeable behaviour of certain local officials. Her house was at one stage taken over by the Germans and at another by the English, In the meantime she housed a quantity of refugee children from the industrial towns and supported partisans and Allied advance troops at some considerable risk to herself, being always under the suspicious surveillance of the regime. One of the English army officers whom she had known at this time was a friend of Conrad's, and so the message on her Christmas card had eventually reached Orlando. 'If any of your friends want to escape from austerity England,' she had written, 'houses here are astonishingly cheap and life is getting back to normal at a great rate (thanks largely to a perfectly splendid black market which has got the economy on the move) and there's nothing like Italian *cortesia* in spite of everything.'

Conrad in the course of time had passed the information on to Orlando, of whose difficulties he was aware, and Orlando, with the sense of failure beginning to interfere with his sleep, had thought that there might be no harm in spending a week or two in Florence. He had followed up the roundabout introduction to Theodora, and since his eyesight was not good enough for him to drive a car, she had driven him round Tuscany in hers, and had taken the opportunity to organize him into buying Lecceto, for the preservation of which she had long wanted to provide.

'It'll be the hell of a job of course,' she had pointed out. 'But you've got the money and you need something to fill up your time.'

Not to let her get away too easily with such bluntness, and reminding her of the melancholy justification for his having so much time on his hands, he said, 'I may die before I finish it.'

'Lucky you, if you do,' she said briskly. 'It's the ones who finish before they die who are in trouble.'

'What do you think of my daughter?' Orlando asked Miss Bates.

'Beautiful.'

'Her mother was very beautiful.'

'I think she looks like you.'

'She doesn't seem to have a great deal to talk about.'

'Self-absorbed. They are, at that age.'

[*]

'Dear Paul, it's like a mixture between Anne Bridge and Agatha Christie. The social life, I mean. Soon there will be some kind of genteel murder. William Holmes' good-looking secretary will be one of the suspects but we'll all know he didn't do it because any fool can see he's there to provide the love interest with the gauche young English girl who's come to spend the summer with her father, the eccentric recluse. (To tell you the truth I haven't met him yet – the g.l. sec, I mean – but I can tell that's going to be his role.) Probably the victim will be the Consul's wife who lets the British community down so dreadfully by not getting her *ous* quite right. The murderer, I'm sure, will be Miss Theodora Bates, the archetypal thwarted spinster, secretly in love with said recluse as well as with three perfectly appalling female pugs. And of course the Consul's wife's vowels would be all she'd need for motive because she's the biggest snob you ever imagined and unbelievably boring about the Socialist Government and the Welfare State and giving away the Empire – but I haven't said a word – no embarrassing arguments – Uncle Conrad would be proud of me.

'As for Father, I don't know. His health doesn't seem too bad and he sees reasonably well, but he's what I'd call morose. Relations between us seem a bit strained. I haven't dared to ask him your thing about the shares yet. I'll try and work up to it. The trouble is he's such an unintimate kind of person. Perhaps I am too.'

It was as if a delicate instrument were resting on that region of his brain in which his youth was stored. He was Orlando, middle-aged, unsound of body, having sustained a severe eye injury which had permanently damaged his sight; and at the same time he was Orlando, fifteen or so, physically

perfect except for his hammer toes, riding the strong tide
in his sailing boat, feeling the salt wind against his face. In
both capacities he was linked with King; the difference was
in his degree of consciousness, both of himself and of King.

The years between, the ten years during which he had
lived in England, married, made money, forgotten King,
become a successful politician, those years seemed to have
lost their substance. It was as if he had not been himself
during that time. He had been happy, but could not now
remember the faintest flavour of that happiness. It had all
ended badly, because he had been one of those who were
now universally vilified as 'Munichites'. Also he considered
himself to have been a bad husband: at all events his wife
had died in a lunatic asylum.

The feeling of success, of leaping, as it were, with what
seemed now such childish joy, from one pinnacle of
achievement to another – it was a feeling of which now
even the memory escaped him – hurrying into the House
of Commons, his big speech ready, knowing his supporters
would cheer it and his enemies be thrown into disarray; his
establishment, children, nannies, cooks; the shooting in the
country, the dining out in London; the weekends in country houses, powerful among the powerful; more than that,
the continuing impulse by which once having started one
was impelled from one action to the next without need for
thought except on an agreeably superficial level; the whole
atmosphere of that time seemed from his present isolation
remote and unreal, nor could he now understand how he
could ever have taken any of it seriously.

His boyhood had been real, but ignorant, the years of
action another man's dream. The great and lovely turning
point, when the physical world outside his window had
seemed flooded with light from his hospital bed, had been

when he had realized he was returning from the world he had been in for the past ten years to the world of King. The subsequent loneliness, the struggle with a depression he had persisted in regarding as a purely physical symptom, the curious phenomenon of the shrinking world about and within him, had not detracted from the remembered glory of that moment, a glory which for years now he had been waiting to see renewed. Sometimes his hopes had fallen very low.

'I know the answer in my head,' King had written, 'but not in my bones. I cannot act it out, I am not good enough.

'September 13th. 7.30 Breakfast with Orlando.

8.30–12.30 Build tower.

12.30 Lunch.

1.30–3.30 Reading.

3.30 Take boat for shopping, etc. or sometimes fishing. Other things to pursue: 1. Improve French (ask the Curé for two evenings a week instead of one?).

2. Finish monograph on Gibbon & Christianity.

3. Send for *The Golden Bough* from the London Library. Re-read Coleridge.

4. Enlarge veg. garden with Sid before the spring.

5. Learn the flute?'

He had not learnt the flute, Orlando was sure of that.

'September 15th. Yesterday I went into St Nazaire to get some stores. I went to the usual bar. Neither of these actions was either necessary or, as far as I know, premeditated. I had gone into Vannes to do the shopping. I don't remember how I found myself on the bus to St Nazaire. I went to the ship chandlers. It is some way from the bar and yet I cannot remember taking any conscious decision. I simply found myself with a glass of pernod in my hand, aware of the sailor on the other side of the room, at the start of a familiar sequence of events.

'Orlando's time is much taken up with school and friends – rightly so – sometimes for days on end I see him only at breakfast and perhaps for half an hour in the evenings when he comes in. He's popular with his schoolfriends. At their houses he eats well. Their mothers make a fuss of him because he's good-looking and has no mother of his own. I am glad of all this and would not wish it to be otherwise, but I suppose when he was younger he kept me away from adventures.

'The sailor was a nice boy, glad of the money because he is saving up to get married. He was docile and experienced. Only my own anxieties prevented it from being a bearable experience.

'Back over the calm pale sea. White desolation licks the shores of my island mind.

'September 16. Blank.

'September 17. Blank.

'September 18. Better.

'September 19. Astonishing day. Orlando and I went for a fishing expedition. The weather was mild and the light extraordinarily beautiful. We went all the way to Belle Ile, landed for lunch. Orlando swam though it was cold. I sat in the sun on the little sheltered beach and watched him. There was no one else there. We came back in the evening over a calm sea with a good catch, some of which we cooked for supper.

'We talked about a great many different things. Somehow we came to my recollections of Queen Victoria's Diamond Jubilee in 1897, which I remember clearly and which seems incredibly strange and distant to him. He would have made a good Empire-builder once – perhaps in India, before the

Mutiny. There were some extraordinary Englishmen there at that time. He might have found it very satisfying, because he's a thoroughly competent man of action, extrovert, responsible, and yet in a way, though perhaps he doesn't know it, poetic. It's interesting for me to have to make the effort of imagination necessary to understand someone so totally different from myself. The Empire's beginning to be discredited now – rightly, I'm bound as a liberal to think – but long ago what scope there must have been for such a man as Orlando will be. He needs scope, though there again he doesn't know it himself. His greatest ambition is to be a fisherman with the Lanoë brothers when they all leave school. But today for once I could not worry about him. He is so confident and open and good. What luck to have a day like this, and to know what luck it is.

'September 21. How can one achieve that desirable state of being contained within the diurnal without becoming a cabbage? Insincere question. I would willingly become a cabbage, if I could.

'September 22. He has gone to stay with the Lanoës for a week – for no particular reason – I suppose it is boring for him here with no one but Sid and me, a couple of morose cranks – the only difference between us being one of age, and perhaps of honesty – Sid makes no pretence at being anything else but a morose crank, I do – well, I must admit another difference – I believe Sid in his own extraordinary way is perfectly happy, I believe when he wakes up in the morning he says to himself, "Thank f-ing Jesus Christ I'm not in f-ing Australia," or something of the sort – and that's all he requires.

'When I suggested to Orlando that he should ask the Lanoë boys here instead, he said their mother would rather he went there. I don't understand why. I didn't like to pursue it. Does she think they aren't safe with me? What kind of monster can she suppose me to be? Does she imagine I have no self-control whatever?

'September 23. Last night I drank two bottles of Muscadet, alone. Sid found me where I had passed out, after being sick. He put me to bed. My head is very bad. I can't go on. I can't live like this. A few days ago I loved Orlando. I can't now. More and more there are days on which I can't love. I have nothing to love with. I am not a real person. I AM NOT. I am NOTHING. I dissolve into my aching room. Everything within the glass dome is ME and I am NOTHING.

'September 25. Better. As if … The only answer to life is to live as if … So I can tell Orlando those things which I want him to believe, and hope that when later he finds them all to be fairy stories he will remember my frequent use of the subjunctive tense.'

The spring was hesitant. In the evenings they sat on either side of the olive-wood fire, reading, each afraid the other might be bored. Orlando was in mind of King, Agatha of her cousin, Conrad's son Henry. He would burst open the door, she thought, stride across the room. 'I love you,' he would say. They would kiss.

'Henry's been staying here for a couple of days,' Paul wrote to Agatha, 'bringing the famous Caroline. Serena and she spent most of the time trying on each other's clothes and S. has quite come round to her and hopes Henry will marry her. Since I've never managed to exchange more than the briefest of banalities with her – she doesn't really talk, in the ordinary sense of the word – I can't venture an opinion, though of course she's stunning to look at. Henry treats her in a fairly off-hand manner, as he does everybody. He's got a beaten-up-looking old MG which he drives appallingly badly and is as mysterious as ever about his doings. He doesn't seem to go to Mount Sorrel much.

'I quite understand that it's difficult to talk to Orlando, but if and when you can, please try and interest him in the business. As soon as you let me know that the moment is ripe I can write to him with every possible detail and I'm sure I can persuade him to see things my way. No doubt he feels very detached from it all and thinks that he's handed over all the responsibility to Conrad by making over all his shares to your and Imogen's trust, but surely it must be possible to make him interested in something which was entirely built up by him. I don't suppose, for one thing, that he has any idea how immensely the value of the holding has gone up. Legally perhaps there's nothing he can do, but in fact of course his influence would weigh enormously with Conrad.

'As I see it, the way to approach him is this.

1. His dear stepson Stephen is running Logan Holdings into the ground (due to his boneheaded lack of imagination).

2. His dear other stepson Paul, rather than precipitate family unpleasantness, left the business to seek his fortune elsewhere.

3. Having in the course of time married the girl of his choice, Paul (or rather I, because the third person bit is difficult to keep up) discovered that her father, for whom I was now working, was chairman of a large and flourishing firm on the verge of even further expansion, well able to take over Logan Holdings and run it far more efficiently, to everyone's advantage.

4. The only barrier to this is the obstinacy of Conrad, the trustee on your and Imogen's behalf of the largest shareholding, who supports Stephen because, frankly, he never got on with me.

'It's probably better not to emphasize the possible benefit to me, which is problematical anyway (I don't particularly trust Serena's father, for one thing – anyway, if he did want me to be Managing Director instead of Stephen you know me well enough to know Steve wouldn't suffer). What might arouse his interest is the idea of the really big things that might result. There's no doubt Serena's father is about the shrewdest operator in this country at the moment. He was the first person to get on to the property scene at the end of the war – now he's moving in on commercial TV, which is going to be the next big thing though no one knows it yet.

'Anyway, see what you can do, but don't let it worry you. I shall absolutely understand if you feel you can't even mention it to him – or not yet. I leave it entirely to you.

'How are the Italian lessons? I certainly envy you the sun.

'You are a saint to have lent me that money. I've bought Serena a marvellous evening dress for her birthday. I know that wasn't what you lent it me for but I'm still going to manage to pay you back by the time you come home in the autumn – especially if the great deal goes through.

'Henry sent his love by the way and says he misses you – so do I. You are the *only person* I can really talk to – and the only person I know who's always the same.'

'Do you think you might ever go back to England?' Agatha asked Orlando.

'I don't suppose so,' he said.

He was feeling tired. They had driven into Siena in the little Fiat 500 which he kept for other people to drive him about in. He had said he had one or two things to do there and anyway liked wandering about the streets; he would meet her for lunch after her morning class. In fact he had nothing to do. He had not been able to face the decisions he would have had to make if he had stayed at Lecceto. The masons were working on the terrace for the priest's house and he did not know how big it should be because he did not know whether he was going to live in that house himself or in the tower house; and if he was going to live in the tower house, then who was going to live in the priest's house, and if nobody was going to live in it what was the point of spending all that money on it, and perhaps it would have been more sensible to have allowed it to fall down.

On the way to Siena Agatha, who was not an experienced driver, had taken a corner rather wide and had had to swerve to avoid an approaching lorry. Fortunately they had hardly skidded at all on the dust road and the incident had amounted to very little, but it had been enough to send a familiar pricking feeling down his arms. At once he had thought, perhaps it will be today. He had already had two heart attacks and had been told he might have another. As he understood it, this could be expected to kill him.

When Agatha had left him he walked down the street towards the Campo, where he thought he would sit and drink some coffee and read a newspaper, which he could do quite comfortably with the use of a small magnifying glass. As he walked along he was suddenly engulfed in a crowd of sober-suited men emerging from a building. They were talking with animation about what sounded like the prices on the stock exchange, and for a moment as they pushed past him, gesticulating and ignoring him, he lost his bearings and found himself in the middle of the street which, being the widest in Siena, was the only one in which he could be momentarily uncertain as to where the sides of it were. Before he could reorientate himself there was a furious hooting and screaming of brakes. As he made his way quickly towards the dark wall of a building he heard the driver of the bus shouting. In Italy they are kind to women and children but not necessarily to the infirm.

He kept close to the wall as far as the newspaper shop, bought *The Times, La Nazione* and *Time Magazine*, and made his way to a table at the side of the Piazza del Campo, of whose great shell-shape he was aware even though its outlines were beyond his scope and which he usually found even in cold weather a harmonious place in which to sit. Today there was sun and he sat there for some time, reading, until suddenly, with a familiar flash as of a shutter opening and closing in his mind, terror of death took hold of him and then released him.

He waited. Then he went back, as to an abscessed tooth, to that part of his mind where the event had taken place. Nothing happened. He probed. Nothing. He breathed more easily. Death was something he had once been near and in whose shadow he had felt peace. Death was a stopping point merely, not very relevant to life, the common end.

The nerve twitched again.

It was no more than a moment, a turning sickeningly towards black earth, which muffled breath and burst the heart by means of suffocation; but more than physical defeat, more than the helpless flight head first into the black tunnel, the terror was in the disintegration of the surrounding world. For it was that he felt in those moments, the crumbling silent swift irrevocable vanishing of everything about him, tables, chairs, pigeons, waiters, tourists, they would all go, all be superseded by infinite vacancy. In the moment before he died he would be the last man left alive.

'I can't,' he said.

'*Signore?*' The waiter, for once, was at hand.

'*Il conto.*'

There was no escape. But it was better to walk about than to sit still.

He was not alone. King was with him. This was perhaps what haunting was. King was his familiar. They walked together, isolated from the crowd by their blindness. King must be blind too because he was dead. He walked a little behind Orlando's right shoulder, making no sound in his shabby plimsolls. Guilt is the enemy of liberty, King had said. Orlando could not turn to look him in the face because of guilt, guilt that he had not loved King enough (but he had been too young to love anyone), guilt that he had not understood his own importance to King (he had known about King's fits of 'boredom', they had used to worry him), guilt that he had failed to live up to King's expectations when the chance came ('he is so confident and open and good'), most of all shared guilt ('I know the answer in my head, but not in my bones. I cannot act it out, I am not good enough'). One could not start to be good quite suddenly in middle age; it needed a lifetime's practice. Should he learn the flute?

But the pain had gone again. He smelt fresh bread, passing a baker in a dark steep street. Sid used to make bread on the island, dark brown, rather sweet. They ate it with the fish they had caught that day, or with clams cooked in garlic butter, or mussels with white wine; and there were the vegetables Sid used to grow, peas and broad beans so young they ate them with the pods on; he had never tasted vegetables as good as those. And all the time King had talked, a flood of information, anecdote, exhortation, to which Orlando had sometimes listened and sometimes not. 'I am passing on the ancient message,' King had said. What could he have meant? Now he walked in silence behind Orlando's right shoulder, his lamentations not lending themselves to the spoken word. 'It is like a glass dome whose vast emptiness

echoes with the sound of my own breathing – I would willingly become a cabbage, if I could – everything within the
glass dome is me and I am nothing.' And Orlando could
remember only days of sun and movement, water under the
dinghy, wind through the bent grass, the unity of being he
had seemed to share with King who in the afternoons had
slipped away to rendezvous with sailors.

Orlando could remember no incident from his youth
which pointed to King's affliction (for affliction he would
have thought it himself, therefore to him his homosexuality
had been an affliction). There was nothing to which even
hindsight could give a new significance. The fact revealed
King's self-control, which presumably was admirable, but
also the depth of his shame, which called for tears.

A linnet sang loudly, tightly caged on a balcony high
above the street. Orlando turned in the direction of the
trattoria where he had arranged to meet Agatha for lunch,
hoping to come across the right street by hazard, being
now lost. He remembered two Swedish girls in Florence,
greedy for sensation, which he supposed he had given them.
As far as he remembered, he had felt better after it. They
would both make horrible wives one day: their advanced
techniques were unlikely to be kept for their husbands'
sole delectation. But he was smiling to himself. Had he felt
ashamed? He could not remember. The next day he would
have liked to have gone home to his wife, had she not been
dead. There was his shame. He had as much guilt to carry
as King's, and a great deal more cause for it. Death, he
thought. But the shutter did not open. He tried to imagine himself running into a burning house, jamming on his
ARP warden's tin hat, but it was impossible. I couldn't do
it now, he thought, my nerve has gone. Altogether and in
every way I have lost my nerve

By the time he found the place where he was to meet Agatha he had walked so far that his legs were aching.

In answer to her question, he said he did not suppose he would ever go to England again.

'I believe the Logan business is not going very well,' said Agatha.

'Isn't it? It ought to be all right.'

She had seen him sitting at the table as she came in and he had looked as if he were suffering in some way and she had not known what to do about it.

'Stephen's running it now, you know,' she said.

'Conrad's still on the board, presumably?'

'Oh yes, but I don't think he has an awful lot to do with it. He does so many other things. And he's been busy with politics. They think they can force the Government to have another election this year.'

'I daresay they will. It's obviously on its last legs. But Stephen's very steady and reliable, isn't he?'

'Yes, but he's not very adventurous. Paul says he's much too cautious. Not that I know much about it.'

'Paul's jealous, probably. They never got on very well, those two.'

'He says he left to avoid a quarrel.'

'If he thought Stephen was doing the wrong things he should have had a quarrel,' said Orlando unsympathetically.

'He wouldn't, he's not like that,' said Agatha, springing to Paul's defence. 'He's awfully kind, especially to his own family.'

'He's doing all right himself anyway, isn't he? He's the son-in-law of a millionaire, so Conrad tells me.'

'Yes, but it's not all that easy. He's tremendously tough, the millionaire. There's no question of Paul's getting anywhere except on merit.'

'What's the wife like?'

'Paul's wife? She's terribly pretty.'

'Nice?'

'She's a bit sort of old-fashioned. I daresay she'll grow out of it.'

'Out of what?'

'Well, what I mean is, she's very much an ex-deb and all that sort of thing. Her father gave a huge ball for her and got a lot of publicity, and she was always being photographed by the *Daily Express* and she really thinks all that sort of thing matters. She's on committees for charity dances and gives interviews to magazines about what she gives her guests for dinner, you know the sort of thing. It's not at all like Paul. She's the sort of person who wouldn't have a baby in case it spoilt her figure. Which is so stupid because the first baby usually improves your figure anyway.'

'Does it?' said Orlando, beginning to be amused. 'You don't really like her much then?'

'I do in a way. I try to anyway for Paul's sake. No, well, as a matter of fact I really don't. As a matter of fact I think she's a real empty-headed vain selfish idiot. She only married Paul because she was impressed when he took her to stay at Mount Sorrel, and the sooner she runs off with somebody grander the better for Paul. She certainly will too.'

'I've just remembered something,' said Orlando. 'When you were very young you used to stamp both your feet at the same time. Do you remember that? As soon as you got angry you started to jump. You often did get angry too. "It isn't fair," you used to say. You used to shout it at Nanny. She was rather frightened of you, I think. I remember you shouting at her once because that little nursery maid we had – what was her name? – anyway, she'd stolen some eggs or something, and you were furious because Nanny told me.'

'She hadn't stolen eggs, she would never have done such a thing,' said Agatha, indignantly. 'We used to save buns and things from tea for her to take home to her little brother and Nanny said that was stealing and it wasn't.'

'What happened? She wasn't sacked, was she?'

'Of course she wasn't. You were very nice about it. You arranged for her to take home a dozen eggs every week. Her father was on the dole.'

'Did I?' But he remembered. 'Her name was Jen.'

'Yes.'

'Do you still jump in anger?'

'I might, I suppose. I certainly wouldn't do it if anyone was looking.'

'Go on about Paul. He has no interest in Logan Holdings now then, except presumably a few shares?'

'He works for the millionaire father-in-law, whose name is Daintry, and who's a property tycoon. But he seems to be every other sort of tycoon as well, I can't quite make it out. Anyway apparently it would be a perfectly sensible thing for him to take over Logan Holdings, of which he has quite a lot of shares already somehow or other, and Paul thinks it would be a good idea because everything Daintry has anything to do with does so frightfully well, but Stephen's against it because he just likes running his business in a conservative sort of way by himself and doesn't want all sorts of exciting things to start happening to it.'

'And he doesn't want to lose his job.'

'Oh but he wouldn't. Paul specifically said so.'

'And what does Conrad think?'

'He's on Stephen's side, but then that's probably because he's not all that interested. I know you think Conrad must always be right, but after all you haven't seen him for a long

time. He may have changed. He's very obsessed by politics now, I'm sure more so than he used to be. He really
does think the Socialist Government's a national disaster.
He gets quite depressed at times, brooding about England
and longing to get back into power.'

'He always used to be very detached about his own part
in things. Too much so, I used to think. He used to want to
retire to Mount Sorrel all the time. It took a lot of persuading to get him to take an active part in politics.'

'He may have changed. After all he had a lot of authority
in the war. Perhaps he got to like it.'

'Perhaps. Interesting.'

'If you told him that you thought the takeover was a
good idea, he'd listen.'

'But I've been out of things for years now. He'd be
amazed if I suddenly started to take an interest.'

'But pleased. He's always told Paul and Stephen how
brilliant you were, specially in comparison with them.'

'I've no rights in the matter. I handed everything over.'

'That doesn't make any difference to what Conrad thinks
of your opinions.'

'I don't know anything about it all now. I can't possibly
start involving myself again.'

'Why don't I get Paul to write you a proper letter,
explaining the whole thing?'

'I'd have to go and see for myself and I can't do that.
There's the difficulty of getting about, and my wretched
health, and besides what about you? You're here for six
months and I couldn't go until after that. And by then I'll
probably be dead.'

'I'd be perfectly all right by myself for a bit. And perhaps
it would be fun to go to England again after so long. Paul
says Daintry's a fascinating man.'

'He doesn't sound it. Besides, if I died in England there might be tax complications.'

'Oh how could that possibly matter?'

'It could matter to you and Imogen. You'd have less money.'

'We don't need money. If Uncle Conrad can just manage to pay for my medical training, I'll be all right after that, and Imogen can earn a fortune as a model any time she likes, apart from the fact that she's bound to get married the minute she leaves school – or before, knowing her.'

'You're trying to persuade me. You've been put up to it by Paul.'

'I'm not trying to persuade you. I'm just telling you about it. I have been put up to it by Paul but I don't see that there's anything wrong in that. He thinks the takeover's a good idea and he wants your support. That's all right, isn't it?'

'Yes, of course. You're quite right. All the same, I don't think I'll go.'

King had written, 'I have no interpreter; the language of the people I meet is a foreign one to me; I speak it as a foreigner, missing the nuances.'

Rain rushed from the far distance upon Lecceto, the sound of it running before it across the valley.

'I'll look after her,' said Theodora Bates. 'We're all so interested in her in our little community. Leave her to me.'

'I'll try,' said Orlando. 'I'll go for a week, if you'll keep an eye on Agatha.'

'Good-oh,' said Miss Bates.

'Darling Paul, I've done it and I want congratulating. He's coming back to England in a couple of weeks' time. I'm going to be chaperoned by Miss Bates, imagine that. In

fact for your sake I am to undergo the disagreeable experience of sleeping under her roof – that's all I'm going to do
though because I shall certainly spend my waking hours
either at school in Siena or here. This is really the most
beautiful place on earth, so much so that at first you don't
notice it. It has a kind of standing still feeling about it like
the eye of a whirlwind. It's not romantic like English country. It doesn't fill my soul with unknown yearnings like the
smell of Mount Sorrel woods does – it's the only place I
think I've ever been to where I don't find myself for ever
making plans and resolutions – but resignation is too weak
a word for what I feel, which is not mindless joy either but
the kind of feeling I might have if I were tremendously old
and experienced and had come right round again to liking
scenery and herb smells and earth colours and the shapes
people make in the clear light in distant fields.

'I've looked at the pictures and realize I'm too ignorant
and untrained about them. The Sienese ones are too styl-
ized for me. I'm so self-centred, I want everything to relate
closely to ME before I can start to respond to it. When I am
very old I might be different. But I did walk through the
first rooms in the Ufizzi in Florence and think what a beautiful religion this must have been, forgetting it was anything
to do with Miss Hobson taking Prayers. But really I haven't
any visual education. I like the look of things I'm used to,
that's all. It's quite nice in a way to think one has a whole
sense undiscovered – only that I don't see how I'm ever
to have the time to discover it. Perhaps I'll just take in the
landscape for a beginning.

'Please be nice to Orlando. The thing is, I am only just
beginning to get to know him, though I know it's a wise
child that knows its own father – what could that possibly
mean? – what I mean is, I know children can't know their

parents, there's some great bar to real intimacy (terror of incest, do you think?), but perhaps it's different if you've had such a long gap in your acquaintance as -we've had. Anyway, it seems to me on getting to know him a bit that what he did in giving up and coming here was even more extraordinary than I thought it was, because he isn't that sort of person. He's not really as introspective as, say, me, or as given to philosophizing as, say, Uncle Conrad – in fact when he talks about "ideas" he becomes quite banal. He ought to be busying about in the world of affairs – I bet his health would improve if he did – and I don't believe he's half as disillusioned as he thinks he is. We talked a bit about politics the other day and he's not nearly as right-wing as Uncle Conrad – in fact honestly he said some perfectly intelligent things. But it takes him a bit of time to relax – he's awfully stiff at first – and quite unhappy I think. That's why it would be so nice if you could interest him in things again. (Anything rather than have La Bates as a stepmother.)'

Miss Bates drove Agatha and Orlando to lunch with William Holmes in the former Medici villa outside Florence where he lived in the summer. Orlando was to leave for England in two days' time.

Miss Bates said of their host, 'He's too divinely international and amusing.'

Agatha was beginning to suspect that some of the things Miss Bates said were intended ironically, but since they were said without a smile she had not yet liked to laugh at them.

'He's an art expert,' Orlando said. 'Self-styled, I think it would be fair to say. Almost fair, anyway.'

After lunch Agatha escaped from the house, of which she retained an impression only of high dark rooms and brown marble, and followed an overgrown little path through the woods, which, curving soon under the hill beneath the house, led her into a valley from which no house at all could be seen, where there were small oak trees, and yellow-flowered broom, and new spring grass. The path led downhill. She kept her eyes on the ground for fear of snakes, because the wood seemed unfrequented.

Recognizing now the familiar loud liquid voice of the nightingale she walked on through the wood and the inter-mittent warm sunlight towards the sound of water. She could see poplars ahead of her, perhaps beside the stream. Their leaves had not yet opened fully into their summer green and were a dark reddish gold which reminded her of the bare winter branches of English water willows. Behind them, as well as the pale green of the new oak leaves and of one or two taller larches, there was occasionally the more solid darkness of a single pine.

When she reached the stream she left the path and pushed through some low oak trees to where a small waterfall rushed down two boulders into a shallow pool with sandy borders, from which the stream hurried into a deeper and narrower bed between small smooth stones.

Agatha remembered the stream in the Mount Sorrel woods, which had a waterfall too but a steeper one; the wood through which it ran was darker, with tall elms and sycamores which kept out the light; the air there smelt of wild garlic and mud.

'I want to go home,' she said aloud, but it was not exactly what she meant.

She leant against a tree-trunk, allowing the sound and rush of the stream to engross her. She had hated the lunch party. She had been quiet and polite, but had thought how wrong they all were. Leaning against the tree and gazing at the stream, she could breathe freely. She thought of the future, without precision. One day I will flow like that, she thought, one day I will burst my banks. Tears came into her eyes and she felt intensely happy.

She might have stayed for hours, staring at the stream, but a sound disturbed her and she turned to see Hal Newman's bent head as he approached her beneath the low branches between the path and the stream. By the time he had straightened up and looked at her she was smiling politely again, but more sincerely than at lunch, because she liked the look of him although they had hardly spoken.

'Wow,' he said, pushing back his hair. 'What a place.'

She nodded.

'Just beautiful,' he said.

He was William Holmes's secretary.

He sat down beside the stream and looked up at Agatha, smiling.

'How did you find this place?' he asked. 'Have you been here before?'

'I just followed the path.'

'We're only just moving in to the villa,' he said, in excuse for his knowing so little about its surroundings. 'He only lives here in the summer. There's no heating. Even with all those fires I nearly froze to death last week when we first arrived.'

'Where does he live the rest of the time?'

'He has this beautiful apartment in Florence, near Santa Croce. He has wonderful things there. You should see it. That's where he keeps the library I'm cataloguing.'

'It must be a very big library if it's taken you so long.'

'I guess it's kind of an excuse for my being here. I like it. Are you in college or something?'

'I'm going to medical school in the autumn.'

'You're going to be a doctor? I didn't know that. That's great. That's something I admire very much. I never would have known that.' He looked up at her indeed in evident astonishment, pushing back his hair, which was long and dark and fell over his forehead. He had shining dark eyes and a wide beautiful smile.

'What would you have thought I would have been going to do?' she asked a little foolishly, smiling back.

'I don't know. Some kind of artist I suppose. A painter. I used to know one or two girls in San Francisco who were painters and they had your kind of way of looking at things, you know, as if they really saw them. They weren't like you in any other way though.' He laughed as if the idea were very funny. 'You're so English.'

'I know, I hate that,' she said. 'But I can't help it. It's something to do with English schools.'

'What kind of a school did you go to?'

'Oh a stupid one. Stuffy and awful. Did you like school?'

'I went to kind of a funny school. We didn't wear shoes or do anything we didn't want to do.' He laughed again, joyously. 'It was kind of crazy, you either survived or you didn't. Terrible things happened, suicides, abortions. It's funny, I don't seem to remember too much about it even though it wasn't so long ago. I used to love the dancing classes, I remember that. We had no rules or anything, we just wandered around this big garden, we didn't even have to wash. The garden was beautiful, all of a great hillside in California. It was kind of an experience. Like I say, if you could survive you were fine, it really opened you up. Most of us had personality breakdowns one time or another. It was really wild.'

The sun was on his face. He looked completely comfort-able, sitting cross-legged on the grass. Perhaps it was something he had learnt at school. She tried to imagine a green hillside covered with exotic vegetation, and beautiful barefooted young people wandering in loose robes through camellias and palm trees.

'I don't think I even know anyone who's been to California,' she said, almost desperate in her longing to imagine it.

'It's great,' he said. 'But I'd rather be here.'

'Would you?' she said, surprised. 'With people like Mrs Waring?'

'Mrs Waring.' He bent back his head and stared up into the trees, exposing his smooth brown throat. 'She's strange. I guess she's not too happy.'

'She seemed very happy to me,' said Agatha, remembering Penelope Waring's vivacity. She had darted brightly forward from the group on the terrace, saying, 'Orlando! What a treat! I couldn't believe it when Wicked Will said you were coming.' Orlando had looked puzzled. She had reached up to kiss him, holding his face in her hands. 'It's me, my dear,' she had said, very close to his face so that he could see her clearly. 'It's Penelope.'

'Penelope!' Agatha had been astonished to see his look of embarrassed delight, the slight flush which came into his cheeks. 'My dear Penelope, how perfectly wonderful to see you!'

And she had led him off, all jingling as she was with bracelets and fluttering with chiffon scarves, to sit and talk, ignoring everyone else. Agatha had been left standing uneasily beside Miss Bates, a glass of vermouth in her hand, half listening to what she could hear of their conversation, which seemed to her to be rather one-sided, Mrs Waring doing the talking and Orlando merely smiling, a bit foolishly, Agatha thought.

'Too marvellous, you're looking divine, so thin and distinguished, my dear, much better than when you had all that rude health. I saw it in the paper about poor darling Judith. Oh no, we were out of prison by that time. I said that specially loudly so that Guy could hear because he's forbidden me ever to say that word. Aren't you glad you're not in England? Oh no, darling, we sold everything and moved to Ireland. Guy's sure the Communists are coming any minute. We keep our boat always at the ready in Limerick harbour, all the stores and everything, wine at the right temperature and a crew of four – so that we can go straight over to America, of course, as soon as we hear the Commies have taken over. Couldn't you come and stay with us? Oh do, such a pretty house and real steaks, not that you know what that means to people who've been living in England.'

She had blonde curls (dyed, Agatha thought) which bounced beside her face as she talked. Her face was roundly pretty though she must have been well into her fifties and wore rather a lot of whitish powder.

'I want to know so much. Why am I doing all the talking? I want to know whether you're happy here. Is there a beautiful peasant girl or have you turned queer like everyone else these days? Do talk to me, Orlando, you're being so terribly reserved.'

Orlando was laughing, but when he began to speak Agatha could not hear what he was saying, and being anyway afraid she might overhear something about herself she turned away and tried to concentrate on what Miss Bates was saying to Mr Becker.

Mr Becker was a little old man wearing a blazer, white trousers and a silk scarf. Everyone knew that he was very rich and owned a bank and had lawsuits running in several countries to try and straighten out his financial arrangements with his two grasping ex-wives. He took Agatha over to meet his present wife, who had long hair like Veronica Lake and very red lips and nails.

'Ralph's always worried because I never meet anyone of my own age,' she said. 'But I think older people have so much more depth.'

She was twenty-five and Agatha thought she ought not to be married to Mr Becker, and even when her otherwise dull eyes brightened at the mention of her two-year-old son Agatha was not prepared to forgive her, and preferred the Austrian princess who was certainly seventy and slept no more than three hours a night, she told Agatha, 'on my travelling camp-bed – I take it with me wherever I go – at six o'clock I have my cold bath, spend two hours writing my letters, then I'm ready for anything ... ' She lived half in St Moritz and half in Portofino – or perhaps that was Pierino, who had trouble with his liver and was married to Mimi who was an American heiress and had been a top Paris model and had a headache – and perhaps the Austrian princess lived half in Kitzbühel and half in Venice.

'I saw you in your cradle,' Penelope Waring said. 'You were only a few months old. I was so jealous I remember I nearly scratched your darling mother's eyes out. You're sitting next to Guy at lunch, you must tell him everything so that he can tell me afterwards; important things you must repeat because he's not very clever, but talk to him all the time and not to horrible Max on your other side because he's an international currency smuggler and not at all suitable for a young girl to know.'

But horrible Max was not on her other side because she was sitting between Guy Waring and William Holmes himself. The Austrian princess was on their host's right, and talked a great deal, which was a relief to Agatha, who found him extremely alarming. He had a long greenish-white face which seemed half as wide as anyone else's and on it he wore a perpetual half smile which slid away into nothing up one side of his face. His pale brown hair was not long but it lay in large curls over his forehead, in the style of a man about town of the 1830s. The effect was elaborate and made Agatha wonder if one of the three silent Indo-Chinese boys who were serving the lunch applied curling tongs every morning. She thought she could imagine the unsmiling ceremony, the smell of singed hair and freshly made coffee.

By the stream she thought of it again.

'Or does he use rollers and a hairnet?' she asked Hal. 'And hairpins?'

'Who?' said Hal, who had been gazing at the waterfall and was unprepared for the question.

'Mr Holmes.'

'Oh. Oh sure, the whole lot. It's a big new thing. Bunny made him do it. He's a hairdresser.'

'Who's Bunny?'

'The Indo-Chinese boy. He's a hairdresser in Florence. I don't think he's too successful, though; it seems there are an awful lot of hairdressers in Florence. Did you see that bird in the big room where we went after lunch?'

'I don't think so.'

'A beautiful great thing made with paper, dark dark red; maybe you missed it, it's so dark in that room anyway, especially when you come in out of the sunlight. Bunny makes those, he's a very talented boy. William's been wonderful to him.'

'That's nice. I can't imagine Mr Holmes being kind.'

The questions he had asked at lunch had seemed motivated by so cold a curiosity.

'Have you seen the Pieros?' he had said.

'I don't think so,' she had answered, not certain who or what they were.

It was a bad answer.

The smile slithered up the side of his face. 'Art bores you, I expect. You have had it thrust at you after no sort of education. The English totally ignore the visual in their education, wouldn't you agree? But even you would have remembered the pregnant Madonna if you had seen her. You must get your father to drive you there. Can he see well enough to drive?'

'No, he doesn't drive.'

'He's very wise to live here. Don't you agree that this is a perfect place for a blind man to live?'

'I don't know. He's not really blind.'

'One has the smell of herbs and the sound of the nightingale, the feel of warm rock, the taste of the fig. What more could a blind man want?'

'Well, friends, I suppose,' said Agatha, disliking him extremely.

'You don't think he has those? Do none of us qualify? Miss Bates, now, certainly, she's a very close friend, wouldn't you say?'

'She's been very kind.'

'And now he's met another old friend, Mrs Waring. Had you met her before? They knew each other well in London, it seems, before the war. She's very social. Do you enjoy social life, parties?'

'No, not very much.'

'Have you a kind relation to bring you out, present you at Court and so on? Your mother's dead, isn't she?'

'Yes.'

'And your uncle is also a widower.'

'Yes, his wife died years ago, when their son was born,' said Agatha, wondering why he should know so much about her.

'Then who is going to chaperone you in London?'

'Good heavens, nobody. I mean, nobody bothers about that sort of thing any more.'

'Don't they? I had heard it was all coming back. My informants must have been wrong. You don't care for that sort of thing? It's all very shallow and trivial, isn't it? I chose a very different life myself, but then I had the misfortune to be intelligent, which is not acceptable among the English upper classes.'

'Isn't it?' said Agatha, trying hard to imply that she knew nothing about such categories.

'Of course not. England is the most philistine country in the world. And now that it seems to be settling down to be a second-rate Scandinavia it will no doubt also be the dullest. And yet there is something about the English spring. I still have an occasional yearning for the spring at Madingly.'

'Where is Madingly?'

'In Sussex,' he answered rather shortly.

'Those wonderful pictures you have of it,' broke in the Austrian princess helpfully. 'To me it seems the dream English country house, the mellow Georgian stone, the cricket on the lawn.'

'I suffered terribly through cricket,' said William Holmes, looking appeased.

'Did you spend your childhood there?' asked Agatha, politely.

'Practically,' said William Holmes, and did not elucidate.

'You must see his pictures of it,' said the Austrian princess. 'So beautiful.'

'In the spring I must admit it was rather heavenly. Those lime walks. But I'm terribly glad to have got away from all that. In Italy one can be quite classless, don't you agree? The locals have no idea who one is.'

'I don't think anyone ever has any idea who I am, even me,' said Agatha. 'But I suppose you can behave more as you like in a foreign country because there's an accepted role for the mad Englishman, especially in Italy.'

'You think we can get away with anything by pretending to be Lord Byron?' said William Holmes. 'But imagine swimming in the Grand Canal, and in those days, when I'm sure everything was thrown into it. He used to send his gondola on ahead,' he explained to the Austrian princess, 'after a late night, and swim after it. Perhaps he was too drunk to care about the sewage.' And then he had been drawn by the Austrian princess into a detailed discussion about the sanitation in Venice, with which she seemed to be intimately concerned, and Agatha had been able to turn to Guy Waring and say, rather breathlessly because she was anxious to start a conversation with him before William Holmes should speak to her again, 'You know, it's very interesting for me to meet you because I hardly ever seem to meet anyone who knew my mother.'

'She was very beautiful,' he said, the words popping out like cherry-stones from under his little fair moustache. 'But tricky. Always on edge. Edgy, I think you could have called her.'

She was like me, thought Agatha.

'Always had a lot of admirers,' he popped. 'Used to play them off against each other. They gathered round like flies. Broke a lot of hearts in her day.'

'I think my younger sister Imogen's going to be rather like that.'

'Oh. Bit of a vamp, is she? Let's see now, whose daughter was she? Robin Barwick, was it?'

'No, no, she's my sister. My mother was only married twice. I've got two half-brothers older than me, and then Imogen my sister.'

'Stupid of me. We used to see a lot of them. Orlando stopped with us when he first came to London. Old King, who brought him up, was my tutor at Cambridge. He was a great companion for Penelope, Orlando I mean, when he first came. She introduced him to a lot of people. We were very fond of him. Awful tragedy, his knocking himself up like that in the bombing. Penelope always said it was some kind of guilt, you know, that made him do it, I've forgotten what for, I mean what the guilt was for, but no doubt she'd remember. Rotten thing anyway. Great loss to the country, politically, of course; could have been Prime Minister in time, I always said, but for that fellow Churchill dragging us into the war. Better than those maniacs they've got at the moment. My God, when I think of the Empire, don't you know?'

Down by the stream Agatha said to Hal Newman, 'I don't really like those sort of people.'

'You mean you don't like William?'

'Oh, William I don't understand at all. Except that he makes me think art must be something thoroughly disagreeable and useless. No, I meant all those others.'

'Oh the others.' He was crowned with mildness, cross-legged under his tree. 'They're quaint.'

As the time drew near for his departure to England Orlando made an effort to abandon himself to the course of events. He felt a strong reluctance to leave Lecceto, but having decided to do it he was prepared to let himself be controlled by the airline ticket which lay in the drawer of his writing-table.

He had brought a few pieces of furniture with him from France – two big elaborate Provençal cupboards, a round pearwood table and six good chairs to put round it – but apart from that he had had a certain amount made by a local carpenter, an intelligent and morose craftsman with whom he had established a friendship and who had made him several chests and tables out of a variegated blond nutwood, and it was in the drawer of one of these that he kept the ticket. The drawer was hard to pull in and out; it needed greasing with a candle-end. That was one of the many small tasks from which idleness or lack of concern had kept him. The table was near the window in his bedroom, which was otherwise rather dark. He had kept the small windows which were in the house as he found it, adding only one or two more of the same size. He walked with bare feet across the dark pink unpolished tiles, which were slightly uneven, and sitting down to wrestle with the awkward drawer could see out of the window the small empty shrine, the pear among the vines and the infinite distance. He hoped Agatha was appreciating it all. He hoped she realized that she was very lucky. There must be very few girls of her age, with the minute English travel allowance, who had such luck. Of course young people simply accepted everything. Every morning when he was in London he walked.

Without bothering any more about checking the time on his ticket, he went downstairs and found her sitting on the terrace, hunched over a book of Italian verbs.

'I hope you'll be all right while I'm away,' he said, looking down at her with a slight frown.

'Of course I will be,' she said, without looking up.

'I forgot really to ask you whether you …' He hesitated. 'Whether you're enjoying yourself. I mean, I don't know whether you share my feeling about this place.'

'Oh yes.' She looked at him with astonished eyes. 'I do.'

Hoping she was not misinterpreting his look of slightly embarrassed gratification, she went on, 'I shall miss sleeping here awfully, but I'm certainly going to spend most of the day here when I'm not in Siena. I hope you won't stay away too long.' She spoke faster than usual for fear her shyness should stop her. 'I bet you'll get all involved in everything and not want to come back. I do hope you won't. Do hurry back so we can go on living here like this.'

'Oh I'll be back,' he said. 'I shan't want to stay.'

Conrad Field in the spring of 1951 had lost the lankily youthful aspect which had lasted well into his middle age. He was sixty-one, and had come to look heavier, and a little thicker round the waist; but his dark hair was grey only at the sides and he walked like a much younger man.

Every morning when he was in London he walked in St James's Park with his black labrador bitch Jessie. He walked from his flat near Queen Anne's Gate to the House of Lords to collect his mail and to exercise Jessie. Jessie was an excellent gundog and his constant companion. She was the great-granddaughter of old Janet who used to lie in the side entrance lobby at Mount Sorrel in 1932, snoring and smelling in her basket, thumping her tail once or twice as Orlando passed through on his way to see his dear friend Miss McLeod, the governess. At that time Orlando had not yet met Conrad, who was away in India, on a commission to advise the Indians how to reform their constitution. Jessie had almost as good a nose as old Janet had had in her prime, and a much better temperament.

'Jess!' She was at heel at once, as if the thought of chasing the ducks had never even crossed her mind. 'Good dog.' Walking to work. Luck, he thought, a blessing, a privilege;

we shall learn to appreciate the value of work in twenty years' time, when the technological age gives us idleness and we find it a curse.

When he was alone, he had a habit of almost continuously addressing himself to some imaginary figure: it was the form his thinking took. The figure was changeable, would often change, in fact, as the internal monologue continued, and had no significance except as a focusing point for Conrad's reflections. It was likely to be the person he had last seen, or else the person he expected to see next, and was usually the recipient of confidences which would certainly not have been made face to face. So he could imagine himself talking to a colleague on the Industrial Reconstruction Committee of the Conservative Party, a meeting of which he was to attend later in the day; and the words which came into his mind were half unspoken and half muttered, sometimes to the surprise of passers-by.

So he said, 'Work,' as he walked through the park, 'work.' Exercising one's trained abilities, he thought, like Jess on a good day when the birds are coming over fast. We shall get more of it too, he told his imaginary interlocutor, and soon, before it's too late. The government can't last much longer, with Bevan and Wilson gone. Sixty-one's not old for a politician, I'm fit, thank God, I'll have Mount Sorrel to go home to, rest, restore my sense of proportion. I've got things better organized there in the house at last.

There came a familiar form of mental discomfort presaging the rise to the level of conscious thought of the idea of Henry, his son, who did not go to Mount Sorrel very often in spite of the staff difficulties having been overcome; but because it was a fine morning and he was in an optimistic frame of mind he did not allow himself to think about his baffling son and said, 'Orlando,' aloud so as to redirect his thoughts, 'Orlando,' in a speculative tone.

Jessie looked up at him.

'Good dog,' he reassured her, wondering what would have become of Orlando. It's a long time, he thought. I was very fond of him, you see, he told his imaginary listener, I took some kind of pride in him, I don't know why. I suppose he was my protégé, I brought him on a lot. He was very young to do as well as he did, but talented, you see, and so extraordinarily likeable, that was the thing. Good judgement, too. He changed, got spoilt I suppose, too ambitious. He lost his touch really, lost his sense of values. It could have been Judith's influence, I think I did advise him against marrying her.

The discomfort recurred, because Judith was his sister and of course he had appreciated and admired her good qualities at the same time as finding her less good ones hard to understand. I am not a coward, I will name things, he thought. 'Adultery,' he muttered. 'Lunacy.' Most nights before he fell asleep to the sound of Jessie's gentle breathing from the basket on the other side of his room – she never got on to his bed – Conrad thought, Into Thy hands, O Lord, I commend my spirit. Judith had not commended her spirit into God's hands. I will not judge, he thought, walking a little faster. Why is it harder not to judge where one's own family is concerned? It ought to be the other way round.

'Jess?' He turned. She was sitting a few yards behind him, her ears apologetically drooping, so that her domed forehead looked even smoother than usual. They had reached the entrance into Parliament Square and she knew it was time for him to put on her lead.

Orlando travelled by train to Bath. The train was late. Conrad and Imogen were waiting on the platform in the light of a late May evening. Orlando had been sitting in a carriage near the back of the train and by the time they saw him he was already on the platform, his suitcase at his feet, looking round for them. He can't see us, they both thought, hurrying towards him.

He saw them as they came nearer, the watery light striking them low, from behind the train, and in his turn was seized with pity. He did not know why, but the feeling was so strong that he bent to pick up his suitcase so as not to meet their eyes, momentarily possessed by some sort of intense distress, that they were so familiar and so strange, that Conrad had aged, that Imogen was fifteen and almost entirely unknown to him: he could not account for the feeling but it made him long to be somewhere else, to avoid contact, but it was impossible, and he had to pick up his suitcase, face them, say, 'Ah!' and 'Well!', shake Conrad's hand, kiss Imogen's cheek. And then, walking along the platform, he realized how pleased he was to see Conrad, really absurdly pleased, grinning all over his face in fact, to see Conrad his friend and former brother-in-law, patron in some ways, whom at different times he had admired, been mystified by, differed from, and in the end admired again, without hoping to understand.

'Good of you to meet me.'

'I'm delighted you've come at last. We put it all down to Agatha. We find we all do what Agatha tells us.'

'I suppose you're right. I suppose it was Agatha.'

'Of course it was.' Imogen gave a slight hop beside him on the stairs down from the platform, and laughed rather suddenly. He found he still could not look at her.

'My new car,' said Conrad. It was a Rover, and did not look new. 'Not too bad on petrol. That's one's chief

preoccupation these days of course. I'm afraid you'll notice
the way we all talk about the shortages, it has a disastrous
effect on conversation. Never mind, we hope to change all
that soon, when we get back.'

They drove out of Bath.

'We're all gathering for the weekend,' said Conrad. He
looked pleased. He had always liked the idea of the family
occasions at Mount Sorrel. 'Stephen and Jane are here
already, Henry's arriving in time for dinner, and Paul and
Serena are coming tomorrow.'

Henry did not arrive in time for dinner, but telephoned
halfway through the meal to say that he could not be there
until the following morning.

'Henry's movements are always a little obscure,' Conrad
explained impersonally.

Stephen, Conrad's nephew and Orlando's former stepson, had turned into the kind of adult one could have
foreseen: in fact, Orlando thought, one would always be
able to foresee everything about Stephen. He was probably
running the business perfectly well, if without much imagination. Orlando was predisposed in his favour, as against
Paul, who had been a difficult boy. He wondered how old
Stephen was, and reminded himself that he should have
known, not only because he had once been his stepson but
because, by a turn of events so long unknown to them all
that after its discovery they had unconsciously consigned
it again to the realms of improbability, Stephen and Paul
were Orlando's half-brothers. Their father Leonard had
in the far-off and scarcely imaginable days of his student
youth also been the father of Orlando, a fact rendered
even more hazy in its application to real life in that it had
never been known to Leonard himself. In view of their
complicated but undoubtedly close connection, Orlando

did not like to admit his ignorance as to Stephen's age, but calculated that he certainly could not be more than thirty, although his mannerisms were those of a much older man. His wife matched him in this respect. She was quite pretty and quite pleasant and Orlando thought her quite uninteresting. Somewhere upstairs there was a baby, somewhere near Godalming a house, with a garden that was incredibly improved even in the year or two since they had moved in; or so Stephen assured him, and his aspect was very far from being that of a liar.

'What fun to see old Paul,' Stephen said, laughing as if the prospect were funny rather than fun. 'I haven't seen him for a long time. How's the glamorous Serena? We saw her photograph in one of the glossies the other day, didn't we, darling? What was it, *Tatler* or something?'

'Yes, she looked marvellous,' said Jane. 'Some gorgeous dress. Quite made me wish my father was a tycoon.'

'She has super clothes,' said Imogen in her soft, rather breathy voice.

'Daintry's an amusing fellow, the father,' said Conrad. 'I want you to meet him while you're here.'

But Orlando was looking at Imogen. Conrad was talking about Daintry, Stephen and his wife had put on identical expressions of disapproval, and Orlando watched Imogen, who had flushed a little as she had spoken and was now looking down at her plate. She had come away from her boarding school for the weekend as a special concession in order to see her father. She was wearing a rather tight black jersey, tucked into a black skirt which came well below her knees and was held in round the waist by a broad shiny black belt. These would be what she would consider sophisticated clothes. On the black jersey she had pinned a brooch which he recognized, a circle of pearls which had been given to her as a christening present by her godfather Robin Barwick, a soldier with a fair moustache and a foolish laugh who was possibly her real father. He had no idea what had become of Robin Barwick. She also wore on her little finger a small signet ring which had been Judith's, a cornelian mounted simply in gold. He thought it was the only sort of ring a girl as young as that could wear, and inwardly commended her taste, since she must presumably have some of Judith's other jewellery. When she looked up again from her plate he smiled at her and she smiled back, flushing again, and he saw that she would be a born victim of men for ever and he wondered what in the world he could do to help her.

'Have you met Mr Daintry?' he asked her. 'What did you think of him?'

'I thought he was fabulous,' she said. 'I really did. I thought he was someone who could be really, really kind.'

He almost groaned aloud. Because of course she would have to be terribly stupid as well. Probably she really was Robin Barwick's daughter, in which case it would be inherited. Out of some blind selfishness, he thought, attacked by the same distress he had felt on the station platform, out of some thoughtless indulgence or instinct or God knows what the hell we thought we were doing – if indeed it was me and not Robin Barwick – out of some foolishness we made this creature – or Robin Barwick did. We all had good physiques after all, even if some of our minds could have done with improvement (Robin Barwick's that's to say). We launched her and left her, and she droops her ears like the labrador bitch seeking approval, hoping for love, the truth just dawning on her that she's physically desirable, that is to say wildly attractive, and behind this extraordinary fact she herself somewhere cowers without the faintest idea of what to do about anything and wants to be a model and will sleep with anybody out *of* desire to please and will be treated badly because she's so foolish and will cry spoilt tears and blur the big green eyes and blotch the smooth cheeks. I must talk to Agatha. I know nothing about young girls. Now Agatha, he already addressed her in his imagination, what in Heaven's name are we going to do about Imogen?

It was this disquiet which disturbed his sleep, not the brief description which Conrad and Stephen gave him of the situation in Logan Holdings, nor the much longer conversation which he had with Conrad about political affairs. As to the business, he was suspending judgement until he had spoken to Paul, and perhaps also to Daintry; and he found to his surprise a similar reserve in his reaction to Conrad's exposition of what had happened in English politics since the war. He was, as always, impressed by Conrad, but distance seemed to have given him so much detachment that, clearly and analytically though Conrad stated his case, Orlando found himself bearing in mind what might be the opposite arguments and privately assuming a position somewhere between the two points of view. This was disconcerting because it was not at all what used to happen in the old days.

'One thing's clear anyway,' he said. 'The sooner you yourself are back in office the better.'

'Certainly,' said Conrad, smiling. 'There's nothing more depressing than a long period in Opposition when you've had the fun and satisfaction of being in power, though of course one complained of the hard work, and the ties, and the lack of liberty; and of course I was glad of a rest, but a year or two would have done me. Five years is too long, especially when you've got to watch the dreary spectacle we've been submitted to lately. But what about you? Wouldn't you ever come back?'

Orlando shook his head. 'I've got much too far away from it all. Besides, my health's still likely to collapse at any minute. And then, you know, I could never get the conviction back. I've got outside the framework, if you know what I mean.'

'Yes, I do know. And I'm in it. You used to be in it, you used to know as well as I did why one was doing this sort of thing, what the principles were. In fact you were more involved than I was because it was I who left the Government when I became doubtful about its foreign policy. You thought it was one's duty to stay and get on with one's own particular job. We quarrelled in fact, if I remember.'

Orlando nodded. 'And I was wrong. Which gave me a distaste for the whole business. Perhaps it's just that I can't trust myself. I get too excited and then I make mistakes. You're much better at it than I am, and you have much more faith in the whole structure that you're maintaining. I've lost that. Tell me, what about Imogen? Is she all right?'

'Yes, I think so.' Conrad found himself hurt by the casual phrase which had preceded Orlando's change of subject – 'I've lost that.' He would have liked to talk more about it, but seeing that Orlando evidently thought the subject closed he did not like to go back to it. We shall have time, he thought, I must not hurry him, he's out of the way of talking intimately, we shall talk more later: already his mind was pitching itself at its most alert in answer to Orlando's; there was so much to talk about, he found. 'Imogen,' he said. 'Yes, I think she's all right. She's a frivolous creature of course, as you see. She wants to be a model. They've become respectable since your young day. They're called models rather than mannequins, and they earn an awful lot of money for a year or two and then they marry million-aires. I think she'll do very well at it.'

'She seemed rather helpless,' said Orlando. 'Does she do well at school?'

'She's rather short of brains. Miss Clayton's fond of her though. She's very dependent on Agatha, I think. It's prob-ably not a bad thing for her that Agatha is away for a bit. She'll have to learn to stand on her own feet. Agatha, by the way, didn't get on with Miss Clayton at all. I don't know whether she's told you?'

'A little,' said Orlando, smiling at the recollection of what Agatha had said about Miss Clayton.

Conrad did not smile.

'Agatha doesn't seem to be able to accept authority,' he said. 'She's got quite a good brain but a lot of foolish ideas. She'll no doubt grow out of them. She's determined to be a doctor, as you know, and I can see no objection to her trying it though I doubt whether she'll see it through. It's a long training. I've been quite worried about her at differ-ent times. She's got a rebellious side which can be quite tricky.'

'I can't thank you enough for all you've done for them, I can't even try,' said Orlando. He felt an extraordinary pleasure in the idea that he understood Agatha better than Conrad did. 'I expect a few months in Italy will do her good, give her a bit of a breathing space after leaving school.' Unconsciously he slightly emphasized the slow-ness with which he rose from his chair, so as to underline the reason for his having left so many of his fatherly duties to Conrad. 'I must go to bed, I'm not used to so much activity. I shall look forward very much to seeing Henry again tomorrow.'

'Henry has his own peculiar charm,' said Conrad, also getting to his feet. 'And can be exasperating. They're hard to understand, this generation.'

He looked sad.

'When you were my age,' said Orlando, 'and I was about Henry's age I suppose, or rather younger, you were incredibly kind to me.'

'You were different,' said Conrad. 'And the gap was not so great.' But he smiled.

It was perhaps because it was true that he was not used to so much activity that Orlando slept so badly that night. When he did fall asleep, his dreams woke him. He dreamed about Judith, which he had not done for many years, and about Wood Hill, the house up the valley where they had lived, and over and over again he walked up to the front door and saw the furniture scattered in disarray and the white peacock on its side on the stone floor with its stuffing spilling from its neck and Imogen crying beside it and Judith on the stairs, white with anger, shouting at him, and he woke to hear a voice saying, 'Judith, Judith,' in a tone of unbearable grief and reproach, and recognized it as his own.

When the light began to show through his curtains he got up and dressed and went downstairs, through a house whose familiarity was still that of a dream, or a memory recalled with that sudden unbidden clarity which is sharper than immediate reality. There was a certain excitement as well as disturbance in his mind: this was not that morning despair which he had recognized with such pain when it was named by King in his diaries.

He walked through the hall, which smelt of stone and perhaps some kind of floor-polish: a smell he had never come across anywhere else. It was a grey but clear dawn, which invited him to open the door into the garden and to wonder if it was the weakening of his sight which had made his sense of smell keener or whether it was merely that a particularly heavy dew had brought out the smell of damp earth and spring. On the other side of the house, beside the path which led to the church, the balsam poplars must be opening their leaves: the aromatic smell was on the air. He walked across the lawn and into the park, then through a door in the wall on to the road which led up the valley towards Wood Hill. I'll go part of the way, he thought, I won't go right up to the house, not yet. All the same he would probably have done so had he not seen an obstacle on the road which as he approached closer turned out to be a car, of a rather untidy aspect, being pushed along the road towards him at some speed by a figure who was shouting, 'Now! Now! Try it now!' The car jerked violently, came towards Orlando in a series of decreasingly vigorous jolts, and stopped.

The young man who was standing in the middle of the road watching this attempt, and who was still a blurred figure to Orlando, said very loudly, 'Fuck!'

There was a thumping noise from the inside of the car and a girl's muffled voice said, 'I can't get out.'

The young man ignored this and began slowly to approach Orlando. 'Good heavens!' he said.

Orlando guessed that this must be Conrad's son Henry, but since he could not yet see his face he waited in silence.

'Hullo,' said Henry.

Orlando smiled.

'How amazing,' said Henry.

Orlando could now see his face, which chiefly struck him as thin. He could see some kind of similarity to the child's face he remembered, but would never have foreseen that Henry should have emerged as such an outstandingly bony young man. He looked more like Conrad than he had used to as a child, only every feature was thinner, his aquiline nose was consequently more hawklike and his eyes, which were dark, seemed larger.

When Orlando was quite certain that it was indeed Henry he said, 'Ah, Henry.'

'How amazing,' said Henry again, looking now slightly embarrassed. Orlando wondered whether he might be uncertain as to how to address him. Now that they were close he became aware that Henry was wearing a dinner jacket and smelt strongly of alcohol and tobacco.

'I arrived last night,' said Orlando. 'And not being able to sleep I thought I'd go for an early morning walk.'

'I see,' said Henry. 'It's certainly very early. That's why I was so surprised to see you.' He now began to fling himself with some volubility into explanations. 'We had to go to this thing in London. It was frightfully rude of me not to be here, we'd got involved, you know how it is. The car seems to have stopped, we thought we'd drive straight down afterwards, you know how one gets those ideas late at night. It keeps stopping unfortunately. I don't know if perhaps you could give me a hand, it only needs a push, I suppose it's the battery. The trouble is, it's fatal to stop, and Caroline wanted to comb her hair or something. I told her no one would be around when we arrived, though I was wrong of course because you were. I'm terribly sorry, that handle seems to have gone wrong too. There we are.' He opened the car door. The girl got out, looking cross. She was wearing a strapless black evening dress and her face, which was pretty though at this moment obviously not at its best, was tired and puffy round the eyes.

'I thought I was never going to get out,' she said. 'Like the man in the iron mask or something.' Her shoulders and the bare upper part of her bosom were beautiful. 'Shall I push and one of you put it into gear?' she said. 'I don't think I'm doing it right.' She too smelt of alcohol and tobacco, though in her case it was mixed with some rather exotic scent.

'Why not leave it here and walk?' suggested Orlando.

'No, no, that's just the sort of thing that infuriates Papa,' said Henry. 'Look, if you wouldn't mind sitting in it and if Caroline and I both push

'As a matter of fact I don't see awfully well. Why don't you and I push? We could get more speed up.'

'Well, shout at me when to do it then,' said Caroline. 'And you're not to get livid with me if I do it wrong. Whoops!' She staggered clumsily as she turned to get back into the car, but recovered herself and sat down in the driver's seat.

It occurred to Orlando that they were both rather drunk. He shut the car door for her and noticed that as she reached out to turn on the ignition she tossed back her blonde hair and showed a beautiful long line of profile and neck. It was a pity her mouth was so big.

'Right then,' said Henry.

They pushed. I'm supposed to have a weak heart, Orlando thought, but he did not say it because it did not seem very important. Henry was pushing the car with tremendous determination. They were running quite fast before he shouted, 'Now!' and this time the jerk was followed by a roar.

'Don't take your foot off!' he shouted, running to open the door and take Caroline's place in the driving seat.

When he had made sure that the engine was not likely to stop again he turned to Orlando and said, 'Could we offer you a lift?'

Caroline had already scrambled over on to the back seat where she lay with her eyes closed.

'I'm sorry about the windows,' said Henry.

They were indeed ill attached to the main body of the car, being removable side-screens which had lost most of what means of security they had ever had. The car was a four-seater MG and the roof was rather tattered too. Orlando could imagine that it might look better open. As he was thinking this Henry took the left-hand corner in the village street very fast and the right-hand door swung open with a clatter.

'Christ!' said Caroline but with irritation rather than alarm.

'I'm terribly sorry,' said Henry, leaning right over Orlando to close the door, though without stopping the car. 'That handle seems to be rather unreliable.'

'Look out!' said Orlando.

They bumped on to the grass verge.

'Oh sorry,' said Henry.

They bumped off again.

'I'll hold the door,' said Orlando.

'Thanks awfully,' said Henry, accelerating.

They swung into the entrance with a squeal of tyres, rattled down the drive and drew up with a jerk in front of the house. Henry jumped out and went back to kick the gravel over the deep ruts his wheels had made as he had braked.

'We might as well stay up till breakfast now, I suppose,' he said.

'Oh *bed!*' said Caroline.

'I should go and get a bit of sleep if I were you,' said Orlando. 'It's still quite early.' He was thinking that it might be better for Conrad not to see them until later, when with any luck they would be looking more respectable.

'Perhaps you're right,' said Henry. 'Come on, Caroline, we'll find you a bed.'

'Anything to bring?' Orlando offered politely.

'No,' said Caroline. 'He wouldn't let me go and collect my things. I'm going to have a terrible inferiority complex tomorrow, Henry, going to see the horses in this dress.'

'What horses?' said Henry.

'Aren't there some horses? I'm sure I remember feeding the horses. Perhaps they were dogs.'

'Jane will lend you some clothes.'

'I don't see why she should. Poor woman, an unknown girl arriving in the middle of the night pinching half her clothes. I'd be livid if it was me.'

'Perhaps Imogen could help,' said Orlando.

'Oh, is Imo here? How super,' said Caroline. She was following Henry up the stairs. 'Good night, good morning, *sweet* of you to help us,' she said to Orlando, smiling down at him.

Conrad woke as Henry and Caroline passed his bedroom door. He turned over in bed and looked across the room at Jess, who had not stirred. It can't have been anything then, he thought, wondering why he should have woken so early. He lay on his back, looking up at the ceiling and thinking that in a minute he would make a cup of tea.

In 1948 he had been on a semi-official fact-finding visit to South Africa. He had returned no more confident of that country's ultimate political future but laden with material goods unobtainable in England. His South African hosts had had an exaggerated idea of the rigours of life in austerity England and even now, three years later, remembered to send unsolicited parcels of buffalo butter and tinned pears. Embarrassed by their kindness, he had allowed himself to be guided into making purchases for himself which he would never have made had he been alone but which he felt sure would otherwise be added to the already substantial pile of presents. So such unlikely luxury items came into his possession as eight pairs of silk pyjamas, one of which he was now wearing. His embarrassment at the apparently inescapable self-indulgence had led him to make the purchases as hurriedly as possible, following his hostess obediently from counter to counter in the store to which she had taken him, and making assertions as to sizes and fittings which in most cases turned out later to have been quite inaccurate. The pyjamas, which were in a wide maroon and gold stripe, were far too big.

A big man in bigger pyjamas, he lay and looked at the ceiling, on which the pattern of light which came through the faded linen curtains showed that the sun was up. It was going to be a fine day. The realization gave him particular pleasure because Orlando and all the others were there and the narcissi were at their best.

'O God, give me patience and understanding,' he said.

This morning he felt that God quite possibly would give him patience and understanding, even as regards Henry, and there was no anguish in his prayer. Leaning over the side of his bed, he pressed a button on the mechanism which sat there on the floor emitting a rather ominous muffled ticking, and watched to see what would happen. Quite soon the faint sound of Geraldo's orchestra mingled with the ticking, grew louder and was accompanied by a hissing. Conrad smiled. He had set the machine to wake him rather later, and had not been certain as to the wisdom of overriding its pre-set pattern. He had not owned it for very long and it was a source of great satisfaction to him.

He watched it perform its cycle and pour the boiling water on to the prepared tea-leaves, and then when he had given the tea time to brew, he propped up his pillows and sat up to drink it, marvelling once more at the astonishingly good flavour and the quite excellent tone of the wireless.

His thoughts began to move clearly and smoothly. He could foresee that Orlando might not be easy to deal with over the question of Logan Holdings. At the time he had left England he had made over all his shares in Logan Holdings to Conrad, the idea being that Conrad would use the income to pay for the upbringing of Agatha and Imogen. It had not been possible to make the shares into a trust for the children because of the regulations about foreign residents owning English securities and Orlando had therefore made them a gift to Conrad, but Conrad had always considered that he held them only in trust, and he was determined that Orlando should decide what should be done with them. Strictly speaking, Conrad was the largest shareholder in Logan Holdings, but since in fact the larger part of his holding was formerly Orlando's, he was determined that Orlando should influence events as much as if he still owned what he used to own. He felt this the more strongly in that he had never approved of Orlando's decision to leave England. He understood that a man's way of life must be affected by his health, but that was all. He was unwilling to recognize that there had been other factors in Orlando's reasoning, and he was unwilling now to let Orlando abdicate from what he felt was his rightful position in the Logan Holdings negotiations. Stephen, Paul and Daintry all knew that Conrad's attitude towards the proposed takeover was dependent upon Orlando's. The trouble was that Orlando seemed to be unwilling to take up any attitude at all.

It's unnatural, thought Conrad, putting down his teacup on his bedside table and addressing an imaginary Orlando. A man can't suspend judgement for ever. Rightly or wrongly, with as many qualifications as one cares to make, one's got to come down on one side or the other about everything in the end. 'Good heavens, that's part of the fun, isn't it?' He pushed back his bedclothes rather abruptly, got out of bed and went to the window. He would go for a walk in the woods before breakfast, he thought, there was time to go up to the new plantations and back. Drawing the curtains, he looked down on to the drive in front of the house and saw Henry's car. So he had driven down late after all. Good. Excellent, in fact.

To the accompaniment of Geraldo, he crossed the room with a succession of side-steps vaguely Latin American in feeling, clasping his loose pyjamas round his waist and sending Jessie into what seemed to be an ecstasy of surprise and admiration.

'All right, Jess, all right, give me a moment to get dressed, you fool.'

Stephen walked up and down in the library with his hands in his pockets. 'The man's an adventurer,' he said.

Orlando wondered where he could have come across the prototype on which he was modelling himself: surely, he thought, a man of Stephen's age could only become so pompous and platitudinous by careful study.

'They think nothing of him in the City.'

Orlando wondered when Paul was due to arrive. He must at least be livelier.

'Daintry's not sound.'

Perhaps I could have talked like that once, thought Orlando. Perhaps it is not good to have become such an outsider. He thought of Lecceto and its far distances and a line in a translation from something Greek – 'The horses, the young horses, and the sea'. He did not know what it meant, or to what once familiar symbols it referred, but he held very clearly in his mind the great curl of the wave before it struck the sand and spread, and he thought of the solid beat of the galloping hooves on the firm sand, which would be darker where the wave was receding and where the hooves would splash as the horses verged upon the sea – and it seemed as if all this would drown the sound of Stephen's voice, which was explaining that the City thought Daintry a bit 'hot', though technically he kept on the right side of the law.

Orlando made an effort to concentrate.

'A lot of highly respected figures in the financial world have had that reputation on their way to their first million,' he said. 'It's soon forgotten as long as they succeed.'

'Oh quite,' said Stephen. 'The question is, will he go on succeeding?'

Come not to me again, thought Orlando; but say to Athens,

Timon hath made his everlasting mansion
Upon the beached verge of the salt flood;
Who once a day with his embossed froth
The turbulent surge shall cover: thither come,
And let my grave-stone be your oracle.

He remembered Agatha declaiming by the vacant shrine. Oh Lord, he thought, I don't really belong here at all.

'He made his money out of scrap then?' he said, standing up and walking to the window, so that their paths almost crossed for a moment.

'War surplus, you're supposed to call it,' said Stephen, reaching the bookcase and turning briskly on his heel. 'Only he keeps rather quiet about that now. How Conrad can take him seriously beats me.' He quickened his pace in his irritation. Orlando stood with his back to the window watching him. 'Do you know one of the things he used to do immediately after the war? Buy up country estates for their timber. That's how we first came across him in the furniture business. Wouldn't you think that was the sort of thing which would make Conrad dismiss a man as an uncivilized rogue without waiting to hear any more? Yet for some unknown reason he's persuaded himself that that's the sort of person who ought to be encouraged. It's carrying broadmindedness to the point where it's beyond a joke if you ask me. Still, no doubt you'll make up your own mind.'

'Surely he's got to be taken seriously if he's already bought up a third of the shares?'

'We can cope with that,' said Stephen. 'I've already drafted a circular to the shareholders advising them against selling any more. I hope to get the board to pass it this week.'

'And Paul of course is in favour of the deal going through?'

'Of course. Paul wants to get back in. He and I can't work together; it's not unusual with brothers, I believe. It was a very good thing he left when he did, otherwise there'd have been an explosion. Of course we're the best of friends outside the office.'

Agatha wondered whether Orlando ever thought of her, whether perhaps with Conrad on one of those walks through the woods when Conrad expounded his views on this or that subject, waving his walking-stick to emphasize a point, stopping to inspect a young plantation or watch a hare lope across the ride ahead of him, whether on such a walk, over mud and last year's leaves, the sun filtering through the larches and a couple of squirrels scattering – all of it as familiar to Agatha as her own hands, which were thicker at the base of the fingers than she really liked, or as her rather bony knees, with their scars of childhood scrapes – whether then Orlando thought of her with anything like the kind of immediacy she herself felt when she was away from the few people she loved, or whether she crossed his mind, if at all, in some kind of quite abstract way, like any other thought.

Sitting with her chin on her knees on the grassy terrace at Lecceto with the tower house behind and the great distance before her, she tried to understand that in fact he would be unable to picture her present situation with much exactitude because what she was seeing, which was peculiarly clear to her, would have been beyond the scope of his eyes. This was something she found hard to imagine. It was evening, and the sky was extraordinary. She had been sitting there for some time and, having exposed herself to the totality of what was before her eyes, was trying now to observe the particulars more minutely. Far to the right, the hills were dark mauve, the sky above them the blue of watered silk, banded with dark raspberry cloud and spiked by the black cypress on a nearer hill. When she looked to her left the farm below her was pinkish orange, and above it was the moon in a clear blue sky. In front of her the most distant hills, clearly defined though very far away, were dark grey-ish brown, the colour of a mouse's fur. But already the sky on her right, which had been so pale, had turned to ridges of orange, brown and a deeper though still watery blue, and the hills below it had densified and darkened. Now the greens in the middle distance were stronger, while the nearer farm was an infinitely faded red-gold, under the moon. The sky about the moon was still pale blue, combed now with a few strands of mild violet cloud, while opposite Agatha the great orange stain left by the setting sun had deepened and the pale blue-green turned to yellow, the hills beneath darkening from mouse colour to a sombre purple or plum. Momentarily the middle distance had the look of something seen through deep water, while in the sky the red, lemon and black shredded away into darker grey, and twilight succeeded the sunset.

She felt like a laboratory worker gazing at the experiment which fulfilled the hopes of years. This feeling of wakeful certainty seemed likely to be the highest happiness; then likely too, of course, to be what Orlando was after; but already as she grasped it the certainty had gone. What had she meant? Whatever Orlando was after he did not seem to have found it, and she was cold, and had talked too much to Hal Newman, whom she had met in Siena by chance and had obviously, now that she came to think of it, bored to tears at lunch, burdening him with pointless details of her childhood and youth – how childish and how youthful – but then she thought again, I do know something, but nine minutes out of ten it escapes me.

She stood up quickly and turned back towards the house. She was going to be late for dinner with Theodora Bates. Bother Theodora Bates. There would be a letter from Henry. It would say, I am arriving tomorrow, Caroline has gone, she has exploded, spontaneous combustion, she has burst into a million fragments. He would be there when she came into the room. He would stand up and hold out his arms. She wou'd approach, be enfolded. No, she would hesitate at the door. Hal Newman would appear beside her. Henry would turn white, and still she would hesitate, to make him suffer. She groaned aloud in shame for her thoughts but immediately forgave herself and began the scene all over again in her mind, at the same time hurrying into the little car, waving to Nella – 'See you tomorrow' – smiling. I am well, I am pretty, thick Florentine bracelet on my sunbrowned arm. The little engine roared and the Fiat bumped over the stones. I can drive, speak Italian, do almost anything; beneath and behind my exasperating weakness is all the strength in the world.

There was no letter from Henry, but there was one from Paul: 'I had forgotten how well I remembered him. He is amazingly like he used to be and amazingly different. I never saw him after he was hurt because I was away in the Army, so I hadn't seen him since the early days of the war when he was completely unapproachable, because he was so angry with everyone for proving him wrong about the necessity of war and with our poor mother for going out of her mind (at least it looked like anger) – so really my recollections of him are rather of the years just before the war when I was in my impressionable adolescence and when from being quite a jolly person to have about (oh, I ought to be honest and admit I was always embarrassed by his relationship with my mother – he was too young – she made herself ridiculous – I know I always felt that really) – anyway he did turn into a heavy-handed step-father. It was odd, that – I think he may have been more or less carrying out Mama's instructions – she always believed in men being authoritarian. Anyway the result was that I did dislike him quite considerably and I had forgotten that until I saw him again. And now of course all the hostility has gone, on both sides. But, my dear, a lot else has gone. I think you underestimate his decline. We went down to Mount Sorrel on Sunday – Stephen and Jane pretty stiff, Henry whiter than ever with *la belle* Caroline, Conrad with his grieved look on because H. hadn't told him he was bringing C., Imo out from school on her best behaviour – and there sat Orlando, polite, much more romantic-looking than in his sleek younger days, but a million miles away – I think he's a deeply and hopelessly disillusioned man – I don't believe he cares in the slightest whether any one of us lives or dies. I'm taking him to meet Daintry this week and I'll do my best to win him over to our side, but I think we're wasting our time. He'll stay uncommitted because he hasn't got anything to commit himself *with*. You won't like my saying this but I think you should be warned. Don't make him one of your lost causes. He's not worth it.'

Agatha and Miss Bates were sitting opposite each other in Miss Bates' dark dining-room, bowls of soup before them. Agatha had asked Miss Bates if she might read Paul's letter, because it was likely to contain news of Orlando, but since she frowned as she read it Miss Bates did not ask her what it contained but said instead in a helpful tone of voice, 'Flora's definitely not in whelp, it's a hellish bore.'

'Oh dear,' said Agatha abstractedly.

'All that ghastly drive to Rome for nothing. I bet it was the dog's fault, too inbred if you ask me. I thought as much at the time. A typically epicene Roman pug, I thought.'

'Aren't there any nearer suitors?'

'I wanted this particular cross. It should have been good.'

'What a pity. You'll have to try again. Couldn't you make him come up here this time? Perhaps he'd pull himself together in the country air.'

'I suppose I could try,' said Miss Bates doubtfully.

'Orlando seems to be all right,' said Agatha. 'But I don't think Paul thinks he's going to be on his side about the business.'

'Is that a pity do you suppose?'

Agatha shook her head non-committally. 'Paul's often wrong.'

'But I thought he was the one you were supporting?'

'He is, but he's probably wrong.'

'Then why support him?'

'I usually do. Perhaps it's because no one else does. Besides, he is my brother.'

'So is Stephen.'

'He doesn't need me.'

He was a weedy little shit, Orlando thought, as might have been expected, but attractive, which might have been expected too.

They were sitting in the Ritz, waiting for Daintry. Paul had ordered drinks. There was a little table with bowls of crisps and olives on it between their gilt chairs. They were on a large raised platform between potted palms and pillars, observing the entrance.

'You must do something for Agatha,' Paul was saying.

At Mount Sorrel Orlando had liked him better, if merely in contrast to Stephen.

'You must be a father to her.'

He was certainly free with his advice.

'You won't believe this but she comes to me for help.'

Orlando didn't believe it.

'Me! I mean, Christ, if anyone needs help, I do. You just don't know what a cock-up I've made of my life. And yet she asks my advice. She depends on me. Of course that's fine for me, it's very good for me in fact, but it doesn't help her much. She needs someone – you know, a real person, not a shadow.'

This was a new line. At Mount Sorrel he had been confident. Now he seemed to be asking for pity, hinting at secret disasters. It was suddenly completely familiar to Orlando, so much so that he gave an inappropriate smile and offended Paul.

'You've no idea what I'm talking about.'

'I was thinking how little people change. I'm sorry. Go on.'

But Paul's eyes, which were a startlingly pale blue in Judith's thin face, were angry, and his mouth had turned down at the corners. According to Conrad, the Army had made a man of him.

'As a matter of fact,' said Orlando, in a conciliatory tone of voice, 'I'm really delighted to see you doing so well. You forget I haven't seen you since the days when you'd just left school and were supposed to be a bit of a problem to us all. Now I find you thoroughly established in the world – a beautiful wife – highly interesting job.'

'She is beautiful, isn't she?' said Paul, responding at once. 'Agatha doesn't really like her, at least she doesn't think she's a good thing for me. She thinks I don't realize how vain and snobbish and shallow she is. She doesn't understand that that's just why I like her.'

Orlando was not sure how to answer, but was saved from having to do so by Paul's suddenly rising to his feet as a tall man came through the door and walked towards them. Orlando could at first only make out that he was tall, and being used to the tricks which distance sometimes played on his eyes he momentarily suspended judgement as to how tall, but as he reached their table and held out his hand Orlando realized that his eyes had not deceived him and that Mr Daintry was enormous.

Paul called a waiter and without consulting Mr Daintry ordered him a double martini as a matter of urgency.

Mr Daintry grasped Orlando's hand, said, rather surprisingly, 'Hiya!' and sat down.

Apart from his immense height, he was fair, pink-faced, inclining to plumpness, and wore a bushy handle-bar moustache and a well-cut dark pin-striped suit.

'Super,' he said in a contented tone of voice.

He reached for his martini, said 'Cheers,' drained the glass, ordered another one all round and said, 'Conrad joining us?'

'No, he's not actually,' said Paul, rather flustered. 'I thought ... um ...'

'I like old Conrad,' said Dainty. 'Meg OK?'

'She's very well,' said Paul. 'She sent you her love.'

'Met my daughter yet, have you?' Daintry asked Orlando.

'I have indeed. She's very beautiful.'

'Super, isn't she? I still call her Meg sometimes though she's been Serena for two years now.'

'She changed her name while she was at the Monkey Club,' said Paul with satisfaction. 'From Margaret Rose.'

'Born a year or two after Princess Margaret,' said Daintry. 'Her mother was always reading about the little princesses. Simple creature, she was. Still is, as far as I know.' He laughed cheerfully. 'She was the boss's daughter. When I pushed the boss out she went too. Anyway when I started sending young Meg to posh schools she decided Margaret Rose was common and became Serena.' He gave another shout of laughter. 'I'm not complaining. That's exactly what I was paying for. Do you know I paid Lady Early twice her usual fee to make that girl a debutante? I'm not complaining about that either. She did a good job on her, eh, Paul?'

'Excellent,' said Paul.

'Bottoms up,' said Daintry, draining his glass again. 'What about a spot of lunch?'

He led the way into the restaurant. Orlando found himself smiling slightly as he followed, but when his glance happened to meet Paul's the smile was not returned.

Orlando had been thinking how negligible he and Paul
must appear as they were drawn along in the wake of the
vital force which preceded them. Daintry swept his glance
benignly over the half-empty room and moved as of right
to the best table near the window, stopping on the way to
clap on the back a man who looked like a senior Cabinet
Minister lunching with his mother and who flinched quite
considerably under the blow but returned Daintry's greeting with something like deference and introduced his
mother: she reached protectively for her handbag.

'One of my merchant banker friends,' Daintry said in
explanation as they sat down. 'He's terrified of me. I hope
you don't mind this old place. It's convenient for my office.
In fact I stay here quite a bit too.' A waiter in the grip of
a conditioned reflex had already opened a bottle of champagne. 'I got to like it in the war. Used to come here a lot
on leave with the boys. There was a chap in our bunch who
knew it before the war, used to bring us all here. I was in the
Raf, you know. Coastal Command.'

'You must have flown Shackletons,' said Orlando.

'And Sunderlands,' said Daintry. 'Decent old buses. We
were an awful bunch of roughs. Still, I made a few contacts.
Got several of the boys working for me now. They're a
good bunch. You had to learn to use your wits in those
days. The Air Vice-Marshal's a bit of a bind, but he looks
good on the paper.'

'He makes the tea very well,' said Paul.

'I don't like that, I don't like it at all, I never meant
him to make the tea,' said Daintry, looking embarrassed
and indeed quite downcast. 'It's really not on the cards
for him to be making the tea. I don't like it. I'm not at all
unconventional, you know,' he said to Orlando seriously.
'I'm a dyed-in-the-wool conservative traditionalist. I like

everything to be as it should be and in order. It's only quite a temporary arrangement for the Air Vice-Marshal to be making the tea. He offered to do it. There's no doubt he does it much better than the terrible old bag who was doing it before, but I'm not going to allow it to go on. He turned out not to have much of a head for figures, that's the trouble. Make a note of it, Paul. He must have a better office, a room to himself, even if he only makes the tea in it. We've got to have a proper respect for rank.'

'Right,' said Paul, nodding seriously.

'That's why I like Logan,' said Daintry to Orlando. 'You play by the rules in that set-up, that's why it's a logical step in my development to become involved. I want to consolidate my own affairs as well as bring some dynamism to yours – which I know bloody well I can do. I'm not a modest man, as Paul here will tell you, but I don't make false promises either.'

'This is what I haven't so far seen, the logic of it from your point of view,' said Orlando. 'You're already a public company yourself, we're going to be very expensive for you, and our interests and activities seem to be only marginally allied.'

'Let me explain,' said Daintry. 'Hang on a moment.' He turned to the waiter who was standing at his elbow and spoke to him quietly for a few moments before turning back to Orlando. 'You have to know your way around these days if you want a decent meal. There's still supposed to be rationing in this bloody country. I think you'll like what I've ordered. I'm a public company, yes, I'm not short of finance, I'm backed by two merchant banks who've been super to me; so you don't see the logic. The first point to make is that this is a personal thing. When Paul married my daughter and I began to hear a bit about Logan Holdings –

and when I met Conrad too, because we mustn't underestimate the charm of that man – well, then I began to get
interested. First of all it turned out I'd done a deal with
them back in '48 when I had some timber to dispose of.
Then I heard from Paul about his difficulties there and his
disagreements over the way the thing was being managed
and, you know, this is my life, the air I breathe – show me a
balance sheet and my old grey matter starts to hum – I'm a
financial wizard or I'm nothing, boy.' He gave a loud shout
of laughter and as suddenly became serious again. 'No, but
when I went into it I saw what was needed there. I'm not
running down the management, though I'd say it's been a bit
too conservative in the last few years. But this is something
I guess I know as much about as any man in the country
and that's property. The furniture retailing side of Logan
Holdings, Logan Furnishings, owns property in high streets
all over the country which is vastly undervalued and vastly
underdeveloped. When the Conservative Government gets
back into office and lifts some of the restrictions – which
they'll do, ask Conrad – there's going to be a building boom
in this country like nothing you've ever seen – and this is
my field. My first deal when I came out of the Raf was to
sell my office – I had a little estate agency – and lease it
back, and with the capital I went into war surplus and with
the capital from that I went into property. It's had to be
mainly Government offices so far because of the restrictions on building licences – boy, did the Government boob
when they decided to rent space instead of becoming property developers themselves! – but I've a tame architect who
can find the loopholes in any planning legislation they can
think up, and that's the kind of architect we need today,
believe me. He knows those bloody Acts better than the
people who drew them up. They've had to put in special

clauses because of us, but they're always too late. We've made our killing by the time they get on to us. He can tie those planning offices into knots. He's the only architect around who's a businessman as well. Now all I want Logan to do is to be ready to capitalize on its assets. I don't want to interfere with Logan Furnishings. That should remain separate, self-contained and autonomous, though there can be no objection to brightening one or two things up a little bit.' Mr Daintry paused for a moment as a huge steak was set in front of him, said 'Whacko!' and went on addressing himself to Orlando. 'I'm being completely frank with you. I want you to understand exactly what there is in it for Logan and exactly what there is in it for me. But more than that I want you to understand that this is a matter of personalities, it's not just a paper proposition, and that's why I've come out in the open. I'm not interested in the deal if it's going to be fought, because I want the firm as it is, with all its integrity and character. I want to work with that board of directors and none other.'

'I think you have a third of the shares,' said Orlando, seizing a pause in the flow of words.

'I have a third and I have my offer ready for the other shareholders, but I don't want to send it out without the board's approval. Conrad also has a third, quite a large part of which he holds on your behalf; it's Conrad's approval I want and it's clear to me he's not going to give it unless I get yours. You know Derek Faber?'

'Slightly.'

'Derek's about the most reputable merchant banker in the City as well as the shrewdest. I think it means something to Conrad that Derek's backing me to the extent he is. Have you been to their place in the City?'

'Not since before the war.'

'I love that place. Going into that dining-room with those family portraits and knowing that some of the biggest deals in the world have been done in that room over the last two hundred years. And they're all gents and they're all hot as hell. Super!' He gave his jolly shout of laughter.

Paul smiled proudly. He had been sitting in attentive silence, completely ignored by Daintry but watching him closely and from time to time smiling his approbation. When Daintry turned to speak to him he was all deference.

'I meant to telephone Banks,' said Daintry, 'to tell him I didn't want those phoney shares he was trying to sell me.'

'I'll go and do it now,' said Paul, getting to his feet. 'He'll just about be back from lunch.'

Daintry merely nodded and turning back to Orlando said, 'Ever gamble on the Stock Exchange?'

'Very seldom.'

'Nor do I. Waste of time. I'm a gambler by nature though, I'm afraid. Do you know this friend of Paul's who runs these gambling parties?'

'No, I don't.'

'I'll take you along some time. They're super parties even if you don't gamble. He does the whole thing in style. In fact I think there's one tonight. We'll check up when we go back to the office. I'll probably go along after dinner if it is tonight. I'd be very happy if you came along with Paul. I don't know what plans he has for your evening. Anyway don't commit yourself now. Tell me, how do you find this poor bloody country after living abroad?'

Orlando allowed his glass to be refilled and agreed with Mr Daintry that in spite of all appearances to the contrary it was still the best bloody little country in the world, which made it rather hard for him to make his reasons for not coming back to live in it sound convincing, the more so as he was aware that his thought processes were becoming fogged by alcohol. Mr Daintry evidently believed in doing everything on a large scale, including his eating and drinking, and Orlando found that the sense of unreality which Daintry induced in him was to some extent eased, or relieved, by his becoming rather drunk. If Mr Daintry was to be seen as only one feature of an altogether unreal world, he lost, with his uniqueness, some of his significance.

'Why are you smiling?' said Mr Daintry sharply.

'I'm so sorry, what a maddening thing to do. I was just thinking how irresponsible I'm getting in my old age. Tell me, how do you see Paul fitting into all this? I can't tell you how glad I am to see him so keen on his job.'

'Nice boy,' said Daintry. 'He and Meg are well suited.'

'And he's good at his job?'

'Excellent, quite excellent,' said Daintry, expansively. 'Dead keen, as you say.'

'Oh good.'

Daintry looked at him and burst out laughing.

'That boy would sell his own grandmother,' he cried happily. 'What's more, it wouldn't be because he needed the money.'

Orlando laughed too, but without Mr Daintry's exuberance. He was not sure whether or not there was any criticism implied in that last remark, but thought it probably just as well that Paul's temperament should be known to his employer, for better or worse.

Daintry rose to his feet as Paul approached. 'We were just talking about you,' he said benevolently. 'Your stepfather wanted to know whether we appreciated you at your true worth in the organization and I assured him that we did.' He clapped Paul on the shoulder and said, 'We thought we'd go back to the office for a glass of brandy.'

Orlando felt himself effortlessly drawn by Mr Daintry's
magnetism down the long passages, in and out of the
gentlemen's lavatory, past the bowing commissionaire and
into the waiting Rolls. Corners, steps and baffling mirrors
in the walls, at all of which he would normally have hesitated in order to avoid the errors of judgement into which
his bad sight, let alone his present slight inebriation, might
have led him, seemed to present no obstacle: it was only
necessary to keep Daintry's powerful back in view, and to
submit himself to being magnetized. It was quite a pleasant
sensation; but as Paul bent his head to climb into the Rolls
beside him Orlando surprised on the face briefly very close
to his own an expression of euphoria which rather shocked
him. It wasn't *that* pleasant, surely?

But they were already being magnetized out of the Rolls
and into a lift, Daintry's office being only five minutes from
the Ritz. It was on the first floor of a house in Half Moon
Street and not large, though obviously expensive. They
padded after Mr Daintry over the thick fitted eau-de-nil
carpets into his own room. It was furnished entirely with
eighteenth-century furniture which Orlando immediately
recognized as being very valuable indeed.

'What a charming table,' he murmured.

'I love furniture,' said Mr Daintry simply.

He sat down at a Chippendale desk which was too small
for him, pressed some buttons on a machine in front of
him, said, 'I'll take that call at 3:30' – to which the machine
answered, 'Righty-ho,' rather cheekily – and waved a hand
vaguely in the direction of a cupboard in the wall, from
which Paul obediently extracted the brandy and three
glasses.

'Like it?' Daintry asked Orlando. 'Not too posh? Quiet
good taste? No, I'll tell you something, these pieces of

furniture in this room give me real pleasure. Quality, excellence, that's what I like. Otherwise this office is a waste of money. I don't need it. All I need is a telephone and a secretary. It's all I had for many years. But people seem to want all this, they don't know what to make of you if you haven't got it, don't quite trust you. It's worth it for prestige, I suppose, and then we have to have our own proper accounts department and all that lark now we're a public company. But I'm against proliferation of staff. I'm all in favour of letting other people do the work for you, outsiders. I'm an economizer on running expenses and all the trappings, you can get rid of a lot of money that way. Send the Air Vice in, would you?' he said to the machine.

'Will do,' it sang.

'That's another thing people seem to expect,' said Daintry gloomily. 'A sex bomb in reception.'

The Air Vice-Marshal was very much smaller than Mr Daintry. His moustache – neat, well-brushed, exactly covering his upper lip – was not more than a third of the size of his employer's.

He slipped quietly round the door and said, 'Ah.'

Daintry introduced him to Orlando and he said, 'Ah,' again.

Daintry referred briefly to the purpose of Orlando's visit.

'Ah yes,' said the Air Vice-Marshal. 'Expansion.' And he gave a melancholy little smile.

'Super,' said Daintry.

'Rather,' said the Air Vice-Marshal, looking at him admiringly.

'He lives in Italy,' said Daintry, nodding towards Orlando. 'Has a smashing castle in Tuscany.'

'Ah,' said the Air Vice-Marshal. 'Hoopoes arrived yet?'

'A few weeks ago,' said Orlando.

'Beautiful,' said the Air Vice-Marshal, looking pleased. 'Beautiful. Well, I think, if you'll excuse me.' He looked at Daintry. 'It's getting on for half-past.'

'Super,' said Daintry.

When the Air Vice-Marshal had shaken Orlando's hand politely and slipped out of the room, closing the door silently behind him, Daintry said, 'Half-past?'

'Three,' said Paul. 'Time to make tea.'

Daintry grunted. 'Who are the Hoopoes then?' he asked suspiciously.

'Birds.'

Daintry brightened. 'He's a world authority on birds, did you know that?'

'Perhaps that's why he was in his element in the air,' suggested Paul.

'He's too bloody unambitious,' said Daintry. 'He's got a job here for life though, if he wants it,' he added sharply, looking at Orlando as if he suspected him of doubting his word. 'There's such a thing as loyalty, you know.'

Orlando found himself on the point of remarking that that was super and decided that it was time to go. 'I'm seeing Conrad later this afternoon so we'll talk about all this,' he said. 'And no doubt we shall meet again. Thank you for a delightful lunch.'

'Any time, any time.' Orlando had the impression that Mr Daintry's mind had switched itself to the next subject – perhaps the call he was expecting at 3:30 – for his farewells, though still bonhomous, were very slightly absent-minded.

Paul came down in the lift with Orlando and said as he left him on the pavement outside the office, 'We're expecting you to have dinner with us of course, as well as stay the night. Why don't we meet at Muriel's about 6:30 or so and go on home? I usually look in there on the way back from work.'

'You mean that drinking club? Is it still going? Good heavens. Yes, all right, I'll see you there.'

As Orlando walked along the dark corridor leading towards Conrad's flat, which was in a vast and gloomy late-Victorian service block, a sound travelled towards him which brought into his mind so quick a succession of images that he had realized that the stool in the library at Mount Sorrel had been re-covered since before the war (a fact which he had quite failed to notice when he had been there last weekend) before he recognized the music as the Cavatina from Beethoven's String Quartet Opus 130.

He stood still. He could hear the grinding sound of the ancient lift which had brought him up to the fourth floor as it returned to ground level. It was operated by a little old aggrieved woman in a uniform more or less that of the Salvation Army, who manipulated a rope in one corner of the lift by means of which she manoeuvred it into a position never less than six or seven inches above or below the required floor, in stepping out on to which the inexperienced visitor was likely to be uncomfortably jarred, if not to fall flat on his face. There was a slight smell of stale cooking, whether of cabbage, porridge, toast, or all three he was unable to decide; and there was the thin pure unhurried music, which brought back into his mind the library at Mount Sorrel, a fire, Conrad's feet in their impeccably shiny shoes on the big stool, which had been covered then in some sort of faded tapestry and had now a serviceable linen cover which was not an improvement. He would not move his feet, that had been the problem, but had stayed sitting back in his armchair, and they had stood waiting, he

and Judith, until the end of the movement, knowing that
Conrad knew that they had come to tell him they were
going to be married, and that he did not want to hear them.

He had told Orlando months before that Judith was too
old for him.

Standing in the gloomy corridor, the dark cream paint of
whose walls needed renewing, and remembering this scene,
Orlando felt so completely a victim of uncontrollable
forces that he could for the moment hardly have brought
himself to imagine what a sense of responsibility for his
own actions might feel like. He had been 'in love' with
Judith, and at the same time with a whole way of seeing
things, a whole life of action and influence, which it was
the chief effect of Judith upon him to make him imagine
went with her and was implied in being in love with her; or
had it not rather been she who was implied in his being in
love with it? However it was, possessed by this obsession,
he had certainly been quite powerless, and the exhilarat-
ing sense which he had had of being in control of his own
destiny had been illusory. But then there was always some
similar framework which one unconsciously imposed upon
reality, a matrix by means of which one selected from the
evidence of one's senses, and of course this meant that one's
grasp of anything at all must be to say the very least partial.
I know nothing, he thought, I know nothing at all.

The sense which came to him of being stripped down
seemed to have exposed him totally to the music, each
note of which now came to him with extraordinary clarity, so that he felt himself absorbing from each harmony,
as it followed its own laws and inevitably superseded the
one before, an indecipherable but nonetheless knowable
message which came to him without the intercession of any
of his interpretative faculties; it was only necessary for him

to remain exposed to it. I know nothing, he thought again, but this time with an alertness, a physical quickening of the pulse, which might have seemed more appropriate had he been thinking, I know everything.

He found that he had walked as far as the last door in the corridor, which was marked D and which he therefore knew to be Conrad's. The latch was up and, pushing open the door, he said, 'May I come in?'

Immediately ahead of him seemed to be a wall of frosted glass, but manoeuvring himself rather awkwardly in the small space round the door he realized that behind the glass must be the bathroom and that a door on the right led out of the area of total darkness in which he found himself. He opened it, and found Conrad lying on a sofa in a surprisingly light and pleasant sitting-room.

He could see the back of Conrad's head, which was propped up against one arm of the sofa, and his feet, in highly polished black shoes, which were resting on the other; the intervening part of his body was covered by a rug. Approaching, Orlando saw that his eyes were closed and that his face wore an expression of deep calm.

Suddenly he opened his eyes, and at once threw off his rug and stood up.

'I'm sorry, you've caught me out, I found I had a bit of free time, my meeting was cancelled. I've got this wretched cold so I thought I'd take things easily.' Looking guilty, he pulled a huge white handkerchief out of his breast pocket, releasing a strong smell of Vapex, and loudly blew his nose.

'Quite right,' said Orlando. 'I remember that was always a favourite of yours.' He nodded towards the now silent gramophone.

'Yes.' Conrad went over to turn it off. He removed the record and put it carefully back in its sleeve. 'Marvellous. It's the sound of pure thought. It reminds me of that Yeats poem, "Like a long-legged fly upon the stream, his mind moves upon silence".' He closed the lid of the gramophone, and repeated, 'His mind moves upon silence! This is the new Pye Black Box. Wonderful tone, don't you think? I'm very pleased with it. We'll get some tea.' He pushed a bell in the wall. 'Sit down and tell me what you thought of our friend Daintry.'

Orlando sat down in a chintz-covered armchair by the fireplace. The room had a large bay window, which made it light, though the view outside, consisting as it did mainly of the back of St James's Park Underground station, was uninteresting. The cream paint had here been much more recently applied, the chairs were comfortable, the writing-table in the window he recognized as having come from Mount Sorrel, as also presumably had the books which lined the walls. The whole made a perfectly pleasant if slightly austere bachelor sitting-room. He said something to that effect.

'It suits my purpose,' said Conrad. 'They give one a perfectly good breakfast. It was really impossible trying to keep up two establishments. Out of the question, in fact. I simply couldn't afford it.'

Conrad, unlike Mr Daintry, was poorer than he used to be, and though Orlando imagined that in spite of heavy taxation he must still be relatively rich he obviously, again unlike Mr Daintry, did not think of himself as a rich man. Since, allowing for all Conrad's assets in the way of possessions, their degrees of wealth were probably much the same, the difference was largely psychological.

'I've had to let the shoot to a syndicate, did I tell you?' said Conrad as if he had been following Orlando's train of thought. 'I get quite a lot for it, and I really wasn't getting the time to shoot myself.'

Orlando was surprised. Conrad had been a brilliant shot.

'Times are hard, you know,' said Conrad, seeing his expression. 'They're kind enough to ask me out a couple of days a season. Well now, what about Daintry?'

'He seemed rather splendid, I thought. In a way.'

'Isn't he? I thought you'd like him. A pretty tough negotiator too.'

'I should imagine so.'

'That's the type we need these days.'

'Is it?'

'There's a lot of thrust there, a lot of impetus. There's been a social revolution here, you know, since the war. It's not necessarily going to be the orthodox who are going to do the things that matter in the next few years.'

'I've heard talk of a social revolution, but to tell you the truth I can't see much evidence of one. Except for the National Health service of course.'

'There's the Welfare State, yes. There's no doubt that's here to stay. All thought up under Churchill of course, though the Labour Party takes the credit for it now. But that's set up. There's no need to bother about it any more, except for minor details. What we've got to concentrate on is economic recovery and playing a decent role in international affairs. The Labour Party know nothing about economics or foreign affairs, they never have done. I know old Ernie Bevin was respected because he was a good man, but there's no one else on that side.'

'Are you in the running for the Foreign Office?'

'Not a hope. Not as a member of the House of Lords. No, but seriously, heavy taxation and death duties need time to take their toll – so does education to make its effect – but there's a big change going on, believe me.'

Orlando said teasingly, 'I believe all your social revolution amounts to is that there'll be a few bright grammar school boys where there used to be Old Etonians.'

He was relieved when Conrad laughed. 'How dare you sit on your distant rock and laugh at my social revolution? Don't you understand that that's what English revolutions are like?'

There was now an approaching rumbling and rattling, followed by a crash as the outer door of the flat was thrown open, hitting the wall beside it, at the same time as a good deal of crockery was apparently bashed against some other wall. This was followed by a thunderous knocking on the sitting-room door.

'Ah, tea,' said Conrad, springing to his feet and opening the door.

There entered, bearing a loaded but at first sight not appetizing tray, the sister, in the spirit if not in the flesh, of the lady of the lift, who determinedly hooking one small but formidably shod foot round the leg of a little table twirled it out into the middle of the room, dumped the tray on it with a vengeful groan, and stood back to contemplate her achievement.

'Tea is not really their strong point here,' said Conrad mildly.

'I had far too much to eat for lunch,' said Orlando politely.

The attendant directed her glance briefly at each of them with the expression of one who has had thoroughly disagreeable suspicions confirmed, and turned on her heel. The outer door crashed behind her.

There was a pause.

'The tea itself might be all right,' ventured Conrad.

There was a gentle bump at the door and Conrad opened it.

'Ah Jess,' said Orlando. 'I was wondering where you were.'

'She keeps her basket in the bedroom here. They're inclined to make a bit of a fuss about the hairs. She's come in now because she has rather a *penchant* for those nasty little paste sandwiches.'

Conrad put the plate of sandwiches on the floor in a corner of the room and then poured out the tea. Jess ate the sandwiches.

'So you think Daintry's offer should be accepted?' said Orlando.

'I'm coming round to that view, yes. I was against it at first, partly because I hadn't then met Daintry and partly because I thought I ought to support Stephen, and he's very strongly opposed to it, as you know. I'm still uneasy on that score. Stephen's been running the firm reasonably efficiently but I haven't much doubt that he'd lose his job under Daintry.'

'Paul says that that's not so.'

'Paul is not necessarily reliable. They don't get on, those two brothers.'

'Paul seems to be fascinated by Daintry.'

'I think it's a very good thing. Daintry has no illusions about Paul but I think he'll get the best out of him. As to Stephen, I've no doubt he'd get another job without too much difficulty. He's got a perfectly good record.'

'He'd get a good price for his shares. And compensation probably.'

'That could be written in. Logan Holdings has been in danger of stagnation under Stephen. This would open up all sorts of possibilities. What do you think?'

'I really don't feel at all involved. But if you think it's a good thing ...'

Conrad nodded. 'Let's do it then. I'd better be getting back to the House. I must say I've been thankful not to have been in the Commons lately. The atmosphere's not pleasant. They have to keep such long hours with this small majority, everyone's tired and bad-tempered, the standard of debate's gone down terribly since your day – a lot of pointless abuse and name-calling goes on. The trouble is, we can't be at all sure of getting a decent majority next time, if indeed we get a majority at all. There's got to be a very big swing indeed, and I think a lot of people on our side are too optimistic. It's a worry, you know, it really is. God knows what kind of mess they'll get us all into if we don't get them out.' He looked across at Orlando rather speculatively, as if not quite able to believe that he was not as involved in all this as he had used to be.

'Then I hope you do,' said Orlando, getting to his feet.

'You'll at least come down for the weekend?' said Conrad. 'Is it no use trying to persuade you to stay longer?'

'I'm booked back on Tuesday. But I'd very much like to come for the weekend.'

After he had said good-bye to Orlando outside Daintry's office, Paul went upstairs again and looked into Daintry's room to see if he was needed. Daintry was talking on the telephone, so Paul picked up the glass of brandy which he had refilled before he went downstairs and went into his own room, where he finished it and read the *Evening Standard*. Later on Daintry sent him a message to say that if he cared to bring Orlando to the gambling party any time after ten o'clock would he please do so and that he himself was off to meet Mr Cotton at the Dorchester about the Birmingham deal. There seemed to Paul to be no point in hanging about the office, so he went to the club

where he had arranged to meet Orlando and drank two
gin and limes; then, remembering that Serena was always
very angry when he came home drunk in the early part
of the evening, he went to the telephone and rang her up.

'We're rather involved,' he said. 'It looks as if it's going
on all night.'

'Aren't they agreeing then?' asked Serena anxiously. She
was very much in favour of the proposed merger.

'They're getting on like a house on fire,' said Paul. 'That's
the trouble.'

'How marvellous,' said Serena. 'You are clever, Paul. Will
you all go out to dinner or something? Shall I not expect
you?'

'No, don't expect us. We may be late. You go to bed.'

'All right. Good luck. 'Bye-ee.'

Paul put down the receiver feeling as reassured by her
evident approval as if it had not been elicited by falsification
on his part, and went back to the bar.

By the time Orlando joined him there he was looking
rather white, but Orlando, who was pleased to be able to
see his face at all through the gloom, did not notice anything
unusual. He had had to more or less feel his way up the
stairs, and when he arrived at the top he had a moment of
familiar panic, thinking himself lost. There was smoke and
darkness and strange voices. He felt his affliction as if it
were new, and put his hand to his eyes.

'Darling, there's a terribly attractive *blind* man behind
you. Do *do* something. Must you just *sit* there like a
drunken *sot*?'

The voice, low and husky, and the enunciation, clear and
exaggeratedly emphatic, was familiar, but only, he thought,
generically so. He had known people like that. She was
sitting quite close to him, and appeared, as far as he could

discern, to be good-looking, about forty-five, with pale hair and red lipstick.

'You are the most *god*-awful shit,' she was saying to the man with her, whose back was towards Orlando.

He was reminded – but of whom? – of a mixture of people – or perhaps, he then thought, of Angela Payne, with whom he had had an affair in about 1935. She had not been quite like that herself but she had taken him to places where there had been people like that, pubs and clubs which were part of her life as a journalist and occasional writer for the BBC, a kind of open, drunken, shabby, sometimes almost despairing but often quite funny world which Judith thought tawdry and in which he had several times found himself involved in long conversations with people he had really liked but had never seen since. He had made Judith very unhappy by his affair with Angela. Poor old Angela, she'd be about that woman's age – perhaps in fact she was that woman, she'd always liked a drink. He turned quickly away and at once saw Judith's face, hurt and suspicious, glimmering out of the surrounding darkness; then he realized with relief that it was Paul, who now came towards him and helped him to find his way to the bar. Orlando sat down on a stool and said, 'Oh dear, oh dear.'

'Why?' asked Paul. 'What will you drink?'

'Oh, what you've got, thanks. I don't know. I seem to have been rather critical of people since I've been in England, and I was just remembering that life's so difficult one hasn't much right to criticize.'

'It's not difficult for everyone,' said Paul firmly, evidently unwilling to sacrifice the uniqueness of his own problems. 'Not for Uncle Conrad, for instance. Or for Daintry.'

'I don't agree. I think for anyone to be of Cabinet rank in politics, whether in or out of office, is unbelievably difficult. You're bound to lose some of your freedom by becoming committed to that extent, and you have to keep a daily watch to know exactly how much you have lost, otherwise you're in trouble. It's not a bit easy.'

Paul was not interested in Conrad's problems.

'Serena's got one of her migraines,' he said. 'I thought we might go out to dinner somewhere and then look in at this party Daintry was talking about. He asked me to bring you.'

'Excellent,' said Orlando, who had been looking forward to a quiet dinner in Paul and Serena's little Chelsea house and early bed among the rampant rosebuds of their minuscule spare bedroom.

'Have another drink,' said Paul.

The party was in a first-floor flat in Eaton Square, and as soon as Orlando had handed over his coat and followed Paul into the drawing-room it struck him that it was years since he had been to a party and years since he had been so drunk. Neither realization was unpleasant, particularly in combination with the other. The party might have been an alarming prospect without the sense of irresponsibility induced by the drunkenness, and the drunkenness might have contained the seeds of embarrassment but for the party, which more or less required it, and where indeed he almost immediately noticed one or two men considerably drunker than himself. His own state, which was not acute, was merely the result of a slow but steady intake of alcohol since his first martini in the Ritz with Paul before lunch, broken only by his interlude with Conrad and culminating in a glass of brandy in the restaurant where Paul had taken him for dinner. The brandy he did slightly regret, but had accepted at the time because Paul had ordered it and because his resistance had been lowered by Paul's conversation during the latter part of their not very good dinner. Paul seemed to be convinced that the war in Korea was going to lead quite soon to a world war in which either Russia or America would drop a hydrogen bomb, and though Orlando was perfectly aware of the possibility he was irritated by the apparent satisfaction with which Paul insisted on its inevitability.

So now he took a glass of red wine from a proffered tray and looked round him with a disposition to be amused. There seemed to be no sign of Daintry, and the immediate impression he gained was of people a good deal younger. He made his way carefully through the crowd to a chair. By the time he had reached it he had decided that the party was to be compared with the slightly raffish gatherings that Penelope used to take him to in his earliest years in London rather than with the more high-powered affairs he used to frequent in the later thirties when as a Cabinet Minister he was supposedly some kind of minor notability. This conclusion pleased him. There did not seem much danger of his meeting anyone he used to know in the old days.

'Delightful party,' he said to the man sitting near him, who was slumped back in an armchair under the shadow of the sturdy back of a girl dressed in green taffeta. She was sitting on the arm of the chair and was engaged in conversation with a man at her feet.

The man in the armchair grunted, or possibly groaned.

'Amazing how seldom one feels really relaxed, don't you agree?' said Orlando. 'I've been living rather a quiet life lately and I'd quite forgotten that as a matter of fact I feel much more relaxed in a crowd than by myself. Do you find that at all?'

The man in the armchair appeared not to have heard and stared straight forward with a completely blank expression from beside the bastion of green taffeta until unexpectedly he said, 'I suppose I'm always pretty relaxed really.'

The claim was immediately proved not to have been exaggerated by the girl's knocking over the glass of wine which she had put down beside her on the arm of the chair and which emptied its contents over his leg. He slowly bent over to inspect the damage, turned down the cuff of his trouser-leg, which spilled a small quantity of red wine into his shoe, and leant back again in his chair. The girl, however, had by now jumped up with expressions of solicitude, the man at her feet had produced a handkerchief, and the three of them being thus united by an event from which Orlando felt himself fortunately excluded, he rose to his feet and set off in the general direction of a door which led into another room, apparently also full of people. He had had time to notice that the girl in green taffeta was not at all pretty, and now looked around for better favoured girls, a quest which involved going up very close to quite a number of them. As he did this with an expression at once optimistic and serious, it was assumed that he was looking for someone in particular, and one or two people, taking pity on his obviously poor sight, even offered to help him find whoever it was. He refused these offers politely and continued on his way.

'Delightful,' he murmured from time to time. 'Delightful.'

Once he had got over his surprise at how young most people looked – hardly older than Agatha – it seemed to him that the standard of looks was high. There were more pretty girls than he had seen in all the time he'd lived in Italy. He liked the way they wore their hair, too, longer than had been the fashion before the war, and curled either under or outwards only at the ends. He remembered the crimped look of the ubiquitous permanent wave of the thirties – though of course Judith had never done anything to her hair except have it very expensively cut, being, he thought with a recurrence of old pride, the kind of beauty that breaks the rules of fashion. He liked the prevalence of bare shoulders – that was Edwardian, surely – so for that matter were the men's tight suits, which looked rather uncomfortable and seemed, as in the case of the man who had had the wine spilt over his trousers, to be adorned with more cuffs and pockets with flaps on them than had been considered fashionable when he had last visited his London tailor.

He remembered how much of his time with Judith used to be spent on gossip and comment about social life, an interest which was completely absent from his life in Italy, where even if he had been to parties he would not have been able to understand the subtleties of behaviour which conveyed the information on which the gossip and the comment were based. It was a question, once again, of frameworks. This was one he had once known well.

'Are you looking for someone?' Dark hair and eyes, rather plump cheeks but beautiful neck and shoulders, a choker of pearls, dangling pearl ear-rings, a haughty expression.

'Not specifically.' His smile, he thought, was probably irresistible.

'Oh.' She looked at him coldly. 'In that case aren't you being rather rude? You've been going round staring at everybody, I've seen you.' She had rather a high little voice.

'What you call staring is what I call just looking,' said Orlando. 'I'm virtually blind, you see.'

'I don't think blindness is any excuse for bad manners,' she said.

He burst out laughing and went on his way, encouraged. Years since he had been to a party. Even more years since he had behaved badly at a party. He wondered if there was dancing in the next room, and hoped there was.

In fact there was gambling in the next room, and it was there that Paul had gone, to look for Daintry. In the doorway he had come across his cousin Henry, with Caroline, and the three of them were standing together when Paul said, 'I hope my dear stepfather is not going to become a liability.'

Orlando was at this moment approaching them, though without having yet seen them, his glass of wine held high to protect it from the crowd and an expression of pleased interest on his face. There was something definitely at odds between his distinguished appearance and his unabashed curiosity as to the attributes of the girls he was slowly circumnavigating.

They watched his progress for some moments, then Henry said in an interested voice, 'How very splendid,' and went forward to meet him.

By the time Henry had worked his way through the crowd, stopping once or twice to greet acquaintances, Orlando had become involved in conversation with two girls, one of whom was extremely pretty, the other, he was beginning to guess, rich. It was this latter who, as Henry approached, was inviting Orlando to a party. She was a tall girl, Greek she had already told him, with an unusually elongated head and a high carrying voice, the tone of which was nasal, so much so that when her conversation, which was rapid and rather breathless, failed her and she filled in with 'mns', which happened frequently, the sound was of a small persistent buoy in a perilous sea, warning of sandbanks: it seemed to be an integral part of her method of communication.

'You must come to my party, mn, yes do, really. I'll send you an invitation, mn. Anyone got a pen? Have you got a

pen, Jane, mn? Anyway, mn. Here we are. You write it, mn.
You must come. The 25th, mn.'

Orlando was pleased to be invited to a party on such
very short acquaintance, and accepted, although the date
was well after that on which he was due to return to Italy.

Henry touched him on the shoulder, and he turned to
greet him.

'Delightful party, delightful.'

The girls had become involved in a discussion of the relative merits of Tommy Kinsman and Chappie d'Amato, the
Greek expressing astonishment that there should be any
question as to the supremacy of Tommy Kinsman and the
pretty one quietly insisting that she'd been to a party in
Cambridge where Chappie d'Amato had played and that it
had been the best party she'd ever been to.

'Why don't we sit down?' said Henry, leading the way
towards the other room.

'I've been asked to a deb dance,' shouted Orlando in his
ear as he followed him through the crowd.

'It'll be a good one,' Henry shouted back. 'They're stinking rich.'

The atmosphere in the next room was rather different.
The centre of attention was a long table in the middle round
which about twenty people, mainly men, were sitting. They
were playing chemin-de-fer. A number of people were
standing about behind the players, watching the game,
which was evidently being organized by a fat pale young
man with a snappishly authoritative air. The players were
on the whole older men, among whom Orlando recognized Daintry, and a middle-aged peer notorious for his
wealth, and a man with a fair moustache and a rather high
colour whom for the moment he could not place though
he associated him with Judith. He would have preferred to

have gone back into the other room, but Henry was leading him to a far corner, where chairs and tables had been so redisposed as to make the dozen or so young people sitting in them into a self-contained group. Although the rest of the room was comparatively quiet out of deference to the gamblers, this particular group seemed to have no inhibitions as to the amount of noise they felt free to make, or indeed as to the lengths generally to which they felt able to go in pursuit of a sense of relaxation. Feet were on tables to some extent, bottles of champagne were liberally disposed among them, and two large jars of caviare had been appropriated from the nearby buffet and were being handed about. The talk was continuous and punctuated by loud laughter, and on the whole male. There were girls, but they did not seem to be expected to contribute much to the conversation. One of them, whether or not as a result of the champagne, seemed to be in a more or less permanent state of giggles. The two young men closest to her apparently found this satisfactory, and when she stopped they looked at her anxiously until some flying witticism started her off again.

Caroline rose from somewhere in the centre of the group and, coming forward, kissed him warmly on the cheek. She was wearing a tight little black bodice which left her arms and shoulders bare, a big shiny black belt round her waist and a full white skirt. She was evidently someone who looked her best when dressed up for a party; and Orlando, flattered by her friendliness, nevertheless found himself wishing that her pretty greeting was less obviously meant for him merely in his role as Henry's uncle by marriage, not that he could have done much about it had her attitude been different. Henry could certainly be quite formidable if crossed.

'Delightful,' he said, repeating himself, as he accepted a glass of champagne.

They were introduced to him, the group, but he did not really listen to their names. They accepted his presence amicably but were not much interested, being absorbed in their own various conversations, which ranged and changed, became general and then splintered again. A correctly handsome man in a rather vulgar white dinner-jacket was sitting on a table loudly enlarging on an incident with a garage mechanic, whom he had apparently short-changed; with a good deal of self-mockery and exaggeration, and some ridiculous imitations, he built up the intrinsically uninteresting episode into an exotic fantasy which evidently gave great pleasure to some parts of his audience, though by no means all. A small man with a rather fine head, a hugely hooked nose and a high forehead, who was talking softly in one corner, looked up in irritation at the raconteur's loud laugh. At that moment a pert little female face, with straight hair and a pretty nose, popped up from the floor beside his chair and said in a high voice, 'My trouble is I simply don't need God. I feel absolutely no desire for Him at all.'

'I should think not,' said the man on her other side decidedly, as if the Deity had been caught importuning.

He had a pale, rather anonymous kind of face, this man, and was systematically working his way through a pile of letters which he had on his knee and which he was slowly opening, tearing up and throwing over his shoulder on to the floor. Occasionally he would glance through one of them before tearing it up and then he would break into quiet pleased laughter.

'He's been in hospital for three weeks,' said Henry to Orlando, as if in explanation.

'One's been at death's door, my dear,' said the ex-patient in a voice like Noël Coward's. 'Would you care to see my scar?' He made as if to undo his trousers but was prevented by a number of strongly expressed opinions in disfavour.

'They're all bills,' he said, going back to his mail. 'They must be out of their minds, sending me all these bills. Laundry! I never have a clean shirt to lay my hands on and they send me a bill for £39! £39! It's since 1948 of course. 1948!' He lay back in his chair with a screech of laughter, recovered himself enough to tear the bill into small pieces, still muttering '1948' and shaking his head, then he threw it over his shoulder to join the rest.

'Slut,' said a pretty young man lazily. 'Sloven. Slattern.'

But somebody had started to relate an incident of immense complication to which almost everybody else seemed to have some scrap of knowledge to add. It concerned a stolen car, and a poor old man, and a figure apparently well known to them all whose doings sounded quite reprehensible but seemed to be spoken of with admiration as well as amusement. The poor old man had come very badly out of the encounter.

'You don't know this character?' said Henry. 'He's rather eccentric.' He tried to explain. He had been at Oxford with most of them, this monster, and was a legend, that much Orlando could understand. Now it appeared that he was involved in a big deal selling forbidden goods to Iron Curtain countries and might be sent to prison at any moment. But Orlando had stopped listening: it was all rather hard to follow if one did not know the personalities involved; and, besides, he had been struck by a note in Henry's voice which took him back quite unexpectedly to the oyster farms of his youth, to the little bar on the quay at Locmariaquer, his friends the Lanoë brothers (one of whom had been killed in the war – the other had emigrated to America) and their pretty sister: though they would never have called it so at the time, they had constituted of course a group, and had been, just as these were, passionately interested in their own and the others of the group's personalities. The salt winds of that desolate sea had blown on just such legends, monsters and heroes as now emerged in a drawing-room in Eaton Square, talking of debts and God, cars and each other's astonishing behaviour. At the same time he remembered Conrad saying, 'He tells me nothing. I'm afraid he's got in with a very undesirable set.' He realized that Henry was introducing him to his friends.

At that moment one of them turned to Orlando and began to talk about Italy. He was hoping to go to Florence, was an art historian, had an introduction to Bernard Berenson.

'Then of course you must come and see us.'

As Orlando began to give detailed directions as to how to find Lecceto, he noticed that Caroline, who had been kneeling on the floor quietly picking up the torn pieces of paper and putting them tidily on a table, was now looking anxiously in the direction of Henry. Turning, Orlando saw him moving towards the chemin-de-fer game.

Caroline came and sat on the arm of his chair.

'You're worried?' he asked her.

'I wish he wouldn't do it, it's so silly. He's in such trouble already.'

'Through gambling?'

'Didn't his father tell you? He's terribly angry with him. He's paid his debts twice, and he's refused ever to do it again. I know he means it. It's partly his own fault, you know. He won't trust Henry with money, he never has. He gives him the tiniest possible allowance, and it's so unfair because people think he must be rich because he's Conrad's son. And then he's absurdly generous. He's always in terrible

money trouble, and now his father says he's going to stop
his allowance altogether because he's left Oxford and ought
to be getting a proper job, and it's so silly when lots of
people with fathers like that have had everything made over
to them already, to avoid death duties. It's terribly hard on
Henry, it really is.'

'Has he ever had a job?'

'Oh lots, but not the sort Conrad counts. He's working
for Brian now – that man over there in the white dinner-
jacket – they do up vintage cars and sell them. I suppose
it isn't really a full-time job, but he works terribly hard
sometimes.'

Orlando moved slightly in his chair, so that he could
see Henry, who was now standing by the table watching
the game. At that moment he looked up and saw Orlando
and Caroline watching him. Immediately he moved to an
empty chair at the table, sat down and without any change
of expression called out, 'Banco.'

'He knew we were talking about him,' said Caroline.

'Wouldn't he like that?'

She shook her head, wrinkling her nose in irritation.

'He'd think he was being impinged on.'

She turned her back to the gambling table and reached
out for her glass of champagne, but as she did so she caught
sight of a middle-aged man of decidedly sinister appearance who was approaching their corner of the room, and to
Orlando's surprise put down her glass, jumped to her feet
and ran to kiss him on both cheeks.

'Charlie!'

The others looked up and greeted him, if not with quite
as much enthusiasm as Caroline had shown, certainly with
friendliness. He was a stocky, heavily built man with sticking out ears who looked like a burglar.

'This is Charlie Edwards,' said Caroline. 'He's a burglar.'

'How do you do?' said Orlando.

'Who did the Antibes job, Charlie?' asked the man in the white dinner-jacket whom Caroline had called Brian.

'French mob,' said Charlie, sitting down and accepting a glass of champagne. 'Had some English friends of mine working for them – they're the only ones they can trust to do an honest job – but it was a French-organized show. How's the game going then? Our Henry's sticking to it, I see.'

'Waiting for you, Charlie,' said Brian. 'How are you feeling tonight?'

Charlie, who was wearing a dinner-jacket with very broad shoulders shot his cuffs, straightened his bow-tie and crossed himself. 'Not bad,' he said weightily. 'Not too bad.' He drained his glass, stood up and moved towards the table. Brian and one or two others of the group followed him. The man with the big nose was talking about Existentialism.

'Isn't he sweet?' said Caroline, smiling affectionately after Charlie Edwards' broad back. His ears seemed particularly protuberant from behind.

'Quite only, I thought,' said Orlando.

'Oh you don't understand, he's terribly kind and generous and his stories are marvellous. He's retired now really, except for a few special jobs. He's going to start an antique shop and write his memoirs.'

He had certainly moved in on the game in a thoroughly businesslike manner.

In a few moments Henry left the table and came back to sit beside Orlando and Caroline.

'Isn't it super to see Charlie?' said Caroline.

'He's in good form,' said Henry. 'I said we'd all have dinner together on Wednesday.'

'Aren't you playing any more?' asked Orlando, who had been surprised after what Caroline had said to see Henry leave the table so soon.

'I don't play with Charlie,' said Henry pleasantly. 'What's become of Paul, I wonder?'

'I think he's in the other room.' Orlando was rather impressed by what struck him as a certain grandeur in Henry's attitude. He was also reminded that perhaps it was time to find Paul and go home. He stood up, but was prevented from explaining his purpose to Henry by the arrival of the fat young man from the gambling table, who was now paler than ever with the effort of controlling what appeared to be extreme rage.

'Which of you lot asked that man here?' he said, coming uncomfortably close to Orlando and Henry. 'I know perfectly well it was one of you.'

'I've no idea,' said Henry coldly.

'It was either you or Brian, I know it was. I suppose you think it's funny. You know perfectly well ...' He was interrupted by Daintry, who put a hand on his shoulder. 'Marvellous party. I'm afraid I'm pocketing my winnings and going on my way, it's long past my bedtime.' He shook Orlando warmly by the hand. 'We'll be in touch. Super that you came along.'

'You see what I mean?' muttered the fat young man furiously to Henry, and indeed almost immediately afterwards the rich peer whom Orlando had recognized rose to his feet and a minute or two later left the room.

'You'll all have to go,' said the fat young man. Orlando had not until that moment realized that he was in fact their host. 'I won't have my party broken up like this. You all seem to think you can do anything you like. Half of you weren't asked. Go on, get out, the lot of you ...'

A startling burst of sound interrupted him.

'Put another penny in,

In the nickleodeon.

All I want is loving you

And music, music, music

Flushed, Caroline rose from behind a chair, where she had succeeded in plugging in a gramophone and saving the situation. For although the change of atmosphere was not immediate, and the host merely raised his voice in order to go on berating Henry – who shrugged his shoulders with a smile and indicated that he was unable to hear, though one or two people standing near were evidently not suffering from the same disadvantage and were seen by the host to be exchanging amused glances at his expense – nevertheless within a quarter of an hour or so some furniture had been moved, several people were dancing, and the party had changed its tone.

The host, out of control of events, swallowed the contents of the nearest glass and turned back towards the gamblers, several of whom were carrying on without paying any attention to the increasing noise in the other part of the room. Orlando followed him towards the gambling table, with the idea of passing it and going on into the other room to look for Paul.

He paused for a moment, looking down at the green baize cloth, and as he looked up again he saw opposite him the man whose face had seemed familiar when he had seen it earlier, but this time he was close enough to recognize that the pink cheeks, grown pinker and plumper since he had last seen them, and the fair moustache, a little faded now, belonged to Robin Barwick, his late wife's military lover and the putative father of Imogen. Almost immediately he was aware of Imogen's face, misty with distance and wearing an expression of exaggerated alarm, swimming in the air behind Robin Barwick: and the two faces, gazing towards him with differing degrees of the same wondering alarm, were without any doubt alike.

So now it was hallucinations. His ever-present wariness about his health made Orlando put Imogen's manifestation down to that, and since he did not particularly want to talk to Robin Barwick he turned quickly away from the table, and to avoid the latter's gaze moved round until he was behind him. It was too late. Robin Barwick had risen to his feet with some kind of explanation and now put a hand on Orlando's arm. At the same time a stir in the corner of the room closest to him drew Orlando's attention. A figure was moving quickly away from him, pushing people aside rudely. He could not make out whether or not it was Imogen, but with a quick readjustment of his suppositions the possibility did occur to him.

'Is that a girl over there?' he asked Robin Barwick. 'Just behind those two there. Can you see?'

'Blonde girl, young-looking, you mean, in blue?' said Robin Barwick.

'Yes, that's her. Forgive me, I must just ...' He left Robin Barwick baffled and vaguely gesturing, and pushing past a couple seized a girl by the arm – the wrong girl, but so unlike Imogen that she could never have been mistaken for her. His problem was unsolved. He pushed on and suddenly found that he had cornered her. Her back was to the wall, her eyes expressed the most urgent guilt and fear, and she was undoubtedly Imogen. She waited in silence, while he came close enough to convince himself.

Having by now got over his first surprise at the idea that she should be there, his strongest feeling was one of relief that Robin Barwick had obviously never seen her before.

'Why are you looking so frightened?' he asked her.

The question surprised her.

'Well, I – I'm not meant to be here.'

'I suppose not.'

'I mean, I thought you'd be angry.'

'How did you get here?'

'I came by myself.'

'That's not true, sir. I brought her here, sir.'

Orlando peered at the youth who was standing beside Imogen, and who he had not realized was associated with her. He was slightly smaller than Imogen, had dark hair cut very short, a poor complexion and small brown eyes with which he stared unflinchingly at Orlando during the latter's examination. He was wearing the virtuous expression of a schoolboy owning up to a misdeed, and seemed to be standing to attention. Orlando took an instant dislike to him.

'What's your name?'

'Jamie Henderson, sir, I'm a Grenadier.'

'How perfectly ridiculous,' said Orlando, since this was indeed how the information struck him. 'Come along, my dear, we'll go and get a drink.' He took Imogen by the arm and began to lead her away. The young man followed him.

'Look here, sir, I don't think you ought to blame Imogen. I'd like to take full responsibility.'

'Yes, yes, never mind,' said Orlando irritably.

'Jamie, I think actually it'll probably be all right,' said Imogen breathlessly over her shoulder.

'I don't want you to get into hot water. I'd like to explain.'

'Tell him to go away,' said Orlando.

'Go away, Jamie,' said Imogen obediently.

'That's better,' said Orlando.

Imogen giggled. 'I hope he'll come back though. He's got to drive me back to school.'

'They don't know you're here presumably?'

'Oh no.' She was shocked at the thought.

'Do you do this often?'

'Oh no,' she said again, less spontaneously.

'You know it's appallingly late. What time do you have to get up in the morning?'

'I expect I'll manage,' she said.

'You can have half an hour and then I'll take you back to school.'

She looked at him, and he saw her wondering whether to question his decision, on the grounds, he felt fairly certain, of his own incapacity to drive rather than of any desire on her part to be alone with Jamie Henderson, but the fact of half an hour at a party won over all other considerations and she said, 'Thank you' enthusiastically, drank some of the champagne which he had given her and which immediately turned her cheeks a good deal pinker, looked round with excited interest and then said through her nose, 'It looks a terribly boring party actually.'

'Why do you say that?' he asked mildly.

'The same old people...' she said in the same voice.

He looked at her. For a moment he thought she might smile and acknowledge her artifice, but instead she scuffed in her handbag, produced a packet of cigarettes and offered him one.

'No thanks.' He tried to remember the legal age for smoking, but failed. I don't know her well enough, he thought; next time she will smile. 'Go away,' he said. 'I'll see you back here in half an hour.'

He turned away himself, meaning to make sure that he was as far away as possible from Robin Barwick, and found himself standing beside the art historian whom he had invited to Lecceto and who was now talking to the Existentialist with the big head.

'I'm glad I ran into you because I'm afraid I didn't hear your name.'

'Raymond Phipps. This is Joe Hertz. Did you really mean that about coming to see you? Joe's going to be with me as well.'

'Of course.'

It was late, he'd had a lot to drink; besides, he liked them. Somehow in the half-hour he had given Imogen he asked most of them to come to Lecceto in the summer. He had a feeling by the end of it that he had at least managed to exclude Brian in the white dinner-jacket, but he was not even sure of that.

Turning back to look out for Imogen, he was confronted by a frowning Henry.

'You shouldn't have asked all those people to Italy. They're the most terrible bunch of spongers and layabouts.'

'I'm relying on you and Caroline being there to keep them in order.'

The frown became less ferocious. 'I suppose I could weed them out a bit for you. I mean, I could tell some of them you'd made a mistake, couldn't I?'

'If you like. You organize it. So long as you come yourself.'

'Will Agatha still be there?'

'Yes.'

'Good. She gets on awfully well with Caroline. She's quite – what I mean is – she's not like anyone else, Agatha. I'm very fond of her. I've always been very fond of her.'

Henry was still frowning and Orlando wondered whether it might not be as a result of the concentration needed to keep upright. It seemed to him that Henry was probably, though quite unostentatiously, very drunk indeed.

'I'm just beginning to get to know her,' said Orlando.

'That must be marvellous for you. She frightens me. I've always been frightened of Agatha although I admire her enormously – well, also I know her weaknesses, I mean I know her awfully well in a way, though perhaps I don't really, I mean one's helpless, isn't one, when people are attractive – she's really beautiful now, Agatha – one can't be detached about girls exactly, can one? But I have this feeling about her that one day she's going to get me. No, not like that, I mean, though she does quite like me but she disapproves of me, but what I mean is I think she'll probably kill me one day.'

'Kill you?' asked Orlando, surprised.

'Yes. With a gun or something. She's quite violent, you know. I have this feeling that one day she'll point a gun at me and pow! – through the heart – blood everywhere.' He gesticulated wildly to indicate the blood gushing from his heart. 'I'll have deserved it, of course, no doubt about that.'

He seemed to be quite serious, and indeed was gazing at Orlando with rather alarming intensity, so that it was a relief when Caroline appeared beside him, put her arm through his and said, 'Paul seems to be in rather a state.'

'Pow! Zam! Wheeee-uck!' Henry pulled his arm free and with a succession of horrifying sounds went through a pantomime of having been shot by Caroline, which ended with his collapsing on the floor with a ghastly death-rattle. He then rolled on to his back with his arms and legs outstretched as if in crucifixion and began to laugh wildly.

'Do get up, Henry,' said Caroline.

He jumped to his feet with startling speed, put his arm round her shoulders, leaning on her fairly heavily, and asked her to dance.

Orlando, reminded once more that it was Paul who had brought him to the party, set off again to look for him. Passing near the dancers, he noticed that the lights had been turned out in that part of the room and that the couples had mostly merged into embraces of varying degrees of intimacy. Certain that one of the most entwined would be Imogen and the ghastly Henderson, he skirted past in embarrassment and continued his search. It was useless, because the room was now too dark for him to see who anyone was without putting his face very close to theirs, and the party was at a stage when such an approach was no longer acceptable. More than half the guests had left, and the ones who remained – save for those few who were more or less peacefully sleeping – were in a condition to resent close inspection. Orlando abandoned the search with relief and made his way back to the table beside which he had agreed to meet Imogen.

She was not there, but Paul was. He had turned a strangely translucent greenish white, and was leaning on the table at an awkward angle. He turned on Orlando a gaze which when it had focused itself appeared to be one of hostility.

'I'm a homosexual,' he said indistinctly.

'I thought you'd given it up,' said Orlando as if they were talking about golf.

'Well, I haven't,' said Paul peevishly.

'Have you seen Imogen anywhere?' asked Orlando. 'I'm supposed to be taking her back to school.'

'I'm working for the Communists,' said Paul, his gaze focused slightly to Orlando's right.

'I'll make my own way back to the house after that, so don't wait for me. Do you think I ought to have a key?'

'You don't believe me,' said Paul, swaying towards Orlando.

Orlando put a hand on his chest and gently pushed him back against the table, in time to prevent all the glasses being swept to the floor.

'Give me a key and I'll see you in the morning,' said Orlando. 'I must find Imogen. Heaven knows where the school is. Miles from London, I believe.'

'Doesn't mean anything to you,' Paul mumbled. 'Trying to tell you something, doesn't mean anything, nothing means anything.' His voice was suddenly very loud but then sank again to a mumble. 'Nothing anything. Rotten, rotten through and through.'

'Why don't I get a taxi for you?'

'Through and through.'

'In fact, I tell you what, I'll get a taxi and drop you off and take Imogen on to school.'

This simple plan proved difficult to put into execution because he could find neither Imogen nor a telephone with which to summon a taxi, and he was wandering about with irritation rising rapidly in the direction of panic when he was approached by Henry, who as soon as he learnt the need supplied it. Unimpeded by whatever might have been his state of inebriation, he fished Imogen by the scruff of her neck from the gently heaving sea of dancers, ushered her into a taxi beside the abusively mumbling Paul, went on to persuade the driver to undertake the journey to Virginia Water and back for not too unreasonable a reward and, leaving Orlando grateful and relieved, went back to the party.

'I like Henry,' said Orlando, settling back into his seat.

'Arrogant, brainless and cunning,' said Paul, with surprising clarity of diction.

'Shut up, Paul, you drunken sod,' snapped Imogen.

'For heaven's sake!' Orlando, shocked, sat up sharply between the two contestants. 'Imogen, you can't talk like that.'

'Can't she just?' murmured Paul, resting his head on Orlando's shoulder. 'You should hear her when she gets going.'

'Rubbish. It's only you that brings it out in me.'

'S-E-X. Stamped on her forehead in letters of fire,' murmured Paul drowsily.

'Nothing to do with sex. I just don't like people being unnecessarily unpleasant about people.'

'I shall have to move,' said Orlando firmly, leaning forward to pull down the small seat facing him. Paul, who had been leaning on his shoulder, slid down behind him on to the seat.

Imogen helped to guide Orlando over on to the other seat, and said in her gentlest voice, 'It's only Paul. We always carry on like this. It's not serious. Go on, Paul, sit up for heaven's sake.' She seized Paul's shoulders and with a considerable demonstration of physical strength pushed him back until he was sitting more or less upright.

'Sex-mad, sex-mad, sex-mad,' he mumbled, rolling his head from side to side.

'Oh belt up!' Orlando being out of the way, Imogen could move closer to Paul: she did, and kicked him sharply on the shin.

'Ow! Oh Imo, you are mean!' said Paul childishly. Then he fell asleep.

'I apologize for my brother,' said Imogen.

In his general confusion of thought, Orlando had temporarily forgotten that Paul and Imogen were half-brother and sister, a fact which he might have been expected to remember. He shook his head, wishing that he could get

out of the taxi with Paul and go to bed. Instead, he roused
Paul, took him into his house as quietly as he could, deposited him in semi-somnolence on the sofa in the sitting-room
and climbed back into the taxi for the drive to Virginia Water.

'Please let me go alone. It's so late for you. I promise I'll
go straight there.'

'I don't trust you. I'll take you there myself. How will
you get in?'

'Over the wall. I left a window open.'

'It's very naughty of you to do this sort of thing.'

'I know.'

'Do you do any work at school?'

'I do try. But it's terribly boring.'

He thought her air of repentance, though well done, not
quite genuine.

'Did Agatha work?'

'Oh yes, of course. Agatha's frightfully clever. But she
was always having rows with the staff. They don't mind
me, even though I'm so useless, it's funny. I'm better when
Agatha's about, she stops me being quite so silly.'

He was not sure quite how to take this apparent humility
so he changed the subject and said, 'Is Paul often as drunk
as that?'

'Yes, quite often.'

'How does his wife take it?'

'Oh she can cope. She's tough as anything.'

'He's still a tricky character?'

'Still?'

'I knew him quite well as a child.'

'Oh *yes*. Well, he is tricky, yes.'

'But you're fond of him?'

'Oh of course, yes. I mean he's one of the family, sort of
thing. He's awful in some ways, I know, but he can be so

nice to be with sometimes, and funny. Especially when he's alone, with me or with me and Agatha, when he doesn't have to try, then he's nice. I really like him better than Stephen because Stephen's so disapproving.'

'What a family!'

'I know. Agatha's the only one who's any good.'

Perhaps the only one who's my daughter.

He could not see Imogen's face, because it was dark and they had by now left the street lights behind, but there was a kind of paleness in the air outside the taxi – perhaps the beginnings of dawn – against which he could see the droop of her head, which expressed sadness, unless of course it was merely sleepiness.

'I hope you'll come to Italy,' he said, the feeling recurring that he and Agatha ought to do something about her.

«Oh I'd love to,' she said enthusiastically. 'Raymond and Joe are going, aren't they?'

'Are they?' he said, rather annoyed although he did remember that he had asked them.

'The thing is, Uncle Conrad's arranged for me to go to some horrible French family in Tours because I keep on failing School Cert. French, but I expect we could change that, couldn't we?'

'You could come on afterwards perhaps. I'll talk to Conrad about it.'

'I'd much rather come to Italy instead. I mean my currency allowance will run out if I do both, won't it?'

'There may be an extra allowance for students. Conrad will know.'

'Agatha says it's the most beautiful place in the whole world.'

Irritated, he told himself that it was her sense of insecurity which made her sound insincere and was ashamed of his irritation.

'I can cook quite well,' she said.

'That will be very useful,' he said. 'Really useful.'

They were silent, and he slept a little until the taxi drew up outside some wrought-iron gates in a high brick wall, and the driver offered to ring the bell. Imogen stopped him breathlessly and led Orlando a few yards through the long grass beside the wall to a place where she said, 'If you could possibly just give me a leg-up ...'

She was very light. She looked down from the top of the wall, smiling happily in the slow light of dawn, whispered, 'Good night,' and disappeared. He listened. There was no sound but birdsong.

Acknowledging her skill, he went back to the taxi, whose driver gave him a nod implying scornful complicity; it was obviously useless to explain that Imogen was his daughter. He climbed into the back seat and fell asleep.

Arrived at his destination, he crept to the little spare bedroom and examining his face in the mirror – it was daylight by now – he said aloud, 'What a perfectly ridiculous evening for a man in imminent danger of death.'

But as he got into bed death was not uppermost in his mind.

In the wood where Judith had once tried to kill herself the garlic and the bluebells were both in flower. The white stars of the garlic were scattered in most profusion by the stream; the bluebells grew under the elms and hornbeams on the slope of the narrow valley, and faded into a blue mist towards the summit. The smell was of garlic and damp earth, the sound was of blackbirds and pheasants, a drumming woodpecker, a cuckoo somewhere out in the open, beyond the viaduct; all symptomatic of a vigorous late spring and all deeply familiar to Conrad, who walked through the wood with his dog, thinking of Orlando, who was to arrive in time for lunch.

He had not seen him since the discussion at which it had
been decided to go a stage further with the probable merger
between Daintry and Logan. He had expected to see him
the next day and to go with him to a meeting with Daintry,
but Orlando had telephoned in the morning and suggested
that Conrad should go alone.

'I don't think there's anything I can usefully contribute,'
he had said. 'It's you he wants to see. Besides, I'm not feeling frightfully well.'

'I'm very sorry to hear it. Have you seen a doctor?'

'Heavens, no. It's only a colossal hangover.'

Conrad had gone alone to the meeting, at which he and
Daintry had found themselves in accord and had agreed that
lawyers and accountants should be asked to carry the project
further. It was true that no useful purpose would have been
served by Orlando's being there, once his formal blessing
upon the proceedings had been given. He had, after all, no
official position. Conrad was nonetheless disappointed,
because he was unwilling to accept the fact that Orlando
was not going to be drawn back into things: it seemed to
him so silly, such a waste. Daintry had spoken well of him,
declared himself impressed, which showed that Orlando
had not lost his acumen. Conrad suspected him of using his
semi-blindness as an excuse, and could not understand his
reluctance to return to what, for Conrad, was normal life.
He had thought at first it might have been despair, resulting
from Judith's death and the failure of his career; but now he
wondered whether it was not simply frivolity.

'He has become frivolous,' he said. Jess came to heel, to
be on the safe side. 'A hangover.' He would never have used
a hangover as an excuse in the old days.

Conrad could have understood despair. He had known
it himself, or at least had come very near to it. He had been

thirty-six when his wife had died and he had felt as if he too had been cut off in his prime: it had not seemed possible that his life could continue without her. It was twenty-five years ago now – she had died at Henry's birth – and if there had been anything less than perfect about the beautiful Field-Marshal's daughter (which there was no reason to suppose there was) it was long ago forgotten.

There was an establishment in Curzon Street which Conrad occasionally visited in order to satisfy his carnal needs. It was well run and pleasantly furnished – once you were used to it there was little to offend – and over the years he had had a succession of regular girls there, but he was not a frequent visitor: indeed he probably went there as much because he thought it important that someone who took an active part in public life should be not less than a whole man as because of the urgency of his physical promptings. Sometimes even twenty-five years later he would weep a little afterwards in memory of Alexandra, with whom his brief union had been, so far as he could now remember, flawless, and with whom he hoped to be reunited in death, not in any sense which he could now expect to understand but in some other realm and in spirit.

He had walked sometimes after these night excursions into Grosvenor Chapel in South Audley Street, where he had prayed to be forgiven the sins of the flesh and to be given grace to live in such a way that his spirit should be fit to join with hers on his death. He had been brought up as a Christian and though he had had to re-examine his faith as a very young officer in the trenches in what was still to him the Great War, it had survived. The religion of the Church of England seemed to him beautiful and true, and he was an active member of various lay bodies which worked to support it. He felt it was by the grace of God that he had

been saved from despair after Alexandra's death, and that
the two causes which had helped him to find reasons for
living – the maintaining of his estate so as to pass it on to
his son, and the improving through the exercise of political
power of the quality of life for the rest of his countrymen –
had been sent to him by God. Any estimate of Conrad's
character or motives which left out his relationship with his
God would have been an incomplete one, yet there were
few people who knew him, either in public or in private
life, who would have thought it worth mentioning. It was
taken for granted, in so far as it was considered at all, that a
man in his position could be expected to support the established religion: the difference was unremarked between
conventionality and the personal faith which rules a man's
life. Conrad was a Christian, and he suspected that Orlando
was not (old King after all had been an atheist): Conrad
felt that on the question of Orlando's frivolity his lack of
religion had a bearing because what was there to give him
his mainstay?

'It's very hard,' he said, 'if you believe something, to
imagine what people feel like who don't.'

Jess, who had taken a quick detour up the slope to inves-
tigate an interesting stump which might have concealed a
rabbit-hole, scuttered down the steep slope rather noisily
with a flurry of small stones and loose earth.

'Good dog. In the same way, that he should turn Labour
is just conceivable – well, Liberal perhaps – but that he
should simply not care ...! No, I am very dissatisfied with
myself, Jess, very dissatisfied. I must be showing some lack
of imagination.'

Almost immediately after that he said, 'Poor old Steve'
with a pitying smile, because the idea of lack of imagination

had made him think of Stephen, who certainly suffered from
that defect, and because, too, having settled in his own mind
that further effort on his part could be expected to elucidate
the mystery of Orlando, it immediately became less worrying, and there was a certain relief in dismissing it from his
thoughts for the time being, because there were features of
Orlando's apparent attitude which seemed to question the
bases of Conrad's own principles and this he found disqui-
eting. It was easier to think about poor old Stephen, who
was taking the latest developments in the business situation
very badly indeed and was going to make a fool of himself
by calling in lawyers, when it would have been better to
have accepted Daintry's offer of compensation, which was
a generous one, and to have started to look for another job.

'Dignity,' he said. Stephen was showing no dignity.
'Damn. All the qualities I admire are out of fashion.'

He was vaguely turning over in his mind some phrases
from a speech he sometimes made at schools of which he
was a governor about the ancient Roman virtues, when he
saw a figure moving towards him through the trees. The
steady tread, the downcast glance and the fact that Jess
was hurrying joyfully to meet him, told Conrad while he
was still some distance away that it was Glass, the head
gamekeeper.

This was the oldest part of the wood and the trees grew
tall. The light, though it was morning, was greenly obscure;
translucent sheets of misty sunlight came through the gaps
in the branches, particularly by the stream, where the trees
grew less closely: through the green light the two men
approached each other, over soft damp earth, and moss, and
fallen twigs.

'Jess, good dog then, Jess.'

They greeted each other, talked of the woods, the pheasants. Glass, who was younger than Conrad but looked older, leant on his stick, his wrinkled healthy face immobile. Conrad did not see so much of him now that the shooting was let.

'And I suppose – no more news?'

Glass slowly shook his head.

Conrad was silent.

'The wife takes it hard,' said Glass.

Conrad nodded.

'It's the uncertainty,' said Glass. 'Though I say it's not uncertain, we'd know by now.'

'I remember the same thing in the war – the other wars – it was worse when one's friends were missing than when they were reported killed.'

'Missing, that's it.'

'It was a splendid thing they did, a fine campaign. Everyone knows the Second Battalion of the Gloucesters now, all over the world.'

'That's the kind of thing consoles a father maybe. Not a mother.'

'No.'

'He'd have done what he was ordered, no matter what.'

'He was going to stay on, wasn't he, after National Service?'

'Signed on for another seven years, last August. He liked the travelling, there wasn't that much for him to do here, he'd not have stayed. He'd not have stayed in these parts, whatever happened.'

'No, they don't stay, these days.'

'It's a long way, Korea, she feels that.'

'Can you take her away for a bit? Coombs can manage, can't he?'

'We could maybe get over to her sister's place in Taunton. Not that I've ever seen eye to eye with her husband, but I could keep my own counsel for a few days I daresay, if I take my old pipe.'

'Ah, relations.'

'I did hear Mr Orlando had been down.'

'He's here this weekend again. I know he'd like a word with you. We'll try and come past some time and see you.'

'That would be a pleasure. It would be a real pleasure to see Mr Orlando again.' His face showed that his feeling was genuine. They parted, Conrad to walk on towards the gate which led out of the wood into a sunlit sloping field, Glass to penetrate deeper, walking with a steady rhythm, although his shoulders were bent, into the woods from which Conrad had come.

The sun was hot, uninterrupted in the field, and Conrad sat down on a stump for a few moments and raised his face towards it with his eyes shut. Jess came to push her head between his hands. He bent down to put his face against the top of her head.

'You smell nice.' She wandered off. 'Why is life not more often good and great and glorious? Why am I not a better man?'

Orlando was rather quiet at lunch.

The chairman of the local Conservative Association and his wife were there. There was dissatisfaction with the sitting Member and a plot to induce him not to stand again at the next election: a keen young local man was ready to take his place. Conrad's guidance had to be sought, and he came down on the side of sticking to what they had.

'The fellow never opens his mouth in the House of Commons,' complained the Colonel.

'He's a conscientious private Member,' said Conrad. 'I know of several cases where he's really put himself out to help a constituent, and got something done too.'

Mrs Mayhew looked gloomily under her hat at Orlando. She thought he looked very handsome and sad and wondered what he was thinking about when from time to time a faint tired smile crossed his face – the past, she supposed, that poor wife.

In fact he was thinking how awful it would be if he were suddenly to make violent amorous advances to Mrs Mayhew, and have to be dragged off by Colonel Mayhew, who would no doubt be purple in the face and shouting military epithets. It was an irrelevant concept because Mrs Mayhew was not at all enticing, although gifted with green fingers, and Orlando knew that instead of indulging in foolish fantasies he ought to be helping Conrad with a rather difficult conversation. The trouble was that even his friendliness for Conrad could not overcome the deadening effect of his own total boredom.

He exerted himself and contributed a remark to the effect that the most useful function of a Member of Parliament these days was as a sort of welfare officer. Here Conrad differed, but did seize the opportunity to diverge from the immediate problem. He entered on a long monologue about the functioning of the House of Commons, which Orlando had heard before and considered that Conrad did very well, so that he himself could safely relax again and, when he did, he found that he was longing to return to Lecceto. There was so much to do, and if he was going to get enough rooms ready for all these people who were coming in the summer he would have to get on to Rossi the moment he got back. He had already written to Agatha asking her to arrange for Rossi to come up and see him the day after his return, but the letter would hardly reach her before he arrived himself. Thank goodness she was there to help him, he could not possibly manage without her, beds, curtains... Ought he to arrange for anything to come out from England or was it better to get everything there?

Conrad was quoting from William Morris. He had gone on from the familiar speech about the House of Commons to the familiar speech about what the private Member without great political ambitions should be aiming for, and this was when he usually used the quotation from William Morris, especially when speaking to the young, Sixth Forms and the like, because it showed how open his mind was that he should quote from the works of a Socialist – for whom, nonetheless, Orlando knew perfectly well his admiration was genuine, just as he knew that the views he expressed in these familiar pieces of exposition were his true opinions, for neither repetition nor the seeking after calculated effects in order to make his points had dulled the sincerity of his purpose: Orlando was sure of this.

'"... how men fight and lose the battle,"' Conrad was quoting in a thoughtful voice, and though Orlando could not see his face clearly he knew the expression on it very well: he knew the kind of serenity which came upon his forehead as the muscles just above his ears tightened with his emotion, 'and the thing they fought for comes about in spite of their defeat and when it comes it turns out not to be what they meant, and other men have to fight for what they meant under another name."'

There was a pause. 'That's political action for you.'

The Colonel had heard a bit about William Morris and did not like what he had heard although he could not for the moment remember what it was. His wife, however,

had raised her keen long nose with an expression of unexpected liveliness and now exclaimed, 'It's *terribly* true of
gardening.'

Orlando walked up to Wood Hill. He took a stick, but the
way was so familiar to him that he hardly needed to use
it. He walked up the valley, and a mile or so from Mount
Sorrel paused and turned, by habit, to look back at the view
of the house; he saw only mist, a rather bright and dazzling
mist because the sun was shining.

He knew the house was there. He knew the valley folded
down to where it sat in its slightly cold grandeur facing its
park. He knew the woods on his right concealed the entrance
to Wood Hill and the copse of beeches on his far left crowned
the round green hill which partly framed the distance from
the windows of Mount Sorrel itself. He knew that behind the
house the closeness of the grey stone village pleasantly belied
the exclusiveness of its elegant facade, and gave way to a milder
hill, green fields, an open distance. He knew all this, and could
see none of it, and he did not mind that he could not see. He
could think of no reason why this should be: he accepted his
not minding as a piece of good fortune and went on to find his
way into the little road which led to Wood Hill. Probably, he
thought, he was used to his disability at last: though after all
this place had been of much significance to him for the most
important part of his life, and he had not revisited it since his
accident: no, it was unexpected good fortune to find himself
with no inclination to rail against his fate.

He made his way towards the house through the trees,
hoping the present inhabitants would not happen to pass.
Conrad had told him that the house was let, but he had taken
the risk of going there without first telephoning in the hope
that he would manage to avoid the tenants. Where the trees

stopped and the lawn began he hesitated. He could discern the outline of the house. An unfamiliar child's bicycle was lying on the grass close to his feet.

It was near enough. He remembered the feeling of it. His house, his pride, Judith, dreams of King. He had forgotten that. All the time, it now seemed, he had had these dreams of King. Or was it afterwards, in hospital? His life had been underwritten with his dreams, as if some part of him had been a secret scribbler on walls, skilled in the hieroglyphics of another tongue. And King had stalked, mourning his lost message, his misunderstood signals, all over this house in Orlando's dreams, dreamt at a time when Orlando had no conscious knowledge of what he was later to read in King's diaries; this message which he had failed to pass on perhaps because he had not been able to decipher it himself, or else because he had not been able to believe it, for what was it that he had written about the subjunctive case, about 'as if'?

In the context of this house – or rather of the bright mist which he knew to be at once house, memory and dream – King seemed less pathetic and more courageous. Almost, Orlando could feel he might be able to guess at what it was he had been so concerned about, though all of it was in a language unfamiliar to Orlando until his middle age, and even now hardly learnt; nevertheless remembering how Agatha, at three or so, had sat near where he now stood, about where that unknown child's bicycle had been abandoned, and how Jen who had looked after her with such singleness of purpose had bent over her with a biscuit or a daisy chain, and he had watched from the trees, Judith on his mind, all his bright achievements in his hands, King in his dreams, he could approach a guess as to the level of existence on which King had been striving to find for them both a footing.

Vague though this apprehension might be, it seemed
to make a closer approach to the house unnecessary, and
with a feeling of renunciation, the same admission of ignorance which he had made when he had listened to the music
outside Conrad's flat in London – which admission in an
extraordinary way had the effect of seeming to strip his
physical being for action, as if a valve had been opened
in his heart – he turned back into the woods and began
to walk quickly, unable now for some reason to think of
anything except practicalities: how soon he could see Rossi,
how many rooms in the tower house could be made habitable within a few weeks, whether the plumbing would be
finished in the priest's house by the time of his return.

'I suppose he thinks I'm a pompous ass.'

They were sitting in the library. Orlando had come in
from the garden to find Conrad, who had been at his desk.
They had been brought tea. It was Sunday afternoon.

They had talked a great deal. Leaving politics at the
point where all that mattered was that the Labour Party
should be got out before they ruined the country – nothing
else being from Conrad's point of view worth discussing
until that had been achieved – they had talked about business, Conrad again advocating adventurous capitalism,
as represented by Daintry and such other entrepreneurs
as could properly exploit technical expertise – 'why do
we have to run ourselves down all the time – aren't we
ten years ahead of anyone else with the Comet?' – and
then they had progressed to Orlando's plans for Italy,
and here Conrad, once he had expressed his view that the
whole of Europe was liable to turn Communist though
he was prepared to admit that this was less likely than it
had seemed a year or two ago – began to feed Orlando's
enthusiasm; this was something with which he could

sympathize. The possibility of a new vineyard set them off; in no time the economics of a venture a good deal more complicated than Orlando had envisaged until that moment had been worked out and put on paper and the details of transferring money and obtaining the necessary permissions gone into. Conrad was quick to grasp Orlando's intent and to anticipate the direction of his thoughts; he appreciated too the role of Agatha as heiress to these endeavours. He had pronounced the whole thing excellent, for Orlando, for Agatha, for the neglected terraces of Chianti; and then had found himself drawn by a natural progression into admitting to Orlando his disappointment in his own son.

'I can't understand him,' he said. 'He doesn't seem to be interested in anything. Or if he is he doesn't talk to me about it. I suppose he thinks I'm a pompous ass. Perhaps I am a pompous ass.'

'He seems to have quite a lot of charm,' said Orlando cautiously.

'Oh, he can be quite amiable. He didn't even get a degree, you know.'

'The person who seems to me much more of a problem is Paul. The other night when he was drunk he told me that he was still a homosexual and for good measure working for the Communist Party.'

'He's always been an exhibitionist.'

'You think he was exaggerating?'

'That wife can cope with him. There was an unfortunate episode just at the end of the war when I had to get him out of trouble. Public Lavatory, Leicester Square. I was able to hush it up. I think it taught him his lesson. I daresay all he was leading up to was a long maudlin account of that – or perhaps you got it, did you?'

'No. I wasn't very encouraging. What about the Communism?'

'Rubbish.'

'Poor Paul. I can't help liking him in a way, though I know there's nothing to be said for him. I always did like him better than Stephen.'

'Stephen's an ass.'

'I was never in the least good with either of them.'

'You were too young to be expected to know what to do with two thoroughly difficult boys. They've survived all right. I haven't much sympathy with either. Over this whole Daintry business they've both been pursuing their own selfish interests entirely, without a thought for anything else.'

'I suppose so.'

'I've got to go over to Evensong. I don't suppose you want to come, do you? I'm reading the Lesson, so I've no escape. Look here, you know, if ever you get sick of it out there, you'll come back here, won't you? I mean, this house is far too big for me. Or else you could have Wood Hill back again. Daintry would give you a seat on the Timberwork board any time you wanted it – you're going to need the money with all these plans for Italy.'

'I can't thank you enough. As usual. The thing is, I've got to start on this Italian business and see how it goes. After that, in a year or two, who knows?'

Miss Bates walked slowly into her house in the noonday heat carrying a heavy shopping basket. The house was dark and quiet and she supposed that Agatha, who had no lesson in Siena that day because it was Saturday, must be out on the terrace reading in the shade, unless of course by any chance she was already in the kitchen preparing the lunch. But she was not in the kitchen and Miss Bates set about preparing the meal without her, which was a good deal easier because though Agatha was willing she was not very efficient in the kitchen. Chopping-board, knife, an onion from the rack, its purplish inside already showing through the outer skin; but then there were no tomatoes, so she took her little vegetable basket from the hook and opened the door into the garden, and then she heard Agatha crying in the bedroom upstairs.

She hesitated, went quietly back into the house, hesitated again at the foot of the stairs and saw the letter on the table.

She picked it up without compunction and read, '... The awful thing is that they all seem to be coming, but I think it won't be until about the middle of July so we should be able to get enough rooms habitable by then. It looks as if it will be Henry and Caroline, both of whom I like very much, Raymond Phipps, Joe something-or-other, I know you know him ...' Miss Bates did not bother to turn over, but putting the letter back where she had found it and calling the dogs in a loud voice went out into the garden to fetch the tomatoes.

By the time she came back Agatha was chopping onions in the kitchen.

'I'm terribly sorry. I meant to have it all done by the time you came back from doing the shopping.'

'It only takes a minute. There we are. Why don't we have some of that nasty vermouth on the terrace while it cooks?'

'All right.'

'No one else's home-made vermouth is quite so revolting as Willie's but I'm too mean not to drink it when it's free. If your father sees it he'll make us throw it away.'

'He seems to have asked everyone he's met in England to come and stay for the summer.'

'He'll have to hurry up with the work on the house in that case.'

'It can't possibly be finished in the time. And they're all terribly selfish and complaining people. And Nella won't be able to manage all the cooking and my cooking's so ghastly.'

'I'd better give you some more lessons. Who are all these people?'

'Well, Henry my cousin really, and all his awful friends, and a girl called Caroline.'

'Can she cook?'

'I shouldn't think so.'

'Why are they awful?'

'They aren't awful really. In fact they're very nice. It's just that they frighten me.'

'Why don't you send them over to Wicked Will's and then they can all frighten each other?'

'That's a good idea.'

'Is she quite pretty, this Caroline?' asked Miss Bates, tentatively.

'Terribly. She's a model.'

'Skinny, I suppose, like that Barbara Goalen one sees in all the papers?'

'Not quite so sophisticated-looking. Prettier really.'

'Of course they all have awful complexions.'

'Do they?'

'From wearing all that make-up.'

'I hadn't noticed that.'

'It shows up more in the sun. Is she fair?'

'Oh yes, absolutely blonde.'

'Poor thing, she won't be able to take the sun at all.'

'Won't she?'

'Oh no. In fact,' said Miss Bates, 'I should think she'll probably come out in blisters all over and have to be sent straight home.'

'Good heavens, what a terrible idea!' said Agatha, bursting out laughing.

'Isn't it?' agreed Miss Bates, beaming.

When Orlando arrived at the house in Chelsea, he was greeted by Serena, who told him that Paul had gone out.

'One of his drinking friends is in trouble,' she said, as graciously as if she were explaining that he had been unexpectedly called away to a Royal Garden Party.

'Oh dear,' said Orlando, wondering in that case how soon he could go to bed.

He had timed his arrival for after dinner so as to minimize his imposition on their hospitality, but he would have liked to have seen Paul again before leaving. 'What a pity, I shall probably miss him. I shall have to leave long before you're up in the morning to catch my aeroplane.'

'He may be back. I think he only went out for half an hour or so. Won't you help yourself to a whisky and soda?'

She was wearing a very pretty dressing-gown, or possibly negligée, or even wasn't it what he could remember Judith calling a tea-gown? Anyway it had blue flowers on it and a good deal of *broderie anglaise*.

She apologized for it. 'I was simply exhausted. All day rehearsing this stupid charity dress show. So I thought I'd have a bath and put on something comfortable and relax with my dear husband in front of the telly.'

'Do you find you watch it a lot?'

'Glued to it, from the moment I come in. Uncle Conrad's still too snooty to have it, I suppose, so you won't have seen it since you've been in England. You know Daddy's convinced they're going to allow commercial soon?'

Her face was perhaps a little too round, but she had nice brown eyes and a pretty mouth, on which she wore bright red lipstick. Her dark hair was brushed back and held in a band; she looked clean and wholesome and like an advertisement in an American magazine.

'Does Paul have quite a number of drinking friends then?' he asked.

In fact he was reluctant to enter into a discussion about Paul's habits with her and regretted his question as soon as he had asked it.

'I ration the time he spends with them very strictly,' she said, smiling. 'Just the odd evening every now and then.'

'I see.'

'I think husbands need to get away occasionally with their own cronies, don't you? And our life together is really so much of a social whirl, it's nice for him to relax sometimes with his friends from the old days. He doesn't enjoy the social life as much as I do – or at least he pretends not to.'

They were interrupted by the telephone ringing. Serena picked up the receiver and immediately assumed an expression of cool surprise.

'I can't, I'm afraid. I'm doing something else. No, on Thursday I'll be much too tired, I've got this boring thing the night before. Well, all right then, Friday. One o'clock, yes. See you. Bye-ee.'

She put back the receiver and said, 'Bunny Hayford. He really is becoming rather a bore.'

'Who's he?'

She looked surprised. 'Oh, I'd forgotten you'd been abroad so long. Well, you know, his father's that shipping magnate, the richest man in England or something, and Bunny's a racing driver and fabulously good-looking and always written up in things. He's quite sweet really but terribly spoilt of course.'

'Of course.'

'D'you know, I think I'm going to be frightfully rude and go to bed? The thing is, I've got this show tomorrow and if I arrive with bags under my eyes I'll get terrible stick. Do have lots to drink, won't you, if you're going to stay up a bit? I should think Paul probably will be back quite soon. I know he was looking forward to seeing you.'

Orlando rose to his feet to say good-bye and to thank her.

'We're dying to come and stay with you in Italy,' she said.

'You certainly must do that, just as soon as we've made it habitable for civilized guests. I'm afraid that won't be for a year or two, though.'

'Let's hope you'll be over again before that,' she said with her formal smile.

Orlando sat down again to wait for Paul.

When he finally arrived he was sober but obviously worried.

'Has Serena gone to bed? Thank goodness for that. I'll just go and see if she's asleep.'

He came down again almost immediately, saying in a rather abstracted way, 'She's got to look her best for tomorrow, you know. Have you got a drink?'

He went over to pour himself out some whisky, then putting the glass down on a table he began to walk up and down the room snapping his fingers. 'She's got this dress show, you know. It's very important to her.'

'She seemed to be quite relaxed about it. In fact I'd have said she was thoroughly enjoying her life.'

'Yes.' He stood still for a moment, looking at Orlando; then he snapped his fingers again and walked quickly over to the table where he had left his glass. 'Yes, she thoroughly enjoys life. Never stops complaining but she enjoys life.' He laughed briefly and began to pace up and down again.

'She certainly seems much less worried than you do,' said
Orlando.

'I'm not worrying about her wretched fashion show, not
at all. I've got a problem. Unfortunately I can't tell you
about it.'

He sat down in an armchair opposite Orlando, leant
back his head and closed his eyes for a moment. Almost
immediately he opened them again and sat up.

'It's not really my own problem.'

'It doesn't always help to tell other people anyway. In
fact in my experience it's often fatal.'

'Oh of course. One should never tell anyone anything.
There's one exception to that rule, and that's Agatha. Agatha
is the only completely reliable person I know.'

'You tell her things?'

'Not much. But I know that I could. In the last resort,
she'd always be there, the only person.'

'It sounds rather desperate.'

'She believes in something, that's why. You have to
believe in something. All these other people have nothing,
nothing at all, except self-interest. It's the capitalist ethic,
drummed into them from birth, rabid self-interest. Despair.
Total despair.' He jumped up from his chair and began to
walk up and down the room again.

'Don't you think there's quite a lot of latitude in the
capitalist system all the same – the post-war variety, anyway?'

'Latitude? Lassitude. Apathy. No wonder they're terrified of Communism. It's infinitely more powerful, now
that the Russians have the bomb. All the entrenched,
they're terrified, in spite of their arrogance.' He began to
snap his fingers again, still pacing up and down. 'All my life
I've suffered from the arrogance of the privileged. Isn't that
my justification?'

'Oh come, I should have thought you were privileged yourself.'

'With dear cousin Henry on my doorstep, sneering at me as a poor relation?'

'Henry? But at the time he was living on your doorstep you were all children and it was you who patronized him because he was so much younger than you and Stephen. You were rather fond of him, I remember.'

'You don't understand, you don't understand at all. I never belonged. One must belong somewhere. Everyone needs the same things.'

'Do you really expect me to believe that at this moment of time you'd prefer to have your destiny ruled by Stalin?'

'It's not a question of preference, it's a question of history.'

'I can't make out what you're saying. Did you mean it when you said you were a Communist the other night?'

'I never said that.' He stared at Orlando, then came to sit opposite him again. 'I never said that.'

'It's what I understood you to say.'

'I was drunk.'

'Certainly you were drunk.'

'I'm not a Communist.'

'I had a great friend who was a Communist,' said Orlando, after a pause. 'He was killed in Spain. He worked in Timberwork in the old days, before it became part of Logan.'

'Did you ever know a fellow called Guy Burgess? He'd be about your age, I suppose.'

'No, I don't think so.'

'Serena can't stand him.' He was silent, staring in front of him, drumming his fingers on the arm of his chair.

'I think I'll go up to bed,' said Orlando. 'I hope your worries will dissolve. At least the Logan situation looks good for you.'

'Yes,' said Paul. 'Yes. I'm going to become very rich. Very rich indeed.'

'You don't look very happy about it.'

'Happy?' Paul's very pale blue eyes, expressionless, met Orlando's for a moment. Then he stood up. 'Oh yes, I'm happy about it. Tell Agatha, will you, that I'm grateful to her for persuading you to come over and take a look at us all.'

Nella's family had been joined by another and on the slope above the road leading to Lecceto they were cutting the hay, seven or eight men and women sweeping long scythes through the grass, bending to scoop it into their arms, stretching to throw it on to the mounting heaps with which half of the slope was now dotted. All this movement stopped when they saw Agatha on the road below them. She had walked to the village and was on her way back with a full shopping basket. The village was two kilometres distant and she was tired and thirsty, but she had been determined that she needed the exercise. There were no scales either at Lecceto or in Miss Bates's house, Orlando and Miss Bates being both indifferent to considerations of weight, and Agatha had been able to persuade herself that too much *pasta* had made her fat, possibly disgustingly so.

When they had heard from Orlando that he was coming back Agatha had insisted on moving back to Lecceto on the grounds that she ought to get the house ready for him and that she would only be alone there for three days. Miss Bates, who trusted Nella anyway, had felt that her promise to Orlando would be fulfilled as long as a visit was made on one side or the other each day. Agatha had taken time off from her lessons in Siena, thinking, arrogantly but correctly, that she was so far ahead of the other students that it would not matter.

The haymakers, some leaning on their scythes, two of the women with hands on their hips, watched her from above, and when they saw her turn her head to look towards them raised an arm or crooked it to make their customary inward-turning wave of the hand, and someone shouted a greeting. Agatha shouted back and waved, arm stretched and openhanded, like an English schoolgirl. She felt she had their approval, as indeed she had, for her smile and her progress in their language and her eagerness to come and live alone amongst them: relations were so far sunny and full of promise.

She walked on, under their close observation, left her shopping in the kitchen and came out of the house again to walk up to the priest's house. She was worried by the fact that all the building operations seemed to have stopped while Orlando was away, and felt foolish to have been unable to discover whether this had been by arrangement with Orlando or not. When she had heard from Orlando that he wanted to see Rossi immediately on his return she had, in passing on this message, also asked that at least the masons should start work again on the terrace of the priest's house, but so far there had been no sign of them.

She walked as if to the tower house but at the space before it where the well was she turned left so as to go into the priest's house through the chapel. It was already obvious from the absence of appropriate sounds that no one had arrived and started work while she had been shopping, but she went on all the same, down the few steps which led to the chapel door. There were two or three empty shell-boxes there, left behind after the fighting in the war. Agatha

had found the shrivelled remains of flowers which someone had once planted in them, so she had filled them with
trailing geraniums, whose leaves half covered the mysterious letters and numbers which referred to their previous
use: they made quite adequate flower-pots. Behind them
now she saw to her surprise – and stopped still at once – a
hare, crouched on the doorstep of the chapel. The double
door, a faded blistered green, was half open behind it,
showing the cool darkness of the chapel. It was overhung
by the vine, which had grown tall in the sheltered corner
between door and wall and now almost covered the worn
pediment over the door. The hare, though, was in full
sunlight on the step. It had opened its eyes but did not
move.

She stood in silence for what seemed such a long time
that she began to wonder if the animal might be ill, about
to die perhaps from old age or poisonous food; but then it
stood up, and turned, and loped away over the low wall and
into the long grass without hurry, so nonchalantly in fact
that it made her laugh, and she ran down the last two steps
and went to feel on the stone the warm place where it had
been lying.

The chapel had been robbed long before Orlando had
acquired it: now the scars left by the despoilers had been
plastered over and the walls whitewashed. The only signs of
its former function were a plain little balcony on the wall,
with a door behind it through which the priest had been able
to come from his house to overlook what was below, and a
stone in the floor with a big iron ring by which it could be
moved to disclose in a deep square hole a number of bones,
presumably human. Agatha walked through the chapel and
pushing open a door behind where the altar had stood went
into the priest's house, where there were still piles of rubble

and fallen plaster, and a heap of old shoes in the big stone
fireplace in the kitchen. She walked on through the kitchen
to the new terrace, three-quarters finished but abandoned
when Orlando had been unable to make up his mind about
its exact dimensions. There seemed an impossible amount
of work to be done.

She bent her head under the branches of the pear tree,
hurrying, and raising it was surprised to see Hal Newman
standing in her path.

'Worried?'

'There's so much work to be done here, and I don't know
whether the workmen were meant to be here this week or
not. I don't know how he's ever going to get it finished, do
you?'

Hal swept his bland gaze over the view.

'It's beautiful.'

'I do like the way you say things.'

He smiled at her. 'Like how?'

'The way you can say very banal things quite straight
like that. I think it must be American.'

'Thanks,' he said ironically.

'How are the books?'

'Finished for the moment. Willie's gone to Venice.'

'Are you alone there then?'

'No, there's three or four of us. He's taken Bunny and
Enrico. Willie knows a lot of people in Venice who might
commission Bunny to do things for them.'

'Those birds?'

'Or anything, like for their houses, you know. He's a very
talented boy. Listen, you know what I could do? I could
come over sometimes, and help you here. I just love that
sort of thing, building, it makes you so calm. I built a house
with my brother once, between Carmel and Monterey, only

a beach house, but it had two rooms, fireplace, chimney, we built it all.'

'Do come, what a good idea. Oh look, Miss B.'s arrived. I shall make you both some lunch in that case.'

Orlando came back with sheaves of plans and calculations. The first evening they sat late on the terrace, he and Agatha and Signor Rossi, distracted only by the fireflies in the darkness in front of them, and with a map of Lecceto spread out on the table.

The workmen had reappeared on the morning of Orlando's return, a reinforced body of them who were making such astonishing progress by the time he arrived about the end of the afternoon that he was easily reconciled to the fact of their not having been there while he had been away – a piece of calculation on Signor Rossi's part which had enabled another client to be kept happy without Orlando's having had the annoyance of knowing what was going to happen in advance.

Signor Rossi had a certain cynical sense of humour which Orlando found sympathetic. He was a small sallow hypochondriac with an extremely sharp intelligence who as well as handling the local labour force seemed to hold all the other reins of power in the immediate neighbourhood. He had come more and more to act as Orlando's adviser as well as agent: how much the foreigner's provision of much-needed employment for the region helped him in his campaign to be mayor, how much exactly of what Orlando paid for the labour went as commission to Signor Rossi, these were somewhat vague areas. The mutual understanding as to the interests and personalities involved was so good that definitions were unnecessary. Each respected the businessman in the other as well as liking the man of good sense and easy apprehension.

The detailed map which they were studying showed each terrace divided into numbered segments of varying sizes. By the end of the evening it had been decided which should be cultivated and which left to grass, where should be corn, where sweet corn and artichokes for their own consumption, where cypresses and where, much more important, the new vineyards. The means of harvesting and selling the wine, and applying for the special mark which showed it to have been grown in the true Chianti region, all this had to be gone into in great detail. Agatha, now withdrawn a little and half asleep, heard Orlando saying in Italian, 'You and Agatha will have to see to it.'

'See to what?' she asked.

'Getting me buried in the cemetery over there. You know, the one with the little wall and the cypress tree.'

'Is that what you want?'

'It's marked here, look: Cimitero di S. Donato. That's where I want to be. I don't want Conrad carting me back to Mount Sorrel or anything like that.'

'All right. I'll remember.'

'What bothers me is that there doesn't seem to have been a vineyard on that slope before, and yet it's the obvious place for one. Do you think there's something we haven't thought of?'

'It will be very stony,' said Signor Rossi. 'In the days when they had to do all the work by hand it was not worth cultivating those terraces when they could use the ones nearer the houses, but now, with a machine, we can get that ready for planting in a day, two days at the most.'

'And they're how much a day, you say, those bulldozers?'

There was a period of hard work. Agatha cut her Italian lessons down to two a week, and most days Hal came over and worked with the masons. It turned out that he

was a perfectly competent workman and won the approval
of the experts, but Orlando, who worked with them too,
complained that he was lazy: certainly he spent a good deal
of time lying on his back gazing at the sky. He was better
when it came to furniture. He and Agatha, after many
hot afternoons searching among the little side streets in
Florence, found two huge infirm sofas suitable for the big
room in the tower. Hal proved able not only to mend but
to re-upholster them; and then Agatha found a pair of faded
damask curtains which Orlando had brought from France
years ago and never found a place for, and she and Hal
patiently measured and cut out and banged in a hundred or
so brass-studded nails and ended up with two good, even
splendid, pieces of furniture.

Stephen wrote from England, still hoping to solicit help
from Orlando though it was far too late. 'Conrad is hypno-
tized by Daintry,' he wrote. 'He loves the idea of a man
vulgar enough to do all the things he hasn't the face to do
himself and who yet remains in awe of him, Conrad, the
man of privilege. He's bewitched by all the promised accumulation and expansion, as if accumulation and expansion
were ends in themselves, whereas what is actually going to
happen is that Daintry will quite ruthlessly sell off everything in the Logan group which shows less than 20 per cent
return on capital employed.'

'He's probably right,' said Orlando, throwing the letter
over to Agatha. 'He's thought it all out, his grievance has
made him marshal his thoughts, but what can I do, in my
position? It's his battle, and the trouble is I don't really care
who wins it.'

'Paul seems to be winning it.'

'Perhaps. But, then, what about Paul? When I saw him
again, I found I couldn't understand him any better than

I had when he was a child. He doesn't seem happy, but one can't see quite why, nor will he tell one – only those same portentous hints and mysteries which I remember from the very first moment I met him, when he was about ten. And what's all this about Communism? Do you know anything about that? And then these people that have disappeared, you know – the papers were full of it the day I got back here – he'd mentioned the name of one of them to me just before: Burgess. I'm sure it was the same.'

'Paul knew Burgess?'

'Apparently.'

'I've never heard him mention him, but I suppose it's perfectly possible. I mean, it said in the papers, didn't it, about him being in drinking clubs all the time? And of course Paul does that sort of thing too. He has all sorts of odd friends he meets in pubs and never sees anywhere else.'

'He was definitely worried that evening he mentioned his name. He admitted he was worried, and said he couldn't tell me why.'

'I wonder if he knows something about it. I don't believe they've gone behind the Iron Curtain, do you?'

'Not really, it's too melodramatic. But what do you think Paul means when he talks like that?'

'He likes mysteries and teases, sometimes quite cruel ones. I don't know. He never talks about politics with me except to have a general grumble about reactionaries and so on. He doesn't get on with Uncle Conrad, of course. He feels that Uncle Conrad despises him. He does, too.'

'I did just raise the matter with Conrad. He was quite sure that it was all exaggeration on Paul's part.'

'I should think he's right. Paul does talk such rubbish sometimes. And I have a feeling that if he was in real trouble, whatever it was, he'd probably have told me. Not that

we ever discuss anything much, and I'm sure he'd be astonished if he knew how much I know about him – he thinks
I'm very innocent – but at the same time if there is ever
anything serious he does tell me.'

'He said he did.'

'If you could ever know him properly, and he could just
stop showing off to you, you'd like him too, I know you
would. He hasn't been loved enough.'

'Ought. I to have done it? I suppose so. But he was eleven
when I married your mother and it wasn't a very easy situation. Now I feel rather as I do about Stephen. Well, all
right, of course I do like Paul in a way – but I feel he's in
the middle of all sorts of complications of his own, and if
I knew his motives I'm pretty certain I shouldn't approve
of them, and it's simply not for me to take it on myself to
interfere.'

'I'll write to him. No, don't worry, I won't ask him
about the missing diplomat. I'll just leave it open for him to
mention it if he wants to. He'll be all right. Why should you
worry about him? I can see you're worried about Imogen
and she's much younger and your own daughter.'

'We'll get her out here, won't we, and put her in order?'

'Of course we will. And truthfully – I mean, you don't
really agree with him about Logan, do you? – what did you
think of Uncle Conrad?'

'Conrad's my friend. You can't ever know how kind
he was to me, years ago, or what a marvellous person he
seemed to me then, even though a little remote perhaps.
This time, having become a million years old myself in
the interval, I was less impressed by him, but perhaps that
made it possible for me to like him even more. I kept finding myself smiling affectionately at things he said. I'd never
have done that in the old days.'

Agatha sighed. 'I hope I get to be a million years old quite soon.'

'You probably will. But I see how he might strike someone young and intolerant.'

'I'm not intolerant. Just terribly irritable.'

'And impatient.'

'And impatient.'

'I thought doctors had to be very patient.'

'No, no, it's the patients who have to be patient, obviously. The doctor can be perfectly foul as long as he cures people.'

'How can he cure people if he's too impatient to get his diagnosis right?'

'Then he has to be like a poet, patient as an ox. I know. That's what I shall start learning in October. I will learn it too.'

'I believe you.'

Finding Orlando so confident about his own plans for the future of Lecceto, and gaining practical support both from Hal and from Miss Bates, Agatha lost her nervousness about the approaching visit and gave herself up to the pleasures of preparing for an arrival.

Bedrooms were whitewashed, beds acquired, shutters painted. Seeing the place in anticipation through his eyes, she thought how Henry would love it. The weather was hot, there was less green in the landscape and the distance was hazy: she wished he could have seen it earlier. But then, just before they were all due to arrive, there were three days of thunderstorms. The thunder rolled round and round the hills, lightning struck the fuses and there was no electricity, the rain rushed from the north-west and destructively pelted the growing grapes. When it was over the far distance was clear for a day or two and the air full of the smell of herbs;

a crowded Land-Rover, followed by a white Jaguar XK, bumped along the road to Lecceto, and the visit began.

Agatha had been watching the cars driving along the road. Orlando was up at the tower house and Hal was lying down in the shade somewhere indoors. As the cars approached Agatha dashed back to the terrace, sat down and picked up a paper.

'Hal!' she called urgently.

He did not answer.

She jumped up to go into the house to find him, but the cars were already in sight. She hesitated, could already see Henry's face, began to hurry towards them, stopped again, half turned back, and then they were there and out of the cars, exclaiming; and Henry with his look of being dazzled and astonished – which was familiar to her though none-theless flattering – was remarking as to her brownness and implying as to her beauty and ending up by telling her she had grown.

Behind him came Caroline and Raymond Phipps and Joe Hertz and the pale man who had had his appendix out and the pretty one with the lisp, and in the XK were a tiny girl with brown curls and huge eyes and the dreaded Brian (who was not expected).

'There aren't enough beds,' Agatha whispered desperately to Henry.

'It's all right, I'll get rid of Brian.'

This did not seem to be immediately practicable, but when Henry had taken stock of the accommodation, which he did with great rapidity, he disposed of everyone with surprisingly little fuss, and as it seemed that Brian and the little brown girl, whose name was Cherry, only needed the smallest of the single rooms between them, and as Joe Hertz had brought his sleeping-bag, there was room for everyone after all. Henry put Caroline into the nicest room by herself, quite a long way from the room which he himself was to share with Raymond Phipps. This was a relief to Agatha, who had been worrying that being abroad might make it seem unnecessary to him to observe the conventions he did observe at home. She assumed that Henry and Caroline were lovers but felt that to have had this acknowledged in their sleeping arrangements would have been embarrassing.

Her happiness at finding that this was not to be the case was added to by the fact that the young man with the lisp, whose name was Ozzie and whom she knew only slightly, turned out to speak perfect Italian and to know quite a lot about Tuscan cooking, so that he quite soon disappeared into the kitchen and made friends with Nella; and then it became clear during the course of the evening that they were all making every effort to please and amuse Orlando and that they were succeeding, so that all that was left to worry about was that they should like Hal and that he should like them. On the first evening all that happened in this direction was that it appeared that Raymond Phipps, the incipient art historian, had an introduction to William Holmes from someone in England and that Hal said that in that case they must all come over some time. Apart from that, his soft voice and slow speech were for the time being submerged. Nevertheless the first evening amounted to a success.

Their life was changed. It was hot, sensual summer. The visitors brought with them many cross-currents of feeling, between themselves, between one or other of them and Orlando, one or other of them and Agatha. Neither Orlando nor Agatha slept well during that time, yet both felt in exceptionally good physical condition.

They went to Miss Bates's swimming pool. She watched from the terrace.

'I don't really know many young people,' she murmured to Orlando.

Brian did a perfect dive.

'A fiver if you do it from the terrace wall,' offered Henry.

'Go on, Bri,' said Cherry. She had a high little voice and spoke very little although she smiled a lot. Brian treated her like a slave and she obviously liked it. Orlando found this disturbing.

Brian won the fiver.

'Go on, Henry, you'll have to do it now,' said Caroline.

'Oh no,' said Agatha.

But he did. It was a dangerous dive, and he hit his head quite hard on the bottom of the pool.

'Is he a foolhardy person?' asked Miss Bates.

'Yes, I think so,' said Orlando. 'Especially when challenged by Brian, who's the show-off of the group, and also the only rich one. They're all rather interested in money.'

'Are Henry and Caroline a pair?'

'Yes.'

'I was afraid so.'

'Why afraid?'

'Agatha's rather keen on Henry.'

'But not … Good heavens, I mean, they're first cousins. Besides, she's much too young.'

'Exactly. But these things sometimes happen.'

Orlando was quite shocked. It had simply never struck him. He felt he needed to think about it, so he changed the subject.

'They do seem rather materialistic to me. I'm sure my generation was more serious. It must be something to do with wanting to have a good time after the war. They don't seem to want to change the world, only the personnel in the seats of power – or do they even want to do that? They don't seem very ambitious. Perhaps it's a good thing.'

'Which is the art historian?'

'Raymond Phipps. He's nice, but not very original, I think. They admire his clothes. Joe's the most intelligent, he's going into advertising, which is a little surprising. Adrian, the pale one, says he's an art thief, which may or may not be true. Ozzie's an interior decorator – they're always with us of course, dear things. Brian is a car sales-man but has a rich father. And Henry is simply seeing how long he can hold out before he has to get a job.'

Henry was now lying in the shade, protesting to Caroline that his head did not hurt in the least. Caroline was bending solicitously over him in her bikini, Agatha watching doubt-fully from the other side of the pool.

'Is that Agatha?' Orlando asked, indicating her to Miss Bates.

'Yes.'

'Poor thing, if what you say is true.'

It was bad enough for him, he thought, whose age and ruined eyes protected him from too much torment as Caroline passed him with virtually nothing on to ask Miss Bates whether she had witch-hazel in the house. She wore so little in the heat that there was no disguising the perfection of her body. Far from being, as Miss Bates had optimistically supposed, too skinny, she was even a little on the plump side, but with such smoothness and roundness and youthful delicacy of skin texture as to make Cherry, for instance, who was altogether on a smaller scale, look scrawny. Nor did she seem to have any hesitation about displaying her advantages. In the simplest – it seemed to Orlando – and most straightforward, natural way, she conveyed a whole-hearted pleasure in physical existence. Or was it so simple and straightforward? He could not make up his mind whether it was more than just her sensitivity to his situation which made her come so close whenever she spoke to him, and gaze so directly into his eyes and lean forward to listen to him so that he could see the pressure of her bikini on her smooth bosom and smell the delicious mixture of her scent, always rather powerful, her Ambre Solaire and presumably her own sweet skin.

'Oh dear, oh dear,' he said in an old man's voice, leaning back in his cane armchair as she passed him and went on into the house to look for medicaments for Henry. 'Oh dear, oh dear.'

Miss Bates looked at him questioningly, but he was lost in thought. He was remembering how Caroline in talking to any man did lean forward with that smile and that look of promise; and if, he was thinking, that promise was more often fulfilled than her evident loyalty to Henry might lead one to suppose, well, then, were there not more areas of allowable behaviour than there had, in London, appeared to be?

'Oh dear, oh dear,' he said again, standing up this time. 'I'd better go back home and get on with some useful work. I'll leave the young people to find their own way back. Send them away when you've had enough of them, won't you, Theodora?'

Henry drove Agatha into Siena to do some more extensive shopping for provisions than the nearby village could afford. They had a list, which they had made in consultation with Nella, and it was in reference to this that Agatha said, 'I never would have thought you'd be so good about the house.'

'I've made my bed every morning too.'

'Good heavens.'

'Amazing, isn't it? Do you think we're doing all right? Is Orlando sick of us?'

'No, you're a tremendous success with him, all of you.'

'He is with us, too. Everyone thinks he's marvellous.'

'I really think he's much happier with lots of people here. There's such a difference in him since I first came.'

'That's probably because of you.'

'I don't think I'm anything to do with it.'

'Yes, you are. When he showed me round everything and told me all the things he was going to do, he kept referring to you. It was obviously very much in his mind that he was sharing it all with you.'

'Do you think I can manage the responsibility of that? I mean, I've got to be working awfully hard in England for the next few years.'

'I think he recognizes that all right. I'm sure you can manage it, I think you're able to manage anything these days. I'm rather frightened of you in fact.'

'That's only because I can speak Italian.'

'No, but you've got much more decisive and confident and brown and beautiful and you can drive about and find the way to places and cook delicious meals and be just right with Miss Bates and talk to Giuseppe about the vines and be offhand with that American who's so hopelessly in love with you.'

'He's not. If you mean Hal.'

'I suppose you're in love with him then.'

'I'm not.'

'Of course he's frightfully good-looking.'

'Yes.'

'You're being annoying.'

'No, you are.'

'Am I? I'm terribly sorry. Well, anyway, I do think you're good at all those things and so does everyone else. They're all terribly impressed.'

'Do you mean that? The thing is, you know, I do like it. I mean, I like showing you all round and knowing places and being browner than you all and showing off my Italian, and at the same time it makes me feel guilty because you're all so nice about it and it's only because I've been here longer and I really hate the feeling of showing off and I wish you'd all catch me up and be as brown and as know-all.'

Henry laughed. 'You really don't like privilege, do you?'

'No, I hate it. Don't you?'

'I don't mind it as much as you do. As long as I'm on the privileged side. Don't frown at me like that.'

'Sorry.'

'I don't think you do show off. I think you do it all very well.'

'Thank you. Look out! For heaven's sake, Henry, you must be the most dangerous driver in the world.'

'Don't worry, the Italians are all terribly dangerous drivers too.'

William Holmes returned from Venice and asked them all for drinks. It was rather a stiff and formal occasion, with the host at his most searching and lapidary. Nevertheless he asked them all to dinner the following day.

In the morning they went to San Gimignano, where Adrian, with expressionless face, climbed on to the wall of one of the highest towers and walked three times round it, attracting a small crowd, winning two pounds from Brian and momentarily forfeiting the friendship of Raymond, who thought the whole thing very tiresome and childish. Differences were smoothed over round Miss Bates's pool and then they went back to Lecceto to change: they had decided to wear their best for Willie.

Brian left before the party. He came down with his suitcase as they were waiting on the terrace ready to set off.

'We're off,' he said. 'It's been perfectly wonderful and we've stayed far too long. We were supposed to have gone on to Positano days ago.'

There were exclamations, questions. 'What about Willie's dinner?'

'I telephoned from Miss Bates's and left a message.'

'Why didn't you tell us?'

'I didn't want you to feel you had to persuade us to stay. It's better like this. The agony is shorter for all of us.'

'If it's just because of Willie's dinner you could easily get out of that,' said Agatha, feeling guilty because she had earlier wanted Brian to leave.

'No, no, if we're not coming to dinner now's the moment to make the break and turn the nose of the great car south. William Holmes simply provides a clear point in time. I don't feel up to the sophisticated international queer milieu, it makes me feel terribly loutish and crude. Yes I *am* loutish and crude, I know, but I don't usually *feel* loutish and crude.'

'Darling Brian, of course you're not loutish and crude.' Caroline put her arms round his neck. The others gathered round them, expostulating in one way or another.

'Does he really want to go?' Agatha quietly asked Cherry.

'He told me back in England we were going on to Positano on the fifteenth. It is the fifteenth, isn't it?' she said.

'Yes, I think so.'

'Typical,' said Cherry with a little sniff.

There was no doubt that although he had not been asked, and although Henry had promised and indeed intended to ask him to leave sooner or later, and although there would be too many people for the resources of Lecceto if he and Cherry stayed, and although neither Agatha nor Joe Hertz could really be counted among his admirers, nevertheless his method of departure did leave them feeling uneasy. Should they not have accepted Willie's invitation, was it something that had happened that afternoon, had someone hurt his feelings? When he had gone and Agatha told them what Cherry had said, it became clear that this was exactly how he had meant them to feel: they agreed, with varying degrees of irritation or admiration, that it was typical and set off for the party untroubled by further guilt.

Orlando did not go with them. He thought it might be foolish if he were not to recognize the difference in age by leaving them quite often to their own devices. Besides, he did not really enjoy Willie's parties.

Agatha said that she thought pictures ought to be in museums rather than in private houses. She said in a rather prim voice that she disliked the exclusiveness of connoisseurship.

'My dear, we are poles apart,' said William Holmes, staring at her.

'I know, that's why I said it,' said Agatha, who had been drinking her wine rather quickly through nervousness.

'You're a very strange girl.'

'Let's go back to the lime walks.'

'The lime walks?'

'At Madingly.'

'Ah, you know them?'

'No, but you talked about them last time.'

'Oh.'

'And I never found out what they were.'

'They were in the garden.'

'At Madingly.'

'At Madingly.'

'I asked you where it was last time and you said in Sussex.'

'Yes, of course.'

'But I didn't ask you what it was?'

'What it was?'

'Yes. What is it?'

'My dear child.' He turned to the Austrian princess. 'She's never heard of Madingly.' He laughed hollowly. 'Isn't that enchanting?'

The Austrian princess had brought her daughter, who was not very pretty, and her daughter's friend, an Italian girl who was not very pretty either. Hal was sitting between them, not talking much. He looked towards Agatha and they smiled. Agatha was not happy. She had not known until she had heard Brian's remark earlier in the evening that William Holmes was a homosexual, and she was deeply shocked by her own ignorance and by the possibility that her dislike of him might be something to do with this fact, an idea which filled her with self-reproach. Nevertheless she found herself quite unable to get over her dislike, and was also worried about Hal, since her knowledge of homosexual life came chiefly from having read Proust, and she was afraid that if Hal was a homosexual he was probably not at all happy. Bunny and Charles, on the other hand, the two Indo-Chinese, who this evening were sitting down at dinner, did look happy, and must certainly be homosexual because otherwise it was odd for such a snobbish man as William Holmes to have made friends with an Indo-Chinese hairdresser even if he did make beautiful paper birds. Perhaps they could be happy because of some different attitude towards such things in the East, whereas in England – and then the thought of Ozzie struck her. Was he? He might be. He could be sent to prison.

'You know,' said William Holmes, 'you are really quite a rude little girl.'

'I know. But only sometimes. And much worse than that is that I am very very ignorant and stupid.'

Unable, or unwilling, to say anything to that, he suggested they should all have coffee on the terrace.

There was music. Blue and scarlet macaws swung above them, suspended on threads.

'How beautiful they are,' said Caroline.

Bunny was dancing, but waved to show he was glad she liked them. He was dancing supposedly with the Austrian princess's daughter but had spun her away from him with a skilful flick of his wrist like an awkward humming top and, freed, was gyrating slowly on his own with graceful arm movements like one of his own paper birds.

'Dance,' said Hal to Agatha, moving similarly.

'I can't.'

'Come on.'

'I wish I could.'

'Just move.'

'Outside.'

'Sure. Outside.'

The stone was still warm from the day's heat. Barefoot and in the semi-darkness it was not difficult to move a little and lift her arms. No one was looking, hardly even Hal. She began to feel happy, but then, in case he was bored, she said, 'I must sit down.'

Some of the others had started to play poker in a corner of the terrace. She went to talk to Joe, who was sitting alone on the low stone wall. Later Henry laughed loudly because he had heard her serious voice say quite clearly, 'What exactly is meant by buggery?'

'Agatha, I adore you,' he shouted from the poker game, she could not imagine why.

There was more dancing, more wine. William Holmes sat talking to the Austrian princess. Names fell from their lips like magic runes. They were two high priests telling the holy names according to ancient ritual, slower and slower.

Agatha turned and swooped on the dark terrace, bending her neck, raising her hands to the deep star-encrusted sky – who cared? Hal moved slowly round her, sometimes in view and sometimes out of sight, smiling. Adrian, his white face gleaming in the light from within the house, unexpectedly was there too. 'One two and one and two and ...' he muttered, fingers flicking, toes tapping. He was Fred Astaire and they were two great blue birds of the night. The music was anyone's possession: inside, Bunny was doing a flamenco.

Agatha began to laugh. She laughed so much that she had to hold on to Hal. He put his arms round her. 'I've never seen you so happy.'

They were back in the jeep, driving through the warm night. Her head was on Henry's shoulder. Caroline could not see because she was at the end of the front seat, with Ozzie between her and Agatha.

'Are you drunk?' Henry asked.

'Oh yes,' she answered with the idea somehow that he had said, 'Do you love me?'

'Well, I mean,' Ozzie was pretending to have been shocked, 'that Willie. Camping around like that, I've never seen anything like it. Do you know what Charlie said to me in the Gents?'

'Don't tell us.'

'It's not what you think. Anyway, he's asked me to go to Venice with him on Monday. Willie has, I mean.'

'Oh, Ozzie.' Agatha sat up in dismay.

'To meet the *haut monde* and the *crème de la crème* in person, my dear. Drop by drop.'

'Will you go?'

'I'm thinking it over.'

'Oh dear.'

Adrian said languidly, 'I have been asked to go horseback riding with the Austrian princess's daughter's friend.'

Agatha put her hand on Ozzie's. 'I'm a bit frightened of Willie.'

'I don't suppose I'll go.'

She looked so anxious that he was pleased.

'I don't think I'm old enough, do you?'

'Oh no.'

'I don't think I'm *ready* for Wicked Will.'

'I'm so glad.'

After a bit she began to sing.

'Out of tune,' said Henry, who sang rather well.

'You sing.'

They sang all the way home. When they got to the bumpy road they were singing 'Keep the Home Fires Burning', except for Adrian who was being Al Jolson singing 'Mammy'. When they got to the house Henry did not stop, but drove on, up the grassy road to the tower house, which was only just passable. They went on singing. At the open space he drove slowly round the well and down the hill again, swirled round at a dignified pace in front of the terrace, back up the hill, round the well, down, round, up the hill, round the well, 'while our souls are yearning, my Ma-a-a-mmy'. Every time he turned again instead of stopping Agatha was helpless with laughter. It seemed so funny. She was holding Ozzie's hand, leaning on Henry's shoulder, head back to see the swirling stars, the tops of the buildings looming, turning, cypress points wheeling. She thought it must be the only moment in her whole life which she had recognized at the time as being perfectly happy.

Orlando, woken by the appalling noise, looked out of the window. He watched the wandering lights of the jeep in some astonishment, hoping Agatha was not in actual danger. At last it stopped, more or less under his window. They tumbled out, went into the house. But there was someone still there on the terrace, looking up at him.

The white dress fluttered. Agatha had been wearing something dark; it must be Caroline. Her face was raised towards his, but he could not see the expression on it. Could she see him? He did not move. She raised her arms, opened them to him. The moment extended, then was over. She lowered her arms, bent her head and walked slowly into the house.

There was a day when Raymond and Joe took the little Fiat into Florence, to take their studies more seriously, and the rest of them were sitting on the terrace after lunch, wondering whether to go and sleep until the day became cooler or whether to do some painting in the upper rooms of the tower house, which were comparatively cool and needed whitewashing, when unexpectedly Caroline and Agatha had a quarrel.

There was idle gossip, in the course of which Ozzie said of someone or other, 'Of course she went to Switzerland, you know, and had twins. They were adopted.'

This wild assertion was denied.

'Besides she's not that sort of person. She'd have had an abortion.'

The trivial conversation would have flowed on and petered out had not Agatha chosen to make an issue of it.

'How awful,' she said. 'I think it's much worse to have an abortion than to have illegitimate twins.'

'Oh rubbish,' said Caroline, lazily. 'You haven't thought about it.'

'I have thought about it as a matter of fact,' said Agatha, firmly. 'Because although I am not a doctor or anything near it, not being even a medical student yet, still I do think of myself as one, and I have thought about those sort of things, and when if ever it is permissible to take life, and in the case of an unwanted baby I don't believe it is permissible.'

She had spoken pedantically, and when she had finished there was a pause. She glanced quickly in the direction of Adrian and Ozzie and saw that they were looking embarrassed. She did not look at anyone else.

'I still think you haven't thought it out,' said Caroline, clearly annoyed. 'You're just being emotional about it.'

'It is an emotional subject,' said Agatha stiffly.

'You can't imagine people less fortunate than you, you can only think of it in terms of yourself.'

Agatha looked up, pushing back her hair. 'Myself? You mean as if I ... ?' Outrage gave depth to her voice. 'No one can imagine impossibilities. I could never ...' She was lost in incoherence, out of which came, 'And if I loved someone ...'

She stopped. Orlando, watching in distress, felt that it was already too late. It was out in the open that she was just too strong; that if she loved anyone, he was for it. She felt her error herself, as if she had brandished a sword which should have been sheathed all her life.

To his surprise, Orlando saw that Henry had sat up and was looking at her with rather solemn admiration. Aware of this, Agatha said to him hesitantly, still flushed, 'Well, you know what I mean ... ?'

Henry nodded.

Caroline jumped up from her chair, said, 'I think you're all being perfectly ridiculous,' and went into the house.

Henry lay down and shut his eyes.

Agatha got to her feet a little stiffly and walked away from the terrace towards the tower house. Halfway to the trees she thought they must all be staring at her. She walked on slowly but self-consciously, with tears in her eyes.

When Orlando quietly opened Caroline's bedroom door she was sitting at the table, writing a letter.

'Are you very angry with my poor daughter?' he said, wandering in.

'No,' she said distantly.

'She's only seventeen and she wants to get everything clear-cut and right. Sometimes it makes her sound priggish.'

'Sometimes?' asked Caroline bitterly.

'Ah well.' He sat down on the edge of the bed.

Caroline looked at the letter she had been writing.

'It's the sight of Henry gazing at her goggle-eyed,' she said after a bit. 'Of all people.'

'Why of all people?'

She tried to speak lightly. 'He must be the only man in London with an account at that terrible abortion clinic.'

'An account?' said Orlando mildly. 'Surely not?'

She laughed reluctantly and sniffed. 'Perhaps not an account then, I don't know. All I mean is that he is thoroughly unscrupulous and callous himself and yet he can talk the most utter drivel about Agatha being *good*. When all she is is cautious and priggish. Oh, I know she's your daughter and awfully sweet really. What am I talking about? Do you think I ought to leave?'

'I don't want you to.'

'I'm supposed to be back in London by the end of the month. I've got some modelling jobs to do.'

'Don't go.'

She did not answer.

'Will Henry go too?' he asked.

'I don't suppose so. Henry is a very difficult person.'

'Is he?'

'He is a hundred per cent selfish.'

'Will you marry him?'

She shook her head. 'It's not like that. It never was.' She sounded sad and he wondered if she meant it.

'It's coming to an end really,' she said.

'I hope you'll be all right.'

'I'll be all right.'

'I like you very much.'

'I know. I like you too.'

Agatha had cried, pressing her face into her knees, crouched on the grass the other side of the tower house. Tired, she lay down, breathing the smell of the wild mint she crushed; then decided to go for a walk.

One could plunge over the edge of the promontory and find that surprisingly there were only a few feet of stony slope to slide down before reaching a path which led through scrubby bushes out on to a lower terrace. She followed the line of the terrace, past olives and two or three bushy fig trees, and at the bed of a tiny dried-up stream turned downhill to cross the valley. High up on the opposite side and to her left, hidden from Lecceto by an intervening patch of wood, was an empty farmhouse, square and plain, its barn beside it, inaccessible by any road yet only very recently deserted by the family that had lived there and had transported everything they had needed by donkey from the road a kilometre or so distant. The absence of road, let alone electricity or more water than one meagre well could supply, as well as the inhospitable height of the place, meant that it was likely to be a ruin within a few years. In the meantime the lizards sunned themselves on the doorstep, scarcely bothering to move for the visiting stranger. Perhaps there were snakes too. Agatha picked up a stick and tapped it on the stones as she approached.

It had taken her nearly an hour to walk there. On the way she had tried to think only of what she was doing and of her immediate surroundings. She had almost succeeded, and sitting at last on the warm doorstep, looking down the length rather than across the breadth of the familiar valley, she felt as if the space might be clearing round the issues she now felt courage enough to reconsider.

She had spoken too vehemently and regretted it. That had happened before, and the extent to which she always regretted it might sometimes have been thought disproportionate. But there was more than that. The burning issue was Henry and Caroline, and she felt she must dredge from out of her own wretched depths the thing she had refused to contemplate, and name it jealousy. She groaned at having to do it, and did it, and groaned again: she banged the doorpost with her clenched fist, cried, denied it, felt her heart must be physically bruised as she tore it open again to admit of Henry and Caroline's loving each other, and called up her will to accept that, and unexpectedly, tired though she was, found a kind of enjoyment creeping in.

Squatting on the doorstep, clasping her knees tightly to her bosom, she said in a precise tone of voice, 'Skin by skin I will peel the onion of motive,' and smiled. If there reared its head a little feeling of self-congratulation on the grounds of being at least honest and in that respect hardworking,

she ignored it. Henry and Caroline loved each other. It
was possible that Caroline had had an abortion rather than
oblige Henry to marry her: this was a tragedy which could
be redeemed. She herself loved Henry; but they were
cousins, and might have lunatic children if they married;
nor had Henry ever shown any signs of wanting to marry
her. They had merely a certain special relationship, which
they had always had and always would have. Henry had
no physical feeling for her. He had for Caroline. Agatha
had therefore to overcome her jealousy for Caroline. A
first step in that direction was to acknowledge it to herself.
Having done this, she could allow for it in assessing the
situation between Henry and Caroline, and could then
admit that, her own prejudice apart, there was nothing
against their marrying. Caroline was beautiful and charming, liked by all Henry's friends: probably it was time he
got married. Her mind now raced ahead to embrace the
role she foresaw for herself; it was an acceptable one, a
sensible one, one she felt able to undertake. She could be
the special friend, dedicated to her work (fortunate indeed
in being able to give so much of her time, undistracted, to
her work), who would always share with Henry – what? –
a certain mental companionship, perhaps, which he might
never have with his wife; whose friend she would also be,
and whom she could help with the children. If she put
her mind to it, time would transmute all the relationships
according to her plan. Her imagination rushed on to show
her the distinguished consultant physician on an afternoon
at the Zoo, smiling down at the little face, engrossed in
bears or hippopotami, in which she could see reflected
the two people she loved best: they would certainly have
beautiful children.

'I love Caroline,' she said tentatively.

She did not mean it. She knew she did not mean it, but she could feel that the necessary sincerity was not far away, that it would, with continued effort, come through to back up the reiterated statement.

'I can change things.' In possession of this power, she walked through the overgrown orchard, plums, apples, fallen vines; touched the hard little peaches on the trees. 'Only so can movement move.' She thought of the turning world, the streaming stars. 'I'm talking rubbish.' A dash of goldfinches from the thistle-tops up into a pear tree. 'I have an instrument, seated in my heart, which can turn everything into a triumph, with trumpets.' Laughing, she jumped on to a pile of stones and frightened a lizard, wandered off and felt a fig not yet ripe. Exhausted by exaltation, she began the long walk home.

At last the opportunity came to talk to Caroline. Ozzie and Raymond had volunteered to do the day's shopping, Joe was reading in his room, which being in the priest's house was out of earshot of the terrace, and Henry and Adrian were helping Orlando to paint the inside of the tower. Caroline was sunbathing on the terrace, face downwards and apparently asleep.

Agatha, approaching her, went so far as to put her hands together in a sort of prayer, like an Indian greeting, which would have surprised Caroline had she chanced to look up.

Caroline's dress, of pink cotton, was lying on the chair near the wall on which she lay. Moving it to sit on the chair, Agatha said, 'I love this dress.'

Caroline moved her head so as to be able to see her.

'Did you make it?' asked Agatha.

'Yes.'

'I only asked because I know you do make them. I mean if anyone asked me that, it would be the most appalling insult.'

Caroline gave a little grunt, presumably of amusement.

'Where's Henry?' asked Agatha, who knew the answer.

'Painting, I think.'

'They've worked quite hard, haven't they?'

'Mn.'

'I'm amazed. Henry's so lazy usually.'

Caroline did not answer.

'I hope you don't think I'm very boring about Henry,' said Agatha.

'What?'

'I mean, we were practically brought up together and I'm awfully fond of him in a way, though of course I can't help feeling he'd be pretty awful to be married to, but what I mean is I think it would be wonderful if you did.'

'Did what?'

'Marry him.'

'Oh. I didn't think you were going to say that.'

'I think he'd like to marry you very much.'

'Do you?' Caroline carefully rolled herself over so that she was lying face upwards on the wall. She had been surprised at Agatha's approach and a little curious, but all that gave way to a new interest in what she was saying. She had been truthful when she had said to Orlando that her relationship with Henry had never looked likely to end in marriage, but she would have had no objection at any time to Henry's wanting that it should. What might happen after that was another matter. 'Do you really think that?' she asked.

'Yes, I do.'

'We're not very well suited.'

'Why not?'

'He's so difficult.'

'Remote, you mean?'

'I suppose so.'

'Not trusting, that sort of thing?'

'Exactly.'

'I expect he'd get better with practice. I mean, with years of practice, and if you were very fond of him.' Agatha stopped, afraid she was being trite.

'Oh I don't know.' Caroline settled herself more comfortably. 'I hate complications. But it is nice of you to say you think it would be a good idea. I mean, awfully nice of you.'

It seemed to Orlando that there was a sort of fine tension about Agatha's looks which had not been there before and which made her quite beautiful. He hoped it was not too much to do with the presence of Henry. He hoped she was happy, and believed she was, because sometimes he saw her laughing with every appearance of enjoyment, especially with Adrian or with Ozzie. She did not seem to be with Henry particularly often and Orlando was inclined to think Miss Bates had been romanticizing that situation. She had, however, silences and times of dreamy remoteness. He would not be sorry, he thought, when they had all gone and he and Agatha were left in their former companionship: now it never seemed possible to talk.

He liked having them all there, liked being drawn, as he felt he was, into their various problems and interests, but when they left there was another thing that presumably would go and that was the turbulence in his own senses. It was not agonizing, sometimes it was agreeable, but he would not object now to being relieved of it. He felt that he knew that in the right circumstances Caroline would sleep with him. He also knew that the right circumstances would not arise and that as far as he could see for the moment it would be quite wrong of him to try to make them arise. Caroline was going back to England in a few days' time, because of her commitments there. Henry and the others were staying longer. Henry seemed to be being particularly nice to Caroline during her last few days, which was as it should be. Orlando tried to concentrate on his manual labour and wrote a long letter to Stephen full of advice about the Logan situation which he knew he would not take.

Agatha wondered what it would be like to die. She had had for a long time an obscure feeling, which she rarely examined, that there was going to be a cataclysm of some kind. If she did think about it at all, it felt as if it must be the end of the world that was coming, and fairly soon. This presentiment, which was very strong, ran parallel with her plans for the future, which, since they involved her in qualifying as a doctor before the serious events of her life could even begin, were necessarily long-term. The presentiment being irrational, she tried to ignore it. It nevertheless underlay everything else, so that in spite of her apparent decisiveness all her plans were in fact provisional.

Whatever it was that was coming – and she was particularly conscious of it during these days which seemed to her more than usually doom-laden – it seemed to be not death so much as disgrace that threatened her, some kind of mental or moral disintegration rather than a physical one. Death was more or less unimaginable, and therefore of no interest: the other sort of collapse was only too easy to envisage. She thought of torture, the Russians over-running Europe, interrogation in a little dark cell, day after day. Would not her tiny store of love and knowledge be exhausted in an hour? What kind of abyss would open then? Who else would survive, could anyone meet the test? She must be always working to prepare herself; but then, if she tried to think of it rationally, what did she mean by that? The palpable horror could be apprehended but not understood; it was too vague.

This cloud was round her in the little car as she drove away from Lecceto looking for Hal. Henry had taken Caroline and Orlando into Siena. She left the others and braved William Holmes in search of what seemed likely to be comfort. Besides, Hal had not been to see them or to help with the work, which was unusual.

She found him alone, asleep in a swinging seat under a tasselled canopy on William Holmes's terrace. When he woke up and saw her, she thought no one could have a more beautiful smile, and wished she had been in love with him instead of Henry.

'Where have you been?' he asked.

'That's what I was going to ask you. You know I'm much too frightened of Wicked Will to come here except in desperation when we haven't seen you for days and days and think you may be dead.'

'We've been working so hard here. He's been re-hanging all his pictures. Besides, there are so many people at Lecceto these days, I thought I'd better keep away. How's Nella managing?'

'She's been marvellous. And they're quite helpful. Ozzie's an awfully good cook. Come for a walk.'

'You're always so energetic. To the stream then, where we first met.'

'We first met here on this terrace.'

'Yes, but I mean, you know, talked.'

They walked down the path through the wood. The stream was smaller now. They sat on the bank in silence.

'Unhappy?' asked Hal.

She nodded.

'Want to say why?'

She shook her head.

The stream was so thin it made no sound. She went over to put her hand in it, turned back and lay down close to him. He lay beside her. She turned towards him and they lay face to face.

'Would you like to take your clothes off?' he asked.

She nodded, sat up slowly, and took off her clothes. When she lay down again the moss felt cool. She moved a stick from under her back, and lay still. He was naked too.

'How beautiful you are,' she said.

'You too.'

He kissed her face all over very gently, then slowly lowered his head towards her breast. She shut her eyes, hoped she would do all right.

After some time she realized that her chest was wet. For a moment she kept her eyes shut, the thought alarmingly in her mind that it might be some physical manifestation she had not read about, then opened them, understanding that he must be in tears.

She tried to raise his head, but he resisted. She gently rolled him over, so that he lay on his back with her arm under his head. His eyes were shut and his face, which was quite calm in its expression, was suffused with tears.

'I'm sorry,' he said.

'It's all right.'

She lay with his head on her shoulder, wondering what had happened. She could look down the length of his body and see his genitals resting peacefully between his thighs. She remembered then the soft feel of them against her knees. In her ignorance she had forgotten that the male organ was supposed to stiffen.

'Hal,' she said. 'It's quite all right.'

At the same time she felt a distinct annoyance: she had thought she was going to be relieved of the burden of her virginity.

'I can't,' he said.

'It doesn't matter.'

'I can't ever.'

'Ever?'

'Not for about two years.'

'Was it all right before that?'

'Yes.'

'Did something awful happen?'

'No.'

She paused, then asked, 'Do you like boys?'

'Oh sure, anything.'

'What do you mean?'

He raised his head from her shoulder, and moving a few inches further away stretched his arms, then bent them and rested his head on his hands, staring up towards the tops of the trees. He sighed, his body in repose.

'I guess I just overdid it,' he said. 'Boys. Girls. Since I was nine.'

'Nine?'

'What do you do if somebody wants you?' he said. 'I guess I just got used up.'

She raised her head and, propping it on her elbow, looked at his face. He was still gazing up towards the barrier of leaves over their heads, or towards the clear sky which was discernible through them. His body, stretched on the shaded moss, was evenly brown, showing that he had sunbathed naked; it was flawless.

'Didn't you ever say no?' she asked mildly.

'Not often. Why should I? I like it. Or at least I used to.'

She went on looking at him in silence, trying to reconcile what he was telling her with the extraordinary pure beauty of the look of him.

'So you see,' he said, 'I'm just some kind of a shell.'

She lay down again, turned towards him, pillowing her head on her folded arm.

'You've been exploited,' she said slowly. 'Used and exploited because you're too nice and too beautiful and do you know, do you know what? I was going to do it too, I wanted to make use of you, I did, I... Because I really can't get free of Henry, who doesn't love me, and I thought that you could help me to get free of him. I was going to exploit you too.'

'Don't you cry as well.'

'I hate all this in love business, it's nothing to do with really loving people, I wish we didn't have to do it. It's so greedy and disgusting, I wish we could be free of it, I wish we could be free.'

She cried in his arms.

He said, 'It's not so bad, it sometimes works out.'

Later they helped each other carefully up the steep path. At the top they embraced and said good-bye, so that Agatha could go round the back of the house to her car and so avoid Willie in the event of his having come back from Florence.

'I feel useless,' she said.

'You're beautiful.'

'I want to love you without ever wanting anything from you at all. Can I?'

'Sure. Me too.'

Orlando had walked with Henry to fetch some sheep's cheese from the old woman who made it and who lived a mile or two away. When they came back Henry said he was hot and would like to swim. Some of the others went with him.

Orlando, crossing the terrace on his way to the tower house (he was spending a good deal of time up there now because he was making himself a room, where he was going to keep his books and his desk), heard Agatha and Joe talking; or rather Joe was talking and Agatha was listening. They had been discussing a book of Sartre's he had lent her and now he was telling her about some other books he thought she ought to read.

'What is the sickness unto death?' asked Orlando, hearing the phrase as he passed.

'A book of Kierkegaard's,' said Joe.

'No, but what does he mean by the sickness unto death?' asked Orlando.

'Despair.'

'Ah.' He nodded and walked on, his stick tapping lightly on the familiar stones.

He smiled, thinking of Agatha's seriousness. As if she could know anything about despair. He knew she took things hard, he had noticed that, but the real thing – not grief, depression, melancholy, but despair – that she could not know about. Which was of course the sickness unto death. There were many different kinds; he supposed the book would go into that. He had certainly known one, though whether he would ever have recognized it without old King he did not know. He had never been, on his own account, as introspective as the diaries showed King to have been.

He had taken the worn notebooks over to his new room, and when he reached it he pulled them out of the pile of books which was waiting to be sorted out and put in the shelves, and taking his magnifying glass out of his pocket he turned over the pages of one of them, reminding himself of the state of mind in which he had first read them. He had been beside himself, in what felt like a literal sense; and now was back in his own skin.

'More and more there are days on which I can't love. I have nothing to love with. I am not a real person. I AM NOT.' There he was outside, howling. 'The only answer to life is to live as if ... So I can tell Orlando those things which I want him to believe, and hope that when later he finds them all to be fairy stories he will remember my frequent use of the subjunctive tense.' But scientific laws were provisional too and yet workable theories were built on them; so supposing you first believed and then acted out a fairy story, what was the difference between the fairy story and the truth? Orlando smiled again. He was not really interested in speculation. He was back in his own skin, he had a framework – something to do with Agatha and Lecceto – within which he could function, and whether or not this could be taken as having any relevance to what King had written was quite unimportant in the face of its obvious workability.

He felt in fact, shutting the notebook and putting it to one side, ready for anything. Including Caroline; in the sense that he realized that if anything came of that it would be an extra, and would not shake the structure of the framework.

Signor Rossi came up in his dark suit with a message for Agatha.

'Your father has telephoned me to say he is detained in Florence on business. He thinks it is better that he spends a few days there. He will not be away long.'

'Oh yes, he said he might have to do that. It's something to do with the bank.'

'A few days?' said Adrian. 'What can he be doing?'

'I don't know. Banks are very complicated.'

'Perhaps he's having a wild affair with Caroline,' said Ozzie.

'Don't be silly,' said Agatha, laughing.

Caroline had announced that she had a phobia about being seen off on trains and had arranged for a taxi to collect her from Lecceto and take her to Florence. She had stood firm against all attempts to make her change her mind and allow Henry to drive her to the station or any of the others to go with her in the taxi; but at supper on the evening before her departure she had said quite casually to Orlando, 'If you've really got those business things to see to you could have a lift in my taxi in the morning,' to which he had replied, 'Thank you' in a matter-of-fact tone of voice, although he could not remember having any business things to see to in Florence.

Without thinking too much about it one way or the other he had taken the precaution of mentioning to Agatha that the mythical business might take a few days and of taking with him a good deal of money; so that as they drew nearer to Florence he was able to tap the driver on the shoulder and ask him to go to the Excelsior Hotel instead of the station. He did this because Caroline had turned to him as they drove away from Lecceto and had said, 'Well, there we are,' and he had said, 'And very nice too,' and put his hand on hers. They had then talked for most of the journey to Florence about Miss Bates, whose house they passed, and whose history was unknown to Caroline, so that Orlando was able to tell her at some length all that he knew about her; they were quite amusing in a kindly way at Miss Bates's expense. It seemed clear to Orlando that enough had been indicated earlier on to make it obvious that as soon as they

reached Florence they should go to a hotel and go to bed.
They did.

They allowed themselves three days, changing her
train reservations in the hotel that first evening. To avoid
the possibility of running into Raymond, who was still
taking his Florentine sight-seeing quite seriously, Caroline
decided that they must go to very expensive places, except
for lunch, when they could take a picnic into the country as
long as they kept away from works of art. Orlando agreed,
and when they went to the expensive places he loaded her
with expensive presents. He was very happy.

'Why did you do it?' he asked her.

'I could see you wanted to.'

'That's not good enough.'

'Because I wanted to, then.'

He discovered that she had a surprising lack of interest in
motives. At first he thought it might be a result of secretive-
ness or discretion, but he soon decided that it was neither
of these things and that she was a person with an extraordinary sense of immediacy: it probably accounted to some
extent for her physical attraction.

'Do you know, I think you must be the only person I've
met who really genuinely lives for the moment,' he said.

She considered it, and agreed that it was probably true.

'You must be careful not to be too reckless.'

She smiled. 'You mean I mustn't do to anyone else what
I did to you.'

'Exactly.'

'I can't promise.'

'Please be careful.'

'I'm very good when I'm with someone. I was faithful to
Henry for a long time.'

'I wish you could be with me.'

'It isn't really practical, is it?'

He shook his head.

'Shall I come back some time? In the winter, to keep you warm?'

'Yes.'

'I might. I might be hating London by then.'

'You'll have some frightful young lover.'

'Nobody could ever be as good as you. No, you think I'm flattering you, but I'm not.'

'These young men haven't much experience.'

'I've never seen you look smug before. It's very funny. Do it again. Is that what you looked like when you were Minister of whatever it was?'

'Probably.'

He not only told her about his political career, but also about his childhood in France with King, his illegitimacy, his going to London and being taken up by Leonard and going to work for him, Leonard's death and his marriage to Leonard's wife Judith. She was very interested in Judith.

'She sounds so dashing, in the way women could be then. I can't imagine Conrad being her brother.'

'They didn't really get on very well, although they saw a lot of each other. She was too extravagant a personality for him. I find it very hard to describe her satisfactorily. Perhaps it shows I never understood her.'

'You must have. I never met anybody so understanding.'

'I might understand her now. Certain things have taught me more patience than I had then.'

'Poor Leonard. Never to have known you were his son.'

'I believe he would have been pleased really. Although he was very bad with his legitimate sons.'

'And if you had known do you think you would still have fallen in love with his wife? If she had been your stepmother?'

'I don't know. Who knows when it will strike, or whether it will or won't?'

'It struck a bit with me, didn't it?'

'Of course. When Henry made me push you in the car. I saw your lovely neck when you were getting in.'

'I was in a filthy temper then. But I saw you coming towards us with the patches of mist lying just above the grass in such a funny way because it was so early, and I said to Henry, "Who's that marvellous-looking man?" and he wouldn't pay any attention because he was so furious about the car not starting.'

'What will Henry do now?'

'Nothing, I should think. Gamble. Avoid responsibility. One day he might do something quite unexpected if he can just get really free of his father. He's like some kind of hawk that needs training. I don't know if anyone will ever do it.'

Alarmed by the shadow, or possibility of a shadow, on her face, he said, 'I'm terribly sorry but I'm afraid I'm going to give you another present.'

She was carrying it over her arm when he took her to her train, a leather bag half covered by a silk scarf he had given her another day.

'Please take care of yourself,' he said.

She looked at him with tenderness, a little tearful.

'I'll come back in the winter, really I will.'

'Yes.' He nodded.

'You will want me?'

He kissed her, wondering how he could survive until then without her.

'Be careful.' He held her away from him a little, thinking of the dangers that lay in wait for her; and as he did so he noticed the other scarf on her arm, knotted loosely with his, a green and blue one which he remembered Henry buying for her one morning in Siena, and then he noticed that round her neck she was wearing a piece of bronze jewellery he had given her, but that round it with admirable instinct she had twisted a thin enamel chain, a pretty little object which someone had no doubt chosen with affection. She was looking at him anxiously, a long strand of fair hair blowing across her face. He smiled, his anxiety fading. She would always have her trophies. She would be all right.

He touched her cheek. 'I am very fond of you indeed.'

He helped her up the steep step on to the train, and by prearrangement did not wait until it left before walking away, down the platform and out of the station, in search of transport to take him back to Lecceto.

After they had all gone, Orlando and Miss Bates walked in the valley. They had been to the site of the new vineyard and were walking back, slowly because it was nearly the middle of the day and very hot. Apart from their voices and the sound of their feet on the dry ground and the thin electric shrilling of the grasshoppers, everything was quiet under the sun.

'It's the silence of noon,' said Miss Bates. 'Rather bad.'

'Bad?'

'It always frightens me a bit. It's when the gods come out, satyrs and things, you know. Don't like the feel of it.'

'I see.'

'Not to worry. I'm sorry I missed Agatha.'

'Come back and have some lunch. She'll be there by now.'

'I've got a man coming about a dog. I left my car along here at the bottom so I'd better go straight back. But perhaps I might look over tomorrow. I haven't seen her since they all left.'

'She seems to be bearing up all right. In fact unless she's fooling me I think we're both feeling rather relieved. It's nice to have the place to ourselves again.'

They had been in fact as they had been right at the beginning, only with the difference that there was ease between them where there had been awkwardness. He wondered how he could have been so obtuse as to have thought her an insufficient personality: she now seemed to him to be full of depths and possibilities.

'You'll miss her.'

'She's coming back at Christmas, perhaps with Imogen. We shall see about that next month when Imogen comes. Henry's threatening to come over again to drive them both back to England. I don't know that I'm very keen on that, he's such an appalling driver.'

'With Caroline?'

'No, I think that's probably drifting to an end, with no hard feelings.'

Caroline did not lend herself to hard feelings. Not that he himself had got away without some sadness. He had missed her the first few nights, had not slept in fact. The second night after his return from Florence Agatha had suggested helping him with his books after dinner. 'It's cooler if we do it late,' she had said. 'And we're never going to get it done otherwise.' They had been up until two, and then he had slept for several hours, waking very early as he had used to do long ago when he was first reading King's diaries. The

following night Henry said he would help them and by one
o'clock all the books were sorted out and in their proper
shelves. It was satisfying to have got it done. He did not
know whether Agatha had heard him pacing his room the
night he had not slept, or whether she had really thought
it was time the books were put away. Whichever it was he
was grateful.

'I'm sorry I had to leave you so long,' he said to her.
'Were you all right in a house full of men?'

'Of course I was.'

'I believe Henry has a terrible reputation.'

'I know. But it's different with me because we're cousins.'

Remembering this conversation, he now said to Miss
Bates, 'You know, I think you were wrong about Agatha. I
don't think she is interested in Henry.'

'Don't you? Just as well perhaps. That Caroline was a
nice girl, I thought, in spite of all the sophistication.'

'Yes, very nice.'

She had brought him nothing but happiness – well,
hardly anything but happiness. And she had better find
someone of her own to settle down with, and if Agatha
and Imogen were coming in the winter it would perhaps be
better if she were not to be there too; not that he felt there
was anything he needed to do about that because he was
sure that some time in November or early December there
would come a letter in that dear huge writing to say that
after all she could not get away. Perhaps, later on, some
nice thirty-year-old that Agatha approved of ... He began
to laugh.

'I don't seem to have thought of my health much lately,'
he said.

'I've noticed that,' said Miss Bates. 'I should think you
ought to, in this heat. You've been working much too hard.'

'I can't seem to worry about it somehow. I'm so reconciled to everything, I'm probably even reconciled to dying as long as it's quick. Look, if you're really going back to your car, I'll take the short cut here. Come to lunch tomorrow, all right?'

'Lovely, but it's awfully steep up there in this heat. Why don't I take you round in the car?'

'No really, I like walking.' He smiled good-bye, turned to walk up the steep path on to a higher terrace, then unexpectedly turned back towards her and with rather a preoccupied look on his face held out his stick to her and said, 'Here, take this. I don't need it.'

Surprised, she took it, and watched him walk away from her up the path – certainly with sure feet – and disappear over the top of the slope. Carrying the stick, she walked on to her car.

He moved slowly through the great silent heat, over ground familiar and loved, so that it was for the parched earth he hoped for rain, not for his own heated blood. The open grass terrace crossed, he paused by a little fall of stones from the wall above, where his path turned to lead uphill again. An old pear tree overhung the miniature cliff made by the stones above the dried-up bed of a tiny stream which in some weathers ran across these rocks. He waited a moment in such shade as it afforded – which was very little because the sun was high – and thought how perfect a conformation, miniature and so all within the scope of his eyes, the tree, the stones and the bed of the stream made. There was a tiny chasm, miniature steps of rock, and the ancient dry sweet-smelling land. He began to walk up the hill, but a step or two out of the shade of the pear tree turned again to look back at the microcosmic landscape.

As he did so he was seized by an extraordinarily violent physical shock.

There was a bright white light inside his head. Outside he could see the pear tree, white too, and shimmering. He understood at once that someone had done it; someone in the mad world of unreality where logical deductions were made, policies pursued, action taken, someone on one side or the other, some Stalin, some Truman, had been and pressed the bloody button.

Agatha must not know. Thunderstorm, he could say, and hide her eyes. He seemed to be on his knees, but scrambled up. The effect of the radiation was to make everything shimmer so much that he could hardly see the path, but would; and would hold her, could feel the part of his shoulder where her head would rest, not frightened because he would be there, the white light spreading unbearably bright, stretching his arms to reach her; and the light, spreading, was outside as well as inside, and rearing up had become a wave of a white appalling sea, and as he stretched his arms and worked his legs to run to find her the white wave drew him back and roared and even as he fell engulfed him. He was overpowered.

Agatha came quite soon, through the heat and the grasshoppers' whirring, thinking he was late and she would meet him.

She saw him from above, where he had fallen, near the pear tree but in the full heat of the sun, and understood at once that he must be dead. Her feet made hardly any sound on the dry ground as she approached and slowly went down on her knees beside him.

He had fallen slightly sideways and was bent in a sleeping position or like an unborn child. His face looked peaceful but infinitely absent. He's gone, she thought, this is death. The grasshoppers like singing wire were still the only sound. She could smell the warm earth and the wild marjoram that was crushed under his body. How I love my father, she thought. She looked towards the pear tree, the fallen stones and dried-up stream bed. Hearing the click of a stone, she looked along the wide terrace and saw a hundred yards or so away Giuseppe approaching slowly, carrying a long scythe. She looked round and saw Nella standing above her on the hill, carrying a bundle of vetch which she was taking home to her rabbits. As they both with infinite slowness and solemnity approached her under the relentless sun, Agatha thought, They know about this, they know more about death than I do She bent her head, gazed again at Orlando's face, and felt while they were still some way away a kind of adoration, or perhaps merely acceptance; but when they were near and she looked up to see the pity in their faces, she felt she had to put out her hand and touch Orlando's forehead, and when she did, and felt that he was indeed dead, all the symptoms of grief began.

There was no doubt that Miss Bates was excellent in an emergency

A message having reached her through one of Signor Rossi's emissaries – appealed to by Nella – she was over at Lecceto in no time, organizing everything with the most reassuringly authoritative air She carried Agatha off to stay with her; and at her own house she sent the necessary telegrams, telephoned her friend the British Consul, and assured Agatha that everything was in order and would be done as Orlando had wished.

'What would I do without you?' asked Agatha weakly.

'That's one thing you don't have to worry about because you are not without me.'

Miss Bates took the stick Orlando had given her up into her bedroom. With some care she chose a place for it where it would not be in the way but where she could see it from her bed. She was older than Orlando, and she had to die herself some day, and sometimes in the night she woke up and thought about it. She thought it would be nice if on those occasions she could turn on her light – the pugs would stir at her feet, grumbling, then settle back to snoring sleep – and look across to the stick, to remind herself that with the consciousness of approaching death – how else explain that look of preoccupation? – he had handed it to her and had said, 'Here, take this. I don't need it,' and then he had walked away, at that mysterious hour of noon, and lain down on the burning stones and gone to his death without his stick: she took comfort from the thought, and kept the stick as a talisman.

Conrad had met the Consul before, but he could not remember where.

'It might have been in Rome,' he said. 'There was a lot of official entertaining when I went to that conference. Could he have been there then, do you think? I know I remember the name. Was there something about the wife?'

'She's common,' said Agatha.

'Was that what it was?' said Conrad vaguely, hoping Agatha was not going to be aggressive.

He had come for the funeral, collecting Imogen on the way from her French family near Tours, and had been surprised to find on his arrival at Miss Bates's house that Henry was there already, and having driven all night in the jeep was by this time – it was after dinner – asleep on the floor. Conrad thought that this was rather rude to Miss Bates, but Agatha found it reassuring. She had already got into the way of treating her grief as an illness, and normality, in the shape of Henry, face downwards on the floor, his head in his arms, a position he always readily assumed after dinner, was probably good for her. She felt better since his arrival, but the trouble was that however much

she told herself that Orlando's death had been expected
her imagination kept turning back to the actual event,
to how it had happened, how he might have felt, to the
frightening privacy of his last moments: it was the thought
of these last moments that made her want to cry; and
Imogen, who had known Orlando so little, hardly helped.
Although Agatha felt her usual proprietary sympathy for
her sister – she had noticed at once that her hair needed
washing – it did constitute a barrier between them that
Imogen had not shared the summer at Lecceto. She could
not be expected to understand, and Henry and Miss Bates,
who did, seemed to Agatha for the moment much closer to
her than the other two.

Conrad was tired after his journey too and though he
made an effort – wholly successful – to charm Miss Bates,
who seemed to him a person of superlative kindness and
efficiency, without whom they would all certainly have
been quite lost, he could not somehow strike the right
note with Agatha. He had the feeling, as he often did with
Agatha, that she was all the time resenting him for some
reason that he did not understand, and though he wanted
to be kind to her he felt she would not let him. She had lost
a father and he had lost a friend, but her face was closed to
him: she would not share her grief.

So he found that he had told her much too brusquely
that he had booked a return passage for her with Imogen
and himself in two days' time and when she said she would
rather stay until the end of September he said that he had
heard that the country round Lecceto was very remote and
wild – he had been talking to a friend of his about it, who
knew that part of Italy very well and said that land values
were going down. As soon as he had said it he realized that
it was extremely tactless and that he would never have said

it if he had not been so tired or indeed so sad, or if she had been a little more cooperative in her attitude.

The situation was not saved by Miss Bates, who cheerfully said, 'Ah yes, and the minute they've gone down they're going to come straight up again. Signor Rossi knows all about it. He'll be able to tell you tomorrow.'

It was not convincing.

Agatha saw Imogen's eyes, lit with secret enjoyment, gazing at Miss Bates, then rolling very slightly in her direction. But she did not want to laugh at Miss Bates, and if Imogen, whose mind she knew well, was also building up a fantasy in which Miss Bates and Conrad were to be paired off in some kind of ludicrous romance, she was not in the mood to be amused by that either.

It was an uneasy evening, partly perhaps because the funeral had not yet taken place. There was to be a service in the English church in Florence the next morning and in the afternoon the committal of Orlando's body to the grave he had asked for in the little cemetery across the hill from Lecceto. This Conrad had agreed to on the telephone to Miss Bates while he had still been in England. He had hoped that Orlando could be brought back to Mount Sorrel, and felt hurt that he had obviously not felt that to be his home: but he wanted, of course, to fulfil Orlando's own wishes.

Miss Bates offered quite early to show Conrad and Imogen to their rooms, and while they were upstairs Agatha, who had not moved, stretched out her foot and poked Henry, who was apparently still asleep. He rolled over and looked up at her.

'I suppose you want me to drive you there,' he said.

'Where?'

'Lecceto.'

'Now?'

He nodded.

'I wasn't going to ask you to.'

'But you would like it?'

'Yes.'

He got up quickly and led the way out to the jeep. It felt like an escape.

'Were you asleep all the time?'

'Not all the time.'

He did not speak any more on the journey, which took them about half an hour. Twice they swerved to avoid nightjars sitting in the middle of the warm road.

There were no lights on at all in Nella's house. Presumably the whole family was in bed. Henry turned the engine off so that they passed quietly. They left the jeep and walked on to the terrace. There Agatha hesitated. The chairs had all been put away, and it looked unfamiliar. Henry put a hand on her elbow and guided her towards the tower house.

They walked in the moonlight up the grassy road, through the open space beside the well, and round the corner of the tower. The distance opened before them, lit by the moon and interspersed with stars and the lesser lights of hill villages and isolated farms. They leant against the building side by side in silence until Henry turned to look at Agatha and she became aware that he was going to kiss her. She did not know why it should be now, whether he hoped to comfort her, or had perhaps some kind of feeling that Orlando would have liked it, but she felt she must not move. He merely looked at her. She would have waited indefinitely, but he slowly bent his head.

As his face approached hers, she saw the fear in his eyes.

Agatha

Orlando died; and Agatha was the first to find him, under the bent pear tree in the full heat of the sun.

If in the course of an exploratory operation a surgeon had touched that part of her brain where those particular moments were stored they would have recurred to her with a clarity which patients who have experienced it have described as quite different from the normal action of memory; which seems to show that when five years later Agatha walked, rather quickly because she did not want to be seen, through the woods at Mount Sorrel in the first cold weather of the autumn of 1956 those moments, as well as all the other moments, of her past, though not for the time being present to her conscious mind, were physically contained within her. Her kneeling down beside Orlando on the dry ground which smelt of the herbs he had crushed by his fall, together with the powerful emotion of those first minutes before Nella and Giuseppe came, the clarity, excitement and, it had seemed, unlimited love, were in some minute but scientifically factual way a part of her physical being. As were, presumably, of Conrad's, his distant Indian mornings.

She looked down at Mount Sorrel from the trees at the end of the valley. He was already at his desk in the library writing about India. The house faced her across the park. She did not much like its cold façade – her memories of it, immediate or more distant, were mixed and not predominantly happy – but it had a place in the landscape there, the valley folded to accommodate it, the village clustered behind it and the distance beyond framed it in an eighteenth-century landscape; one which for the moment seemed mostly in tones of grey, except for the low white mist which lay on the floor of the valley concealing the stream. The house was higher than the bed of the stream – lawns sloped down in front of it – and the light on Conrad's desk could be seen from the opposite hillside.

Surprised that he should be up so early, she turned back into the wood and began to walk quickly uphill away from the open valley. Perhaps he did get up early now, old people after all needed less sleep than younger ones, and he was sixty-six this year. She was no longer familiar with the daily routine of his life: she had stayed at Mount Sorrel only once since her marriage. He had leased them a little damp cottage in the woods which had belonged to old Glass the gamekeeper, who was dead now. Conrad very seldom came to see them and probably did not know or care whether or not they were there this particular weekend; or did she only assume his indifference to suit her own purposes, because she distrusted him, had too much to conceal from him, who was after all her husband's father and her own uncle? She had better concentrate on what she had to do.

'Dora?' she called quietly. 'Dora!'

It was a morning for only getting through, for plodding through the fallen leaves with a purpose, not expecting that on this grey day the woods should turn beautiful, as they had been for the past few weeks when there had been sun through slight mist and a haze of cobwebs over everything, even, pattern on pattern, sunlight through dew-whitened cobwebs on old man's beard, on hazel or thorn, and the smell of damp leaves; but now she must not be late and must call Dora too from time to time, who had provided her with an excuse for being up so early, should she be required to give one, by getting lost the night before.

She hoped the dog might come dashing down some ride to greet her, was conscious in fact of grey (like the morning) anxiety because Dora was not yet a year old and had never before been out all night, but she had something else to do before she could concentrate on looking for her, and even as she thought of traps, or rabbit-holes, or roads, she had to hurry on to the appointed place: only, passing as she had to do by the entrance to Wood Hill, she could at least turn in there – it was a short cut to where she had to go – and skirting the back of the garden, keeping to the trees, see if there was anything to be seen of the vile seducer, the ugly brute she suspected of being behind the disappearance, the utterly appalling Sandy.

The house, Wood Hill, where she had spent the first eight years of her life, was still shuttered and curtained against the night. There was an elderly couple living there now: not much was known about them except that they were the owners of an unpleasant, undisciplined dog. There had been children once but they had grown up and gone. Agatha waited for a moment, concealed in the trees. Would Dora, an early riser, scratch at a door, bark? There was no sound and she turned to go. Unexpectedly a door opened. He emerged, sniffed the ground, a yellow dog, cross between a labrador and something smaller, nastier, a hyena perhaps; bristly along the back as if his hackles were always up, little eyes, unnecessary whiskers; and alone. The door shut behind him.

Agatha moved as quietly as she could through the trees and over the top of the hill. She heard him bark, but half-heartedly. He was not even a good watch-dog.

Her anxiety was now acute, but she must not be late.

Conrad wrote, 'My father was very distressed by Lord Curzon's resignation. He felt that the Government at home had completely failed to understand the grandeur of Curzon's concept of Empire. But by that time I had been sent home to school.'

Seven, his life the heat and smell of India, parakeets, flying foxes, brilliant red flowers in darkest deodar trees, soft rain on early morning rides over the foothills of the Himalayas, sounds and smells of the camp, following his father as he dispensed justice. At school he would learn to be wise, good and immeasurably grand, like his father. The untouchable was his mother's smell in some kind of soft drapery which covered her warmth as she kissed him good-bye. It was as if they had cut off his arm and said, 'Grow another to prove yourself worthy.' The memory was stored away somewhere, part of him but not to be recalled, though he could remember very clearly the feel and smell of his pony Sam. His father had represented to him that owning meant being dedicated to serve. He had honoured his father and mother and in the sweet-scented Indian morning had cantered along mountainous paths followed by his faithful syce.

Conrad wrote in his memoirs, 'I have very happy memories of my childhood in India.'

Over the top of the hill there was a plantation of conifers, only a few years old and too thick to walk through. Agatha followed the fence round the edge of it and joined a track leading downhill, into the small valley in which were the ruins of the old Timberwork factory. The part that still stood was the eighteenth-century stone structure, roofless now, which had been built as a paper mill. The additions which had been made in the nineteen-thirties, when Orlando had been turning the little furniture factory into the highly profitable organization it had later become, had collapsed now and lay in heaps of rubble, encroached upon by the willow herb. Through the tall trees beyond she could see the viaduct which took the railway line across the narrow valley. Here again there was a lurking mist; the trees emerged through it with an effect almost of a Chinese landscape, the occasional huge conifer dark among the elms and hornbeams.

She took an overgrown path halfway down the hill and crossed the hillside parallel to the stream until she reached a point from which she could look down through the trees to where the road curved under the tall arch of the viaduct. Here a car had drawn up on the grass verge. There was a thermos flask on its roof and the three men standing near were holding mugs. Two of the men were wearing hats and rather long belted overcoats; the other, who was standing a little apart from them, was Agatha's half-brother Paul, a convicted traitor.

He looked a good deal smaller than the other two, hatless and wearing over the navy-blue suit he had worn at his trial a short duffle coat bought from a government surplus store, originally more or less white, but dirty now. His shoulders were bent and both hands were clasped round his cup as if to keep them warm.

Agatha walked slowly towards them down the hill, her hands in her pockets, reluctant to reach the moment when he must look up and see her. The sound of her own gumboots against her legs – a sound she usually liked because of its agreeable associations – seemed loud to her as she approached, but none of the three men looked in her direction. She was almost out of the trees and on to the grass before Paul saw her, said 'Ah!', put down his mug on the bonnet of the car, and came up to put his hands on her arms and kiss her quickly on both cheeks.

The men in hats hardly glanced at her. It crossed her mind that they might have been aware of her approach all the time.

Gesturing vaguely in their direction, Paul said as if in introduction, 'Bill and Ben, the flowerpot men,' and with a hand on her arm led her away from them to the other side of the car.

'It worked all right then?' said Agatha.

'Yes. Thank you.'

'I'm glad you've got some coffee,' said Agatha, rather quickly. 'I was going to bring some but then I thought I'd be sure to wake the children.'

'Have some.'

'Is there time?'

'Of course, come on,' said Paul, but as he reached for the thermos he shot a quick glance towards the two men, and she realized with a slight shock that he was frightened of them. She tried a polite smile in their direction – *she* was not a criminal after all – and one of them nodded back. Perhaps it was the one who had come to see her to ask her for the money for the escape. She was not quite sure because of the hat, but it could have been the same; he had the same look of consciously assumed anonymity, as if all sorts of other expressions might cross his face when he was not on the job. She thought he seemed efficient and reliable – always assuming that one was on the same side – and was annoyed with Paul for being frightened of him.

'You know you could get five years for this,' said Paul.

Agatha, who had not realized the penalty was so great, although she had known – in spite of having temporarily forgotten it – that in fact she indeed was a criminal too, paused for a moment before answering. Then she said, very calmly, 'What a lot.'

'Oh yes,' said Paul as if he found the idea obscurely satisfying. 'Helping a criminal escape from prison. Very serious offence.'

Agatha looked at him, finding his mood, as so often, hard to gauge.

'What weak coffee,' she said.

'Hot though.'

'Where will you go?'

'You'd better not know. They'll keep me somewhere for a bit before they get me out of the country. It's safer that way. I'll send you a message when I get there. We could probably meet somewhere or other.'

He said it without conviction. Everything about him except his businesslike suit seemed pale: the grubby duffle coat, the thin face, slightly greasy in complexion, the fair hair, shorter than usual (had they cut it in prison?), the eyes avoiding hers, light blue eyes whose gaze in better times had sometimes been dazzling. The word 'desolation' came into her head, at the same time as the thought that he had no one but her.

'We must,' she said. 'We must meet somehow.'

He turned away a little.

'I don't know where I'll be.'

'Tell them to let me know when you're safely out of the country. They can do that somehow or other, can't they? Otherwise I shan't know when you're safe.'

'OK.'

'And then you send me a message. I'm always here.'

But he was fumbling in the pockets of the duffle coat, bringing out a packet of cigarettes, extracting one with difficulty because his hands were trembling violently. 'Even now?' he asked with the cigarette in his mouth, as he grappled with the matchbox.

'Of course even now.'

'But you don't –' He had managed to light the cigarette, and paused to draw on it deeply. 'You don't approve of what I've done.'

'Of course I don't approve of what you've done. I think it was an awful thing to do. But I've often not approved of you.'

He nodded, half smiled; but she noticed with horror a tear trickling down the side of his nose.

'Paul, listen, get through these next few days, do what they tell you. Here, I've got a bit of money, take it. Get them to buy you books so you don't get depressed, hiding. And then when you get there, Paul, have a nice time, do.'

He looked at her questioningly.

'No, it's important. Don't have guilt and all that, it's such a bore. Have a nice time. You know – those things you like – drink, and boys and things.'

He shook his head, but giggled weakly, looked at her again, and laughed outright.

'Well, you know –' said Agatha, smiling reluctantly.

'What a business,' he said, shaking his head again. 'What a lark, what an episode.'

'Work would be the best thing of course,' said Agatha, relieved to see his spirits improving. 'And your money might run out soon, mightn't it? Can't you write a book, Paul? You're much cleverer than most people who do.'

'A travel book?' he suggested ironically.

'Yes, a travel book, why not? They're what everyone reads these days. There's a new thing, just started, I read about it somewhere, a Book Club just for travel books. That shows... Oh do, Paul, and send it to me and I'll find a publisher and make all the arrangements and everything.'

'I might.'

'Do.'

'How are the children?' he asked quickly. Each was as nervous as the other that there might be a gap in the conversation.

'All right.' Beginning to smile, she added, 'Very well in fact.'

'And that awful beagle?'

'She's not awful.'

'You'll never be able to keep her in London.'

'Of course I will!'

He shook his head. 'Too boisterous. You won't be able to control her.' He sounded pleased again, as he had at the thought of her going to prison for helping him.

She did not answer.

'And our dear uncle?' he asked, his hard ironical tone not concealing from her his anxiety to know how Conrad was bearing the shame.

'Very busy I think,' she said.

'Starting a war, I suppose.'

'No, he doesn't seem particularly belligerent. If you mean about Egypt. Not that he's exactly unbelligerent.

I don't know what he thinks really. He's starting to write his memoirs.'

'Good Lord, I never thought he'd do that. Early days, Eton and Oxford and all that?'

'I suppose so.'

'Perhaps that's what I should write. My memoirs.'

'Could you?'

'No. No, I couldn't. They'd be a pack of lies, wouldn't they?'

The men in overcoats were moving, one merely shifting from foot to foot to keep warm, the other approaching the car with two mugs. They watched him open the car door, bend to put the mugs inside, straighten up again to reach out for the thermos.

'Look here,' said Paul hurriedly, taking her by the elbow to turn her slightly away from the car. 'I've got more money than you think. I'll be all right. You'd better go now. I'll send you a message. Give my love to Henry and the children. Tell Henry to buy Logan shares if he can raise some money. They'll recover. Daintry's still the hottest operator in the business.'

'I will give them your love,' said Agatha. 'Later I mean. I'd better not now.'

'No, quite right. Keep your mouth shut. Now don't worry, will you?'

'No.'

'I'd better go then.'

The men were waiting by the car, one with his hand on the handle of the door by the driver's seat. This one's face had assumed a rather more amiable expression; perhaps he was relieved that they were about to move on.

'OK?' he asked.

The other one was getting into the back seat.

'Yes, yes, here we are, off we go,' said Paul fussily.

The driver took his seat, shutting the door quietly. Paul kissed Agatha quickly on the cheek and got in beside him, winding down the window. When he had shut the door he lent out and said, 'Don't forget, get hold of some Logan shares. You'll be on to a good thing.'

She nodded, raised a hand. The car started. Paul waved and smiled and the wind blew his pale hair away from his face as the car moved off. She thought he looked younger than thirty-five. She waited by the road. The sound of the car faded. The sky was lighter; there might be some sun after all. A very slight breeze stirred the trees behind her. Leaves fell, and a chestnut hit the damp earth.

'I have no money,' said Agatha aloud, as if she were patiently explaining. 'Because I spent what I had and a good deal more on getting you out of prison.'

Perhaps it was an exaggeration – pushed to extremes, there was probably something she could sell – but she could not help minding that none of that seemed to have crossed his mind for a moment: he did take things for granted.

She shook herself slightly, as if she had been wet, and began to walk rapidly along the road in the opposite direction to that in which the car had gone; having now no need of concealment, she could walk back by road and hope to find Dora on the way, or if not on the way then back at the cottage, for she might just possibly have spent the night in shelter somewhere and come home at daylight. Or she might have gone to Mount Sorrel – that was a new idea, quite hopeful – someone there would certainly have taken her in if it had been late – they would not have been able to let Agatha know because there was no telephone at the cottage – and Conrad would walk up with her before breakfast, with his fat old labrador – he would not have come earlier even though, as she knew, he had been awake, because he would have thought they would still be asleep, unfamiliar as he was with the early-rising habits of small children... She concentrated on these possibilities, walking rapidly and not thinking about Paul; she would not allow herself to think about Paul; on that subject her mind was tired, nor did she like the prospect of having to admit to herself – and certainly she would never do so to anyone else – that she almost despaired of him.

She passed the ruined mill and followed the track into the woods behind it, approaching the sound of the stream. Earlier in the autumn the track had been very muddy but now after the first few frosts of winter it was easier to walk on. It led her past the waterfall and through the darkest part of the wood, where the trees were tallest and the valley steepest, and out into a field made muddy by the bullocks who looked up at her curiously, their breath steaming from their nostrils, and through another rough little copse out on to the road which passed Wood Hill and went on into the village, and turning a corner on this road she saw Dora and turned back at once, stood on the grass verge, waited, pressed her hands against her face. Certainly the dog must be dead.

Agatha walked up and down on the grass as if by refusing to go round the corner again she could deny what lay beyond, which was Dora dead by the roadside, killed by a car. Fighting with the information, she heard a car in the distance. It was coming up the hill, must be passing the dog now, came round the corner, a Land-Rover with a man driving it who slowed down. Stiff, her hands in her pockets, she was frozen in fear that he might stop; until catching a glimpse of her face, he accelerated, embarrassed, there being nothing he could do.

'It's only a dog after all,' said Agatha firmly and walked round the corner.

Dora lay by the edge of the road, apparently unmarked. Her limpness showed her to be dead, but her compact little body looked otherwise unchanged and her coat which had seemed as if it must have been polished with silk, though it was only youth and health which made it shine, was unspoilt; even people who had found her too energetic or who didn't like dogs had admitted she was beautifully marked: only a fleck of blood by her mouth: it seemed such a pity.

Beside her on the grass was a piece of paper, torn from the back of a book. Agatha picked it up. On it was written in pencil, 'Sorry about this little foxhound, jumped out very fast and killed at once. There was another dog but he ran off.' Sandy the murderer. Looking up, she saw the blood on the road. She could only have failed to see it before because her eyes had been fixed on the corpse – a great bright scarlet splash down the middle of the pale grey road, oh she'd spilt her blood all right, and Agatha began to sob, crumpling the note in her hand, momentarily overwhelmed by love and admiration. She'd stood on a hillside, autumn bright on the long grass with low yellow sunshine and Dora had scented sheep, being unfamiliar with them, and from right across the big field – she below Agatha on one side, the sheep on the other, grazing – had begun to give chase. Her firm deep-chested body built for speed, tail for once a backward-bending curve, she bounded through the tall grass as the silly sheep began to fluster, hustled together, ran, the sound of their matted pelts against their legs possibly intoxicating to a pursuer. Agatha shouted – why should she obey? – but without slackening her pace a moment she came in a great bounteous sweep of movement to her feet as if, running so beautifully, it made no difference to her where she ran. And so she'd dashed at death like that and spouted all her warm bright blood on to the road.

Agatha crouched to pick up the limp body, head against hers, then carried it to the edge of the wood by the road. She would return later with a spade to bury it, but in the meantime, unaware that there was now an observer among the trees behind her, she covered the body with fallen leaves.

'We can only bleed,' she said.

The familiar tone, calmly authoritative, as if precise diction could conceal its sadness, came to the man watching her. He turned away, moving quickly back through the trees the way he had come.

Agatha knelt on the damp ground, piling high the dead leaves.

Conrad wrote with a relief nib, smoothly and fast, in a firm Palmerstonian hand. The task bored him. He found that speech was a much more natural means of communication than this remote refined process of thought, manual labour and solitude. He was not a voluble man but had spent a lifetime working for various aims by means of verbal persuasion, whether at private talks or public meetings. He was used to the action and reaction involved, and without it found the writer's task too unresponsive, in a sense perhaps too arrogant; there 'was no interplay of personality, no way of gauging an audience's reaction or bending to it. How much should he describe of India in the 1890s? There was no listening face whose expression could tell him the answer. Was that life – on tour, in Simla, in Delhi – of interest to anyone nowadays?

'There's rather a vogue for travel books,' he said, frowning and wondering whether it was time for breakfast. But the Empire was out of fashion. 'It will come back of course,' he said, beginning to address an imaginary audience of attentive youth, 'because it's a very interesting subject. The life that was led, the type of individual that was produced to wield these huge responsibilities, to live this life of in some ways enormous self-sacrifice and in others extraordinary fulfilment, all this will be seen in due course to be uniquely fascinating. Uniquely fascinating.'

Should he describe Government House, Calcutta, modelled on Kedleston, its fantastic gardens, the Viceroy's bodyguard, his Indian servants in their scarlet livery with the Viceregal monogram embroidered in gold? Instead he wrote, 'I am far from nostalgic. I had always said that Independence must come, and was one of the people working to see that it came sooner rather than later. Of course I regret many things about the manner of its coming, the bloodshed, the Labour Government's precipitance ...'

'I'd have liked to have done it myself of course,' he said slowly, putting down his pen. 'I'd have liked to have stage-managed the handover myself.' He smiled indulgently at his own vanity.

The telephone rang. Apologies. Was he in bed?

'No, no, just doing a bit of writing. Otherwise I'd have been in Church. Dodging it this morning, I'm ashamed to say.'

The Prime Minister wanted an extra Cabinet meeting – 'Of course, yes, tell him I'll be there.'

Putting down the receiver, he said, 'Hope the silly fool knows what he's doing,' disrespectfully but without real anxiety.

Henry walked back through the wood to the cottage. It was small and yellow-washed with wooden lattice work round the roof of a pointed gable, a seaside boarding-house in a forgotten Victorian resort rather than a gamekeeper's cottage. He pushed open the back door and looked into the kitchen where the children were eating cornflakes.

'I'm just going to telephone a minute. You'd better come.'

They looked shocked.

'We haven't finished our breakfast.'

'Where's Mummy?'

'She's just coming. Here, take this.' He cut two pieces of brown bread, put butter and honey on them, and gave one to each child. They took them and climbed into the back of the car.

'I thought we were going to have sausages,' said George.

'We are, when we get back. I didn't want to leave you alone.'

'We'd have been all right,' said George.

'Supposing Lucy had cut her finger?

'I'd have held it under the cold tap until you came back,' said George.

'She might not have let you, you know what she is.'

'I'd knock her out, and then hold it under the cold tap.'

'I'll knock you out,' said Lucy. 'And chop you in bits and put you down the lavatory. And pull the plug, I will.'

'Don't be silly, Lucy,' said Henry. 'People don't leave people of five and four alone in houses anyway. I don't know why but they just don't. Now I'm going into the telephone-box and you can sit here a minute and if you quarrel I'll be very angry.'

'*You'll* be very angry?' said George loudly. 'You mean we will.' This seemed to strike him as immensely funny and he began to roll around, laughing, in the back of the car.

Henry watched them from the telephone-box and soon Lucy began to wave her hands up and down frantically, making horrible faces. George reached into the front of the car for Henry's coat, searched through the pockets and gave her a handkerchief: she must have had honey on her fingers.

'Sally? Oh I'm sorry, you were asleep.'

'Of course I was asleep, it's very early.'

'I'm sorry. Sally?'

'Mn?'

'I'm sorry.'

'Well, all right then.'

'I wish I was there.'

'Is that what you rang up to say?'

'No. The thing is, Dora – you know, that dog – she's been run over.'

'Oh poor thing. Is she dead?'

'Yes.'

'Is Agatha very upset?'

'Yes. At least I think so.'

'You think so?'

'I haven't spoken to her. I just saw her, picking her up. It must have happened in the night. I came back. Agatha looked so ... I didn't want to go up to her.'

'Henry, you must. You must go and look after her. Poor Agatha, she really loved that dog. I know what it is. Go on, Henry, go and find her.'

'You're very kind. I will go. The thing is, I may not be able to get away tonight after all, I'll have to see how it goes.'

'Yes, I see.'

'Sally, darling, I'll ring up later.'

'I'm going out.'

'I'd better say I'll see you tomorrow night. About nine. Without fail. Sally?'

'Yes?'

'You're very nice.'

'Oh *Henry.*'

'Sorry to be so hopeless. Good-bye, Sally –'

He went out, smiling affectionately, and got into the car. On the way back to the cottage he told the children that Dora had been hit by a car when she was crossing the road, just like the badger who had been killed a few weeks ago, and that they must be very kind to their mother who would be feeling sad about it.

Agatha had become pregnant quite soon after their marriage. It threw her into a relationship of unaccustomed intimacy with her own body; she was embarrassed as well as fascinated, too embarrassed to go to the relaxation classes which her doctor had recommended but fascinated enough to read everything she could find in the Chelsea Public Library on the subject of childbirth, from which she had gleaned the general impression that if having a baby hurt you it was your own fault. Confirming as it did her inclination towards guilt of any kind, this misapprehension left her free to assume, after a last-minute anaesthetic and a forceps delivery, that she was not much good as a natural woman. This might have worried her more than it did had not quite another realization begun to dawn upon her, which was that through no virtue of her own, for the virtue was all on the other side, she was a good mother.

It appeared to her that George was a perfect organism, requiring only her intelligent co-operation in order to complete his biologically pre-ordained progress. That being so, she could not see her task as a very difficult one; but it did require a certain discipline, a watchfulness in case she should, instead of interpreting, impose. She already had an idea of all loving activity as involving self-restraint, and in this sense her

newly discovered and previously unimaginable maternal love
seemed of a higher quality than her love for her husband. If
love between adults was a process which only began when
one's love was returned, it implied two selves, liable to make
demands: in maternal love self-abnegation could be complete.
Thus she was grateful to George for her first breath of freedom from herself, a breath that at certain of her more ecstatic
moments she could imagine might in the course of time prove
to have been a first gasp of the great white air of death.

The baby was breast-fed at first. The doctor had
pronounced views on feeding. He was a dark-haired young
man with a sternly professional air and a kind of restrained
fanaticism about social justice, which meant that he accepted
no private patients and that Agatha had to sit for a long time
in his surgery waiting room before seeing him. She did this
gladly, because she admired him without qualification and
had erotic fantasies about him which she allowed to run
riot because she had heard that it always happened between
maternity patients and their doctors. At one month, cod
liver oil and orange juice; at six weeks, mashed banana.
Then came yolk of egg, then apple purée, then Farex mixed
with cow's milk (at the cottage she boiled this for three
minutes in case the milk was not so purified as in London).
Rose-hip syrup for sweetening, never sugar. Soon the two
o'clock feed consisted of egg-yolk and mashed carrot, fruit
and orange juice, and by the time George was two and a half
months' old he was no longer breast-fed but drank cow's
milk from a bottle at his first and last feeds. The method was
crowned with success; each meal was a triumph. George
grew plump and took on a sort of overall gloss, or sheen,
outward manifestation of a superlative mechanism within.
He smiled now, and thumped vigorously with his heels on
his red kicking rug. From the privacy of his first months of

ORLANDO KING

life he emerged, buttoned into a sort of bag with arms, on
to the streets of Chelsea in his pram.

She walked the same streets with both of them later.

'Keep away from the road.' 'Wait for me at the edge of
the pavement.' '*Stop*, Lucy!' 'Hold my hand to cross the
road.' Carrying her shopping basket, always afraid they
might be run over.

But when they got to the shops they were still her
licence to existence, the experience shared which admitted
her to ordinary life – 'Oh they *are*, at that age' – and I am
one of you, she sometimes thought, saying, 'Two pounds
of granulated,' smiling because another child is staring at
mine from behind a pile of soup tins. We are the same,
we see they get decent meals and have their noses wiped;
that is to say, we've knelt, 'Come on, push,' we've said, the
plump foot dangling nonchalant, laces to be tied, and been
aware of this sometimes as such an act of love as dazzles
the imagination. 'Go on then run,' we've said. 'Not too
fast, you'll fall; oh you silly little thing, what did I tell
you?' So we tire ourselves out, as an arm aches, held for a
hawk to fly from.

These feelings expressed themselves only in a smile or
two, a word perhaps to a strange child, a standing aside
for someone with a heavier basket. She knew very few of
her neighbours by name. The street was a poor one, in the
course of being transformed into something smarter: the
process had not gone far as yet, but there was a property
company which owned or was acquiring a good many of
the freeholds and was selling long leases after repairing the
houses. The milkman had told Agatha that fourteen families had been evicted from two of the houses opposite,
which were going to be turned into a vicarage. Agatha had
written to the Vicar, who replied that there was no truth

in the story. He thought her quite mad. Nor was the milk-man pleased when she told him; he preferred to believe the calumny.

Henry gave her coffee, said he would cook the lunch, offered to go with a spade and bury Dora.

She drank the coffee.

'I have to give her her due, don't I?' she said apologetically. 'I won't go on about it.'

He reassured her, said she was quite right. He cooked the children their late breakfast of sausages, dressed them in their duffle coats and gloves and boots and sent them, the little shock of Dora's death already easily absorbed (her claws had always been rather sharp), to play behind the cottage, where they had made a house in what used to be an outside privy.

'It's unbelievable, how kind you are,' said Agatha, moving closer to the fire he'd left.

He kissed her cheek gently. 'I am quite good sometimes, aren't I?' he said, rather pressing the point.

'Incredibly good.'

'I know you think I'm useless,' he said. 'But did you see those sausages? A bit split, not at all burnt, perfect. I'm going to do the lunch too. You're just going to sit there quite quietly. Papers, do you want? I've got them already. They're there when you want them. I'm just going to peel the potatoes now.'

'You won't forget the burying?'

'As soon as I've peeled the potatoes I'm going.'

She could imagine scavenging noses pushing at the soft flesh.

'It has to be deep. Foxes dig.'

'I know, don't worry.'

'You won't let the children follow you?'

'I'll go out of the front.'

'Thank you very much, Henry.'

He smiled, patted her head, and left.

He walked straight ahead, to keep the cottage between him and the children, and then when he reached the trees turned right and, skirting the road, joined the track he had taken earlier in the morning and which was a short cut to Wood Hill. When he had woken up to find Agatha gone, he had assumed that she had walked to Wood Hill in the hope that Dora might have spent the night there, and he had left the children to start their breakfast and walked in that direction expecting that he might meet her on the way back. He had walked all the way to the road before he saw her kneeling on the ground, piling leaves on the dead dog and saying, 'We can only bleed.'

He knew very well to what she was referring. Her vision was such as to see everything in parallels and correspondences, and he knew that she had in mind not only Dora's death but her own unhappiness as the result of the pain he inflicted on her by his love for Sally, and in reference to which she had once said, 'I only have one reaction. I think I only have one cell. I can only let out an awful black cloud of love like an inkfish when you prod it. I'm not proud of it, it's so useless and tiring. Also, why should I involve you with my entrails? It's an imposition.'

It was not that he did not understand Agatha. He did, a good deal better than she understood him. But he did not know what to do about her.

Agatha's sister Imogen, who was twenty at this time, had certain mannerisms which Agatha found irritating. For instance, when she met Agatha and the children in the street, the day that Agatha had agreed to find £700 to finance Paul's escape from prison and journey to some unknown foreign country, she had swooped down upon Lucy, with jingling bracelets and flying scarves, lifted her high in the air, hugged and kissed her, bent to return her to the pavement and said, 'Instant blissikins.'

George stood watching, rightly (to Agatha's mind) embarrassed. Imogen then kissed him, and said, 'Georgie Porgie, pudding and pie, kissed the girls and made them cry,' a rhyme he particularly disliked. In fact, though, he was very fond of Imogen, and responded warmly to her unusual prettiness: he was prepared to accept that there should be, especially at moments of greeting, a certain amount of superficial nonsense to be got through: he even sensed, though he had never thought it out, that there was some kind of initial nervousness involved.

'How's the magazine world?' said Agatha, implying criticism.

'Phoney,' said Imogen, forestalling it.

It was still summer, and she was wearing a yellow dress tightly waisted and full-skirted. She was employed by a fashion magazine, her contributions being mainly towards a column on accessories: a good many of these she sported herself, a thick shiny plastic belt, for instance, two diaphanous yellow chiffon scarves, and the jingling bracelets. She was never still, shook her long fair hair back from her face or tucked wandering strands of it behind her ear, fidgeted with the bracelets, twined the scarves through her fingers, her face meanwhile, even when she was speaking with breathless animation, preserving a kind of absorbed serenity, like a dancer's, inherent perhaps in its own perfect structure.

'Do you know who I met last night?' she said, beginning to walk along the street beside Agatha.

'No?'

'Gary Cooper.'

'What was he like?'

'Fabulous. He asked me to have dinner with him.'

'And did you?'

'Not then. Some time, he meant. He said he'd ring up. Do you think he will?'

'I expect so. I mean, if he said he would ...'

'There was this man who'd been in Monte Carlo with him and he had a tummy upset, and he went into the chemist to get some medicine and Prince Rainier came in, and he said, "Hey, Prince, I been throwing up all over your kingdom."'

'Probably he was a friend of his.'

'No, he'd never seen him before. I think.'

'Oh.'

'Well, anyway –'

'Yes, well, how funny. Where was this?'

'Some party. I don't know whose party it was actually. I went with Adrian.'

'Oh yes.'

'He's getting a new flat. It's awfully nice. In Chesham Place.'

'Let's go in down here. The door's open. Careful, Lucy, hold on to the railing.' They went down the steep steps into the area, past the dustbins and through the basement door. The kitchen was at the back, looking out on to a square of garden on its own level. The children went out to dig in the sandpit and Agatha began to unload her shopping basket.

'You'll have lunch, of course.'

'I can't really, I'm supposed to be looking at a whole lot of places in the King's Road.'

'Can't you look at them after lunch?'

'I suppose so. I'm supposed to meet a photographer at two o'clock in a stocking bar.'

'Unless it's a place where you eat stockings you might as well have lunch first. We always have it quite early anyway because Willy comes at two.'

'How's all that working?'

'Rather well. She does all sorts of useful things that I've never asked her to do. The children love her. And I like the bookshop.'

'Do they still only pay you three pounds a week?'

'Yes, it isn't very much, is it? Perhaps they'll give me some more at Christmas or something.'

'It's an awful long time until Christmas. Why don't you ask them?'

'They look quite poor. I shouldn't think they make much money out of it.'

'How's Henry's job?'

'Boring, I think, but he seems to be getting used to it.'

'Perhaps he'll get a rise.'

'I think he thinks more in terms of not getting sacked.'

'So do I,' said Imogen with feeling.

'He'll do something quite different one day, and be quite different about it. But I don't know what, or when.'

This was as near as Agatha ever came to discussing her problems with anyone, and the feeling of the nearness, as she sliced tomatoes with a sharp knife, was momentarily worrying, in case she should go further and talk about Sally, which she had never done to anyone except Henry – and not very much even to him – but she did really know that the temptation would pass and that she would be glad not to have succumbed to it, and that anyway after the conversation she would feel as comforted as if they had discussed everything and been mutually reassured. Sliding the knife cleanly through the tomato, she did not hurry to raise the subject of Paul, though she knew she would have to do it before Imogen left.

'There's room for me there,' said Imogen, fiddling with her bracelets.

'Where?' asked Agatha, who was still thinking about Henry.

'In Adrian's new flat,' said Imogen.

Agatha did not pause in her slicing, concealing her reaction, which was negative.

'He wants me to move in,' said Imogen.

'What about when Gary Cooper rings up?' said Agatha.

'That's nothing to do with it,' said Imogen.

'Yes it is. If you're living with someone you're supposed to be their person, aren't you?'

'You don't think it's a good idea.'

'Why don't I ask Henry what he thinks?'

'All right. I can see you're just being tactful, but, yes, ask Henry. I'd like to know what he thinks.'

'Lucy likes cauliflower,' said Agatha. 'And spinach and cabbage and all the things children are supposed to hate.'

'I get so sick of the flat,' said Imogen. 'And I do like Jane and Diana but they get on my nerves sometimes. And it's always so untidy.'

'I don't think that's a serious enough reason for going to live with Adrian.'

'I'm not a very serious person.'

'I know,' said Agatha, putting a saucepan on the stove. 'Why doesn't a millionaire come and marry you?'

'I don't think I'm the sort of person people marry.'

'Rubbish,' said Agatha angrily.

But Imogen was looking down, her hair hanging forward over her face.

'I mean I absolutely wouldn't dream of marrying Adrian,' she said, fiddling with her bracelets. 'But I think in a way he might have asked me, don't you?' Her face screwed up and tears fell softly on to her hands.

'I *hate* him!' said Agatha, stamping her foot.

She turned back to the stove and began to bang saucepans about unnecessarily.

'Yes, well, anyway,' she said, 'I don't really think you should move in with him in that case, and also you know it is entirely your own fault people don't treat you better, you're much too humble. You ought to be nastier. Do try.' Talking to allow Imogen time to recover from her tears, she meanwhile put chops under the grill and mixed oil and vinegar as a dressing for the tomatoes. 'You could do it all so much better if that's the sort of thing you want to do. Look at all the opportunities you missed after those marvellous photographs in *Vogue.* You could be a famous model, a film star or something. What about spending less time with Adrian and more on your job, for instance?'

Imogen was staring dreamily out of the window.

'How can I get people to like me for myself, not for what I look like?' she said.

'Women,' said Agatha, turning the chops. 'What's to be done about them?'

Neither expected an answer.

After a few minutes Agatha felt able to raise the subject of Paul's escape. She and Imogen both had a small income from money left by their father in trust for their children, but they were unable to use the capital. Conrad was their principal trustee and as his belief was that young people should make their own way in the world he was unapproachable on such subjects, as he was also unshakeable in his resolve to give his own only child Henry, whom he considered a wastrel, nothing at all, except the lease of the gamekeeper's cottage at Mount Sorrel, until he had in some sense or other satisfactory to his father proved himself. The raising of a ransom for Paul was therefore not a simple matter.

Imogen was shocked at the suggestion.

'I don't think he ought to be got out,' she said. 'He committed a crime.'

'I know he did. But he's our brother.'

'I thought it was all over. Have we all got to start worrying again?'

'We don't have to do the escaping. All we have to do is raise the money.'

'And then what? Does he expect us to look after him?'

'They're going to get him out of the country. That's part of the deal.'

'It's illegal.'

'Of course.'

'I don't want to go to prison.'

'You wouldn't. But think, if you don't want to go to prison, imagine being sent there for fifteen years.'

'He'll get remission, won't he, for good behaviour?'

'You know he'd never survive it. He's not resilient, Paul.'

'Nor was Stephen, was he?'

'What's that to do with it?'

'Paul killed Stephen.'

'You can't say that. No one can ever be blamed for someone else's suicide. It's something in them, I mean in the people who kill themselves. Besides, no one could have expected it. We all thought Stephen really tough, so pompous as he was with us all. But he must have had an inclination that way. After all our mother did.'

'They're only our half-brothers,' said Imogen, shying away from the thought of their mother's death.

'All right then.'

'Well, Agatha, I really don't think you should. I mean if people break the law, they have to pay the penalty.'

'That's not what I think,' said Agatha. 'Not everybody. Not every law.'

'You surely don't suggest that the law was wrong?'

'Of course not. But the law has its sphere, its role. There are other spheres, and other roles.'

'I don't understand you.'

'It doesn't really matter.'

She had been walking along in Bath once, on an afternoon when it had been raining and had then brightened towards evening, so that the sun which lit the wet street was low and took the passers-by from the side casting long shadows; and the people, buildings, cars and pigeons took on an unaccustomed gleaming significance, as if they had been in a film and Agatha had read the reviews and knew there was going to be a bank robbery; or, rather, as if something had already happened, something which they all knew about and which was going to change the world.

During the few moments that this effect of the light (or whatever it was) lasted, she passed the police station and saw a car drive up with three men sitting in the back with a rug across their knees. All three got out, holding the rug bundled up between them, and she could see that the one in the middle was young, with a thin face, lank hair, and a blue shirt open at the neck, and that the other two, though wearing ordinary suits, were obviously policemen, whose solemn faces and awkward movements with the rug showed that the man between them was handcuffed and that they thought it proper to try to conceal this. All three seemed to be involved in a ritual which linked them by an interdependence far more solemn and inevitable than the handcuffs, as if their own concern was that they should play the parts assigned to them without faltering, and as if this concern, being common to them all, bound them together by affection rather than by steel.

In a few moments she had passed them and 'was round the corner, conscious of the weight of her shopping basket, and hurrying towards the car; but the visionary aspect of the little scene stayed in her mind and on the way home she tried, without success, to find a significance for it, because although she was an atheist she at the same time vaguely expected some kind of personal message from God which would upset all her beliefs and give her a special dispensation never to die.

Having missed Communion, Conrad had meant to go to Evensong, a service he liked and seldom went to, but now that there was to be an extra Cabinet meeting he would have to drive up to London instead, so he telephoned the Vicar to ask if he might read the Lessons at Matins rather than at Evensong and having obtained his agreement felt relieved from the obligation to go on with his writing, and decided instead that there was time to take Jess for a short walk before Church. In this way he could both avoid having to read the Sunday papers, which would be full of tiresome pre-judgements of the issues which were no doubt to be discussed at the Cabinet meeting, and make sure that he would be out if any of his colleagues were to telephone.

His political decisions had always been slow and solitary ones. He could also put forward quite a convincing case for politicians making as few decisions as possible, maintaining that this was the harder but wiser course, and that a politician's proper task was to react rather than to act and that in his reactions it was his feeling for events, for history, his instincts (based on experience) rather than his science, which should guide him. When he developed this theme, which he did sometimes when people came to lunch, his admirers were impressed by his wisdom and authority and by the humility with which he bore them, and more critical guests thought his theory too obviously applicable to his own career in politics, which was long and perhaps too free from controversy.

As he walked round the garden with Jess before church, he filled his mind with thoughts of his immediate surroundings and of his plans for cutting down even further the maintenance involved, of having only grass to be cut and no beds to be dug, because of the scarcity and high cost of labour. Every now and then Jess, who was old, would stop and give a brief choking cough. Each time he watched her with concern and spoke to her gently before they walked on. The trouble was, her heart was going.

Back at the house, there was a message from the Home Secretary, asking him to telephone. He put it off until after church, thinking that it would only be a question of discussing the Middle Eastern crisis before the Cabinet meeting – would he not join in making strong representations to the Prime Minister and the Foreign Secretary for more information, did he not agree that some of them had really been left disgracefully in the dark as to what the hell was going on? In fact he was wrong; the purpose of the Home Secretary's call was to tell him about his nephew's escape from prison.

Conrad enjoyed reading the Lessons. He had a good voice and such a loving familiarity with most of the Bible that he knew he read it well. This particular Sunday his enjoyment was marred by his catching sight of Daintry in the congregation. Five years ago, when they had first met,

Conrad had been fascinated by Daintry: he now found him a bore, and knew that he would be unable to avoid talking to him after Church. Toad, he had come to call him, in reference not only to his vulgarity but to the fact that he now seemed to him to be a toady, or creep; and the great Georgian house which Daintry had resuscitated at immense expense Conrad amused himself by thinking of as Toad Hall. When Paul and his then wife Serena, Daintry's daughter, used to stay there and organize social activities which were supposed to amuse Daintry, Conrad used to allow himself a feast of sneering: he rather missed it after Paul's divorce. His connection with Daintry was not severed after Paul's quarrel because he was still a considerable shareholder in one of Daintry's companies, of which he had been a director until he became a Cabinet Minister when the Conservative Government took office in 1951. He retained a certain admiration for Daintry as a business man, if only for the immensity of his operations. In spite of his equivocal attitude towards Daintry as a neighbour, as the saviour of a worthwhile piece of local architecture, as the lessee of his, Conrad's, pheasant shooting, Conrad had no hesitation in giving him his due as a brilliant financier and a very rich man – two facts which Conrad fully recognized as giving him a great deal of power. It was only in superficial ways that he disapproved of Daintry: fundamentally he had not much against him, as long as he did not have to speak to him after Church.

It was, however, as he had foreseen, inevitable.

'A word in your ear, old chap,' said Daintry, taking his arm in a confidential way and walking with him along the path which led only to the door through the wall into Mount Sorrel garden. Conrad dragged his steps, hoping to avoid having to ask him in for a glass of sherry.

'Bang on, that sermon, I thought, didn't you?' said Daintry, whose nostalgia for his happy times in wartime Coastal Command was still only too often reflected in his speech. 'We're lucky to have a chap like that. Hard cheese about his legs. Look here, about this Canal business – have you a minute or two?'

'I'm a bit tied up this morning as a matter of fact. I've got someone coming to see me before lunch.'

'Valves,' said Daintry.

'I'm sorry –?'

'If the Canal is closed there'll have to be a pipeline. Daintry Automation must supply the valves. No need to look at me like that. I know you. Might as well ask Her Majesty the Queen for prior info. I'm only thinking ahead. If it comes to that point we want to make sure it's an English firm that gets that order. It will be an international effort of some sort. We'll put in a competitive tender and we want full Government co-operation.'

'You certainly are thinking ahead.'

'Why not? Things can move fast, you know.'

'You're talking about a possibility which is highly problematical.'

'Telling me. I'm perfectly in favour of giving Nasser a bashing for his cheek but on the other hand it's not a bit of good without American support, and you'll never get that with Ike so near a Presidential election. That being so, if the Gyppos have first got to learn to run the Canal, then as like as not have a war with the Israelis, I see no reason why the Canal might not be closed for years – and why the world's shipping might not manage perfectly well without it. Just so long as there's a nice pipeline for the oil.'

'I think most people would find that a pretty unpalatable solution.'

'That's as may be. There's a lot of unpalatable things around these days especially for the poor old English who won the war. That's life, isn't it?' said Daintry, sounding as if it suited him well enough in spite of everything.

'Of course if the time comes I'll talk to the President of the Board of Trade. You should write to him too. You know him, don't you? But not yet.'

'Yes, I know him. But he needs to be nagged. Short on guts I find him. He ought to be out there selling us. That's the patriotic thing to do these days. Well, I'll say cheerio if you've got something on. Don't want to butt in.'

He turned back just as they reached the door in the wall, saying loudly over Conrad's faint polite protest, 'Look in any time you're over my way. I'm always there at week-ends. Give you a glass of champagne any time you like. You can see the latest tricks this decorator fellow's been up to. You wouldn't believe it. Paint mixed by the Adam Brothers' own fair hands – must be, to look at the bill – see you.'

He strode vigorously away, huge in his new winter tweeds. Conrad opened the garden door, on which the white paint was chipped where the sun had blistered it and greened along its lower edge by rising damp from the flagstones beneath, and walked through, smiling slightly.

'He's no fool,' he said aloud, giving the door a push to make sure it was properly shut behind him. 'You may not like him,' and here he was talking in imagination – as he rarely did in fact – to his son Henry. 'But he's by no means a fool.'

Agatha had once said in her annoying way that she admired Daintry for not having become any less awful with success, but Conrad knew that Henry would have preferred East Stainton to have become a ruin rather than be inhabited by Daintry. 'There's no point in houses that size these days, anyway,' he had said.

Conrad now saw very little of Henry and believed himself to have accepted without bitterness the fact of having a ne'er-do-well son; nevertheless in the course of his musings, which often, probably because he lived alone, took the form of imaginary dialogues, usually half silent and half muttered aloud, he sometimes entered into long explanations and justifications with his son; a fact whose significance never occurred to him.

'You can't just write off a man like that,' he muttered. (Henry, rather than listening, was digging Dora's grave.) 'He's shrewd, backs his judgement, gets things done. You have to have people like that.'

The telephone was ringing again as he approached the house.

Henry was cooking the lunch and Agatha was talking. He had given her a large glass of rather unpleasant Cyprus sherry and told her that she was to sit by the fire and read the papers, but she had said she did not want to be alone and had followed him into the kitchen, where she now sat on the table, unwisely warming her sherry by clasping the glass in both hands, slightly swilling the contents about inside it as if she were tasting a rare burgundy. She had begun to talk in the rather excitable and exaggerated way in which she sometimes expressed herself to Henry and which left her the option of pretending she had not meant a word of it should he begin to look disapproving.

'First of all we have to liberate ourselves – by thinking a lot – from illusion and insincerity,' she said in a lecturing tone of voice. 'In other words from deception about outer reality and deception about inner reality. And then, you see, what we have to do is, we have to link ourselves to the history of our species.'

'Must we?'

'Yes, because you have to have movement. You can't resist movement. It's all the universe is, all our history is. Flow, and flux and things. Love allows flow, non-love dams it.'

'It certainly does,' said Henry, who meant to imply that therefore she was not to stop loving him in spite of any grounds she might think she had for doing so.

'But love doesn't allow – mustn't allow, or it will go wrong – mustn't allow for the proper play, in action, of our individuality. So we have to have work. And everything else is absolutely irrelevant. Love and work. It's all there is.'

'What about art?' said Henry. 'Move, will you.' He opened a drawer and began to take out knives and forks.

'The less it's thought about the better,' said Agatha, shifting sideways along the table. 'If there's love and work there'll be art. Loving and working you're bound to dream, and your dreams will be myths about your deepest preoccupations worked out in dream language, and that is art.'

'Good Lord,' said Henry. 'And I don't even have dreams.'

'Oh you do, only you forget them. If you don't dream you die. They've proved it, with experiments.'

'I hope this hasn't got anything to do with politics,' said Henry.

'Well, that's only a question of organization, isn't it? Giving theories names and getting emotional about them is all a great bore. Whatever system makes it possible for the most people to love and work with the greatest freedom of choice and the least feeling of injustice must be the best, that's all. There are probably several different systems that are equally not bad, several that are equally terrible. But it's no use thinking any government is going to be worth supporting whole-heartedly – it's like being a prefect at school – I mean one's on the other side of things.'

'I expect you're right,' said Henry. 'You always are.'

'Oh no.' Agatha looked upset. 'I've been talking too much.'

Henry came over to the table and put his arms round her. She leant her head on his chest and said, 'I wish you loved me.'

'I do.'

'I thought I was going to be married and live happily ever after. It's only because it isn't like that that I had to start all this thinking.'

'It is like that,' said Henry. 'You must believe me. You must.'

'Yes.'

'You must trust me. You believe in taking risks. You must trust me. I love you.' He squeezed her so hard that she began to cough.

'Can't we go to bed?' he said.

But the children were coming in, cold.

Agatha took their coats off.

'The baddies were on a train and I shot them,' said Lucy.

Agatha picked her up and sat on the table again with Lucy on her knee.

'Once upon a time –'

'Mn?' said Lucy.

'There was a little girl who lived in the middle of a wood with her mother and father and her elder brother and one day her mother was so hungry –'

'No, she didn't.'

'That she cut her up in little pieces and put her on a plate and poured gravy all over her and ate her up.'

'So then,' said Lucy, nodding several times, 'the little girl jumped herself together again, picked up the gravy, poured it all over the mother, wrapped her in brown paper and put her in the dustbin.'

'She didn't really, did she?' said George, whose nature was such that he found it very hard not to believe what people said even when he knew they were speaking of impossibilities.

'Of course not, silly. Come on. Lunch. Your father has cooked lunch for you.'

'Did Daddy really cook it?'

They were impressed, ready to believe that because he had cooked it it must be exceptional. He fussed about, covering up with activity the thought that he might be in danger of accounting to Agatha for his selfishness by presenting it to her in the sort of light in which it could be expected to appeal to her. Looking at their faces, Agatha's pale and tired and therefore touching, the children's beautifully healthy and expectant, he felt very fond of them all.

Part of the bargain which Agatha had struck with Paul's deliverers was that they should bring him immediately to the assignation in the woods. She had attached great importance to seeing him once before he went into an exile which she supposed would last for ever. For reasons of their own the men had chosen Swindon as the place in which he was to be concealed until they took him out of the country, and it was there that they drove after leaving Agatha.

About the middle of the morning Paul was put down in a crowded shopping street. Following the directions he had been given, he walked steadily for some distance, took several turnings and came into a quiet street of small houses which looked so respectable that he wondered at first whether he had memorized the directions correctly, but since it was important not to linger or look around or in any way attract attention he walked on at the same even pace, past little garden gates of slatted wood, squares of grass and minute flower-beds in which roses were still blooming, and front doors with an oval of frosted glass at face level. One or two of the front doors had faded canvas curtains in front of them, such as he remembered seeing in his childhood on the doors of seaside boarding houses. Whether their purpose was to protect the paint on the door from the effects of the sun or to provide privacy and shade when the door was left open in the summer he had never known, but he remembered the smell and feel and faded look of one such in the doorway of the boarding house in the Isle of Wight to which he had been taken every summer until the war, first by his mother and father and then, after his father's death, by his mother and Orlando, who was later the father of Agatha and perhaps of Imogen, and who was at that time in his heyday. Pain gripped him in the stomach and would have stopped him had he not known he must not stop – 'Oh poor thing, poor thing,' went through his head, meaning, Poor Paul, poor me.

Without hesitating he pushed open the low gate of number 39, went up to the door and rang the bell. The door opened at once and he went in. It was shut behind him and a quiet figure moved past him in the dim hall, said 'Upstairs', and led the way. He followed and was taken into a small back bedroom painted pink with a brown dado and containing little but a double bed covered with a slippery brown bedspread.

'Here,' said the woman.

She was small and fiftyish, wearing a green nylon over-all and bedroom slippers. The expression on her face was quite clearly one of distaste but he thought he could see a subdued excitement too.

She jerked her head towards the door.

'He's coming with the clothes.'

She was not interested in him. The excitement, if it was there, would be for the money. He wondered how much of Agatha's money she was getting.

'You haven't such a thing as a cup of tea, I suppose?' he asked, smiling.

She went out without speaking and shut the door. Almost immediately she returned with a bundle of clothes.

'He says to change,' she said, putting the clothes on the bed.

She went out again without looking at him. She was going to be hard to charm. He would try though. His mother had been able to charm anyone. He looked into the mirror which hung over the mantelpiece, but after one brief gaze into his own eyes he moved away and began quickly to change his clothes. The suit they had given him was the right size, though nasty: certainly they were efficient.

The woman came in, put a mug of tea down on the bedside table – 'How kind,' he murmured – and took away his own clothes. He hoped they would remember their promise to let him have them back on the boat. It was a better suit than anything he would be able to get where he was going.

He heard the stairs creak and then a door was quietly shut. That would be the man who was wearing his clothes, distinctive duffle coat and all, and who was to leave the house and walk back along the street for the benefit of any inquisitive neighbours, so that if necessary he could be passed off as – what, he wondered? – the man from the hire purchase perhaps.

Paul drank the tea, which was tepid and for which he had only asked in an attempt to strike up some sort of relationship with its provider. He tried to fight down his depression and fear by telling himself that the plan was working, that the most difficult part was already over and that there could be no doubt that Charlie Edwards, who had put him on to this organization, was right: they were highly efficient and worth the expense. He congratulated himself for his foresight in having approached Charlie the moment he knew that his arrest was imminent. He was going to get away with it. He was going to be all right.

Later the woman brought him two cold sausages, some bread and cheese with pickle and another mug of tepid tea. She also brought the paperbacks for which he had asked the men in the car, but she still refused to be drawn into conversation. He foresaw that the three days in this little room might be a kind of Purgatory. He asked the woman for paper and a pencil and began a long letter of justification to Agatha.

Henry worked for a firm of insurance brokers in the City, a job which bored him and for which he was paid £8 a week. He had no qualifications, since he had failed to pass any exams at Oxford, but it had been vaguely hinted to him at the time when his forthcoming marriage to Agatha had forced him to look for a job that there might be 'prospects' in this one. They had not yet materialized, and since Conrad thought it right not to let Henry have any of the money which he would have at Conrad's death until such time as he had shown himself capable of looking after it, his financial situation was bad. Agatha had a small income of her own from the money which her father had left in trust for her, and it was on this that they mainly lived, while Henry's salary went almost entirely towards the paying off of the mortgage on their house, the deposit on which had been released by Agatha's trustees.

They had a blue Ford Thames van, on the hire purchase. The visibility from the driver's seat was not good, or at least not good enough for Henry, who was a driver who could use a lot of visibility, but to have had windows cut in the back part, which would have improved matters in that way, would have meant that it was liable to tax as a private vehicle rather than as a commercial one, as which in its present state it was able to pass.

When he had driven Agatha and the children back to London on Sunday evening, and had helped Agatha to give them some food and put them to bed, Henry said, 'I might go round to the pub for a bit, to see if there's anything on television about Hungary.'

'Do, yes. I'll go to bed, I think,' said Agatha.

He went out hurriedly so as not to see the expression on her face, and drove off in the van, over-revving the engine.

When he had Agatha and the children in the car he drove with a modicum of circumspection, but alone he reverted to his pre-marital road habits, which were undesirable. So, turning out into the King's Road, he did not wait for a pause in the stream of Sunday night returning traffic, but accelerating noisily lurched out into the middle of it, passed a couple of cars on the wrong side of the road so as to avoid the avenging fury of the Jaguar he had caused to brake uncomfortably hard, and was then forced back to his own side by an oncoming van, whose furious hooting mingled with that of the car in front of which he was obliged to squeeze. He then unexpectedly shot across the road again (not having had time to get the right-hand indicator mended), down Smith Street, where he narrowly avoided a minor television personality and his psychiatrist wife who were crossing the road rather slowly after a meal at the Indian restaurant, screamed round the corner into St Leonard's Terrace and drew up in front of the house where Sally had a flat: his expression throughout the drive had been abstracted but serene and he had been whistling the tune of a calypso of which the first words were 'Brown skin girl, stay home and mind babee'. He would have been irritated if their possible application to his own case had struck him, but if it had been that which had influenced his choice it had certainly been unconsciously, because the few minutes of the drive had been a break in conscious thought, which seemed to return to him only as he pressed the bell and felt the happy disquiet which the immediate prospect of seeing Sally always induced.

She was wearing a black dress, drawn in rather tightly round her knees and without much back, so that her own beautiful one was exposed, high-heeled black shoes and a tiny sequinned hat with a green feather in it.

'How lovely you look,' he said when they had reached her flat, which was at the top of the house.

'You don't really like it, do you?' she said, turning to look at him, posing slightly with her hand on her hip.

He felt indeed on looking at her such a sharp sense of disappointment that he could hardly speak. He thought she looked ridiculous.

'I think it's lovely,' he said. 'Very smart. Can I give myself a drink?'

'Of course. I'm meant to be going out to dinner.'

'Oh.'

'With Johnny Marner.'

'Oh.'

'He rang up to say he was just back from America and would I have a little quiet supper at the Aperitif– can you believe it?' She picked up the telephone, and dialled, took off her hat and shook out her golden hair. 'My *mother* – would you believe it? – and so *ill*, I'll have to put her straight to bed, this awful spring' flu – my dear, it's so much *worse* when you get it in the autumn – that's the whole point – and to drive up from the country, can you believe anything so silly? – oh I must, she's so *old* and so helpless – tomorrow would be lovely – 'bye – he's mad about me.' This last seemed to Henry to have been said, quite loudly, before the receiver had been replaced, and therefore probably to have been overheard by the handsome middle-aged peripatetic political peer who had been so lightly dismissed. He began to feel better.

'Do you know what he told me when he rang up before? Just like that on the telephone – they are so indiscreet, those sort of people.' She went through into her bedroom, still talking. 'He said that the French and the English are definitely going to declare war on the Egyptians any minute and that they're banking on the Russians being so worried about Hungary that they won't butt in. Don't you think it's quite extraordinary to tell me that? It's going to be short and sharp, over in a minute, he said. It's all been planned down to the last detail. Don't you think it's rather exciting?'

'I suppose it's only his opinion,' said Henry. 'I mean, surely only a very few people know a thing like that for certain?'

'He sounded awfully sure about it,' said Sally, coming back into the room wearing a white cotton dressing-gown. 'It seemed a good idea, I thought. I'm sick of England being pushed around, aren't you? I mean, people seem to forget who we are, don't they?'

She looked serious as she said this, standing in the middle of the room, transformed into such ravishing beauty as a few minutes ago might have seemed too much to hope for, and gazing at him earnestly.

'Who are we?' said Henry foolishly, full of delight. He kissed her gently on the temple, gave her her drink and said, 'Tell me about your weekend.'

'My dear,' she said, settling down in a comfortable chair. All the chairs in her flat were comfortable; it was warm and well lit and had pleasant colours on the walls and Indian rugs on the floors; it was also usually very tidy and clean, for Sally was an efficient girl and in respect of housework would have made an excellent wife, as she quite often pointed out. 'My *dear*, I didn't know such people existed. Quite close to you too, I'm amazed you don't know them.'

'Gloucestershire is a world apart.'

'Well, anyway there they all were. So many of them too. We went from house to house and each was richer and grander than the last. And so big and so handsome – the people I mean, the women as well as the men – and I've never had so many passes made at me in two days, all the men and most of the women. It must be something to do with horses, all that *straddling* must be suggestive. Anyway they were terribly kind to me. You wouldn't have liked them though.'

'Did you?'

'Well, I suppose they're a bit square, really. But you know me. I like anywhere where there's money and lovely things and people are nice to me. It's my deprived childhood or something.'

'And will you be seeing much of him do you suppose?'

'I suppose so. Although really I ought to find someone who's not impossible, oughtn't I? I mean I'm getting old. I'm twenty-four.' Actually she was twenty-five.

'I don't think so. I don't say that out of self-interest, though you might think I do. It's quite hard work being married, for the wife I mean.'

'Not for the husband?'

'All the advantages are on the husband's side.'

'Well, I could marry someone very rich. I mean, I can't go on messing about for ever. Soon I'll be wrinkled and horrible and no one will want to take photographs of me and I'll starve.'

'I'll support you in your old age. I'll be richer then. I'll buy you a little house in Maida Vale and come round once a week with a bag of gold.'

She sighed. 'How many times have I told you I'm not that sort of woman,' she said. 'What am I going to do with you, Henry?'

'You're going to jump into my arms,' he said, putting down his glass and holding them out to her.

Agatha had inherited from Orlando a cluster of half-ruined buildings on a remote hillside in Tuscany, where he had spent the last years of his life. She always hoped that one day she and Henry would be able to spend more time there, and had resisted Conrad's argument that the most sensible thing to do with the place was to sell it; but for the time being they had let the house where Orlando had lived for a small rent to an English couple who both worked for an international organization in Rome. They used it for week-ends (without taking much care of it), and the land was farmed by the peasant family who lived in the only other fully habitable house. For the last two years Agatha and Henry and the children had spent their fortnight's holiday camping in the tower house which Orlando had been in the process of restoring at the time of his death.

Agatha never dreamt about the tower house, but the other one, the one where Orlando had lived, appeared frequently in her dreams, usually empty, sometimes with a wind blowing through it and banging the doors, sometimes as the scene of a search in which she hurried from room to room and failed to find what she sought; and though the dreams were invariably worrying ones, they left behind them a feeling which was in a way satisfying, a feeling that they were in some sense true.

It was from one of these dreams that she woke to the realization that the alarm had failed to go off and that Henry was going to be late for work. Unless she hurried, George would also be late for school, which was worse, because George hated being late for school.

She woke them all, and hurried to make the breakfast. George and Lucy were eating their cereals when Henry came into the kitchen. Agatha saw from the expression on his face that he was uneasy about having come back so late the night before. She turned away from him sharply, suddenly angry, and poured out some coffee for him. He took it from her and put an arm round her shoulder. She moved away quickly, took away the children's empty bowls, and began to dish out their scrambled eggs. Henry made a sound indicative of reproach.

'We're late,' said Agatha, not looking at him.

'I was only trying to be friendly,' said Henry.

'If you have to try, it seems hardly worth it,' said Agatha.

Henry drank his coffee and left.

She ran after him up the stairs and stopped him by the front door.

'I don't mind your being late,' she said. 'I'm used to that. I mind your coming in with a stupid self-conscious face when all that matters is getting George to school on time. You're so frivolous. What does it matter? What do we matter? What right have we to personal happiness? It's quite irrelevant.'

Henry looked at his watch.

Agatha turned and ran upstairs into the lavatory. She heard the front door shut and clutching her stomach as if in physical pain sank to the floor in a crouching position, her head bent on to her knees. After a few moments she stood up, washed her face, stared into the mirror saying, 'God forgive me' and then ran downstairs into the kitchen saying, 'Oh, God forgive me. Jesus Christ forgive me for my manifold sins and wickednesses.'

'Why have you got wet knees?' asked Lucy.

They had finished their breakfast but were still sitting there banging their plates with their forks, co-operating in a complicated rhythm.

'George, why haven't you put your coat on? Quick, we're going to be late.'

'I didn't know,' said George, getting off his chair and looking anxious.

Agatha looked down at her knees and saw that her stockings had in fact been soaked, even in those few moments, by her tears. She smiled, as people will who have cut a finger and feel a certain wonder and pride at the amount of blood they have shed.

'I must have knelt on something. Come on, hurry.'

The school was only three streets away. They ran most of the way. The little yard at the side of the building was empty.

'They've gone in,' said George.

'It's only just after nine,' said Agatha.

'It's all right,' said George. 'It doesn't matter.'

But it did, to him. She could see that it did from his anxious face as he ran in, unbuttoning his coat as he went. She was supposed to love him but could not get out of bed five minutes earlier to spare him this distress.

She could have grasped the railings and shrieked until the fabric of the universe was torn asunder, but said to Lucy, 'We'll buy the lunch on the way home.'

Imogen, late, ran flustered along a passage, to be stopped at the end by a shout from the girl at the reception desk.

'Hey, wait, your uncle rang up. He wants you to have dinner with him tonight.'

Imogen stopped, gasped, clapped her hand over her mouth.

'What's the matter?' said the receptionist.

'Did he say why?' asked Imogen, still looking aghast.

'No. He just said to go to the usual place at eight o'clock.'

'Oh. Well, I can't, but I'll ring him up. Thanks.'

She walked on more slowly. The morning papers had reported Paul's escape from prison and described the search which was taking place for him. Imogen had not been in touch with Agatha, preferring to know nothing about any of it. Surely Conrad could not possibly know that Agatha had been involved? But she, Imogen, knew nothing, must know nothing. She tried to tell herself that Conrad could have no reason to suppose otherwise. It must be money again, she told herself, she must have been spending too much money again.

Familiarity had taken the terror out of that particular situation, and her spirits began to recover. That was what it must be. She would go and have a drink with him before dinner and say she was sorry and it would be all right. She knew that Conrad had always had a kindness for her in spite of the many aspects of her character which he might be expected to find reprehensible: she was much better at dealing with him than Agatha had ever been.

Conrad's first thought on hearing of the escape had been that Agatha might have been involved, and all that worrying day he had at the back of his mind a confused picture of walls, ropes, Paul and Agatha; remnants of the dreams which had seemed to fill the night; Agatha climbing, dressed in black as she had been at Orlando's funeral, Agatha swinging on the end of a rope, banging against a high windowless wall, Agatha on a ladder, himself following, Agatha reaching up to clasp the bars of a prison window and kicking the ladder away behind her so that he fell and, falling, looked down an immeasurable distance to the ground outside the prison building, where under a small thorn tree lay a form curled up in the position of an embryo, and whatever it was, this form, it was he, Conrad, who had let it fall.

The day was a worrying one because it was the first on which he really took in the fact that the international situation, which of course he had known for some time to be serious, was suddenly developing at an uncomfortable pace, that he was not quite certain what the Government of which he was a member was doing about it, and that whatever it was he was not sure that they were going to be able to do it successfully. He was not himself immediately connected either with Foreign Affairs or with Defence, and it appeared that those who were, together with the Prime Minister, had either been moving very fast or, as was beginning to seem more probable, very secretly, into a position where an ultimatum was now to be delivered jointly with France to the Egyptians and the Israelis, the foreseeable result being that the Israelis would accept the terms and the Egyptians refuse them, whereupon there should be a 'short and sharp' attack upon Egypt. Conrad spent the day trying to find out how short and how sharp this attack could be expected to be.

He had not been ignorant of the general thinking of his colleagues about the Egyptian crisis and he was not out of sympathy with it. He would have supported aggressive action against Nasser at the time of the nationalization of the Suez Canal in July. His doubts now – apart from general speculations about the uses or misuses of Cabinet government – were only as to timing and planning.

'It's got to work' was his theme throughout the day. 'We're going to be in very bad trouble if it doesn't.'

He found one or two equally troubled sympathizers but on the whole it was not a popular approach. He felt aggrieved that his reasonable caution should be taken as faint-heartedness; even more aggrieved that his views, which had been freely expressed over the last month or so, should have been so obviously discounted. He was used to the committee system and knew that when decisions were made, particularly ones requiring immediate action, there were always a few members who for one reason or another had their doubts disregarded and were swept along in the current which an action begun soon generates: he was not used to being among their number himself. A brief interview with the highest authority that could be found to spare the time for him that morning resulted only in a display of bad temper and an implication that his own record did not give him the right to criticize. He had resigned from the Chamberlain Government, but not until after Munich, and he was therefore tainted with 'appeasement', a word which still aroused strong emotion and which in his case warred with his reputation for wisdom and high-mindedness.

'It's not the same,' he said doggedly. 'Nasser is not Hitler.'

'I understood we had your support. The service chiefs are absolutely confident.'

'I can't help still being worried about America. You don't think there ought to be one more personal telephone call to Ike?'

'We've considered all these things very carefully. We must be allowed to get on with the job.'

Of course he pledged his support. Anything else at this late stage would have been a personal disloyalty which was not to be considered. He thought that the policy was probably the right one, as long as it succeeded; only he had many years of experience on the periphery of the innermost circle of government and the feel of the thing at that moment was not quite right.

The evening papers carried news of the intensification of the search for Paul. He read them in his flat, having walked back there from the House of Lords to meet Imogen. She was late. He thought about Agatha again. All her life she had been a worry to him. If only his wife had lived, Alexandra, fleet of foot like the goddess Diana, whom animals had but to see to love – and pain began to rise in him as it rarely did now, and the thought of its rareness made him say aloud, 'They think I don't suffer – they don't know – they don't know how lonely I am.' He began to walk up and down in his dull little room. 'I must be tired.' He poured himself out a whisky and soda. 'Difficult times. Difficult times. God help us. Help us, O Lord.' And at once he began to feel calm, and there floated into his mind what God meant to him, which was the stone walls of the church at Mount Sorrel, and the grass on the graves of his forebears, and his deep though ritualized relationship with the men who worked in his woods, and his father gently introducing to him the idea of duty, which seemed one of the most beautiful ideas in the world, and the love of God and the fellowship of men, and wanting the village to be able to be proud of one.

'One does one's best after all,' he said, gazing out of the window at the back of St James's Park Underground station. 'One does one's best.' He took a gulp of his whisky and soda, and looked at his watch, but without too much impatience. Imogen was always late.

When she arrived she was breathless but pretty.

'That's a very fetching garment you've got on,' he said, giving her a kiss on the cheek. 'Have a drink. What would you like? I'm sorry you couldn't dine with me tonight.'

'Yes, I'm going out, I'm sorry.'

'Where do you young people go these days? The Four Hundred? Quags?'

'You might get taken to the Four Hundred, yes, but it's awfully boring. You probably just go to small restaurants – you know, the Matelot or the Ox on the Roof or something. There's a place called the Green Room where everyone I know seems to go a lot – it's a club – underneath Ciro's.'

'Oh Ciro's, yes, I know that. Ah'well, I expect you'll get a much better dinner than I can offer you at the House of Lords. I've got to be there this evening. There's rather a lot on.'

'No, I love going there. It's so peaceful and fuddy-duddy. I feel really safe. I even like the food being bad.'

He laughed. 'I feel like that myself sometimes. But unpleasant facts penetrate even there now and then. I say, what an awful business this is about Paul, isn't it?'

'Awful,' said Imogen feelingly.

'As if we hadn't all suffered enough.'

'That's exactly what I said,' said Imogen. 'I mean, to myself, when I read the paper.' She blushed slightly.

'Have you talked to Agatha about it at all?'

'No, I haven't.'

'You didn't ring her up or anything? I'd have thought you might have.'

'Yes, well, yes I might have. But I didn't somehow.'

'Was that because you thought she might be too sympathetic towards Paul?'

'I suppose so. Yes, I suppose it was.'

'She wouldn't do anything foolish, would she?'

'What sort of thing?' asked Imogen, blushing again.

'Sheltering him from the police, for instance.'

'Oh no. No, I'm sure she wouldn't do that. It would be much too dangerous for one thing. I mean, I suppose they're watching us probably.'

'You don't think she knew anything about it, do you?'

'No.' Imogen shook her head vigorously. 'No.'

'Why are you so sure about it?'

'Well, I – because – well, I mean it would be so silly –'

'Agatha sometimes is silly, with the best of intentions as often as not. She never mentioned to you any plans for getting him out? Even a long time ago, when he was first arrested? After all he must have known he was going to be convicted.'

'It would have been something he'd arranged himself,' said Imogen. 'Before he went to prison. I mean, he had a lot of criminal friends.'

'Who?'

'Oh I don't know. One says that sort of thing. I haven't the faintest idea really.'

'You must have been thinking of someone.'

'Well, I suppose there was that man Charlie Edwards, you know, who used to be a burglar and wrote a book about it. He'd have known all those sort of people.'

'Yes,' said Conrad thoughtfully. 'So you don't think Agatha had any sort of foreknowledge? I must say, that's a tremendous relief to me.'

'I'm sure that if she did it would only be in some quite unimportant way. I mean, obviously Agatha couldn't have worked out a complicated plot involving keeping him hidden and getting him out of the country and all that sort of thing by herself, could she?' She looked at him appealingly.

'My dear,' he said solemnly, 'make no mistake about it. Anybody who knew anything at all and has not told the police is committing a crime. We may wish that Paul hadn't been sent to prison, even more than we wish he hadn't committed the crime which led to it, but the fact remains that it is the law of the land, and that is just about the most important thing there is. Without the rule of law, the whole of our society would fall apart. We have to hope, you and I, that Paul will be recaptured. We have to hope he will serve his sentence. Because that is the law.'

'Oh I do. I do hope that, I really do. I know that you never really got on with Paul, but I did. We had some nice times together, and when he wasn't drunk or being hurtful for some reason, he could be so nice, Paul, he really could. But I know it's no good trying to escape, I mean if you've broken the law there it is.'

'You'll tell me then if you hear anything or think of anything that could help the police?'

'Yes, I will, of course I will,' said Imogen earnestly.

'Don't worry about it too much. The police are a highly competent body of men. It will probably all be over in a day or two.'

'I hope so.'

'Poor Paul, what a fool he was.'

'Yes.'

'I mustn't keep you. What time's your date?'

Imogen looked at her watch.

'Oh gosh, I'm late!'

Conrad laughed. 'He must be used to it by this time, whoever he is. But I'm sorry it was my fault this time. I've been rather bothered about all this. You've set my mind at rest. Now don't you start worrying, will you? We're all in it together after all, aren't we?'

'Yes. Oh yes, of course we are.' She had gathered scarf and bag and stood restlessly running the former through her hands. 'Thank you so much for the drink. It was super. I must run.'

She kissed him and was gone before he could say he was going too. He hesitated for a moment, wondering whether to telephone the police about Charles Edwards. Then he decided that they were bound to have got on to him already, and that anyway he would be needed in the House of Lords; so he followed Imogen, more slowly, down the dark passage outside his flat, waited a few moments for the ancient creaking lift, was hauled down in it by the melancholy lady in what appeared to be Salvation Army uniform who manned its rope control, and walked out into the rather cold autumn evening to see almost immediately in a telephone-box near the entrance to the Underground the distinctive blue colour of Imogen's pretty dress. He did not pause, able without doing so to satisfy himself as he passed that it was indeed Imogen.

If she had wanted to telephone her friend to say she was going to be late, she could easily have done so from the flat. It seemed more likely that she was telephoning Agatha, to warn her of his suspicions.

[*]

All this pain will wear my flesh away, thought Agatha. I'll be all bone, beautiful white bone, blown clean by the wind. Then my pride will have had its fall. Isn't it pride which makes me suffer so? Because someone knows – in some charming room, a delightful girl – that my husband doesn't love me. He says he does but it isn't possible because he also says he loves her – whom I have seen with shining hair across a room. I saw her before he did. I saw her lean forward sitting at a table, slightly hunched, turning to her neighbour '– but you're so *good* at –'. Just that I heard, and saw her dazzled smile and the curve of her cheek and chin and felt a shock of recognition almost indistinguishable from desire, so closely was I, am I, physically involved with him; sometimes my flesh forgets that we are separate. Well, she has a look of Caroline, that's all, who was his girl-friend before me.

If it were all pride I could subdue it. I can dig out pride, jealousy, fear, all maggots in my wound, and still it bleeds. I could cry for ever.

And at other times would shout love, for this I was born to do. I love you and you and you, and you dead and you living, and you heroes and you traitors. Only so can movement move, and love be clothed with flesh. And so can figures neither one thing nor the other be turned to gold.

'The only escape, the only way open to me, was to become everything of which Uncle Conrad disapproved,' wrote Paul. 'In that at least you must admit I have been successful.'

It was cold in the little bedroom. He had asked for some form of heating and the woman had brought a single-bar electric fire. He sat in front of it, with a blanket wrapped round his legs, writing on his knee. He had already covered fourteen sides of the cheap lined writing paper she had brought for him.

There was now a rather unpleasant smell of singeing in the room because he had sat too close to the fire and the blanket had a small brown patch where it had begun to burn. It was getting towards the end of the afternoon, the sort of time when the woman might be expected to bring him a cup of tea. Having moved away from the fire a little, he tried to concentrate on what he was writing but could not help listening for the quiet, slightly shuffling footsteps which would mean she was on her way and would find him out, would sniff, probably, and say, 'You've burnt the blanket.' He would offer to pay. Trapped there with her horrible blanket round his legs, looking up into her horrible unyielding face, he would fumble for money in the pockets of his alien cheap suit.

'If only I had a long-suffering temperament, like you,' he wrote to Agatha. 'You don't know how lucky you are.'

The tone of his letter had so far been detached and even ironical but under the pressure of the persecution to which he now felt that the whole situation of the burnt blanket exposed him, it began to change.

'It's always been the same. Is it my fault that I was the one to inherit our mother's temperament? I know you were only seven when she died and can't have much idea of what she was really like, but she was 'hypersensitive', as Conrad once scornfully put it, long before she went round the bend. Even when she was married to my father there were terrible scenes sometimes. She minded everything so much. Some people do. And think of being like that – a minder – and having to take what I had to take. A neurotic mother, a pompous ass of a father – oh how he grovelled before the system of which he was really a victim, thinking himself a proper little capitalist and never daring to admit what a pathetic slave they'd made of him. Some fool of a psychiatrist before the trial tried to make me say I wanted revenge on my father. I didn't. I wanted revenge *for* him. For the fact that they'd turned him into a stupid little creeping snob. They tried it on Orlando too, and damned nearly succeeded, but in the end he was too intelligent for them and got away. Got right away, you see. That's what I could never do. I always stayed hanging around on the edges, looking through windows, watching other people having a nicer time than me. Oh the cold feeling of that glass that was always between me and them.'

When he had written the last sentence he felt enormously cheered. He read through the whole passage again.

'Excellent!' he said when he had finished it. 'Really excellent.' He laughed aloud, thinking how pleased Agatha would be. Hadn't she said she wanted him to write something? He'd always been interested in that sort of thing. There'd been that time at school when he'd had that really marvellous idea for a film. If only the whole scheme hadn't had to be dropped because of the way he'd been organizing the money-raising, it would have been really good – and incidentally annoyed a lot of people – and then he could have gone on in films and everything would have been different.

But it was not necessarily too late. A sort of picaresque semi-fictionalized autobiography was what he foresaw. And what a film that would make. After the success of the book of course.

The shuffling footsteps had approached without his being aware of them.

She held out the mug of greenish-looking liquid and said, 'Tea.'

'Oh!' He took it, and as she turned away, evidently preferring to overlook the smell of singeing rather than enter into any kind of conversation, he added, 'You're too sweet, you really are.'

Perhaps she was deaf.

It was quite clearly understood between Agatha and Henry that Henry disapproved of introspection and thought that Agatha did too much of it. It was also understood between them that up to a certain point he admired her for it, although there was no question of his taking up that sort of thing himself.

This convention allowed Henry to avoid admitting to himself the extent of the unhappiness which his relationship with Sally was causing Agatha. It seemed to him that neither of them should think about it too much. The bad time had been when he had realized that his emotional involvement with Sally had become too deep to be concealed from Agatha. He had talked to her about it, and had been surprised and sorry to find that while she did already know about the relationship, this knowledge had been able to co-exist with a belief that it simply could not be true: her imagination had been unable to grasp the reality of a situation which the evidence made obvious. Their conversations at that time had inevitably been long and painful and he believed that they were at one in thinking that that had been enough of that. He had agreed with her that their marriage could not stand his being seriously in love with Sally and that the proper thing for him to do was to withdraw, wind the thing down, change it from a love affair into a sentimental friendship. Agatha had said that she could stand a sentimental friendship.

So, driving home after work through the rush-hour traffic, he felt only a minor disquiet in case Agatha should be

in a bad mood when he got back, but was otherwise confident, and resolved to be very nice to her as soon as he saw
her so as to make it quite clear that on his side all was love
and amiability. His optimism was superficial, as perhaps
it always must be in one whose determination to live for
the moment is the result of a conscious decision. Under it
loomed or slowly swirled doubts to which he refused to
give a name, great gloomy sea things beneath the thin ice
on which he skated. Wasn't he behaving well? Of course he
was. At the same time, was it really allowable to spin out
the vaunted withdrawal from the impossible situation quite
so long, enjoying meanwhile the best of both worlds?

It was better not to think about it, to sing, or drive
dangerously, or spend too long a lunch hour with some
friend from the old days trapped like him in a boring job
for the sake of subsistence. Because to take advantage of
two such sweet girls would certainly be wrong: but the
softness of thinking of them in that way had an element of
self-congratulation in it, and also in the case of Agatha an
element almost of daring, because to call Agatha a sweet girl
was not an adequate description.

Part of Henry's charm for women was that in his easy
way he had a very quick appreciation of the intricacies of
personality. It was a gift which entered into his relationships
with men too – and these were the ones which he himself
thought of as proper friendships; nevertheless more than
one pretty girl had annoyed a jealous admirer by saying,
'He's such a *friend*– you couldn't possibly understand.'

This subtle sympathy meant that without ever having
given her character much sustained or detached consideration he had a clear understanding of Agatha's mode of
being, which was very different from his own. There was a
certain element in it to which he was drawn and by which

he was frightened, and which he considered quite inappropriate in relation to anything in his own life or the lives of most people he knew, and that was that she tried to be good. He saw her doing it, and often by her own standards failing, and sometimes it annoyed him on her own behalf because it made her life so much less comfortable than it might have been, and sometimes it made him want to hurt her.

The last reaction was presumably an envious one, because it came to him at times when, returning to her from some mundane activity, or even from being with Sally, he would find her doing something not in itself important, cooking perhaps or playing with the children, or if they were in the country lying on the grass or gardening, and know at once from her calm welcoming smile that she was happy, but with a happiness whose calm was rapt, whose fullness was ecstatic, a happiness which had nothing to do with him, and to which he felt that ordinary people, who lived in the world as it was and did not bother themselves with abstractions or tiresome moralities, had no hope of aspiring. At these times he occasionally said something unkind to her, for which he was afterwards sorry.

This evening when he came back from work he immediately recognized another typical situation. His long lunch had made him later than usual in leaving the office and by the time he got home the children were already in bed. The narrow hallway of the little house was dim and rather cold. Agatha was sitting halfway up the stairs, crouched over the book she was reading and which she was having to hold close to her eyes because of the lack of light. She looked up when he came in, and blinked in a distant sort of way as if she had been concentrating very hard on what she had been reading.

Henry turned on the light, said, 'You don't look very comfortable.' She stood up, jumped down the last of the stairs, kissed him on the cheek and led the way into the sitting-room, where a fire was burning and the curtains were drawn. Having turned on the lights at the door, she went over to the lamp behind the sofa and switched that on too.

'That's better,' said Henry.

She would prepare the room for him but never sit in it herself until he was there: something in her character seemed to prevent her from ever making herself comfortable. She would be cold but not put on another jersey, hungry but not eat anything except a crust of bread unless there was someone with her, tired but not go to bed, sad but not distract herself with idle pleasures; he found that maddening.

Knowing his feelings, she said, 'I was so comfortable on the stairs.'

He frowned.

'Luxury,' she said. 'I was in a bed of luxury.'

'You know I don't like that sort of thing.' But he smiled as he sat down. 'Is Joe coming to supper, did you say?'

After Joe had left, Agatha told Henry that she had helped Paul to escape from prison.

Joe Hertz had been a friend of Henry's at Oxford and had become an equally close friend of Agatha's. At the beginning of their marriage he had been the third who by his appreciation showed up their happiness, a role he played with a slightly wistful and never malicious self-mockery, for which they were both grateful to him; some of the times all three had spent together had been among their happiest. As well as that he was Henry's friend, with a shared past and a shared sense of satire, and Agatha's friend, with a shared tenderness of heart. It was typical of him that he should feel comfortable as an adjunct to their marriage, because his place seemed always to be a peripheral one; touching the circles of love and gain, ambition and self-abnegation, heterosexuality and homosexuality, still more or less uncommitted. From Oxford he had gone into advertising, as many clever people with a slight literary bent were doing at that time. A series of atrocious puns made him one of the highest paid copy-writers in his firm. He liked the money and despised the work. In the same way he enjoyed the company of privileged and amusing people, a number of whom had become his friends at Oxford, and despised himself for spending so much time with them. He felt he had not only an obligation but perhaps a vocation to help others less fortunate, or even to make a more far-reaching contribution towards the improvement of society. Anyone seeing him among the usual group of friends at a party might have been forgiven for not guessing it, but he was not at all sure that he might not be a new Karl Marx. He was always giving himself another month, two months, six months, and then he was going to Leeds to be a school-teacher. Leeds, ignorant of its destiny, was luckily unconcerned by the delay.

Since he was quite honest about all this ambivalence, it gave him a certain ironical way of looking at things which, while it revealed his own discontent, nevertheless made him a very sympathetic companion. Evenings spent with Joe were without tension; and it was easy to go on talking after he had left.

'I've done something rather wrong which I have to tell you about,' said Agatha.

The thought popped up in his mind as if it had been rung up with a *ting* on a cash register, 'If she's been unfaithful she's *out*. I don't want to hear anything about it, she just *goes*.'

'I wish you wouldn't frown so,' said Agatha.

'What is it?' he said through his teeth.

'I helped Paul to escape from prison.'

'Oh.' Relief spread gently through his muscles, easing him more comfortably into his chair. 'How?'

'Some people came to see me asking for money and I gave it to them.'

'Who were they?'

'Professionals of some sort. I think he must have arranged the whole thing before he went to prison. I didn't ask too much about it but you know how he always did know quite a lot of criminals. They told me they could do it all if I gave them seven hundred pounds. They promised it would work, so I did.'

'How did you get the money?'

'Sold my shares. And then I met them with him in the woods the other morning – the time Dora got run over.'

'She wasn't with you?'

'Oh no, no. I hadn't seen her since the night before, when we lost her. So I saw him and he seemed all right and they were going to hide him somewhere and then get him out of the country when the search had died down a bit.'

'Good Lord. I hope it's all right.'

'The thing is, I could go to prison, and I've been rather worried about that because of the children.'

'And me,' he said quickly.

'And you. Do you think it was wrong to run the risk? He hadn't anyone else to help him, you see, and he is my brother.'

'Surely you couldn't be sent to prison for that?'

'Yes, I could. It could be two years. Some things are taken awfully seriously by the law. Look what a heavy sentence they gave Paul. Treachery's very badly thought of, so's helping people to avoid the law. I did think about it quite carefully first. I'd get remission, I suppose. And then

I know you do care for the children very much. I think
the Dutch girl could probably move in permanently – it's a
success, that, the children really like her – and I thought I
could write them a letter every single day which they could
read at breakfast and if there aren't posts every day from
prison I could give you a whole lot at once which you could
give them one at a time. Perhaps, at weekends and things,
Sally would help sometimes, I mean going on expeditions
with them and that sort of thing?'

Henry did not answer, so Agatha went on, 'It would be
rather difficult to explain to George because he's so very
law-abiding but I think if I put it quite simply he'd be able to
understand. I have worried rather about school but I think
five-year-olds are too young to be interested, don't you?'

'Yes, I should think so,' said Henry, but she could see
that he was not thinking about George. He had not liked
her mentioning Sally. She wondered why. They looked at
each other in silence. How easily, he thought, she refers
to Sally, assumes I should be with her; does it mean she
doesn't care? Agatha thought, He never goes for essentials;
what does it matter if he doesn't like my implying that Sally
might do something useful for a change, when what we're
talking about is the children and how to protect them from
suffering if their mother goes to prison?

Henry thought, We can't stare at each other in silence
for ever, and sensing something of her feelings he stood up
and said rather formally. 'I think you were quite right. I'll
support you, of course, in any way I can.'

Conrad walked up and down in the Central Lobby of the
House of Commons waiting for Henry. There was a good
deal of activity. The afternoon's sitting had not started and
there were a number of Members of Parliament hurrying

to and fro looking preoccupied, and some others meeting constituents for whom they had found seats in the public galleries; outside there was a queue of the less fortunate: the Prime Minister was expected to make an announcement later in the day. Conrad paced up and down slowly. Some of the Members greeted him, and hesitated as if they would have liked to talk, but though he was polite he was not encouraging and they passed on, respecting what they felt must be his legitimate preoccupations. He was not happy. His morning's meetings had not been satisfactory. He was tired. He was trying consciously to suspend his thoughts, with the result that his head felt like a nest of cotton-wool in which a few phrases lay supine – 'heavy-hearted', 'deeply unhappy', 'ah, there you are. Let's go through to the other place and have some coffee,' which last lay there in preparation for Henry's arrival, already overdue. He was coming from the City, could not spare the time for lunch apparently, but would come immediately afterwards, by Underground, which was why Conrad was where he was, arousing mild speculation as to which Member he might be waiting for and what it had to do with the crisis; because today there was certainly a feeling that something was going to happen. The Israeli attack on Egypt was filling the newspapers and the House of Commons was expecting to be told that afternoon what the Government was doing about it.

Just as Conrad muttered, 'He's late' he saw Henry, and was struck by how young he looked, walking up the steps among much older people, handsome, suit too tight and hair too long, they all want to look like Teddy Boys these days. 'Ah, there you are. Let's go through to the other place and have some coffee.' He put his hand on Henry's shoulder as if to pilot him through the groups of people standing about; he smiled at the same time, as if he had just said,

'Yes, I'd love to see the Art Room, old chap' on the school speech day. Deftly manoeuvring a passing secretary into a collision, Henry managed to throw off the hand.

'I'm sorry I couldn't manage lunch,' he said.

'Never mind. I expect you're very busy. As a matter of fact we've got quite a lot on here too at the moment.'

'Have you?' said Henry. 'What? Cyprus or something again?'

'The Middle East more.'

'Oh.'

Conrad thought, The young don't read the newspapers, they don't read anything, they go to the cinema.

'I saw an excellent film last night by the way,' he said. 'You really must see it when you get a chance. I got dragged along to this royal command thing, you know, for some official reason. I usually hate that sort of thing but I really enjoyed it. *The Battle of the River Plate.* Perfectly splendid. They hardly embroidered it at all. Awfully well acted.'

'Who was in it?'

'Oh, Quayle I think the fellow's called, and Gregson the other one. Quite convincing. It was a splendid thing of course for the English. The great German battleship, the *Graf Spee* with her eleven-inch guns, outfought by the three little cruisers, *Exeter, Ajax* and *Achilles.* Beautiful. Do try and see it.'

'Yes, I will, mn.'

'Come along then, sit down, it's a bit quieter in here. Just some coffee please for two. Well now, how are you? I haven't seen you for a long time. How's Agatha? And the children?'

'Very well, thank you.'

'And how's the job going?'

'Not too bad. Rather boring.'

'It's a grind at first, I daresay.'

'Yes.'

'Good news about Hungary, isn't it? It really looks as if they've got what they wanted. Not that you can trust the Russians of course but it looks as if they're prepared to give them a go.'

'Yes, it is good.'

'No apathy among the young there anyway. Wonderful how those students seem to have organized themselves. Students, poets, writers, the traditional idea of the revolutionary. Romantic, don't you think?'

'Yes.'

'Now the one among your friends I really do like is that young Jewish boy, Hertz. How is he getting on?'

'All right, I think.'

'Still in advertising?'

'Yes.' For some reason, Henry felt reluctant to tell his father that Joe had said the other night that he was about to set off for Austria with a group of people taking medical supplies to the Hungarians. Anyway perhaps if the revolution was over he would not be going after all now.

'Sugar? Oh no, of course you don't, do you? I ought not to, I suppose; getting fat.' He wasn't. 'Still, what does it matter at my age? I daresay I've only a few more years to run anyway.'

Henry gave him a quick knowing look, refusing to rise, and Conrad laughed, suddenly feeling more cheerful.

'Look here, though,' he said. 'Give me a sign some time. You know what I mean. I could make things much easier for you and Agatha if only I felt the time had come. It would be a tremendous help to me if you could take on some of the responsibilities of Mount Sorrel. It's not that I don't want to hand over, but if only you could take a little interest, or at least show some signs of getting on in the world a bit, the job and so on, you know what I mean.'

Henry nodded, even smiled, but when he raised his eyes for a moment they looked to Conrad wild and far-seeing as an eagle's and like an eagle's full of a remote uncomprehending scorn.

'Well anyway,' said Conrad quickly, 'we must talk about all that another time. I know you've got to get back. The point is, about the wretched Paul. Have the police been to see you yet?'

'No.'

'They will. And what I want to say to you is this. For God's sake if there's anything you know, anything you can think of that could possibly help them, tell them. I know Agatha was Paul's only friend – in the family anyway – and of course I admire her loyalty to him, but Agatha's a person of very strong feelings, as I don't need to tell you, and I dread to think that they might lead her into doing something foolish, like being less than frank with the police or even giving shelter to Paul if he should turn up. That would be disastrous. She's got her children to think of. I do hope she realizes that.'

'I'm sure she hasn't the faintest idea where Paul is.'

'The police know about her special relationship with Paul. If she doesn't co-operate with them she'll be in very severe trouble indeed.'

'He'd be mad if he came to us. He must be miles away by now.'

'This man Charles Edwards. He was a friend of Paul's, wasn't he?'

'He certainly knew him, but I never heard that they saw a great deal of each other. I don't know much about Paul's life during the last few years. He really never cared for me particularly. Agatha and he used to have lunch together from time to time but I'd really hardly seen him for a couple of years before all this.'

'He'd behaved so badly over all that Daintry episode. I don't think any of us should have been seeing him really. However, there you are. Tell her what I've said, will you?'

'Yes, I will. I'll tell her as soon as I get home this evening. And thank you very much for the warning.'

Conrad pushed back his chair. 'I must get on with the various unpleasant tasks I have to do this afternoon. And you must get back to yours, no doubt.'

'Yes, I must.'

They stood up.

'Don't bother,' said Henry. 'I'll find my way out.'

'I'll walk with you.'

As they walked along the dark passage, Conrad thought almost guiltily of Henry's use of the word 'warning'. Had it been a warning? Had he meant to say, 'The police are on their way; get your story straight?'

That morning he had telephoned the Inspector in charge of the case to tell him to get on to Charles Edwards, and had mentioned in passing that if any of the family knew anything it would be Agatha. He had had to do that after seeing Imogen in the telephone-box. He had meant his message to Agatha to amount to an order, that she was to co-operate with the police and not be silly. But if they chose to interpret it as a warning, did it matter? After all he did not want them to suffer. He wanted them to stay out of trouble.

'We've all got to be sensible about this thing,' he said.

'Yes, of course,' said Henry.

They had come to the arch of King Henry's tower.

'Go back in, it's freezing,' said Henry. 'I'll tell her, don't worry. See you soon.'

'Good-bye,' said Conrad, pausing on the top step.

Henry looked back from the pavement, raised a hand, thought briefly, Christ, he looks a million, and after walking a little way towards the Underground station began to run, because he was cold and relieved to get away and incidentally late back at the office. His hair lifted from his forehead by the cold wind, he put on speed, beginning for some reason to smile, and dashed past the now slowly moving queue outside St Stephen's entrance. Some of the people in the queue, trapped in their slow progression, looked at him curiously as he sped by with his smile in the opposite direction.

Conrad had waited at the top of the steps in spite of the cold, and had seen him start to run. It had worried him. Why should he run, except for some suspicious reason?

'People I hate,' wrote Paul: 'Uncle Conrad, Cousin Henry (your husband), all schoolmasters, judges, policemen and taxi-drivers (taxi-drivers are Fascists, don't ask me why but you will never meet a taxi-driver who is not either an overt or a crypto Fascist: at the time of my trial every taxi-driver in London wanted me hanged). People who have done me injury: my dead brother Stephen, my dead father Leonard, my dead mother Judith, Uncle Conrad, Cousin Henry, all schoolmasters, judges, policemen and taxi-drivers. People you might think I would hate but I don't: Daintry, his daughter Serena (my ex-wife), my dead step-father Orlando (your father). People I like: You. Although you are extremely nasty to me. If ever we talk about my problems you are thoroughly stern and bossy. And yet, when we talk, you talk to *me*. With you I am free, you don't force me into a role conceived by you and for you, to suit your own purposes. That is what all the others do. To do that to another human being, what disrespect that shows. Amounting to a gross evil. Only the really smug would dare. But English and smug are synonymous words. Perhaps it was because he was brought up in France that Orlando wasn't so bad. There was a time when I did hate him (oh yes, I have been quite liberal with my hate) and that was when I was finally expelled from Eton and he made me go and work in some foul office in Leicester. Then he wasn't nice, and I was just the tiresome step-son, in trouble again. The war got me out of that. Though the Army was worse of course. But after the war I got to like him again. He'd become free, like he was at the beginning, he wasn't blinkered by phoney frames (in the American sense, spectacles, though hardly in his case rose-tinted, and in the sense too of a correct gold frame edging a picture, and of a frame of mind, a frame of reference, a framework on which to balance all those sacred institutions by which the Conrads order their worlds, frame upon frame – a cold frame too, if you like, to grow a frightful warty cucumber in, and amounting altogether in the end to nothing more nor less than a rotten frame-up).

'Where was I? Oh yes, among people I hate. So much of my life has been spent among people I hate, at home, at school, in the Army, in the office. At the trial my defence made out that I'd sold those papers just for the money, but it wasn't true. I was selling much more than a few drawings, and the money only interested me in the sense that it was the handful of silver with which the traitor is rewarded, and I wanted to feel like a traitor.

'There's quite a certain secret joy in that feeling which you might find hard to imagine. The invisible worm that flies in the night, that's me. That's what I was up to when

I left Logan Holdings, the family firm after all. I knew I
could get Daintry to take it over and push out Stephen and
put me in to run it instead. I married Serena to consolidate
my position with Daintry, thus betraying not only her but
myself as well because I don't like going to bed with girls.
As to that, the funny thing is, I managed quite well at first
while I disliked her, but as I got fond of her it began to
disgust me – so she thought I didn't love her just at the time
that I almost did. I'd never been fond of anyone before, not
in that rather protective, potentially domestic way, and of
course she didn't understand, couldn't wait, thought she'd
better run off with that fatuous playboy Hayford while she
had the chance. Otherwise we just might have made it. She
used to cry sometimes when she'd had some setback, like
not being asked to a party (she took her social climbing so
terribly seriously I couldn't help being touched) and I used
to comfort her and stroke her hair and tell her that never
mind, one day Raine Legge would ask her to be on the
committee for the Save the Idiot Infants Ball, and at those
moments I almost loved her. Perhaps it was because she was
the only person in the world I could help, because I knew
more smart people than she did. I did a lot for her in that
way and she's very good about that, she never forgets to
be grateful. After all she'd never have met bonny Bunny
Hayford but for me, let alone all those shiny magazines and
things I fixed for her. No, she's all right in her way, Serena.
She came to see me in prison, and you know how terrified she was of bad publicity. It really meant something, her
doing that. Do you know what she told me then that she'd
never told me before? I didn't go to the divorce hearing,
as you know, but her lawyers were worried because there
wasn't much of a case against me, she was the one who'd
left and it looked a bit tricky, so they told her all she need

do was write one sentence on a piece of paper and pass it to the judge and it would go through without a murmur. She did and it did. She'd written, "My husband is a practising homosexual." The funny thing was, at that time and for her sake I wasn't practising. I was quite out of practice, in fact. It took me *hours* to get back into the swing of it. No, but seriously, talk about loaded dice.

'I digress. Not that I'm short of time. Time's winged chariot is pinioned for me. But not for you perhaps, with your little ones and your dreadful dog and your handsome husband, those four domestic tyrants. So we will leave the digression, which was marriage – oh God, will you read this far?'

Would she? He pushed away the blanket from his knees, put down his pad of paper and his pencil on the chair, stretched himself, and walked to the window. The net curtains smelt of soot. Opposite was a blank wall of purplish brick. Looking out of the window afforded no relief.

'Lonely,' he said, his forehead against the window pane. 'It's very lonely here.'

He turned back into the room and gathered up the scattered sheets of paper which he had already covered with writing and had thrown behind him on to the thin brown satin bedspread. When he had collected them together he banged them gently on the top of the chest of drawers to bring them into line and was agreeably surprised to see what a fat sheaf of manuscript they made. Of course it was worth doing. Of course Agatha would read it. He had better get on with it so as to have it finished by the time they came to collect him for the next stage of the journey.

He sat down again, wrapping the blanket round his legs. This way the time would pass – ridiculous sad waste of time –

what was that? T. S. Eliot or something – time before and
time after – because of course he always had been really
a literary person and no one, not one single schoolmaster,
not his mother who was too self-absorbed to care, not his
father who wanted him to play cricket and be manly, no one
had ever encouraged him to be himself, or bothered to try
to guess what sort of self himself might be. Except Agatha.

'I'll try to send you some sort of address,' he wrote,
'when I get there, if I ever do. Here in this horrible little
room it's sometimes impossible to believe I'll ever get out.
It's worse than prison, the confinement being more solitary, it feels like a very bad punishment indeed. What if they
never come back for me?

'But I'll go on. About Stephen. You were very kind to
me at the time of Stephen's death, and you were with me
a lot, in spite of all the other things you had to do. I don't
know if I ever thanked you for that. You once said to me
when Imogen was having one of her crises – didn't she have
a brief disastrous brush with Bunny Hayford before he got
involved with Serena, or am I imagining that? anyway, her
heart was broken and she was in floods of tears for three
days – you said – sadly, because you wanted to do more –
"You can never do anything for people in trouble except
lend them your presence," and it's true but people are often
quite reluctant to do that, they'd rather pay for something
or send flowers. But you're good at it. "Wait a minute and
I'll give you my full attention" is what you say when you're
busy, and then you do. You are generous with your full
attention. I'm not becoming maudlin. In many ways you
are quite tiresome as well.

'Anyway, at that time you were very considerate of my
feelings, but you had in fact misjudged them. I didn't mind
very much when Stephen died. People thought I'd as good

as killed him. Perhaps I had, but there was so little to kill. Most of him had been dead for years. He had no real existence of his own, Stephen. From the very beginning he changed his opinions to match those of the most powerful person in the room. When we were children he always agreed with Nanny – he used to sit beside her cutting out pictures of the Little Princesses as good as gold, till he was about fifteen as far as I remember. He was just a sackful of pretentious clichés – and lurking inside it all somewhere was a little vicious undeveloped embryo of what might have been a human being. All that that was capable of feeling was fear, an overwhelming paralysing fear. That part, the only part of him that was almost alive, must have been glad to die.

'Of course I didn't mean him to kill himself. I suppose I overdid it, I got excited, the feeling of power went to my head. I could have eased him out more delicately. I hadn't really expected Daintry to give me the Managing Directorship straight away and tell me to make a clean sweep. It seemed almost too good to be true. Perhaps I felt it couldn't last, and that's why I was in such a hurry. I really had them all hopping, though. And the games I was playing with the share price at the same time – I made a couple of hundred thousand in a week, you know. What I didn't give to Serena I lost later. Serena loved money. No, I should have stuck with all that, I should never have quarrelled with Daintry. I had a good thing going there. The only bad thing was Stephen killing himself. He could have got another job. He'd lost face, that's all, and quite a lot of money, I suppose. But how could I know he'd go home to his frightful house in Godalming and kiss his frightful wife and his appalling fat child and go upstairs and shoot himself in the mouth?'

'Stupid ass,' shouted Paul suddenly, jumping up from his chair. He staggered slightly because the blanket was wrapped so tightly round his legs. He freed himself and began to walk up and down in the minute space between the window and the chair.

'Stupid bloody fool,' he shouted.

Everything had suddenly gone terribly wrong. Furiously, he kicked the chair, which fell over. He bent to pick it up, then stopped, listening. There was silence. With luck the woman was out. She seemed to go out most afternoons, where to he had no idea. He picked up the chair and sat down on it to read the pages he had just written. Agatha would not like them. He would have to re-write them. What a bore. He felt exhausted already. Was it because Agatha would not like that part that he would have to re-write it, or was it because it was not quite true? It was so hard to know. He sat slackly in the chair, thinking formlessly of Agatha, Stephen, what had happened then, what was happening now.

He went towards the bed, to lie down, and as he reached it suddenly collapsed on to it, and clasping the slippery brown bedspread with both hands pressed it against his face. A feeling of appalling loss overcame him. There was nothing to cling to except the horrible bedspread, everything else had swirled away into limitless dizzying empty space, in which he was suspended, nameless and abandoned, in enormous agony of mind. Raising his head from the bedspread, he saw the wet stains of his tears and began to sob, to bellow really, like a child, pressing the crumpled bedspread on to his face to try to muffle the sound. He knew all this. He had had it before. It was the worst pain in the world.

Every weekday afternoon Agatha went to work in a bookshop in the King's Road and Willy, the Dutch girl who lived two doors away, came to look after the children. It was a small bookshop and had been started many years ago by Miss Auriol Bannister and Miss Felicity Wickham, both of whom were still at the helm, or rather Miss Bannister was at the helm and Miss Wickham was a slightly desperate first mate.

Their association had begun in the thirties when they had both been involved in some kind of movement or other – quite what it had been Agatha had never made out, except that it had involved high principles of a left-wing variety, walking tours, pamphlets, free love and fun. They both looked back on that time with nostalgia, which extended to the early days of the bookshop and the wonderful kindness and camaraderie of certain great names at the mention of which Miss Bannister's and Miss Wickham's eyes shone with uncritical love and loyalty. Some afternoons these titans of an earlier age would be recalled over a cup of tea in the chaotic little back office, while Agatha listened and the customers pocketed the books in the shop at their leisure, or finding no one to buy them from, settled down to read them on the spot. Dylan, the most marvellous talker in the world, Augustus John, the wonderful man, evenings in pubs, the beauty of one, the wit of another, the self-destructive fury of a third, all heroes of a glorious lost Bohemia, free, quite often drunk, always inspired with the true poetic frenzy – only 'Bloomsbury we never cared for'. Agatha loved it when they talked like that. The trouble was (from the business point of view) they could find nothing in the current literary scene to command a similar allegiance. More and more often Agatha found herself on her afternoons urging Miss Bannister to do her shopping or to take a publisher's representative into the back office for a thorough scolding, and Miss Wickham to have another go at the accounts, which were years behind, or – and here she had been surprisingly successful – to slip off quietly to the cinema. In their absence she was usually able to sell a few books. If they were there it was harder.

'Grossly over-praised,' Miss Bannister would trumpet from the back of the shop as an innocent customer handed something to Agatha to be wrapped. 'Not a novel at all, mere reportage – I'd wait for the paperback.'

'Not nearly as good as the film,' Miss Wickham would murmur as a customer picked up a book. Confidence undermined, he might put it down and turn to another. 'Auriol says the publisher ought to be ashamed of himself.'

That was another thing. Publishers from time to time incurred Miss Bannister's displeasure: this meant that for a period, usually quite brief, no new book from that publisher was allowed into the shop and those already in stock were so denigrated by Miss Bannister as to deter all but the boldest would-be purchaser.

'We don't stock books from Macmillan,' inquirers would be told, as if the whole of that large and reputable organization had suddenly swung into the purveying of filth, and only an immediate conciliatory visit from the Sales Director (for Miss Bannister had her own little reputation) would make her relent.

Agatha had not liked Miss Bannister when she first went to work in the shop because it had seemed to her that Miss Bannister bullied Miss Wickham. When she got to know them better she understood that their relationship had been going through a bad period. Miss Wickham had just acquired what was in effect a wig, although she herself called it a hairpiece. Her own hair, which was very fair and wispy, had been becoming increasingly thin on top, and the scalp which showed through drew attention to

itself by a curious shininess, so that the wig might be said
to be an improvement, for all that it was so unmistakeably
a wig. Miss Bannister however thought it a mistake, and
said so. All this was just at the time that Agatha was starting to work for them, and Miss Bannister's mockery was
not restrained in front of her. To escape it, Agatha's first
afternoon, Miss Wickham, her long gentle features easily
assuming the expression of a scapegoat going out into the
wilderness heavy with the sins of her people, silently took
up her mackintosh and crept towards the door.

'Going to see what you can pick up at the Doorway
then?' said Miss Bannister with pretended jollity from
behind a pile of books.

The Doorway was a Lesbian club just round the corner.
Neither Miss Bannister nor Miss Wickham, despite speculation among some of their clientèle, had ever been Lesbians.

Miss Wickham seemed to sink several inches closer to
the ground, murmured, 'Must get something for supper,'
and, opening the door a very little, squeezed out. Agatha
wondered how soon she could decently give in her notice.

She was forestalled by Miss Wickham who a few days
later, sitting upright on a hard little chair in the shop, occupied with her embroidery (she was extraordinarily skilful,
and always at her most calm and philosophical when she was
doing what she called 'my work'), said of Miss Bannister,
'She's tremendously kind, you know.'

Miss Bannister was in the back office with the representative of a firm of religious publishers, whom she had
invited in for a glass of port. 'She'll even take some of his
books, I expect, though she loathes religion. His wife died,
poor man, quite unexpectedly, of a cerebral haemorrhage.
She was only forty. They had no children, which makes it
worse, I think, don't you?'

Agatha, dusting shelves, agreed and said, 'So she's not always so fierce?'

'Oh no,' said Miss Wickham, shocked. After a minute she went on in a confidential sort of way, 'I suppose you think she's been a bit caustic about my hairpiece, but the trouble is, you see, she thinks I'm making a fool of myself.' Her long deft fingers moved without pause.

'Isn't that rather interfering of her?' said Agatha.

'Well, but one does interfere when one's known someone a long time. Besides, she thinks it's all to do with some new friends of mine, which it is really. They're awfully nice people. They live in the flat below me in Rosetti Mansions. He's retired from the Colonial Service, and she's so good-looking – it was her idea about the hairpiece. Auriol can't bear them. She thinks they're Philistine and right-wing, which they are of course. And, you see, that really means a lot to Auriol. As a matter of fact,' and here she lowered her voice, 'I joined the League of Empire Loyalists.'

'Good heavens!'

Miss Wickham nodded. 'Glenda – that's the wife – is terribly keen. She even travelled all the way to Glasgow to interrupt Eden and got thrown out of the meeting. That was when Auriol found out about her because it was in the papers. Auriol was so upset that I resigned without ever telling her I'd joined. I realized how much she would have minded if she'd known. Politics have always meant more to Auriol than to me. So I was only a member for four days. You won't tell her, will you?'

'Of course not. Weren't they rather annoyed?'

'Glenda was cross, yes, but not for long. The League was very stuffy about it. I got quite a nasty letter and they only returned half my subscription.' Miss Wickham suddenly gave a sort of explosive giggle and bent down over her embroidery exposing the clear line where the hairpiece failed to blend into the soft grey curls at the nape of her neck.

All this somehow combined with the glimpses of chaos she caught when trying to help Miss Wickham with the accounts to make Agatha feel that to ask for a rise in pay, as Imogen had recommended, was out of the question: besides, three pounds a week was better than nothing.

Following her revolutionary policy of trying actually to sell some of their stock, Agatha moved quite rapidly when the man in the overcoat approached Miss Wickham, holding out a copy of Colin Wilson's *The Outsider.* Miss Wickham peered at him doubtfully, without taking the book.

'Rather French –' she said hesitantly.

'Frightfully slapdash,' said Miss Bannister, in passing.

Agatha, having by now approached the customer, took the book.

'I thought it was very good,' she said firmly, and carried it off to the other side of the shop in order to wrap it up.

The man followed her, watching. 'What time do you finish here?' he asked quietly.

Agatha looked at him, and was immediately reminded of the two men who had been with Paul when she had met him in the woods.

'We close at half-past five,' she said calmly.

'I'll walk home with you if I may,' he said without expression. 'I'd like to have a word with you.'

She looked at him coldly, as if she had no idea what he was talking about.

'It's about your brother.'

She merely looked a little thoughtful, then said, 'I come out just after half-past but I'm usually in rather a hurry because I have to put my children to bed.'

'I won't keep you,' he said. He picked up the parcel and his change and left. Agatha sat down for a moment. She felt certain he must be a blackmailer. She tried to reassure herself: she could have given nothing away, so immediately had his appearance put her on her guard, and besides, her strength must be that she knew so little. But supposing he knew something – Paul's present whereabouts, for instance – and wanted money not to disclose it to the police? She had no more money. As the afternoon went on, she began to feel sick.

That morning she had had one of her failures, a lapse from grace. She had woken up too early, had found her head full of unwelcome thoughts and had lain there at their mercy, hearing the sound of milk-bottles and Lucy's mad morning singing. Henry had been out late again the night before and of course it wasn't fair; if you had a wife who loved you without reserve but also without, she really did believe, any of the diseases which made love non-love, if you had a wife like that and said you loved her, you didn't love another person on the same level. It made no sense, and she was merely weak in suffering it in silence. It was just an awful injury he was doing her. How could she respect him now? How could he fail to realize to what an extent he was using up her goodwill? The feeling of righteous indignation was perhaps to be preferred to the other feeling, the feeling of pure pain. On the other hand it made her so angry that she suddenly sat up in bed and pummelled his sleeping form as hard as she could with both fists.

He did not move but made a faint groan.

'You've used up all my love,' she said furiously. 'You think it's inexhaustible but it isn't. I haven't any left.'

He turned slowly towards her, hunching himself deeper into the bedclothes. Pulling his pillow down towards him, he shut his eyes, apparently settling himself for more sleep.

'Henry!' she shouted.

He opened one eye apprehensively. She immediately thought, What a horrible woman I am.

'You look awful,' she said more mildly.

He turned on to his back, moving cautiously, and opened and shut his mouth two or three times as if experimentally.

'I can imagine more cheery awakenings,' he said.

'Does Sally get angry with you?'

'Yes.'

She was silent, thinking of Sally, whose feet would be like the feet of girls at school, long, bony and bare, in the enforced intimacy of the changing-room, legs thin-skinned tending to be blue before netball, numinous soft bosom exposed for a moment in the struggle with a shirt. She had known a girl rather like Sally at school, Clare somebody, who had had the same mouth turned down at the corners and wide-apart eyes, and would be now an object of desire, like Sally, an object of love, like Sally. What else could one expect?

The hated concept of herself as millstone reappeared.

'You must have what you must have,' she said dreamily.

But then they had made love, and more emotion had been required of her, and he had said ferociously – and he had never said it before – 'You must forgive me,' and she had been shocked, because she did not really want to consider it in that light. She had said, feeling that it referred to much more than just the present situation, 'I forgive you, past and now and to come I forgive you.'

Because of course it was perfectly clear what she should do, or rather, as was often the case and often much harder, not do; and of course she blamed herself, hated herself in fact, when she failed: the trouble was that it was exhausting, and that she sometimes doubted her ability to sustain it. There would be nobody to forgive *her*.

It was all still on her mind when she left the shop – it was always on her mind, that was one of the aspects of the situation which she found impossible to control – so that her fear that her connection with Paul's escape might be discovered had to co-exist with that, as well as with her anxiety to get back to the children as soon as possible in case Willy, who liked to leave punctually at six, should disconcert them by showing her impatience to be gone (which in fact she never did); and so when the man in the overcoat stepped out from the doorway of the dry-cleaners she hardly paused, merely saying, 'Do you mind if we walk straight home?'

'Not at all. There were just one or two questions. I didn't want to bother you at home.' He held out a card in a leather holder.

When she saw it she did stop, but only for a moment, to look at him in unbelief, and then she went on walking.

'You could easily have come to see me at home,' she said freezingly. 'My children aren't afraid of policemen.'

She was furious that his surreptitious approach should have frightened her. She thought that policemen should be kindly people in uniform who told you the way to places and helped you find somewhere to park your car.

'I thought at this stage it might be better,' he said in a firm but detached tone of voice which did not put her at her ease. 'Have you any news of your brother?'

'No.'

He hasn't been in touch with you at all?'

'No.'

Would you expect him to get in touch with you?'

'No.'

'Why not?'

'I expect he's left the country.'

'Why do you say that?'

'Don't people usually, when they escape from prison?'

'Not necessarily, no.'

They walked along the pavement of a quiet road, rather fast because Agatha was setting the pace.

'You've no idea where he might have gone to?'

'No, I haven't.'

'Can you think of any friends or associates who might have been involved in this thing?'

'No.'

'We understand that you were on friendly terms with your brother.'

'Yes, I was.'

'And yet you can't think of anything that might help us in our inquiries, no questionable associates, nothing you remember him saying at any time, after the trial for instance, when you went to see him?'

'No, I can't,' said Agatha in a tone of voice which implied only too clearly that he would be the last person she would tell if she could.

The man was silent for a few moments, keeping pace easily with Agatha. Did he have rubber soles? She seemed to hear only her own footsteps, sharp and cross on the pavement.

'We rather understood,' he said in that tone of voice, soft, indifferent and deadly, which was so much more appropriate for the criminal she had at first thought him, 'from your uncle, that you would be disposed to help us.'

She knew she was in danger, but he had made her angry, so much so that her upper lip was slightly trembling, and the fact that she could not control the trembling made her more angry.

'How can I help you when I don't know anything?' she said. 'Besides, I'm afraid I find your approach very putting off. I don't see why you couldn't come and see me in the ordinary way, without having to be so secretive about it.'

He held out another piece of paper, this time with a telephone number written on it.

'If you think of anything ring this number,' he said. 'Ask for Inspector Skarrett.'

She took the paper and he turned away, walking at the same steady pace down a side-street, past a pub.

She felt she had been childish.

'It's all power,' wrote Paul, 'that's all any of us are after. From the first moment we're born we can't wait to get on to that ladder, and start grappling our way up, and kicking off the people on the lower rungs. Some of us are straightforward about it, like Daintry, and some of us (women, for instance) are more devious, but disguise it how we may it's the only basic driving force we have. And before you start saying it's wicked remember it's the only thing that differentiates us from animals.

'I remember Orlando quoting some French saying about "in order to be happy it is necessary that the others shouldn't be" and being rather annoyed because my mother agreed with him – he thought it wasn't a suitable thought for her, only for him. You don't remember him then of course, but he had a lot of charm in those early days, when he was aggressive and ambitious and rather a show-off. Rather a shit too. No, we don't like people because they're nice, whatever you may say.

'Anyway, that's all I ever wanted, just my share of the feeling that the others hadn't got what I had. And I've always had the opposite feeling. Even you have never understood how much I've felt on the outside. If I'd been inside I should have been a different person – because one is conditioned by one's social circumstances. All right, to some my social circumstances might have looked good, but I was too near to people with better. I was on the fringes of the Establishment, but not in it. That's even worse than being right outside. I was conditioned into being a spy, an underminer.

'Oh, Agatha, you are a good girl to have put this writing business into my head. I've so many ideas now I don't know when I'm going to get them down on paper. Because that's another one, isn't it? "The Role of the Spy in the Modern World" – a *really* highbrow article, full of references to Sartre and Colin Wilson and so on. Do you suppose I can become an Overseas Member of the London Library when I'm in my South American exile? Will you make a few preliminary inquiries? I shall send it to *Encounter*. Then you'll be proud of me, won't you?

'Anyway, that's how I see myself, as a destroyer, and it's up to someone else to do the rebuilding.

'You may ask why I didn't start destroying sooner and why I spent so long in the silken tents of my enemy. Good question. Answer (1) I was always destroying in my heart, with my scorn. (2) Lack of opportunity.

'I did really have a horrible time in the Daintry organization after Stephen's death, although it may have looked from the outside as if I were getting everything I wanted. Daintry despised me. He probably always had, ever since I asked him for a job. He must have seen through me then and known what I was after. He could so easily have found out about the questions I'd been asking. It was obvious to both of us after our first conversation that there was a reasonable possibility of his organization taking over Logan Holdings. It was a logical development, and with me to help him it was quite easy. Besides, I knew that there was something about Daintry which would appeal to Conrad and make him lend the weight of his authority to the whole proceeding. But of course Daintry knew. He let me use him because he wanted to use me, but he must have known perfectly well that I was doing it because I wanted revenge on my brother (my younger brother, remember) for having done better than I did in the family firm by sucking up to Conrad and posing as the honest reliable alternative to slippery me.

'I got my revenge, and my position of power over all the people who had failed to back me when they had the chance. That was good. But all the time Daintry despised me, and used me, and kept me out of his inner councils. So though I had a little power he spoilt it for me. 'In the years after the takeover I worked incredibly hard. I hardly thought of anything else. I neglected Serena. When I came home I was too tired to do anything except drink and go to bed. I drank much too much during all that time. Serena was always out, pursuing her social career, being pursued by Bunny Hayford. We drifted apart. Then when she saw the way it was going, and that I was going to bite the hand that had been feeding me, she thought it was time to get out.

'Not that she knew *how* I was going to bite – she just knew the way my mind was working. You probably don't know this, but in a really big organization, which by then Daintry Enterprises had become, your entire time can be taken up by internal intrigue. In so far as you give any time at all to the supposed function of the organization, it is only as a gambit in this endlessly complicated and intensely bitter struggle for position. The Americans are better at it than we are, but we're learning. English people tend to have a respect for hierarchies – it's probably something to do with the prefect system – but we're breeding it out. The Americans don't have it, and they don't have stiff upper lips either. The upper rungs of the ladder in the average large American firm are a riot of clinging shoving mouthing shrieking blubbering assassins; it's amusing when you first come across it, but gets a bit repetitive.

'Anyway, whether by learning from our new American associations or what, the enlarged Daintry Enterprises became adept at this particular game, and Daintry showed himself quite skilled at taking advantage of it. When we started going into the electronics field – he having quite rightly decided that then was the moment to go in, what with automation coming and so on – he took advantage of one of my private vendettas (I won't bore you with the details) to leave me in charge of one of the electronics firms and thereby, because of the rules of the holding company, lose me my seat on the main board. After that I had to get him into trouble, didn't I?

'"Rubbish," you say, putting on your cross face. But it is not rubbish. The trouble with you is that you have led a sheltered life (oh how angry you are by now) and know nothing of human nature. You are like a visitor from another world. You say, "On the moon all the mothers love their children so much that they grow up to love everybody else." That's as may be. We do things differently here.'

Dora could stand on her hind legs in the larder of the cottage and reach the egg-box, gently nose open the lid and extract an egg, unbroken. Once or twice she carried a whole box out into the garden and spent an hour or so taking out the eggs and playing with them, cavorting about with one in her mouth before abandoning it somewhere in the garden, still unbroken, and going back for another. It was a game which Agatha tried to discourage, but the habit of keeping the eggs on the bottom shelf of the larder was so strong that she often forgot to put them higher.

She could remember sitting on the back doorstep in the sun, the children scuffing with sticks in the dusty remains of what had been a gravel path, drawing houses. Beside her was an egg-box which she had recovered with four eggs still inside it. One of the others had disappeared and one was still in Dora's mouth. Agatha was too lazy to do more than scold. Dora danced about on the grass, making movements with her head as if she were throwing the egg up into the air and catching it again, although it was really still held in the delicate clasp of her teeth: perhaps becoming aware of Agatha's inattention, she trotted up to the doorstep, curling back her upper lip and groaning some sort of invitation to the game.

'No, Dora.'

Agatha held out her hand.

Dora gently deposited the egg in it.

'D'you see how she doesn't even crack them?' She held the egg out for George to see. It lay in the palm of her hand, warm and unblemished. 'How carefully she must have carried it. When I die I'll leave you an egg like that, dropping it into the palm of your hand uncracked, with all the stuff of life still in it.'

The sound of Lucy's stick in the gravel reminded her of Italy, of waking in the morning to the sound of a man hoeing in stony ground.

'I hope it will be cooked,' said George. When the white of his boiled egg was not quite solid, that he hated.

[*]

Sally was wearing a shiny green dress. Across the front was a frill of the same material which dipped under her arms and plunged almost to her waist at the back. At the hem, which was higher in the front than at the back, the same line was repeated by another frill which swayed and rustled round her when she walked. She had matching shiny green shoes with pointed toes, very high heels, and ankle straps. Round her neck she wore a shiny green ribbon with a cameo brooch pinned to the front of it. Her lips and nails were a wet-looking scarlet. She wore a golden bracelet from which dangled dark brown semi-precious stones.

'Black pearls, are they? Pretty – mn,' said the tall young man with sticking-out ears. He seemed to speak through his nose, hardly moving his lips at all, as he bent forward to peer at the bracelet.

'Of course,' said Sally, turning her wrist from side to side, slowly because of the glass of champagne she was holding.

'Of course,' agreed the young man, returning to the height from which he had come. His little eyes directed their feeble gaze down the long organ through which his frail tones appeared to emerge (eugenically speaking, his breeding was a disaster). 'What else could they be?' He gave a short quasi-experimental snicker.

'What indeed?' said Sally, rolling her eyes rather wildly. They lighted to her relief on the face of Joe Hertz, half turned away from her, talking in a group of people. 'Hullo,' she said breathlessly, laying a hand on his shoulder. He turned, looking rather startled.

'Do you know –?' She waved vaguely in the direction of the tall young man, but already a determined couple making their way from one side of the room to the other had interposed themselves. 'Thank God for that. What a nightmare person.'

Joe, effectively detached from his previous conversation, looked at her attentively, as if waiting for further
explanation.

'Why *do* I come to cocktail parties?' she said. She looked
as if she really wanted to know.

'Because you're always afraid you might be missing
something,' he answered firmly.

'That's it.' She glowed at him, as if no one had ever understood her before. 'But every time I find I'm not.'

'But the one time you didn't come he might be here, tossing his raven locks with impatience, jewels winking on his
princely breast, waiting to sweep you up in front of him on
his white horse and gallop out of the room and down the
stairs and away over the burning sands of Arabia.'

'Not much room for a horse in here,' she said, looking
round with a dissatisfied glance.

'He'd leave it downstairs then, tethered to the banisters,
jingling its bits and things. You'd know you'd been right to
come as soon as you saw it there. You'd hurry up the stairs
with your heart a-flutter.'

'You mustn't laugh at me for having a commonplace
mind,' she said. But she looked quite happy about it.

He knew her only slightly, as a pretty girl who normally
had more exciting people than him to talk to at parties.
He also knew her to be in some way or other involved
with Henry. He had not wanted to know this, for various
rather complicated reasons, but it had not been possible
to maintain his ignorance; common acquaintances asked
him what was going on, as the close friend who might be
expected to know, and besides Agatha and Henry were
both thinner, and evenings with them were sometimes
different from the old days, not so much when there
was the odd sharp word as when they treated each other

too delicately, as if they were both convalescent from an
illness which each knew might in the case of the other
recur and prove fatal: this sad tenderness had struck him
more than once as a bad sign. Brian, a worldly friend, had
said it was bound to happen from time to time, Henry
being the sort of person he was: Agatha would have to
adjust herself, he said. Joe supposed this to be true but
wondered how, in practical day-to-day terms, one did
adjust oneself, and knew that it was fear of just that kind
of harsh necessity which made him a coward himself in
personal relationships, a coward who depended on other
people's successes in those directions for his own precar-
ious sense of security.

Sally represented trouble, but he did not feel that he knew
enough about her to know whether he ought to blame her
for that.

'Have you got a car?' she asked.

'Yes. Do you want a lift?'

'If you could just drop me at the nearest taxi-rank it
would be too marvellous. We're miles from anywhere here,
aren't we?'

Smiling at this description of their hosts' rather fashionable address, he led the way out of the room, only to find
that she had not followed him and was nowhere to be seen.
He went downstairs and waited for quite a long time. She
came at last, with a token apology. It turned out that she
was supposed to be going on to another party but could not
be bothered – or perhaps the party was mythical. Anyway
they went to have dinner in Soho, at a quiet restaurant he
liked where the food was good. She said in answer to his
question that she had been there before, and then hesitated. At once he wished he had not asked her, because he
had taken Henry there more than once and it was just the

sort of quiet place, unfrequented by their friends, to which
Henry might have taken Sally.

'With Henry.'

It had been too late to stop her saying it, but at least he
could ignore it.

'What will you have?'

But he could not put it off for ever, and by the time it
came, about halfway through the meal, food and wine and
her pretty face and friendly talk had made him less reluctant.

'You're a great friend of Henry's, aren't you?' she said.

He might even be going to enjoy it. He had been a little
nervous about that too. It smacked of betrayal.

'They're both my best friends,' he said sternly.

'You don't mind my talking about it?' she asked humbly.

He shook his head.

Her tale unfolded, with pauses for encouragement. She
would rather die than break up the marriage. That was why
she had insisted that all physical relations should cease some
time ago. He was not quite sure whether to believe either
of the two protestations. Certainly it appeared that she
herself very much wanted to believe the first, but she left
him a succession of openings for telling her she was wrong.
Was the marriage not perhaps anyway doomed to failure,
were they not too disparate in temperament in spite of their
affection for each other and for the children, did Henry not
need a different kind of person, more easy-going, extravert,
sociable?

At one moment he looked down at his plate, struggling to
control one of those foolish smiles that look like the beginnings of a childish crying fit, because he was curiously and
conflictingly moved, and because he was also almost pity-
ingly amused by his own reaction, by the fact that he was
sitting opposite her in a warm sweat of anxiety, mechanically

putting into his mouth from time to time food which tasted like blotting paper or wine which he gulped too thirstily so that the effect of it added to his general feeling of being about to start giving out some sort of buzzing sound. What shook him was the understanding which came to him while she was speaking of how much his own stability was bound up with that of the marriage of his two friends. Hearing it undermined from a vantage point so different from his own, and with an authority so convincing (because in certain ways she must of course know Henry better than he did, which in itself was a disturbing thought), seemed to be giving him a push towards an independence which he had not known he lacked. It was alarming, but there was also a sense of liberation, and so of excitement. As Sally talked on and on, exposing without any hesitation or embarrassment all sorts of intimacies which he could not imagine any man of his acquaintance revealing in such a way, there were present in his mind not only various straightforward regrets about the whole thing, not only a natural curiosity, but other vaguer, less accountable emotions. It meant that these two were not so much better than he was after all, if the relationship which not only he among their friends had envied could so founder. Was this at last something which Henry could not get away with? Was Agatha's wholeness to be splintered, leaving her weak, accessible? If she should fall into his arms in search of comfort, was that not what he had really always wanted? And if that should annoy Henry, was that not too what he had always wanted?

While he listened, and said 'Yes' and 'No' and 'I see', he was recognizing the involved considerations which might affect his own imaginable behaviour, and then he was realizing that some kind of moral fastidiousness in himself would make such behaviour no more than a possibility,

would make him dismiss it in fact as insufficiently serious:
but the fact that he had even recognized the possibility bore
out his view of himself, that he was not fundamentally a
very nice person.

As he usually did when he despaired of himself, he
focused his attention on someone else.

'Now wait a minute,' he said. 'Let's just look at you.'

He looked at her.

'You're very pretty.'

She smiled doubtfully.

'Now let's see.'

He went on looking at her, with his elbows on the table
and his chin resting on his clasped hands.

'How old were you when you first had a lover?'

'Seventeen,' she said, accepting the invitation to tell him
the story of her life.

Her father was a successful surgeon, her mother, she
said, conventional and boring – 'not that we don't get on
exactly, we just haven't much in common.' At sixteen she
had gone to a finishing-school in London where she took
a course in modelling and began to be photographed for
magazines. She went to work for a fashionable photographer with whom she fell in love, worked incredibly hard,
learnt, she said, everything she knew; but he was not kind,
he treated all his girl-friends badly; to escape, she became
involved with a rich young man whose family thought she
was not good enough for him; he was so sweet, they were
so mean, he had a nervous breakdown, chased her with
a knife, threw her down the stairs. 'Gosh,' said Joe. But
she seemed to have quite enjoyed it. Now here she was, a
successful model, earning a lot of money, asked to smart
parties, pursued by this and that handsome, rich or famous
man. Henry, she said, was 'real', the others were not. Her

life was useless, she felt, her activities trivial, she had no purpose. He had seen her photographed with Lord Marner. Yes, well, of course, that was really quite funny. Her solemnity disappeared as she began to repeat the indiscretions of Johnny Marner, with which apparently he regaled her every morning on the telephone; as like as not a bunch of flowers from him would arrive even as they were talking, for that was the sort of person he was. Of course the whole thing was quite ridiculous, and she wouldn't dream of letting the affair go any further, but at the same time it was so funny, and he was rather sweet in a way and had such lovely manners and took her to such lovely places. 'Do you see at all what I mean?'

He saw. He saw the symmetrical oval of her delicately coloured face, her black-lashed, pearly-painted eyes, the controlled smooth gold of her swept-back hair: a phenomenon. Following an idea of her which was beginning to come to him, he imagined a context of cool rooms impeccably furnished, of pale-skinned odalisques who were prodigies of wit and savoir-faire, of black panthers lounging on cushions, sapphires, subtle lights, infinite afternoons. He began to smile.

'Go on,' he said. 'What else?'

Marner had taken her to stay with a duke. She had noticed everything.

'You're marvellous. You're very clever, do you know that? Go on.'

Oh, but it was all so silly, so unreal. Of course he was rather powerful and was always telling Cabinet Ministers to pull themselves together and calling up smooth chauffeur-driven cars from nowhere. He had asked her to go on some shooting party in Alsace. Of course she was not going. Although it would have been nice to meet the King

of Bavaria or at least the man who would have been King
of Bavaria if there had been a King of Bavaria. 'But you
shouldn't encourage me. You're as bad as Henry. He always
wants to hear what he calls amazing tales. I used to think
it was because he wanted me to find someone else, so that
he'd be rid of me. But only the other day he said something
very strange to me, about wanting me to like his children.
He's never said anything like that before.'

'No, no,' said Joe. His mind was quite made up. 'You
don't want the dreariness of domestic life. You want luxury,
love, beautiful things, expensive things, adventure, intrigue.
You're a perfect beautiful marvellous specimen of a good-
time girl, a courtesan.'

She looked shocked, but there was no stopping him. He
had seen a solution and was going to put all his professional
skill into selling it.

'People don't know how to live any more,' he said
earnestly. 'This is the age of the drab and the dreary and
the conformist and the average man. Our whole society
is suffering from guilt without knowing what to do about
it, so we go on behaving in the same old way but less so,
because we've lost confidence and so we don't dare to have
any fun. You belong to a different age, an age when there
was a proper place for someone like you, where all your
talent for being beautiful, charming and pleasing to men
could unfold and be adored. But you must let yourself be
what you are, choose yourself and become yourself, and
not be ashamed of being unique.'

He paused for breath and refilled both their glasses. Sally
was smiling, enjoying it. Encouraged, he went on.

'What an absurd idea it is that every woman only wants
to get married and have children. Some do and some don't.
Why should custom force them all to conform? You don't

want to waste yourself on one man, cooking, washing, darning, changing babies' nappies, all your lustre dimmed. All right, in ten years, when you feel the moment has come for a little calm, a little routine, you might, with every possible inducement in the way of ease, independence and scope for creating something perfect, agree to settle down. But in the meantime –'

'Yes?'

'You create something perfect. Yourself. Certainly you meet the King of Bavaria. In a man-made world you learn from men in order to turn yourself into a unique woman. Thus you conquer them. But you are kind, discreet, wise. You do not feature in divorce cases. You bring pleasure, not pain; wherever you go you confer an inestimable benefit just by being there. In a certain world you will become famous. A small world. But your name will be mentioned in the history books.'

'You *are* funny. How do I start?'

'This shooting party. When is it?'

'Next month.'

'I may be going to Paris about then. I've been offered a job by an American advertising firm which would mean living in Paris. I probably shan't take it but I could go over and talk to them about it. I'll meet you there. It will be a good thing if you leave independently of Lord Marner. It will show that you're not to be considered as completely attached to him. You're meeting a friend in Paris. A little mysterious. Do you know Paris?'

She shook her head. 'I spent a day there once being photographed for *Vogue*.'

He nodded seriously. 'We must see about that.'

'You mean you're going to train me up somehow. Well, that's all right, I suppose. But you'll have to see it through, you know. You can't give me up halfway.' She spoke teasingly, as if the whole fantasy was still a joke.

'I shan't give you up. I'm going to take an interest in you, you see.'

They developed the fantasy. It went very nicely. They had an amusing evening and were left with the feeling that something had started, though both were vague as to what it really was. Sally pretended to treat it all as a joke, but it was she who was more serious. There was no doubt that she would now accept the invitation to the shooting party.

Joe went home cheerful and rather drunk. He lived in a sort of bachelors' rooming-house on the borders of Pimlico and Belgravia. Because he thought himself always on the point of leaving London he had never bothered to find himself any where more agreeable. He went upstairs rather noisily and let himself into his room, which was neater than might have seemed possible in view of the number of books it contained.

'I really like her,' he said, undressing rather unsteadily and folding his clothes carefully before putting them on the chair. 'I really like her.'

In his pyjamas he gazed into the mirror above the washbasin.

'Why not? A role for her. A role for me. Best for Agatha. Best for Henry.'

He squeezed some toothpaste on to his toothbrush.

'Wonders. I'll do wonders with her.'

He cleaned his teeth, put the toothbrush back into the mug and the top on to the toothpaste, and got into bed.

'I would do anything for Agatha. Agatha, I remember your face as the heaving tides remember the moon.'

He put his head on to his pillow and noticed that it seemed to be heaving very slightly too.

'She'll have to wait until I get back from Hungary of course.'

He reached out for the light-switch, fumbled, found it. He turned out the light and fell asleep.

Conrad could not sleep. Suffering from flatulence and uncontrollable anxiety, propped up on his pillows, he tried to read Herodotus, sipping Bisodol.

He hated his bedroom at the flat. It was too small. On the other hand service flats within walking distance of the Houses of Parliament were almost impossible to find, and staying at the Club was not the same as having one's own rooms. Besides, there was Jess, who was used to the flat and to spending long hours alone there. Snoring now in her basket beside his bed, she added to his anxieties. He shrank from the pain her death, which could not now be long delayed, must cause him; nor had he a successor in view. She had had puppies but he had kept none, thinking she might have another litter, and then what with one thing and another she never had, so there was no young dog to take her place and though he could find a puppy he wanted the same breeding as near as possible, and that might be hard to find. He wrote on the pad of paper which he kept on the bedside table, 'Coombs, re puppy,' which reminded him of Agatha and the beagle which had been run over. There was no doubt it had been an excellent little bitch, that. Bad luck, it had been. If only Agatha wasn't so difficult, he could have given her another one. He would willingly have done it, would have enjoyed it, traced the breeder, found a sibling, it would have been a nice thing to have done; but it was just that sort of pleasant interchange which Agatha's attitude made so difficult.

'Not very co-operative,' Skarrett had said that evening on the telephone. That was Agatha all right. He had thought of having another word with Imogen after that telephone call but could get no answer from her flat, even at half-past eleven. How she managed to hold down a job, keeping such late hours, he could not imagine. He would have to try and catch her in the morning. He had a feeling about Agatha, that was all, but his feelings were usually right.

'Unlike me not to be able to sleep,' he said aloud.

He put down his book and went to the window. Pulling aside the curtain, he saw a line of pale light at the edge of the sky. It was already dawn. He really had had a sleepless night.

The telephone rang.

He picked up the receiver.

'Yes?'

'You asked me to let you know when we got the Egyptian answer in. It came about an hour ago.'

'Rejecting our ultimatum of course.'

'Yes.'

'Ah.'

'As expected.'

'Quite.'

'So we proceed.'

'Yes. Well, thanks for letting me know, old chap. The next ten days or so won't be much fun, will they?'

'No.'

'We'll pull through, I daresay. You must be tired, William. I won't keep you. Many thanks again. Good-bye.'

He put down the receiver.

'Pity,' he said, sitting on the edge of the bed.

He swung his legs up and pulled the bedclothes over them

'We seem to have been swept into rather a rash adventure,' he said, arranging his pillows. At the same time he was conscious that the multifarious anxieties which had been keeping him awake were sliding away from him as if under the influence of a beneficent drug.

Now we shall have to close our ranks, he thought, and fell asleep.

Agatha dreamed about Italy. It had been raining and she was standing in front of the door to the tower house, which had a rough grey stone architrave set into the variegated stones of the wall above it. There were two large grey stones, each a natural pillar, on either side of the door. Last summer she had taken a photograph of the two children standing in the dark doorway. 'Look sad,' she had said and they had, like little refugees. In her dream it was Orlando who was standing there, in the shadow so that she could hardly see him. He was leaning against one of the grey stones and she had the impression that he was ill. 'You haven't maintained it,' he was saying, and though his voice was weak it conveyed an awful urgency. 'You haven't maintained it.' But she knew he did not mean the building.

In the grassy space by the well Henry, wearing a smart suit, was jiving with Marilyn Monroe, backwards and forwards on skilful fast feet, twirling her under his outstretched arm, and she was smiling rapturously; of course, Agatha thought in her dream, that is only right and proper, and she knew that Orlando thought so too. But this business of the maintenance, that was her concern.

Just before she woke another place, very sharply defined, superimposed itself for an instant, a place on an island with blue sea far below. The sunlight was extraordinarily clear – had she ever been there? – there were columns, an ancient ruin, very white and quiet, two broken columns, in the space between which she was going to put something, but had lost it, or forgotten what it was.

'She's taken it. I put it in its special place and she's taken it.'

'Taken what, darling?' she said as she woke up.

It was George, in his pyjamas.

'I put it in the special drawer I always keep it in and Lucy's taken it.' He was indignant; more than that, shocked. 'Just taken it. My second-best red pencil.'

Conrad was on the telephone at eight o'clock in spite of his restless night.

'Charles Edwards, the ex-burglar.' He had dialled Inspector Skarrett's private number. 'He was an acquaintance of Paul's and could have put him on to whoever it was who arranged the escape. It might have been him rather than the Russians – after all Paul was never really one of their men so far as we know. I just give you that idea for what it's worth.'

'I won't bore you with the technical details,' wrote Paul. 'But this little rather rude-looking thing we were making was tremendously useful, not to say pretty well essential, if you were building an atomic reactor. Of course it had other functions as well and I didn't myself appreciate its more thrilling potentialities until I had a mysterious message from someone called Colonel Longfellow who wanted me to meet him for a drink in the Grosvenor Hotel of all places. I feared the worst (my past is even murkier than you think) but I went along and there he was all lean and military with a mackintosh and a whisky and soda, and so I said, "You must be from M.I.5" and he *was furious*. I can tell them a mile off. He wanted to know what foreigners were buying the thing and if they were would I pretend I personally had to supervise the installation and have a snoop round at the same time to see who was making atom bombs on the quiet. So we sat there in our armchairs with our whiskies and sodas being tremendously confidential and responsible and officer class together when all the time he must have known I wasn't in the least like that. I mean they have dossiers on everybody, these people, and he must have known what a frightful officer I was and how only Uncle Conrad's influence prevented me from being prosecuted for that unfortunate little incident in the Leicester Square public lavatory. The silly thing was one was meant to do it all for patriotic motives, and I needed money. I'd made absurdly generous arrangements for Serena at the divorce, I'd spent too much on living it up a bit here and there after she left, and I was being blackmailed. (Under the quaint law we have, by which you can be sent to prison for having sex with a man – well, *you* can't obviously, but I can – most homosexuals are blackmailed most of the time.) So I began to think. If this thing was so interesting perhaps the countries to which it was a prohibited export might like it, and perhaps they might pay for it.

'I knew how to get hold of them. It was all to do with my murky past again. I was actually a member of the Communist party for a short time. You didn't know that, did you? Quite a flirtation with politics I had, after the war. But I could see nothing was going to happen. The English will never turn Communist, they're such snobs. An English Communist could have a duke at gunpoint: if he asked him to stay for the weekend he'd drop the gun and dash off to Moss Bros to hire a dinner-jacket. It could only come by foreign conquest, and I couldn't see that happening for some time, so I rather slid out of the whole thing. But I knew a lot of spies. Incidentally I knew Burgess and Maclean too – well, Burgess really, but that was through drinking clubs more – and I can tell you *that* story's not over yet. Anyway, nothing was easier than to make contact with the people

I needed. And of course they wanted my little gadget and a great deal more besides. My guess is – but I may be wrong – that they knew a good deal about how to make the things anyway: whether they had spies in the factory already or whether it was just that their own people were working along parallel lines I don't know, but I had the feeling that they were just playing me along about that and that what they were much more interested in was exactly how many we were supplying to the British Government, and where. I made them wait for that, which was OK in one way because they put the price up, but in another it may have been my downfall because I had to meet them too often. I don't know what made our people suspicious – perhaps the M.I.5 man wasn't quite such a fool as I thought him – anyway when I saw a man reading the paper in a parked car outside my house two mornings running I went to Charlie at once. I believe in insurance. There's a perfectly efficient organization for getting you out of prison if you're prepared to pay. It's expensive, I know, but worth it, I think you'll agree. My charming hostess this morning vouchsafed a remark while handing me my foul breakfast. "He says you're to be ready to leave," she said. What does he think I am? I've never been readier to leave anywhere in my life. So I said with heavy irony, «I'll start my packing," but she just padded out with her disgusting slippers. If she's not careful I'll leave her something nasty in the bed.'

'They know.'

Imogen's face was perfectly, startlingly, white.

'Sit down.' Agatha pulled forward a chair and with a hand on Imogen's arm firmly sat her down in it.

'They know, Agatha,' said Imogen again.

Agatha looked round quickly. Miss Bannister was in the back room and Miss Wickham, who had seen Imogen's desperately hurried arrival, was tactfully bent over her embroidery at the other end of the shop.

Agatha, having given her chair to Imogen, sat down on the edge of the table and said, 'What happened?'

'They came to see me again, and they know. It's no good. You'll have to tell them, Agatha.'

'Who came to see you?'

'That Inspector.'

'What did he say?'

'He knows about Charlie Edwards and that he arranged Paul's escape and that you gave them money.'

'What did he say exactly?'

'He said he knew Charlie Edwards had arranged it.'

'Charlie Edwards didn't arrange it. It was a friend of his.'

'It's the same thing,' said Imogen impatiently. The colour was coming back into her cheeks now that the horrifying moment of breaking the news to Agatha was over. 'It's no good, Agatha. You'll have to go and see them.'

'Of course I'm not going to go and see them,' said Agatha. 'Just tell me exactly what he said.'

'He said you must go and see him.'

'What did he say that he knew?'

'He said that he knew it was all to do with Charlie Edwards. He said it was only a matter of time until they found out all the details. He said that if you had given them any money you must go and tell him all about it at once, otherwise you'll certainly be caught and sent to prison.'

'*If* I had. He can't have known then.'

'He does know. It's no good. He does know.' She had turned white again.

Agatha looked at her. She has told him, she thought.

She stood up and walked slowly away, turned over a book on the top of a pile on one of the tables and walked back. She was fairly certain that Imogen must have told the Inspector everything she knew but she did not want her to have to say so. She would have liked to have embraced her sister, but they had never been demonstrative in that sort of way.

Instead she said, 'Don't worry. He may not know as much as he would like us to think. I'll wait for him to come to me.'

Imogen had screwed up her chiffon scarf into a ball and was turning it round and round in her hands.

'But if you go to him and tell him, it will be better for you. He said so.'

'I will do that if it seems the right thing. I don't think I ought to do it yet. Don't worry, it will be all right. Leave it to me.'

'But I don't want to leave it to you. I want to help you.'

To Imogen's anxious eyes it was as if Agatha visibly retreated and from a new distance said quietly, 'No, you can't do that.' Then she turned away, without seeing Imogen's immediate tears, and went into the back room where she said politely to Miss Bannister, 'I suppose there wouldn't be any chance of a cup of tea for my sister? She's had a bit of a shock.'

'Of course, my dear.' Miss Bannister at once rose to her feet and set about lighting the gas-ring.

'Tea? Oh goody,' said Miss Wickham, hurrying in from the shop and busily setting out the blue-striped mugs. 'Just what I need.'

They both assumed that Imogen was pregnant and felt very sorry for her, so pretty and so sad. Miss Bannister would have liked to contribute something towards the cost of an abortion, Miss Wickham had already determined to adopt the child. Fortunately both decided that their offers would be premature, and kept them in reserve.

Conrad walked briskly across St James's Park, with Jess at his heels. It was cold and misty but with a faint suggestion of sunshine through the mist and the smell of burning leaves on the air. He wondered if there had been a frost at Mount Sorrel. He hoped the crisis would not prevent him from getting down there for the weekend.

'Come along, Jess,' he said unnecessarily. He felt very well. 'Sometimes I think one sleeps too much,' he said, startling a middle-aged woman in a hat who happened to be walking in the opposite direction. 'An occasional shortage of sleep clears the mind.' He should not have hesitated so much about Agatha. She should be brought to her senses as quickly as possible and the wretched Paul caught and put away. He had told that Inspector it was time to get a move on. Really it was perfectly disgraceful that they hadn't found him already.

This evening the bombers would move in. Alert young men – he envied them in a way – their trained reflexes at work, their faculties stretched, coming in low at dusk to bomb the Egyptian airfields, a competent operation to put the places out of action, a definite move, a clear unequivocal statement. How much he had seen bungled by inaction: Italy in 1935, the Rhineland in 1936. 'You can't be too nice, you know, in this wicked world.' And though of course things changed and one had to move with the times, one couldn't help sympathizing with people who thought the British should never have left Suez in the first place.

'Robust,' he said. 'We must be robust.' His feeling of well-being was so intense that as he walked along he held his arms in front of him and with his hands open horizontally rubbed the palms briskly together at the same time saying, 'Ho ho, ho ho, ho *ho*.'

Jess, delighted by the way things were going, broke into a lolloping canter. A smiling park attendant said cheerfully, 'Nice morning, sir!'

'Excellent, excellent,' answered Conrad.

Of course it was a nice morning. He was going to get a lot done today. He hoped there wouldn't be too much talking, he had a lot of other things to see to, letters to write, arrangements to make, he really wanted to find time to look at the new chrysanthemums in the Royal Horticultural Society's Autumn Show too. Still, he might have to let that go, if there was too much on.

'What an interesting life we lead, Jess, for a couple of old fogeys.'

Henry and Joe had lunch together.

'I had dinner with Sally last night.'

'Did you? How did that come about?'

'We were both at a boring party. She's marvellous, isn't she?'

Henry looked pleased but said deprecatingly, 'Not too bright of course.'

'No, she's quick though, funny.'

'I'm glad you liked her,' said Henry.

Joe felt from the easy way in which he spoke that he meant it, and this seemed significant. If Henry did not feel that there was anything that needed to be concealed about his friendship with Sally, presumably he himself no longer thought of it as dangerous. This augured well, Joe thought. For everything.

They talked about mutual friends, gossiping, before going back to the subject of Sally, and the behaviour of

Lord Marner, and their joint curiosity about this enigmatic but grand figure.

'Incidentally,' said Henry changing the subject abruptly, 'do you know any really discreet solicitors? There's something I want to find out but I don't know who to ask.'

Joe wondered whether he had misjudged the situation. One never quite knew with Henry. On the other hand he had thought he did quite know.

Confused, he said, 'There's always poor old David Matthews.'

'Oh yes, so there is. Poor old David Matthews. Look here, could you ask him something for me? It's a bit difficult for me. Would you mind? Ask him what would be the sentence on someone who was caught giving money to a group of people who organized the escape from prison of someone who had been given a long sentence.'

'Cripes.'

'Supposing the person who had given the money to be a relation of the person who escaped.'

'Yes. Gosh.'

'All quite hypothetical of course.'

'It would probably be only a fine, wouldn't it?'

'Apparently not.'

'Oh Lord. I'll find out.'

'Just so that one knows.'

'Does it look like – um – being found out?'

'I'm not sure. I hope not.'

'So do I. Good Lord.'

He acted quickly. Late in the afternoon he telephoned Henry in his office. They met on a bench in St Paul's Churchyard. Joe unfolded a typewritten sheet of foolscap paper.

'You were quick,' said Henry.

'I stood over him while he rang up his friend in criminal law. This is what he says. "A person who harbours an offender under the Official Secrets Act commits a misdemeanour, and the maximum penalty on indictment is two years. I doubt whether the close relationship, or the fact of a first offence, would really be material My feeling is that the Court would want to give the maximum sentence possible."'

'Why?' said Henry.

'I suppose espionage is considered a bad thing. And helping someone to evade the law. "The matter of bail would presumably be strongly opposed in the case of espionage, and so therefore the person concerned would in practice be starting his prison sentence from the date of arrest."'

'No bail,' said Henry.

They sat side by side on the bench in silence.

'So really,' said Henry thoughtfully, 'a certain line has been crossed. She has put herself on the other side of a certain line.'

'Yes.'

'Interesting. Thanks.' He stood up. 'You won't say anything, will you? Nothing may come of it, at least I hope not.'

He nodded, a little preoccupied, and walked away.

'Keep in touch,' said Joe anxiously. But Henry did not look round.

Joe walked back towards his office, wishing he could ride beside her, on a tired horse, with a tattered flag. When she swayed in her saddle, exhausted from the battle, he would slip to the ground and be at her side; no one else should support her to the tent and sleep across the entrance through the night while her resting soul renewed itself among its own vast ancient images; no one else in the morning should ride beside her when they went, refreshed, to renew the battle in the plain. Or he would stand up in court and plead for her life with such eloquence that the judge would weep. Then he felt ashamed, and wished his daydreams were not always about himself.

Henry suggested that Agatha should go to the cottage early.

'It will probably be the last time we can go before it gets too cold. Let George miss one day's school. They won't mind. He's only five. You take the car, and I'll come by train.'

'It seems rather extravagant,' said Agatha doubtfully.

'I can afford the fare for once. You can meet me at the station. It would do the children good to be there a bit longer this time.'

From his office he telephoned a neighbour of old Mrs Parker who lived in the village and sent a message asking her to go up to the cottage and light the fire and leave a few stores ready. She had done it before for them but they did not like to ask her too often because she was old and though she could sometimes get a lift from the woodmen, of whom her son was one, at other times she had to walk and it was a long way.

When Agatha arrived with the children and found the fire lit and everything made ready, she immediately thought, He must know that I am going to be caught. But it did not lessen her pleasure in the place.

She walked in the woods with the children, available to them in an emergency but in the meantime not listening.

When Lucy said 'Mummy?' she said 'Mn?' but then Lucy forgot what she had been going to say or was interrupted by George. Sometimes Lucy said 'Mummy?' again as if she had something really important to say, and Agatha said 'Mn?' again, and again nothing transpired. It was a routine she was used to and in which she could fulfil her obligations without interrupting her train of thought. Possibly Lucy's train of thought was not interrupted either, always supposing that she had one. Her consciousness seemed still to be almost exclusively occupied by her reactions, often extravagant, to the immediate moment. George, being older, was more given to philosophizing, and when he was alone with either of his parents for any length of time would produce in unhurried but continuous succession the results of his speculations, simple but well-formed concepts on most of the world's great questions, shining fishes from the clear waters of his mind. When he was with Lucy his conversation was on an altogether lower level. This afternoon they were being rabbits, with voices and sentiments of which any right-minded rabbit ought to have been ashamed. When the squeaks and baby talk penetrated to Agatha she said, 'Surely rabbits don't talk like that' in a shocked voice.

'They have witchy fluffy voices,' said Lucy sillily.

'For heaven's *sake.*'

But they had gambolled on ahead, stopping every now and then to waggle their bottoms, which presumably had witchy fluffy tails on them, and Agatha waited until they were out of earshot before following them down the field, hoping that by the time she caught up with them they might have moved on to some less objectionable fantasy.

They were going down to the old Timberwork mill, where the children liked climbing on the ruined walls. It was the first time they had been that way since Dora's death. The fact that Dora had been run over coalesced in her mind with her feeling that Henry must know more than she did about the police inquiry, and produced in her a feeling, not unfamiliar, of her own inadequacy, of there being really nothing else for her to do but take things quietly: she knew that there was a certain sense in which as far as the outside world was concerned she really had no idea how to behave. Henry, on the other hand, had.

The rough wood on the slope above the mill was neglected. Branches which had fallen in last winter's winds had not been cleared away for firewood: the undergrowth was thick and the paths hard to find. It was as if Conrad had not the heart to apply his science there, so near the scene of former disappointments. Elsewhere his woods were beautifully tended, his timber-growing a serious business. Rides were kept clear between plantations, the trees thinned and pruned; but here a thin uprooted wych-elm could lean across the path, held from falling completely by the branches of other trees which supported too huge a growth of old man's beard, whose abundance looked from a distance like a great fall of soft grey roses. Agatha paused, near a tangle of brambles from which a month or two earlier she had picked enough fruit for six pounds of blackberry jelly. She looked for late remnants but after the recent frosts there was nothing. She stood still and could just hear the children's voices. They had run on so far that they might already be down at the bottom, at the mill. Their voices came to her with a slight echo. Otherwise there was no sound except gentle continuous rustling, so much like rain falling on the trees that she looked up towards the grey sky; but it was only the last yellowish leaves falling all round her, singly and slowly through the damp windless air. Here all was well. For once she did not feel out of place.

She liked the feeling of her trousers over her stomach, pulled tight by her hands being in her pockets; the longer strides she had to take because her boots were rather big:

by such little things could messages of liberty be conveyed; also by the touch of damp air on her cheeks, the smell of leaves, moss, fungus, the slow sound of cawing rooks. Her sense of isolation was acceptable here, but must never be relished because that would be pride. There were so many errors into which she might fall, and the God in whom she did not believe had been besought for forgiveness so much lately that it had become a habit to have the words always somewhere near the topmost layer of her mind. If she were to be run over crossing a road she would die with such a shriek of 'Oh forgive me!' that everyone would be left wondering what horrible crime she had committed, not knowing how private were her sins.

One of them she had recently diagnosed for herself as displaced jealousy. Never having allowed herself to feel jealousy of Sally – or perhaps it would be more accurate to say, having most vigorously rejected, because it seemed to her so horrible, her jealousy of Sally – she had allowed the snake she held to recoil and feed on her restraining arm. That is to say, as well as the lowering of morale consequent upon her husband's having fallen in love with someone else she was suffering from an extra anxiety and self-hate which came from her absolute refusal to hate the husband and the someone else. She guessed that by now; and since she knew that the worst was over, that it was largely a question of time, of all three living it down, she sometimes consciously tried to dismiss Henry as selfish, Sally as vain and frivolous, by cursing them aloud. It did no good.

It was easier to believe the fault lay in her own over-estimate of what was to be expected from marriage. She had thought of it as some kind of Holy Grail, in the quest for which, that is to say in the daily renewal of the attempt to do it perfectly, self would be transcended and the soul satisfied. She could see that might be a terrible bore for someone who just wanted to be comfortable. She had no right to be demanding, must therefore adapt. But if, in adapting, a certain amount had to go, what was she left with? Her work was to rear her children, but to lose herself in them would be wrong, not to say impossible, feeling as she did the weight of her own personality. What else? These dripping woods.

She remembered reading about some clever person who had gone to Oxford or Cambridge at a young age and lived in keen daily expectation of meeting the really brilliant people. After a year or so he realized that the really brilliant people were himself and his friends: it was a severe disillusionment. In adult life Agatha had looked for the visions and the certainties; perhaps the visions and the certainties were only the vague intimations of her childhood. Which brought her back to the Mount Sorrel woods. And to those intimations for which she often had to wait so long and which alone had the power to renew themselves.

'Parthenogenesis,' she said, pronouncing the word pedantically, walking downhill now quite fast, her gumboots flumping against her legs, her hands still in her pockets. 'Love must commit parthenogenesis.'

She took her hands out of her pockets and began to run.

When she reached the mill she found that the children were climbing up the most dangerous part of the ruins, behind the mill, where the drawing offices and the canteen had been built on to the more solid eighteenth-century structure in about 1932. This part was mostly a heap of rubble now – willow herb and buddleia had had time to take a hold, a few rank elders too – but a couple of walls were still standing and there was scope for climbing.

'Be careful,' said Agatha but she did not call them down. She knew that Lucy would never pass George, and that George was really quite cautious. Little stones fell, dislodged.

'Careful,' said Lucy, losing her bravado.

If it should be necessary for me to wear an anonymous overall, thought Agatha, sitting down on a stone, and sew hemp with a huge needle in a line of other women, and be in a place where there is always the sound of echoing footsteps and clanging doors and perhaps shrieks, will it make me less ignorant or shall I not be able to bear it? A lot of women did it at the time of the suffragettes and they were not exactly criminals any more than I am. But I have such bruises in my heart where I feel for my children, I cannot bear much pain in that particular area.

She thought she remembered hearing that it always smelt of urine in prison. Every morning she would have to tear open with bleeding fingers the iron curtains which would have closed over her heart in the night, because if once she left them closed she would have failed. But she had had a little practice.

'Listen, children.' It would be easy to prepare them now. She knew she could do it with such confidence that they would be able to accept it, in the easy way of children, but she did not want to do it unless she was more sure than she was at the moment that it would be necessary. 'Listen. I've got a good idea. We'll go back by the village and buy some doughnuts for tea. Then we'll go home and make the house really warm and I'll tell you a long story.'

'Really long?'

'Really long.'

Because although she was full of doubt and difficulty she was at the same time so strong she was sometimes afraid of breaking things just by looking at them, which was why she had to be especially careful to make sure that her glance should be benign.

'By the time you get this,' wrote Paul, on a dark afternoon – only half-past two and already it felt like evening, the air through the window, which he was keeping open now through claustrophobia, soft with rain and milder than lately, bearing a faint smell of the bonfires in surrounding back gardens where the fallen leaves and uprooted weeds smouldered after the weekend's work; not that the house he was in had anything to contribute in that way, having sacrificed its garden to the structure in which he found himself, the doubtful advantage of the spare bedroom – 'I shall be on the move. You can think of me as feeling a physical weight removed, the weight of this foul little house, these pebble-papered walls, my thoughts. I've had enough.

'I got her to buy me an envelope and a stamp and when they come to fetch me the first thing I'll do will be to find a post-box, then you'll know I'm on my way out of the country – they seemed to think when they were bringing me here it would be by boat but they don't tell me much – I don't want to know really, just so long as they get me out. She came in yesterday and said, "He says tomorrow or the next day." I'm afraid I lost my nerve for the first time, I screamed at her, or at least I started to scream and then I remembered the neighbours so I whispered – I said, "Tell him he bloody makes it tomorrow or I'll kill him," and all that sort of stuff; rather shaming, I suppose, but it's dying a slow death being in this room. I said, "Tell him my sister will give him some more money if he makes it tomorrow instead of the next day." I hope to God there wasn't anyone in the next-door house who could have heard, I think they go out all day. You won't mind if he comes to you for more

money, will you? It's that or madness, I can tell you. Not
that he will, I'm sure he was going to come today anyway.

'So when you get this you'll know it's worked and I
haven't had to use my last resort. Oh yes, I've got that too,
I thought of everything. I bloody nearly used it yesterday
too – darkest hours before dawn and all that. I thought they
were coming, you see, and when she said tomorrow or the
next day I thought, rather a quick death than this slow one,
and I nearly swallowed the thing. But I didn't. And if you
get this letter we can both forget about all that because it
will be a letter of triumph, won't it?

'Thanks for getting me out. I couldn't have stood it. I'm
not very strong in any way. You know that. Other people
haven't always known it because of my cutting tongue. But
if people always treat you as if you were nasty, what can
you do but pretend you're being nasty on purpose?

'You on the other hand are beginning to get a reputation
for being nice. So you'll be able to pretend you're being
nice on purpose. But I know you're not really all that nice.
You're too strong, for one thing. You try to tone yourself
down all the time, don't you, so as not to intimidate people.
But I know. You'd like to gather everything and everyone into your own atmosphere and make them be happy
in your own way – you're so sure it's the only right one.
That's why Henry has to get away from you sometimes, to
breathe another atmosphere. You think he's a rat for being
unfaithful to you. He has to, to keep the balance. You're
too bossy, even though you never say a word.

'I've always been very perceptive. The trouble is I've
so far missed my vocation. I ought to have been a writer,
a novelist. Novelists have always been a venal lot, never
outstanding for moral worth, often dishonest, certainly
vain, silly, self-centred, snobbish and peculiar in their sexual

habits. I should be perfectly convincing as a novelist. So as well as a sort of semi-fictionalized autobiography – more or less a new form I've worked out, a bit like Christopher Isherwood with a dash of Virginia Woolf – and perhaps those articles for *Encounter* that I told you about, I'm going to do a comic novel – Evelyn Waugh rather – which incidentally will be a *roman à clef* showing up Conrad's hypocrisy – and that in itself will be rather a lark because it will appear under a pseudonym and won't half set people guessing. Then of course we can leak out the sensational truth. I mean, I might as well cash in on my unsought fame, mightn't I? I thought of the plot last night – I haven't been sleeping well – it just about saved me from the abyss of despair, I can tell you – and now I'm full of optimism again as you can see – they can't keep me down. To add a bit of spice I'm giving Conrad an incestuous relationship with our mother, but otherwise it's all true, virtually. I'm going to have a –'

But there were footsteps on the stairs. He listened. Police. Two policemen. Heavy feet. A pause. The door quietly opened.

'They're here,' she said.

He was white.

'Why?'

'To take you.'

'Who?'

She stepped aside and the men in belted overcoats came in.

'Time to go.'

'Thank God. I thought you were the police.'

He scrawled on the bottom of the page, his hand shaking violently, 'They've come – in haste – imagine my joy – Paul.'

He folded the bulky letter clumsily and was stuffing it into the envelope as he followed the man out of the room and down the stairs.

Conrad had never much liked Penelope Waring. He thought of her as one of Judith's worldly friends, and tried to forget that at one time she had also been a friend of Orlando's, and that indeed when he had first met Orlando he had appeared to be some kind of protégé of Penelope's. It was a long time ago. When one was young one had relationships with women whom one did not necessarily exactly like. Before one was married of course. The fact that in Orlando's case one had had a few relationships with women one might or might not exactly have liked after one was married was an inconvenience Conrad was not prepared to entertain. More and more he found loose morals hard to tolerate. He tried to tolerate them – he believed it his Christian duty to do so – but he really rather hated all that sort of thing. Why did people not concentrate on doing a useful job of work instead? Even his occasional visits to the select establishment in Curzon Street which, undertaken at first from loneliness and need, had come to be no more than a precaution against some kind of imaginable charge at Heaven's gate of having been a prig, were now very rare indeed. So there were one or two aspects of periods of Orlando's life – aspects which had never anyway been obtrusive, since Orlando had not been the kind of person thoughtlessly to give offence – which Conrad preferred to forget. Orlando was his friend; Alexandra, the Field-Marshal's daughter, his short-lived love. They were all he had in the way of the deepest affections and he was not going to let the memory of either be spoilt.

It was for Orlando's sake that he went to Penelope Waring's cocktail party, because for Orlando's sake he felt he ought to do something about Imogen, and Imogen had said she couldn't possibly go without him, she wouldn't know a soul. He had happened to see Penelope a week or so before the party. She had been having lunch in the House of Lords with a peer he particularly disliked, a red-faced bucolic-looking ass whose only interest was in the breeding of racehorses and who was seldom seen in the House of Lords and never in the actual Debating Chamber.

Penelope had hurried over to talk to him with such enthusiasm that he almost forgot for the moment that he did not like her. She was astonishingly well preserved. She must be well over sixty by now and yet she maintained a genuine prettiness. Her hair was neatly waved and curled just as it had been in the thirties – dyed of course by now but well done, so that the ash blonde was only just distinguishable from a possibly more appropriate grey – and her face had still a kind of pink and white softness about it.

She was wearing brown velvet and a pale pink blouse with some sort of scarf effect round the neck. She carried a little fur – sable probably – and diffused, but not too strongly, expensive scent.

'Such *years* –' she said. 'You know we saw darling Orlando quite soon before he died, looking so beautiful and young I couldn't believe it when I read it. I wish we could have a long talk.' She lowered her voice. 'Too boring, old Buffy, isn't he? But, my dear, we're in the racing world now. Guy's dotty about it. We must have a talk about the old days. Oh dear, Buffpots is blowing down his whiskers, I'd better go. Come to my party, now do, and bring that incredible Imogen. I saw her the other night – too beautiful for words – who's she going to marry?'

'She's still very young.'

'She was with the most terrible cad the other night. I don't know many young these days but the people I was with said he was no good at all. I've got several eligibles coming. Andrew Cathcart for instance. Now wouldn't that be suitable? A place, rolling in money, and too good-looking and sweet for words. Bring her along and I'll do the rest. He won't be able to resist her.'

Afterwards Conrad had thought that perhaps he ought to have done more for Imogen. It had not been enough to have once taken her to a Buckingham Palace Garden Party. Who else had she got to see that she met nice people and all that sort of thing? Agatha was no help. Of course matchmaking in Penelope Waring's blatant sort of way was quite ridiculous, but on the other hand if she did happen to take an interest in Imogen and introduce her to a few people, what harm could there be in that?

So they drove up together in a taxi to Wilton Crescent, both preoccupied by concerns very far removed from anything to do with Imogen's chances in the marriage market, though it was with this in mind that Conrad had not been able to repress a slight feeling of irritation at noticing that she was not looking her best. Her face was too pale and tense, lacking its usual serenity, and her constant fiddling with anything which could keep her fingers occupied, whether bracelets or pearls or the ends of her own hair, was even more noticeable than usual.

'I may have to leave you,' he said. 'There's rather a lot on.'

She looked at him as if she was afraid of having offended him.

'Yes,' she said humbly.

'One has to show a bit of solidarity,' he said defensively. 'I shall probably have to speak later on. I'm thankful I'm not in the Commons. Heaven knows what's happened to the level of debate in this Parliament. The Labour people descend to personal abuse in the most improper way.'

'Why are they so cross?'

'Cold feet. They were supporting Eden up to the hilt a day or two ago. Now suddenly they're squealing and talking about the United Nations. As if that could possibly do anything effective at this stage.'

'Is there a war on or something then? I mean, I haven't really read the papers.'

'Police action, that's all. Somebody's got to take a firm line.'

'Oh yes.'

'They blame the Government for not taking a firm enough line with Hitler – though no one would have supported a strong line at the one moment when it might have worked, right back in 1936 over the Rhineland – and then they complain when it does take a strong line with Nasser.'

'But I thought Nasser was in Egypt,' said Imogen, looking alert.

'Well, he is, yes,' said Conrad, rather taken aback.

'Anyway I'm sure you're doing the right thing, Uncle Conrad.'

'It's not up to me exactly. It's not my sphere, I can merely advise in general terms, put my point of view and so on, but my prime responsibility is not in foreign affairs or defence these days. The point is, though, that I have faith in my colleagues who do have the prime responsibility. There's such a thing as loyalty, you know.'

'Yes.' She ached from keeping still, from not running away, not crying out, not allowing herself to think. Two days of it she'd had. But loyalty. Loyalty meant standing by your sister even when you thought that what she was doing was rash, even wrong. Everybody knew what loyalty meant. But it would have happened anyway. The Inspector had said they'd known already that Agatha had had something to do with it. If something awful did happen, it would have been bound to have happened anyway. No one need ever know that she had had anything to do with it. If Agatha did know she would forgive her. I'm only quite young, she thought, getting out of the taxi; if I'd been older I'd probably have known what to do.

'Oh lovely, no, I adore champagne,' though it gives me a headache and I'm going to drink too much out of nerves. 'What a lot of people. Oh yes, I expect I do know some of them. I work on a magazine. Yes, it is, super fun. Oh no, not at all. Everyone's terribly kind.'

'– half-witted, I'm afraid. The sister's rather nice.'

They couldn't be talking about her, they couldn't. They wouldn't, not so close. There must be other half-witted people with rather nice sisters.

'– to be introduced to your beautiful niece –'

But he was a thousand years old, talking in terrifying level tones, his face much too close to hers. 'The Royal Family are an anachronism, don't you agree?'

'Oh *yes*. Well, except I did think the Coronation was rather super.'

'I expect you're part of the Princess Margaret set.'

'Oh *no* –'

'I don't think much of them, do you? Rather brainless, don't you agree?'

'Well. I don't know really, I mean they couldn't possibly be more brainless than I am. Are you someone terribly important?'

'I've been called one of the most acute financial brains in the City. It may be an exaggeration. That's how I came across our host. Wrong about everything else but right about money. Interesting, don't you agree?'

'Fascinating.'

'Your uncle's a very interesting man. He hasn't yet recognized that this country's a third-rate power. But he's very much respected. One of the most respected men in public life, don't you agree?'

Imogen agreed.

'... and Mr Carey the ruthless financier. You're not to monopolize the prettiest girl in the room in your ruthless financial way. Isn't she divine? She's turned down all the most eligible men in London, Andrew, so it's up to you. Come along now, Mr Carey, I'm going to find something much more suitable for you.'

'I must say I do admire that sort of hostess, don't you? It's rather gone out these days, that sort of thing.'

'Yes, I suppose so. It's a bit embarrassing though. I don't think I've turned down any eligible men really. Anyway I never know whether they're eligible or not.'

'That's where someone like Penelope Waring is so useful. She tells you.'

'Yes, but she probably does it in front of them and that's enough to paralyse anyone with shyness –'

'Where's your uncle, my dear? He's wanted on the telephone.' It was Guy Waring, red-faced, ageing, finding the party rather hard going.

'He's over there somewhere, I think. Yes, there. Oh dear.'

'What's the matter?' asked the eligible young man.

'Uncle Conrad's wanted on the telephone.'

'Was he expecting some bad news?'

'Oh no. I mean perhaps he was. I don't know.'

'Are you sure you're feeling all right?'

'Oh yes, it's just – I think I'd better go and see what it is.'

She began to push her way across the room. The eligible young man watched her for a moment but his brief spark of curiosity was quickly extinguished by the approach of an elegant married lady with a satisfactory little scandal to relate.

By the time Imogen found her way to Conrad's side he was talking to a fat man with a moustache – in fact the same peer with whom he had seen Penelope and whom he had been unable to avoid as he came back into the room after talking on the telephone.

'Splendid,' the fat peer was saying. 'Simply splendid of Anthony. As soon as I heard in the Club I sent him a case of champagne and an invitation to shoot. "The sort of leadership we need," I said on my card.'

'I don't suppose the Prime Minister has much time for shooting at the moment,' said Conrad coldly.

'Hasn't he? Is he not much of a shot then? Good Lord, hadn't thought of that. Don't want the fellow if he's not a decent shot. I mean, can't have him banging all over the place, can I, even if he is the Prime Minister.'

'I expect the problem will solve itself. I must be on my way.'

'Can I come with you, Uncle Conrad? I've got to go now too.'

'Don't you want to stay a little longer?' Not a success then, he thought. 'All right, I'll get you a taxi.'

As they walked out on to the pavement and into the cold dark air she said, 'Was it anything urgent?'

He put his hand under her elbow, guiding her towards Belgrave Square in search of a taxi.

'It was Skarrett. They think they're on to something. I'd asked him to keep me informed at every step. They think he's in Swindon. They're surrounding the house now.'

'Now?'

'He's going to telephone me at the House of Lords as soon as he has anything more to tell me.'

'Will you let me know? I'll be at the flat.'

'Yes. Don't worry. It will be a relief when he's caught. It will be over then.'

'Will it? I mean, yes.'

She could not talk about Agatha.

'Thank you for taking me to the party.'

'It wasn't very interesting, I'm afraid.'

'I don't think I really awfully like those sort of people.'

'I know what you mean. Some of them are all right of course.'

'Oh yes.'

'I suppose it's good for one to go outside one's own set every now and then. I have such a round of official dos, in official circles I suppose one would say. Official circles are very small.'

'Yes, I suppose so.'

'Anyway one certainly gathers that the vast mass of public opinion is solidly behind the Government over this Suez thing.'

'Oh yes, I'm sure it is.'

'Not that I suppose one could call that party the vast mass of public opinion. But they must be fairly representative.'

'Oh yes, they must be.'

He saw a taxi and waved to it to stop. When Imogen was inside he banged the door briskly and stepped back on to the pavement with a cheerful wave. She waved back, smiling palely through the window and the darkness. Poor little Imogen, he thought.

Paul was thinking that really the whole thing had been too much for him. He was terribly tired. In the grey cold morning light, waiting to show his forged passport and walk on to the boat which was to take him to freedom, he had no fear left, no nerves at all, was conscious of nothing but indigestion and an iron-grey sky. Overtired. Suddenly he remembered his mother sitting down on the sofa at Wood Hill, stretching out her long legs in front of her on to the stool with the tapestry seat which she had embroidered herself and saying, 'I'm a bit overdone,' and Orlando laughing and explaining that when you had been overdoing things you didn't linguistically speaking become overdone, like a piece of roast beef. But perhaps she had used the phrase often, that he should remember it so clearly, and her sitting on the sofa there and her shoes with their three straps which buttoned and her dark silk stockings, a striped jumper thing belted round the waist, the belt of the same material fastened with a small tortoiseshell buckle, a pleated skirt and the smell of her scent, always the same, always redolent of everything most longed for and most elusive.

'We'll get some coffee on the boat.'

They had said to talk naturally, going through the barrier, and besides he did not want to think about his mother. Indigestion, grey sky, that was all. Also a familiar, settled, inconsolable, uncomprehending, central grief; but he had never been without that.

Even when he saw the four tough-looking individuals waiting beside the two passport officials he thought nothing of it. It was not that sort of morning, everything so drab, so understated, not a morning for dramatics.

«Morning.' Neither cheerful nor uncheerful, secure in his blackened hair, his horn-rimmed spectacles. It was all organized.

Even when they said, 'Do you mind stepping this way?' he did not bother to look at his companion (one of them was travelling with him) for guidance or for reassurance. Obviously it was all meant to be like this, otherwise everyone would not be so calm; probably this was some prearranged manoeuvre to get them on to the boat as quickly as possible. He followed, firm steps, grey sky, into a grey room. And one of them began to speak, using words he had heard before, using his own name, and warning him that anything he said would be taken down and –

Even then he was only able half to take it in. The full extent of the disaster was more than he could absorb. This was something that had been arranged, and when it happened there was something that he had to do. That had been arranged too and when he did it everything would be all right. So he did it.

They had not been on the look-out for it. When he suddenly arched over backwards, at the same time giving way at the knees, as if an invisible rope round his neck had been pulled extremely sharply from behind him at the same time as a brutal knee had been shoved into the small of his back, they were taken completely by surprise. The two nearest to him moved towards him, then stopped.

The one who had been charging him said, 'Christ.'

They stood watching, shocked. He had done himself an incredible violence. He clawed the air with twisted hands, choking, then fell to the ground, eyes turning backwards into his head, a blackened tongue, foaming saliva turning pink. He breathed in retches, twisting to and fro on the dusty floor, jerking and mercifully slowing, quietening, mercifully still.

There was silence. They stood there, staring, as if afraid it all might start again.

'Swallowed something,' said one of them superfluously.

Having no telephone, Agatha received Paul's letter before the news of his death. It was Saturday. Conrad, who had been told what had happened by Inspector Skarrett early that morning, was in London, the political situation being such that for once he was unable to get away to Mount Sorrel for the weekend. Henry was to arrive by train later. He had said that he had to work late at the office and had therefore not been able to come down on Friday evening. He had never worked late at the office in his life, and Agatha assumed he was seeing Sally and was hurt that he had used such a corny excuse. In fact he was spending the evening with Joe, whom he had taken completely into his confidence: if Agatha were to be arrested he wanted to be able to present her with a complete plan, not only for her best defence but for the care of the children in her absence and even for what they should do on her release. He thought that Agatha was as yet ignorant of how close the danger might be, and preferred to leave her so and to discuss things instead with Joe.

So Agatha read Paul's letter alone, in the kitchen of the cottage, while the children played outside; and she went through all the emotions she usually did go through in any confrontation with Paul: irritation, impatience, disgust, as well as sudden optimism, amusement and affection. 'Imagine my joy,' he had written at the end. The phrase might have had an ironic tone, but she did not believe he had meant it like that, she believed he had written it in a burst of hope and excitement, a child on an adventure using words he had heard from a grown-up, creating an unintentionally comic effect. She found it very moving – 'imagine my joy' – poor Paul. Thinking of him as free, as having escaped, she could only wonder how he would manage, how he could possibly find the discipline to turn his fantasies into any kind of book, whether he would survive, whether he would take to drink.

Mrs Parker, pushing open the door unexpectedly, thought how pale she looked, and tired; she often did. Of course the family had all taken it hard, that wretched boy, anybody could have told them he would never be any good, getting himself sent to prison like that; and then her living in London with two children, she wouldn't like to do that herself, and a difficult husband maybe for all his charm, and then losing the little dog like that the other day, a shame.

'I've a message for you. I saw Bob in the village going to drive up with it and I said, "You take me up to the top and I'll go on down with the message and then I can put in an hour or two down there, cleaning up and that." There's probably a bit of washing too, isn't there? I know what it is.'

'Don't bother, Mrs Parker. Aren't you busy?'

'He's out all day today. I don't mind giving you a hand. Saves me on Monday, doesn't it, if I come to have a clean-round when you've gone. Here I am putting on the kettle for a cup of tea anyway so there's no stopping me now. Oh and the message before I forget. Your uncle's coming down late tonight and he wants to see you tomorrow after ten o'clock church because he's got to go straight back to London.'

'Ten o'clock church,' Agatha repeated stupidly.

'First Sunday in the month, they're doing that now, I forget why. Anyway that was the message. Shocking, isn't it, him having to be away all the time like that. He never used to be away that much. Have a cup of tea yourself, why not? You look paler even than when I came in and I thought then you were looking tired. You remember Jen, Stephen's niece that looked after you?'

'Do you ever see her?'

'Ran into her in Marks and Spencer's in Bath last week. I don't often see her, she lives towards Cranmore, married a farmer, doing very well, she said. She certainly looked it. Three times the size she used to be.'

'Did she have children?'

'Four. Nearly grown up the boy must be. She had the little one with her, lovely little boy he was.'

'How old?'

'Six or seven. She was always good with children. Though I often think, nice as her own kids are, it was you got the real caring for. It's different when you're busy and got several. She'd nothing else to do when she was looking after you. We all noticed it. She was only a child herself really, but she'd have done anything for you.'

'Would she?' said Agatha, trying to imagine it.

'Not that she spoiled you. She was quite strict sometimes. You had to have nice manners and that. And when you had one of your temper tantrums she'd just stand there, that patient, and wait until you'd finished. Then you used to have to make it up with her. She wouldn't speak to you for a bit afterwards, it used to really worry you.'

'I remember her quite clearly, but not what she looked like. I suppose I was still very young when she left. I remember nothing but good things about her. All the happiness of my childhood really was with her. Except for sometimes when my father came and played with me. I was only her job. It was awfully nice of her to bother with me as much as that.'

'There was no one else bothering,' said Mrs Parker, who had never much cared for Agatha's mother. 'Anyway she was that sort. You get them like that sometimes, you can tell them anywhere.'

'Yes. Paul didn't have that. No one breathed the breath of life into him like that. He had that awful nanny.'

'That nanny,' said Mrs Parker happily, beginning to slosh about in the sink. 'Now she really was a shocker.'

Agatha usually enjoyed Mrs Parker's terrible tales about Nanny, but today they reminded her too strongly of Paul's troubles and of how early they had begun. On the pretext of needing to collect some firewood she went out of the house and, calling to the children to come with her, set off into the woods.

'When's Daddy coming?'

'Twelve o'clock. We'll go and meet him.'

'Can we go on to the platform and see the train?'

'Yes, if we're there in time.'

'Good.'

They ran ahead of her, forgetting they were supposed to be collecting wood.

'We're cowboys. I'm the captain and you're the sergeant.'

'I don't want to be the sergeant.'

'You can be the sergeant in command of the second rank.'

'I'm called Sergeant Bacon.'

'OK. All troops advance NOW.'

'Second rank ADVANCE.'

'Sergeant Bacon, please take your men over there and form emplacements.'

'Second rank ADVANCE. Form PLACEMENTS.'
Lucy skipped past Agatha. 'I'm forming placements,' she
said, pausing to roll her eyes in a far from military manner.
It was something she had just learnt to do; the effect veered
between lunacy and extreme sophistication.

Sally cried, wanting to go to Hungary.

'In the first place I'm not going to Hungary,' said Joe
patiently. 'It's impossible to get in. The roads from Austria
have been closed.'

'You just don't understand me. You think I'd be in the
way or have hysterics or something.'

'I think you'd be bored, that's all, and cold and
uncomfortable.'

'Women can stand cold much better than men. It's been
scientifically proved.'

'It may be all a false alarm. Nothing may happen.'

'Of course something's going to happen. All those tanks
after they said they were withdrawing.'

'Here, have a hanky. I'll send for you, if it goes on. When
I see what it's like.'

'I don't want to be sent for. I want to come with you. It
won't go on. England and America will stop it.'

'How? They won't risk a world war.'

'Well, moral pressure or something.'

'What kind of moral pressure can we exert when we're
doing the same thing ourselves in Egypt?'

'Oh Joe, how can you say that? It's quite different. We've
got right on our side.'

'Oh yes, I forgot.'

'Please let me come. I want to prove myself. I want to
bend over all those bleeding revolutionaries, deftly bandag-
ing. Honestly I'd be so good at it.'

'There might not be any bleeding revolutionaries. They might not resist. Anyway, listen, there's something else. This is the real reason why I want you to stay here. I can't tell you why, and I don't want you to ask me or say a word about it to anyone else, but I think Henry might need some help soon.'

'Henry? Whatever for?'

'I said don't ask.'

'I hate mysteries.' But she dabbed her face half-heartedly with his handkerchief – the tears had left no trace – and leant back against the pillows of his bed. They were in his warm little room, drinking tea. 'Don't say Agatha's leaving. He'll fall apart, you know.'

'That's not what you were saying a few days ago.'

'I thought I could take him on myself then. You changed all that. You completely changed my view of myself. It's a terrible responsibility for you. But I've always known he was hopelessly weak.'

'I didn't tell you that.'

'No, but he is.'

'I don't agree with you. I think that in some ways he's very strong. He has one of the strongest – I don't know what to call it – personal atmosphere, personality, I suppose – one of the strongest personalities of anyone I know. His trouble is that his father thinks he ought to be an A D C to the Governor General of Australia and won't realize that all that sort of thing is irrelevant, is fading away.'

'What a pity.'

'We're quite lucky, you and I, not to be more upper-class.'

'I think I am rather upper-class. I could pass as an aristocrat, couldn't I?'

He looked at her thoughtfully and then said, 'Not – quite,' which made her laugh.

'Besides,' he went on, 'that's different. To choose to be an aristocrat is quite different from being born one. We're coming to a time when everyone, including the aristocracy, is going to pretend the aristocracy doesn't exist. To choose to be an aristocrat at such a time is a thoroughly intelligent and amusing thing to do. You couldn't do it if you had been born one.'

'Really? Could I have done it if I had married Henry?'

'It would have been unutterably banal.'

'I adore you. I wish you would talk for ever. Which reminds me, I must go. I'm meeting Johnny. I'll ring you up later and let you know how it goes.' She stood up and reached for her coat. 'I'll look after Henry then, and you can look after the Hungarians, but not for long. You must come back quickly so that we can go on our jaunt to Paris and become terribly sophisticated.'

He saw her to the door and hurried back upstairs. Then he opened a drawer and took out the equipment which he had stuffed into it as Sally arrived: a sleeping bag, a box of medical supplies, tins of food and an empty haversack. Into this last he began to put in a random selection of clothes. He was smiling. Sally in a Dormobile with five men. The imagination boggled.

Henry arrived on the evening train, bringing Imogen with him.

As soon as she saw Imogen, Agatha knew that something had happened, but because she had brought the children with her to meet the train she did not like to ask what it was. It was only back at the cottage, when Imogen with slightly ostentatious helpfulness had hurried the children off for a bath and a really long story, that Henry was able to tell her about Paul's death.

Imogen was pleased to have something to do. As soon as she had heard what had happened, she had had a feeling of crisis – of Agatha, whether or not betrayed, needing her help – and a corresponding feeling of being able to cope, because at least she could cook, clean and look after the children. On the way down in the train it had suddenly seemed to her that all her life what she had really wanted to be was a nurse, and she had absolutely made up her mind that the minute the present crisis was over, and when she was quite sure that Agatha did not need her, she was going to start training. She would write off as soon as possible for details. She only hoped to goodness you didn't need School Cert. Maths to be accepted. In the meantime the resolution made gave her an unaccustomed feeling of stability.

'Instead of doing any good, I brought about his death,' said Agatha.

'You did it because you thought he couldn't bear life in prison. I don't think he could. I think he would rather have been dead.'

She brought out the letter and handed it over to him.

'It came this morning.'

Henry began to look through it, turning over the pages rather quickly, not liking the tone of it. It was too like Paul.

'He says at the end about the pill he had,' said Agatha.

Henry looked at the end of the letter.

'Poor Paul,' said Agatha as he read. She looked across at him reading and remembered what else came towards the end of the letter. 'He wrote something about us.'

She was determined to find some consolation other than the bleak consideration that he was better dead.

'He did a good thing. He sent me a really helpful message. Read it. About you and me and me being so bossy and you having to get away from me. Of course he's quite right. I am like that and I shouldn't be. That was a good thing he did, to tell me that.'

To Henry what Paul had written seemed neither true nor untrue, of no interest really, but he did not say so.

'Are they very quick, those pills, cyanide or something?' she asked.

'A few seconds, no more.'

They sat in silence on either side of the fire. They had never managed to get the lighting quite right in the sitting-room of the cottage; there was a lamp by which you could read if you sat beside it, but the rest of the room was shadowy except for the glow from the fire. Agatha felt that she loved Henry, with a love so detached as to be quite close to indifference and yet at the same time it was totally involved, the opposite of indifference. She breathed gently, hoping the feeling would not fade, and hoping he would not say anything, or move. Sometimes he spoilt things by what seemed to her a false gesture, a sentimentality This time he did nothing. She added gratitude to the rest.

Conrad, coming into church late and preoccupied, hurrying up the aisle to his accustomed place in the front pew, was shocked to see Agatha and Henry standing side by side – the first hymn was just beginning – in a pew towards the back of the church. Immediately afterwards he was thoroughly annoyed to see the broad tweed-begirt backview of Daintry a little further up the church; he was not a regular church-goer – what on earth had possessed him to come today of all days? As for the effrontery of Agatha and Henry, whom he knew perfectly well to be heathens – Henry, what's more, if not Agatha, must certainly have a very good idea as to why he had asked to see her afterwards – the whole thing was extremely unfortunate and unpleasant, and, kneeling down for a moment before standing up to join in the hymn, he was so angry, that he muttered, 'Bloody cheek!', meaning it to apply to all of them. Fortunately there was no one near enough to overhear. The church, as usual, was three-quarters empty – which made it worse of course, because when the time came for him to read the lessons he would have to face a congregation in which these three unwelcome faces would be unnecessarily obvious.

'Ransomed, healed, restored, forgiven,' he sang mechanically, thinking, Why should Agatha and Henry be here, what's their game, are they trying to curry favour?

In a way they were trying to curry favour, not so much by appearing in church as by not keeping Conrad waiting afterwards. If they were there, they ran no risk of misjudging the length of the service. They knew that Conrad would be going back to London as soon as possible. Indeed, having read in the morning papers that there were to be Cabinet meetings all day to deal with the Egyptian crisis, they had hoped he might have been prevented from leaving London at all. His presence showed them that things were serious. On that particular Sunday morning it was easy to believe. They both had indigestion. They both, at about the same moment, tried to remember whether Church always gave them indigestion. Neither retained the thought long enough to answer the question; but a truthful answer would in both cases have been in the negative; apprehension was the trouble, and the feeling, until then familiar to both only in the context of childbirth, of being caught in the current of inexorable events. Paul had swallowed poison; it seemed that in the streets of a town not known to either of them men and women were throwing themselves at moving tanks; it was to be expected that upon Agatha and Henry too some punishment should be visited.

Henry's anxiety was largely for Agatha, that she should be spared excesses of grief or anger, but he also dreaded the interview with Conrad on his own account because he was afraid of his father. He thought that Conrad probably knew about Agatha's part in Paul's escape and that the police probably knew about it too. He hoped that Paul's death would be seen to make any legal prosecution of Agatha unnecessary, but he was not confident. Presumably, however, it was for the police to decide whether or not to prosecute and he could not believe that Conrad was without influence on their decision. What he could believe very easily was that Conrad might exact some private penalty of his own, and that at very least there would be a lengthy scolding which would infuriate Agatha. But we are not children, he was thinking, we can go away, after this morning we need never see him again if we don't want to.

Conrad faced them to read the first lesson. The Vicar leant back in his seat behind him, stiffly because childhood polio had left him with both legs in irons and they were difficult to manipulate in the constricted space of a pew. Sunlight infiltrated; two pale shafts, in -which suspended dust was slowly moving, fell on to two empty pews. Agatha, contemplating Daintry's back through one of them, allowed her thoughts to float, like the dust in the sunlight. Old Testament words sounded doom. Daintry's daughter Serena, Paul's wife, had married again, featured in a *Taller* photograph and a feathered hat, petrified perhaps in both for ever, for Agatha had never seen her again. Orlando had once told her that Daintry had said of Paul that he would sell his own grandmother even if he didn't need the money. It was in Italy that he had told her that, where their understanding had been so complete. I am only made, she thought, of what has been put into me by him, who for all his affection for Conrad would have been on my side now, so that I am only following on from him, and from the other mostly forgotten influences of my childhood which have given me the lens through which I focus, so that what surrounds me is not a disconnected blur but a system of signals; other people must see other signals, but I cannot change my lens now and I believe it is the one I would have chosen had I been able to choose. I can only focus as clearly as I can with what equipment I have and in the meantime and for no good reason I may suddenly be required to sing. But she could not remember the psalm and had no prayer-book, so sang 'Der der der' not very well in tune, causing Henry to look at her in surprise. The choir was weak and Daintry no singer; there was old Miss Harrison, catlike at the back, and a voice or two elsewhere, casual and behind the organ-beat, but Agatha was not concerned, thinking about truth and death. And Conrad faced them again, reconciled to a service which for him today was a form observed and no more. He knew he was in a bad temper, or, to put it another way, weighed down by worry – and going to church as often as he did he could hardly expect to feel close to God every time. He wanted to get through with it – Skarrett would be waiting after all – the sooner it was all dealt with the better, so that he could get back to London and his proper duties in this time of crisis, with the Press being utterly unreliable, and woolly left-wing intellectuals whining, and Gaitskell, thank goodness, making an ass of himself, but Bevan, one had to admit, doing the icy contempt bit really quite well. Just let them try, that was all, let them try, the ones who snap at our heels, worry our trouser-legs, yapping abuse, let them try to bear the responsibility, the weight, the incredible complexity of things which we honourable men to the best of our abilities lend our experience and skill towards trying to understand. Who says we're bloody perfect?

Closing the heavy Bible, he looked across the golden eagle's head of the lectern straight down the aisle at Agatha. Shame on you, he thought. Away on a stream of her own thoughts, she had caught only a word or two of what he had been reading and had swept them into her own flow to confirm her purposes. She answered his look with a serenely preoccupied gaze which by no means improved his mood. Henry, on the other hand, rising slowly to his feet beside her for another psalm thought, Christ, he's terrifying.

Daintry, also looking at Conrad, was thinking what a fine English gentleman he was. Daintry was in that sort of mood, benign, a little nostalgic, but full of confidence in the future. He had come to church because he wanted to have a word with the Vicar afterwards and he had not expected to see Conrad. He thought it splendid of Conrad not to give up reading the lesson in his village church because of other business to attend to. What an upright fellow he was, bit cold of course, not much of the old *joie de vivre*. That was what he himself had always had, *joie de vivre*, no one could deny that, and now, just as it was all beginning to go a bit stale, now that he'd got so much that he'd wanted, money, success, power, two stuffed tigers in his front hall, along had come good old Denise to make life worth living again.

This was the news he broke to Conrad outside the church as the sparse congregation filed out into the wintry sunshine.

'Congratulate me,' he said. 'I'm getting spliced.'

'Congratulations,' said Conrad, preoccupied, looking gravely towards Agatha and Henry, who had joined them.

'Super girl, half my age, God knows why she's taking me on. Denise Cornwall-Cope, you probably know her, she's been around a bit. Lovely creature, my type, not too small. I can't take those skinny Audrey Hepburn types. Anyway I knew you'd be pleased. Tell me.' And as Conrad had already turned towards the path which led to his own house, gesturing to Agatha and Henry to come with him, Daintry took his arm and walked with him along it. 'This vicar, is he a fairly broad-minded sort of chap? We've both been married before and quite frankly a Registry Office is good enough for me, but Denise thinks she'd like a church wedding with all the trimmings. He'll do it, won't he?'

'You'd have to discuss it with him. He's very easy to talk to.'

'Put in a word for me, there's a good chap. He'll take it from you. And, after all, you know a good deal about my business morals after what we went through over those takeovers. A takeover of a family firm and still to be on speaking terms – a triumph I call that, a credit to both of us, what? Incidentally' – here he half-turned, reached out for Agatha's hand and drew her close beside him, tucking her arm under his, so that she and Conrad were borne forward together, reluctantly linked by his substantial form and followed by Henry, frowning – 'I've written to you both. You'll get the letters. I was bloody sorry to read in the papers about Paul. Poor wretched chap. I liked him well enough, you know, in spite of everything. We got on very well at one time before he turned against me. He was just bent, that's all. But you couldn't help liking him at times. Rotten luck for you all. But don't forget you've got friends.'

They had reached the door into the Mount Sorrel garden. 'Well,' said Daintry, letting go of both their arms, 'that's it then.' He suddenly gave Conrad a hearty thump on the back. 'Keep up the good work!' Conrad coughed, taken by surprise. 'Show those gyppos where they get off!' He lowered his voice. 'And if he wants anything – you know, new heating system, organ doing over – I did think of offering to do something about the legs, but it's a bit delicate – a new pair of calipers or something, they can do wonders with some of these new materials – so much lighter. Anyway, see how it goes, what?'

They were through the door, and safe.

'He's very kind,' said Agatha.

Henry looked shocked.

'He's very able,' said Conrad distantly.

Henry groaned.

Conrad, extremely annoyed both by the groan and by the encounter with Daintry, led the way in silence down the path towards the house, in through the side door and across the passage into the library. The library windows looked out on to the entrance front. Conrad's black Rover was drawn up on the gravel with a police car beside it.

Conrad sat down at his desk and, looking at Henry, said, 'Inspector Skarrett is in the next room. He has come to arrest Agatha for conspiring to help Paul escape from prison. She will have to go with him.'

Henry turned perfectly white. His eyebrows, narrowed eyes, nose and mouth were sharp lines on his white face. Conrad's heart began to beat faster. Agatha, less disturbed than either, sat down on the arm of a chair, drawing her coat, which she had not taken off, close round her, her hands in the pockets.

'Why?' said Henry.

'Why?' repeated Conrad, as if astonished at his question. 'Because she has broken the law.'

'Paul's dead,' said Henry.

'What difference does that make?'

'It's all over. What point is there in going on with it?'

'Nothing alters the fact that she has broken the law. This is a criminal offence.'

'She gave someone some money. Nothing more than that.'

'She was part of a criminal conspiracy to pervert the course of justice.'

'You could get those charges dropped.'

'What are you saying?'

'You could use your influence to persuade the authorities not to prosecute Agatha.'

Conrad was silent for a moment. Then he said flatly, 'I would not do that if this were a parking offence.'

The lines on Henry's face seemed to draw together into a vortex of rage. Conrad thought, All his life, in spite of all I have done for him, he has caused me nothing but distress. He felt he could hardly bear the accumulation of agony.

'You have never understood.' He was trembling. All right then, if they wanted it like that let there be dramatics. He had been restrained too long. 'You young people have simply no idea of right and wrong. You are utterly and completely spoilt. What would happen if everyone were as irresponsible as you? If everyone broke the law when they felt like it? Don't you understand that without law, without rules, without loyalty to the law and obedience to the rules, everything collapses, falls apart? I am a Minister of the Crown, my prime loyalty is to the State. Paul was a traitor, the worst thing a man can be. Agatha made herself his accomplice. I gave her every chance, I sent her messages, by Imogen, by you, telling her to go to the police and stop fooling about. My duty is perfectly clear.'

'Duty?' began Henry.

Agatha stood up and held his arm before he could go any further. She had hardly listened at first, had been sitting on the arm of the chair wondering whether she really felt as calm as she thought she did; but when their voices were raised she heard, and now said 'Don't,' feeling that she knew exactly what each would say and that it would be a mistake for them to say it. 'There's no point. You can't expect him to understand. He's different from us.'

'Of course I'm different from you. I have a sense of responsibility. I hoped Henry was going to develop one too, but I see that's quite impossible now.'

Agatha smiled. 'I haven't any influence over Henry, if that's what you mean. At least I don't think I have. And I have got a sense of responsibility too, only it's quite different from yours.'

'Evidently.'

'There are quite a lot of people like me, I think. I can see why you don't like us. We're not really on your side, you can't rely on us. We're a sort of underground, a subversive group.'

Conrad looked at her suspiciously.

'To us it's more important that someone's our brother than that he betrays his country. We're not even quite sure what that means, to betray one's country. It's like Paul said in his letter: you're always climbing up the ladder, that's your world, the ladder with rungs in it and everything according to the structure of rules which you've made, respect for the man who climbs the ladder fastest. But we're the opposite of that, we're in a river which flows both ways and has curves instead of straight lines and everything is flow and movement.'

Conrad and Henry were now both looking at her, Conrad with continued suspicion and Henry controlling a wish that she would shut up so that he could start shouting at his father. She was concentrated, not to be stopped.

'We may be anywhere, you see, that's our danger to you. We are worse than any organized revolutionary movement because you never know where one of us may turn up. We don't need to speak to each other. You could put me down in a street in China and I'd know which were ours, just by a turn of the head or a tone of voice. We are the real underground, we will never pay you honour or any of your gods, or judges, or policemen. We've been there always, an ancient alternative way you've always known about and always been afraid of. We're marked with it, we can't be anything else, we were kissed on the forehead in our childhood.'

'Mad,' said Conrad, drumming his fingers on the desk and half-turning towards the door behind which he knew that Skarrett was waiting, re-reading the paper probably, wanting to get on with the job and get back to London.

'Of course I'm not mad. You're not marked like us; your heart was broken when you were a child and reset to fit the pattern. That's why everything you do is just a little false. But when I was a child there was someone in the house from the other side, a girl no one noticed. Even I hardly remember her, but the harm was done, the imprint was made. She kissed my forehead and that's what I have to pass on to my children. To redeem them.' She turned to Henry. 'You know I talk in an exaggerated way, but it is the truth. It's even there in his own religion, but of course they took it over and made an institution, a Church – which incidentally has done more damage than most other institutions – but anyway it's even in that. There are so many different ways of saying the same thing – in fact most things are only different ways of saying the same thing because there are only a very few true things in the world. They come up in different forms and the difficult thing is recognizing them, even when it looks as if they have nothing in common except a certain shape or a ratio between the parts. We don't recognize correspondences. Anyway what I mean is –' She turned back to Conrad. 'It's even there in your own Bible, about abiding in love, you were reading it this morning. "His love is perfected in us." It's another language but it's saying the same thing.'

'Don't quote my own religion at me.' Conrad stood up slowly, leaning his hands on the desk in front of him. His voice was quite dry and cold. 'I shall call in Inspector Skarrett.' He took a few steps towards the door, then turned back to say in the same tone of voice, 'Do you think you have a monopoly of love, simply because you claim it was affection for your brother rather than malice which led you to commit a criminal offence?'

He did not wait for an answer, indeed turned quickly back towards the door into the next room so as to avoid one; but as soon as he turned Henry went over to Agatha, took her hands and said decisively, 'You're quite right. Absolutely right. Don't worry, we'll manage. Everything will be all right, do you understand?'

He dropped her hands as Conrad, having signalled rather imperiously to Inspector Skarrett that he might now enter, turned back into the room. Conrad saw Henry move away, stand by the window leaning his forehead against the glass, then briefly cover his face with his hands to conceal some sort of grimace. He's even going to cry, thought Conrad scornfully.

Henry was not crying, and the expression he was momentarily unable to control was one of foolish joy. He was tremendously excited, too excited to listen to Inspector Skarrett's level tones reciting his piece in the background. He seemed to have had a revelation, which was simply that Agatha was wrong. All his life he had taken it for granted that in all important matters, especially moral questions, Agatha was right, and that when he had diverged from her he had been wrong. He had assumed she was right when she started to speak to Conrad and as his own temper cooled and he began to listen he was full of admiration for what she was saying, which, while it had seemed wild and incoherent to Conrad, was immediately understandable to him because it was an expression of her way of looking at things and, as such, deeply familiar to him. She had started quietly but as she went on without much raising her voice she had become more vehement, swept into the stream of her own eloquence, beginning to gesticulate as she did when she was angry, and he had felt anxious lest she should go too far, lose her temper with Conrad, lose her advantage. Of course she did rage sometimes, had done it to him occasionally, beating her hands together for emphasis, stamping a foot. Like Lucy, who stamped both feet sometimes, partly from frustration at not knowing enough words – 'you *always never* let me do *anything*' – who also danced, responded to music, ran, climbed and made incredible fantasies of which she said, 'It's true because I say so,' annoying George, who would say doggedly, 'It isn't so, Lucy, it isn't so.' And as he remembered George, he suddenly thought, with an extraordinary feeling of welcome for an understanding, that it was George who would save the world, because he knew exactly where he kept his second-best red pencil. Anyone can dance, he thought.

And then he knew that Agatha would be lost in a street in China, for all her goodwill, because a turn of a Chinese head, a tone of a Chinese voice, quite simply meant something different. It isn't so, Agatha, and though I love and honour your point of view it isn't mine, and it isn't the universal truth, and we are both right and I can look after everything perfectly well for a bit and you can plunge blazing into your next necessary experience, which is prison.

'There we are then,' said Miss Bannister, fastening up her cartridge bag. 'On the warpath.'

The cartridge bag had belonged to her father, Major Bannister, who in the years of his retirement in Hampshire had enjoyed a bit of pheasant-shooting when richer neighbours invited him. Her Service background was something Miss Bannister, a pacifist, did not mention: Miss Wickham knew about it and once or twice had ventured a sly reference to inherited officer-class attitudes which had not amused Miss Bannister; who had nevertheless a certain fondness for the cartridge bag, made of good leather, with the initials J.B. on the flap, into which she had been packing not ammunition but ham sandwiches, and as well as those a small silver flask, again inherited from her father and curved conveniently for his hip pocket, into which she had just poured a mixture of Nescafe and whisky.

'That should keep us going,' she said, patting the bag encouragingly, as if it had been a horse.

'Seems a horrible mixture to me,' said Miss Wickham, blowing her nose.

'It's seen me through some tougher times than this, I can tell you. I marched all the way from Jarrow on it in 1931.'

'I wonder if I ought to have put on my other shoes,' said Miss Wickham sadly.

'For heaven's sake –' said Miss Bannister, her irritation exacerbated by guilt, because she had not marched all the way from Jarrow. She had joined the march rather more than halfway down its route. 'Let's go.' But as they were on their way through the front part of the shop – they had met there, although it was a Sunday, as part of a complicated subterfuge to avoid Miss Wickham's Empire Loyalist neighbours, with whom she had been meant to be having lunch, and who had had to be duped with tales of a sudden urgent need for stocktaking – the door was opened in a hurry and Henry came in.

'I thought you might be here,' he said. 'I rang both your numbers and got no answer, so I thought I'd walk along and see. Agatha's been arrested.'

Now that one could never be Viceroy of India, Conrad thought, perhaps there was no longer any point in going into public life. All that having come to an end with those really rather undignified photographs of Lady Mountbatten kissing Nehru, where was the satisfaction, what could anyone look forward to as a glittering prize?

This was what he was thinking as he sat in a smoky room, feeling rather than hearing the repeated and re-repeated arguments passing from side to side around him. He had heard them all before, but there was no alternative to sitting through it, whereas if the world had not changed so inordinately during his lifetime he might have had a perfectly good chance of ending up as Viceroy. He knew he would have made a good Viceroy. Instead, here he was as really quite an insignificant Cabinet Minister. He was respected, of course, had certain things to his credit, certain little fields he had made his own and in which he contrived to make a small effect; he was consulted on this and that, was supposed to have an influence on the party followers, to be admired in the constituencies; but he knew perfectly well that he would never be one of the inner sanctum. Nor was this only a result of the difficulties inherent in being a member of the House of Lords rather than the House of Commons. They think of me as a harmless old steady, he thought, a bit of a trimmer. Once he had been walking along the corridor in the House of Commons and as he approached a group of three of the younger M.P.s who were talking together he thought he heard one of them say, 'Here comes old oil-can,' and then they all moved away. He could not be sure of it, and besides he had once heard that phrase used to describe one of his colleagues, and another Cabinet Minister, and so perhaps even if they had said it they had not been applying it to him. All the same he had wondered.

And wondered now what was the point of it all. Anything that was achieved was always so different from the idea's inception, was always brought about by such a curious combination of circumstances and pressures, mixed motives and muddled reasoning. It was hard not to be cynical, harder still as one grew older to find anything or anybody one could support without many reservations.

Yes, he would do his best to reassure the back-benchers, to still the critical tongues within the party. Of course he would, they knew him. But there were sounds now from outside, sounds he had not heard for many years, distant but recognizable sounds of an angry crowd, then horses' hooves, then booing. Disgusting, he thought.

The first fire-cracker to explode near her feet nearly frightened Miss Wickham out of her wits. She had been trembling a bit anyway from excitement and cold, and now clung to Henry's arm in panic until she saw the youth who was throwing the squibs and decided that he did not look as if he had a bomb in his other pocket. She was wrong in this but had let go of Henry's arm by the time she found out. The bomb was a smoke-bomb and, thrown with a quick sideways flick of the hand, it travelled far and fast to within a foot or two of the watching policemen. Through the resulting smoke two of them ran towards the youth, who dodged them and ran back into the crowd.

'Look out!' cried Miss Wickham excitedly, though it was not clear to whom she was shouting. But Henry put a hand on her arm and said, 'Come on, we're going this way.'

'Where to?' asked Miss Wickham.

'Downing Street,' answered Miss Bannister firmly.

Miss Wickham was impressed, not only by the firmness but by the matter-of-fact tone. Miss Bannister, in her tweed jacket and with her cartridge bag slung on her shoulder, had very much the air of an old hand at this game. The crowd among which they found themselves was predominantly youthful, sober on the whole, not noisy, but young. Miss Bannister had a certain authority. It was Miss Bannister who said, 'Downing Street' as the speeches came to an end and some members of the crowd began to wander away towards Leicester Square or Charing Cross in the tame pursuit of underground trains or buses to take them home to a late tea. That was not how rallies in Trafalgar Square had ended in Miss Bannister's young days.

She was evidently not alone in her resolve because there was a definite movement towards Whitehall – a surge, Miss Wickham told herself. The crowd surged towards Whitehall, she thought as if it were already written in the history books, feeling herself part of the surge, part of a great green mounting wave that was going to break on the bastions of power and change the course of events for ever. Caught up in the course of history, she thought.

'It's terribly exciting,' she said to Henry (not to Miss Bannister because she knew Miss Bannister would have thought her naïve).

Henry looked at his watch.

'I did say I'd meet Imogen and the children,' he said.

He had found the demonstration interesting rather than exciting and would have liked to slip away. He had gone to see Miss Bannister and Miss Wickham ostensibly to tell them that Agatha would not be coming to work in the bookshop the following day, but really because, having driven Imogen and the children back to London, he had felt the need for activity, a desire to do something constructive towards the improvement of the situation. It being Sunday, there was very little he could do. He had telephoned Joe, but he had already left for Hungary, and Sally, but she was away for the weekend. He had managed to get hold of David Williams, the solicitor, and had arranged with him to approach the barrister they had already decided on as the best person to undertake Agatha's defence at her trial. Then he had gone in pursuit of Miss Bannister and Miss Wickham and had found them about to set off for Trafalgar Square.

There had had to be a pause for explanations, because they had not even known that Paul, whose case they had read about, was anything to do with Agatha, who had a different surname, but once they had been told the whole story and had expressed at some length their sympathy and support, they too were frustrated by the absence of scope for immediate action. Not only was Imogen with the children, but Willy, the Dutch girl, had already moved in to help. The next day Agatha was to appear in front of a magistrate to be committed for trial. They could be there, in court, but until then it seemed that the only thing to do was to go after all, a little late, to Trafalgar Square.

Henry went with them. He was not interested in politics and had been too occupied with other concerns to pay much attention to what he had read in the papers about events in Egypt; but when Miss Bannister told him that they were going to a rally to support a campaign for 'Law not War' it did seem that there was something to be said for her point of view. In fact, when one came to think of it, it was odd that England should be dropping bombs on another country without having declared war, and then there was also the fact that if one happened to hear Anthony Eden on the wireless it was a strangely embarrassing experience; and so for these reasons, and because he thought it would please Agatha and annoy his father, Henry had gone to Trafalgar Square. Miss Bannister and Miss Wickham were both very pleased at the thought of having made a convert.

After the rally, though, he would have liked to leave. He had promised to meet Imogen and the children on the bridge in St James's Park at six o'clock, and though it was only just after five and rather cold he would rather have wandered off in that direction than become involved in a march on Downing Street. He could not feel himself to be that kind of person. The meeting had been one thing; he had been perfectly happy to be part of the crowd there. He had not been able to share Miss Wickham's emotion about Anthony Greenwood in his red tie. 'Who *is* he?' she asked, in breathless admiration. 'Tony Greenwood of course,' Miss Bannister had answered as if she had known him all her life, and indeed perhaps she had – but Aneurin Bevan's voice was so clear, so light yet carrying, so musical, that it was impossible not to listen to what he said, and what he said seemed sensible, and when he drew the conclusion that Anthony Eden was too stupid to be Prime Minister, his voice rising to an almost comical squeak of indignation on the word 'stupid', Henry clapped vigorously and shouted out, 'Quite right!' That, he now felt, should be the extent of his demonstration; but Miss Bannister had forged ahead through the crowd and he was left with Miss Wickham, who was in a state of hopeless over-excitement and really, he felt, not capable of looking after herself.

'Now let's just see if we can find Miss Bannister,' he said, hoping to pass on the responsibility.

But Miss Bannister was somewhere ahead, and they were obliged to follow the stream of people moving out of Trafalgar Square and into Whitehall, bunching up closer together as the police, of whom there now seemed to be an infinite number and in a very much less relaxed mood than they had been earlier on, hemmed them in, preventing them from moving out sideways, alerted perhaps by those few smoke-bombs and fire-crackers to a possible change in the temper of the crowd. A young man with a long football scarf round his neck stepped out of order to try to pass the people in front of him. A policeman seized him by the shoulders and pushed him roughly back into the crowd.

'Beast!' hissed Miss Wickham.

The policeman, who had not spoken during the incident, looked at her thoughtfully.

'Hush,' said Henry, feeling foolish and hustling Miss Wickham past. He was no physical coward, had even been rather good at boxing at school, but he was not at all sure that he could control Miss Wickham, and felt he could hardly be expected to take on the entire police force in her defence.

'Where on earth is Miss Bannister?' he said, trying anxiously to see over the heads of the crowd in front of him.

Conrad came out of his meeting with a headache. There was to be a full Cabinet meeting in an hour's time. What a lot of talk. It was clear that the Prime Minister was in an appalling state of nerves, and it was not clear that the military organizers were going to make the action the short sharp affair it had to be in order to succeed. He had walked to Downing Street from his flat and so had no official car waiting for him. Concerned with his thoughts and vaguely thinking of getting a taxi, he had walked a little way towards Whitehall before he noticed that the end of the street was barred by police horses and that the crowd noises which he had been hearing from inside the meeting were a good deal louder and more menacing than before. There was chanting – 'Eden must go, Eden must go' – some angry shouts, and the sound of the horses' hooves as they moved to and fro, evidently rebuffing some kind of advance. He could see that beyond the line of mounted police there were more policemen on foot, shoulder to shoulder, and beyond them another line of mounted police. Suddenly a loud ragged booing began, rose almost to a roar and then died down. The attempted advance had failed and the crowd were expressing their disapproval of the police action.

Two of the policemen who had been standing outside 10 Downing Street had followed Conrad to advise him to go round the other way. He said he would, but paused a moment, still looking towards Whitehall.

'It shouldn't go on much longer,' one of the policemen said. 'They're beginning to clear off already.'

But at that moment there was a sudden disturbance, more shouts and clattering hooves, and a tiny spearhead of demonstrators broke through one side of the first rank of mounted police and pushed back the foot police, who momentarily wavered but then stood firm again. One of them lost his helmet and over his head there reared up – was she standing on something, or being carried? – the excited upper half of a small middle-aged lady.

Conrad had already half turned away to go back up the street, but the appearance of what might be supposed to be the leader of the mob was so unexpected that he paused to stare, and saw the frail form more or less thrown over the head of the policeman by a huge bearded man who now appeared behind her, struggling with the two police-men who had set upon him at the very moment when he had launched Miss Wickham into the air. From behind this struggling group there now appeared another dishevelled figure, who dashed up to where Miss Wickham, unbalanced by her unexpected leap, was picking herself up from the road, meanwhile in imminent danger of being trampled on by a police horse. Conrad recognized Henry. He heard his voice.

'Miss Wickham! Miss Wickham!'

But Miss Wickham was on her feet and hurling herself at a mounted policeman. Clinging tenaciously to a leather boot, she had for the first time an uninterrupted view of Downing Street, of one or two policemen looking infuri-atingly calm and a bowler-hatted figure whom she did not recognize.

'Look out, we're coming,' she shouted to them rather as if it were hide-and-seek and she had just counted up to fifty.

'Miss Wickham!' cried Henry desperately.

Now she clasped a serge-covered thigh, her two feet firmly planted against the horse's side.

'Come on, Henry,' she shouted, wig awry. 'Up and at 'em!'

Aghast at the state of affairs seemingly revealed by the familiar use of the Christian name, Conrad watched in horror as Henry, held back by two policemen, struggled to reach Miss Wickham's side. The mounted policeman next to the one who was the object of Miss Wickham's attack, perhaps disconcerted by the frail aspect of his opponent, took off his glove before reaching over to try to pluck her from her perch. She bit him. He withdrew his hand sharply to put on his glove again, giving her time, still clinging to her victim like a tigress to an elephant, to shriek down the street as loudly as she could to the bowler hat. 'Eden must go! Down with imperialism! Down with the British Empire!' And then it was down with Miss Wickham, into a sea of dark uniforms, and down with Henry and down with the bearded man, and the dark uniforms realigned themselves and the shouting died down, but not before Conrad had turned away, white-faced, and walked towards the other end of the street.

'Only a few fanatics,' said the policeman who was walking beside him.

'One of them was my son.'

Conrad never failed to greet the policemen on duty as he passed them. He even took his hat off to the cleaners.

The policeman was sincerely shocked.

'I'm very sorry to hear that,' he said.

Imogen had taken the children to the Zoo. She had been about to set off when Henry had come back to tell them that he was going to the demonstration with Miss Wickham and Miss Bannister, and what with one thing and another it had been agreed that she should pick Henry up after his demonstration to drive him home. He could of course have gone home by bus, but Imogen felt that she wanted to keep the children in a constant state of activity in case they should start to worry about Agatha, and the idea of parking the car and running in the dark (because it would be already dark) across St James's Park to the bridge where they were to meet had appealed to them, as she had known it would. And now, excited by the darkness and the lights and reflections in the water, they were running about and chasing each other and hoping Henry would not come too soon so that they could go on playing, and Imogen was waiting by a lamp-post, walking slowly up and down to keep warm and listening to the faint but rather disturbing sounds that were coming from the direction of Whitehall and wishing that Henry would hurry up.

She was glad to see the children playing. A few minutes ago in the car there had been a rather awkward little conversation about whether Agatha was coming to say good night to them or not. The trouble was that though they appeared to understand exactly what had happened it was as if they kept forgetting. Agatha had been taken to see them before driving away with Inspector Skarrett and had left them solemn but reassured. Had Grandfather said she was to go, they had asked, knowing of her appointment with him. Yes, she had said, because you were not really allowed to help people get out of prison, but Paul had been very unhappy there and had asked her to help him and you have to help your brothers. 'But you said prison was nice!' And in a way she had, trying to reconcile them to Paul's having been sent there; so she had had to explain that she had not meant that it was nice so much as bearable, for people who liked being alone, and reading, and writing long letters every single day to their children. And they had more or less understood, and had not cried until after she had gone, and then not very much, because Henry and Imogen had been there; but an impression had been quite definitely left on their minds – and Henry, in his present mood, had done nothing to change it – that the whole thing had been by decree of their grandfather, who was the most important person they knew.

So that when, in St James's Park, they suddenly saw him walking slowly out of the darkness into the lamplight, his hands in his overcoat pocket, his bowler hat pulled down over his forehead and his white face set into an expression of extreme severity, they were considerably shocked. His looks seemed to confirm his changed state, from the benevolent if sometimes alarming grandfather from whom, if you remembered to be on your best behaviour, perfectly good presents could quite frequently be expected, to something altogether different, infinitely more distant and cruel.

They stopped in front of him, drew closer together, stared.

He stared back, at first completely taken by surprise and then, as he realized their proximity to the scene he had just been witnessing, horrified. Had Henry completely lost his senses? Was he not only involving himself with a rabble of left-wing fanatics, but trying to bring his children into it as well?

'What are you doing here?' he asked them sternly, frowning at them as they confronted him under the lamp-post.

Lucy bent on him her most terrible gaze. He was the man who had sent away her mother.

'You are a –' she began ferociously but stopped. She had been going to say 'pig' but that was something she very often called George when she was cross with him and she needed a more frightful word. 'You are a SHEEP!'

Imogen had hurried towards them, seeing what was happening, and now stood beside the children, aligning herself with them but uncertain what else to do.

'Take them home at once,' he said to her. He walked away without looking back, but not so quickly that he did not hear Lucy's foot stamping furiously on the tarmac path. Her voice came after him, shrill but without a tremor in it, like an antique pipe.

'As long as I live!' she shouted. 'As long as I live!'

Agatha was in darkness, surrounded by stone. She was breathing in and out, very deeply and very fast, as she had learnt to do in labour. They had said then, 'Don't resist it, go with it,' but it did not seem to work when the pain was mental. She gave up, curled over until her head was on her knees, and hardly breathed at all. She was in a deep well, drowning in anxiety.

When Lucy had a temperature she walked in her sleep, pursued by monsters. Henry never woke. When George was late for school his legs, plump in their thick grey socks – had she mended them, did he need new ones? – pounded on the concrete playground their message of shame – shame – 'Your mother's in prison,' they would say. Because she sacrificed your peace of mind to her selfish brother, who anyway was caught and killed himself.

'Think of Italy,' Henry had said, 'think of Italy.' But she could not remember it. He had said they would go there afterwards; he would give up his job, they would work the land, cultivate the vines and the olives, the children would go to an Italian school, he would teach them English history himself in the evenings. It had made her laugh at the time because it sounded so unlike him. They were still both in the curiously euphoric state that had come upon them immediately after the arrest, as if the smell of burning boats in their nostrils were slightly intoxicating, removing all appetite for food but making the heart beat fastei

But by the late evening the euphoria had fled, to be replaced by fear. Obediently she tried to think of Italy but her thoughts would not settle. They dispersed in fragmented worries. The children. A bruise she ought to stop herself from fingering. Italy. After all had it not been paradise to her mind's eye all this time? Her paradise, though, hers and Orlando's. Was Henry to apply himself to it, make it his? That stony terrace on which Orlando had fallen, crushing the wild marjoram in the sacred noonday heat, must be ploughed up, the weeds must be poisoned, the snakes must slither away to more secret places, corn must be sown between the vines. Of course that was good, and good that the lazy hare should no longer have the ruined chapel to himself and good that the grass should be cut round the stone well and the tower house finished and the convolvulus destroyed. Would any of it be any concern of hers? She had first to be tried and condemned.

Henry had said, 'We'll come back, we don't want to be exiles.' But I am an exile already, she thought. Perhaps I shall always be an exile. People don't recover from being in prison, you can always see it in their eyes. Sally and Joe. Henry had said Sally and Joe could come to stay in Italy, they were friends now. How could she be expected not to mind that a little? Joe was her old friend. Sally was – but how after prison could she face Sally, or anyone else like her? You had to be strong for all that, and strong for marriage, for growing out of being in love, for accommodating differences, for not minding being sometimes bored, irritated, misunderstood, misjudged. How could she and Henry stand up to the emphasis which would be given to their relationship by going to live in isolation in Italy? Leave it to him, he had said. But she had always had to do all the worrying before. Wasn't that one of the reasons why so much of the strength she needed now had been used up? She had reached her limit, that was all. Sooner perhaps than most people. What had they said in her school report? 'She contributes nothing.' That was it. 'She is too reserved. She contributes nothing to the life of the school.' They can always get me that way. Remind me of school and I'm alone in the narrow well of my own inadequacy. What use are the woods to me now, wild garlic and mud, the waterfall? How weak all that is. If I live to be a hundred I will never dare to tell the children a fairy story again.

Think of Italy, he had said. Dream it, dream Italy. After all, she might sleep.

She thought of fallen stones by cypress trees, distance, silence, stars, the snake among the tangle of brambles and wild roses, the path from the wood along which for some mythological purpose of her own she had once imagined a unicorn picking its way between the stones. She might sleep. Even in this well she might sleep and be restored. And there had come into her mind the other place, the place on the island which she could never be certain whether she had seen or not, with the grass growing between the white columns and the sea far below, and she thought, There is a space between two broken columns, I will make up a story about that and send it to the children. In the sunlit space between two broken columns I will place a unicorn so that I may remember him. That at least she could do.

The bearded man was arrested and taken away.

'May I have a word with you, officer?' Henry said in the grandest possible tones.

He walked away a few paces with the senior police officer.

'Most awkward,' he said confidentially. 'My father's secretary. My father's Lord Field, I don't know whether you knew? that. This lady has been his secretary for many years and is most devoted. We were just trying to make our way through to the House of Lords when that great big fellow suddenly seized her and started carrying her along. I'm afraid she became quite hysterical, poor thing. I don't know why she was shouting like that. I rather think she thought he'd do her some violence if she didn't pretend to be on his side. You can see she's in a severe state of shock. I really think I should take her straight home and get someone to put her to bed with a couple of aspirin.'

'She did appear to be assaulting a police officer, sir.'

'I'm afraid she was quite hysterical at that point. You can imagine what a ghastly experience it would be for someone like that, officer, after years of sitting quietly in Kensington typing letters for Cabinet Ministers. She was out of her mind with terror. There are a lot of very distinguished people who can vouch for her character. Perhaps if we left our names and addresses?'

The police officer stifled his doubts. He had a lot on his hands, and Henry's air of authority was very convincing. He didn't want any trouble about wrongful arrest. He took out his notebook.

'If you'll take the responsibility of getting her away from here as quickly as possible.'

'I'll see to it, officer.'

The policeman wrote down the names and addresses of Henry, Miss Wickham and Miss Bannister.

'She's lucky to get away with it,' he said.

'Thank you very much, officer, it's very good of you,' said Henry, grander than ever. He gave a nod which was meant vaguely to imply that he would mention the incident to his father and make sure that the man was properly rewarded; then he led Miss Wickham and Miss Bannister firmly away.

Miss Wickham was beginning to wonder whether she had made a fool of herself. She was white-faced and silent, and could hardly walk for exhaustion. Miss Bannister, however, was still full of fight.

'Disgraceful,' she said as they walked away. Luckily the policeman had already turned back towards the noisy crowd. 'Sucking up to that policeman like that. Felicity should have seen it through and stood trial.'

'No, really, Miss Bannister, we can't have everyone in prison, now can we?' said Henry. 'Comfort yourself by thinking how it would annoy my father if he knew how we'd used his name.'

'I think I can probably be more use to the dear children if I'm at liberty,' said Miss Wickham faintly through colourless lips.

Conrad drove home through the night. He could not forget Lucy, that blazing look, that 'sheep!' The absurdity of the chosen term of abuse only made the insult more bitter. It showed how hard she had had to try to find a word bad enough to describe him.

Mount Sorrel was all he had now. He wanted to get back to it, to sleep there that night, even if it meant driving straight back to London in the morning. At night, with nothing much on the roads, it took him two and a half hours. He had often done it.

'It's all I've got,' he said aloud in the car. 'Everything else they've taken away from me.' His voice shook. He sobbed. Why not? There was no one to hear. 'My son. They've taken my son.'

He had telephoned before leaving London to find out what had happened. When Henry had answered the telephone he had said, 'Are you all right?'

'Why do you ask?' Such coldness.

'I heard – that's to say, I saw you were involved in a demonstration.'

'You saw?'

'I was coming out of Downing Street.'

'I see.'

'That woman – the woman you were with – who is she?'

'Agatha works for her.'

He might have known it. It would have been Agatha. Agatha worked for a left-wing organization and was trying to draw Henry into it too. All her life she had been pulling Henry away from him.

'Henry, we haven't really had a chance to talk. About Agatha, I mean. Of course we must see that she has the best possible defence.'

'Thank you, Father. I have already seen to that.'

'Oh you've got somebody, you mean? Who have you got?'

'A man called Lindon.'

'I believe he's excellent, couldn't be better. If I can help in any way, financially or anything?'

'No, thank you, Father.'

'Now look here, Henry, I don't want this to come between us. We really mustn't let that happen.'

'It has happened, Father.'

'No, Henry, I'm not going to allow you to say that. You're my only son. Just because your wife and I don't agree over something…'

'I think Agatha's right.'

'You can't let her ruin everything between us, after all I've done for you. You're the only thing I have left to remind me of my wife. No, no, this won't do, Henry. You are not as hard-hearted as that. I shall ring off now but you will think better of this. You will see that your attitude is wrong.'

'Yes I may,' said Henry in the same detached voice. 'But not yet. I really think it would be better if we were not to meet for the time being.'

After that he had had to get back to Mount Sorrel. What else was there? He had had to drive with limbs aching with tiredness – he was not young any more, did anyone ever think of that? – through the night towards the West, haunted by those scornful eyes, that confident cry of the child against the dark, 'As long as I live! As long as I live!' Imogen should have smacked her, told her she was a naughty little girl, instead of standing there doing nothing, looking as if she agreed with her. After all he had done for them all, it was hard to take in, hard to believe.

'Alexandra, they don't understand us any more.' But she was in a tennis dress, in 1929. Had she ever existed? Had he? 'Your heart was broken when you were a child, and reset to fit the pattern. That's why everything you do is just a little false.' Splinters of ice into his heart. Did she think his blood was too thin to flow like any other wounded creature's? No one had said that sort of thing to him before. It was simply not a recognizable picture. He was Conrad, wise, kind and just. Everyone else thought so. She knew nothing about training, about discipline and duty, just as she knew nothing about politics or government. You had to have different spheres of action, otherwise rational existence was out of the question. There was a sphere for private faith and a sphere for public duty, a sphere for the heart's affections and a sphere for the great world of affairs. They had to be kept separate, in an orderly and disciplined manner, if stability were to be maintained. What she was asking for was chaos, anarchy. Why did she have to speak as if she alone knew what impulse had first stirred the inert primeval slime?

Phrases circulated in his head. 'A broken man.' 'Nothing to live for.' There was humiliation for his country. The Government had bungled their Middle Eastern policy. What could he have done? Nothing. Over this particular issue the Cabinet had been kept in the dark by one small group. There was nothing left for him but loyalty. He was loyal, but not in sympathy. It was the inefficiency rather than the policy itself which seemed to him so disastrous. Eden was ill, would have to be replaced. He could not believe there could be a Conservative Government for much longer. By the time they got back he would be too old and would have come too badly out of the present situation to be given office again. If he was offered it he would refuse it. A man who had so completely lost heart should give way to someone else. Anyone else. Except a Socialist of course.

All that was over, those years of being always there, always somewhere near the seat of power, a constant influence. As long ago as before the war some newspaper had called him the youngest ever elder statesman. Now that he was old enough for the part he was going to lose it.

There were no lights on in the house as he drove up to it. He had had a Spanish couple, but the housekeeping bills had been so enormous and full of such inexplicably mysterious entries that he had asked them to leave and now had a complicated system of part-time help from the village, which worked quite well but meant that no one except Conrad himself slept in the house at night.

Getting out of the car, he stretched his arms and breathed deeply, as he always did when he arrived at Mount Sorrel, then he stood in front of the portico for a few moments in the darkness and silence. A car passed, somewhere up the valley, and the silence returned. He took the key from his pocket and opened the front door.

As soon as he had turned the lights on in the hall he looked towards Orpen's picture of Alexandra. He always did. Before the war, when he used to travel a lot on Government Commissions and things of that kind, he and Henry used to go together to look at the picture whenever he came back from being away. It was a brief formality – 'Come on, let's go and look at Mummy,' the little boy would say, pulling him by the hand, wanting to get it over so that they could go on to other things, present-giving perhaps or stories of Conrad's adventures in distant parts of the world. They would stand there for a minute hand in hand, looking up at her as if to receive a blessing from the direct gaze inherited from the Field-Marshal and captured so brilliantly by the artist. She was in a garden party outfit. The gaze came from beneath the wide brim of a pale straw hat, which had a ribbon round it, tied in a huge bow at the back. The dress, of some light material in pale and less pale mauve, left the arms bare. Only one arm was to be seen because the artist had chosen a three-quarters view. She sat on a stool, one leg crossed over the other, one hand resting lightly on her hip, a pose which somehow showed her for the woman of action she was. The arm was beautifully painted, lightly dimpled round the elbow, turning inwards at the wrist so that the hand might rest on the mauve material, two fingers just catching the long strand of pearls, his wedding present. The hair beneath the hat was dark and curly, the cheeks a healthy pink, the nose not inconsiderable. The mouth, firmly closed, was a little amused at the corners. Altogether a handsome woman. What would she have made of it all, nearly thirty years later? She had been so honest, so simple and so brave. He tried to remember her voice, the words she used, words from a vanished world, a world where it was decent to be polite to servants and jolly to ride to hounds. It seemed much more than thirty years ago.

He heard a sound behind him, a soft sound as of slippered feet moving slowly across the stone floor. He had an instant of fear, knowing himself to be the only person in the house, but turned and saw Jess coming slowly towards him wagging her tail. Sleep, age and illness were making her drag her feet.

'Oh Jess, poor Jess, did I wake you up then?'

She hated sleeping anywhere but in the house unless she was with him, and the closeness of the house to the village meant that someone could come in in the evening to let her out and then leave her in her basket for the night. He had not been taking her to London with him lately because of her health, and as soon as he saw her he recognized that it had again deteriorated. She was moving badly and her breathing was even worse than when he had last seen her. He crouched down on the floor to receive her welcome.

'Even you, Jess, even you.'

His sorrow became uncontrollable, and he cried. The phrase 'he wept like a child' came into his head. Had he cried like that when Alexandra died? He could not remember. He wept like a child. Jess licked his face.

'Jess, poor Jess, you smell awful. Awful, Jess. You smell of death, I suppose, poor Jess. Perhaps I do too. I wish we could die together. We're no good here. We've got everything wrong, Jess, everything wrong.'

He wept into her soft neck, crouched on the floor beside her in his London overcoat. At last, exhausted, he lay down. She pressed herself against his side. He turned towards her and they lay together on the stone floor, her head resting on his. Mrs Benjamin, the first of the helpers, would find them. 'There they were together on the floor, cold the two of them, stone cold.' Wouldn't they be sorry even then? Perhaps it didn't matter. It was not for that that he wanted to die but because he was finished, destroyed. He prayed, 'O God, let me die.'

'O God, let me die.'

His prayer was not answered. Much later he went upstairs and got into bed.

A Note on the Type

The text of this book is set in Linotype Stempel Garamond, a version of Garamond adapted and first used by the Stempel foundry in 1924. It is one of several versions of Garamond based on the designs of Claude Garamond. It is thought that Garamond based his font on Bembo, cut in 1495 by Francesco Griffo in collaboration with the Italian printer Aldus Manutius. Garamond types were first used in books printed in Paris around 1532. Many of the present-day versions of this type are based on the *Typi Academiae* of Jean Jannon cut in Sedan in 1615.

Claude Garamond was born in Paris in 1480. He learned how to cut type from his father and by the age of fifteen he was able to fashion steel punches the size of a pica with great precision. At the age of sixty he was commissioned by King Francis I to design a Greek alphabet, and for this he was given the honourable title of royal type founder. He died in 1561.